Cookie & Me

Cookie & Me

Mary Jane Ryals

Kitsune Books
Quality books for eclectic readers

Cookie & Me

Copyright © Mary Jane Ryals
July 2010

Kitsune Books
P.O. Box 1154
Crawfordville, FL 32326-1154

www.kitsunebooks.com
contact@kitsunebooks.com

Printed in USA
First printing in 2010

ISBN: 978-0-9819495-6-7
Library of Congress Control Number: 2010927524

Cover design and art: Carol Lynne Knight
Author Portrait: Inga Finch

First edition

To

Martha Beaudoin, amazing friend for 40 years, who generously shared and let me use some of her story

Melanie Rawls, dear friend who encourages me, and who told me it's better to tell the truth

&

Ariel Ryals-Trammell, lovely daughter for whom I got an urgent burst of energy to write this story

Acknowledgments

Thanks, Dad, for your wonderful play with language and stories about your own upbringing.

Thanks, Mom, for giving me the love of literature and for showing me how to tell a good story.

Thanks, Michael, for love, sustenance, great sense of humor, and help with computer matters.

Dylan, you always inspire me, believe in me as I do in you.

Donna Decker, thanks for bugging me about getting this book published.

Donna Meredith, thanks for asking why this book wasn't already published.

Lynne Knight, thanks for your enduring humor and gorgeous cover art.

Laura Newton, Pam Ball, and Delores Bryant, thanks for encouragement and incisive critical reading.

Anne Petty, thanks for keeping me on track, and for believing in this book.
Barbie, Nancy, and Robert, passionate and brilliant siblings all, I am so proud to be your family. Thank you.

Thanks also to the Hambidge Center, which offered me time and space to think and write and rewrite this novel over the years.

And thanks to Laura Young, Lynn Holschuh, and Bill Petty for copyediting the manuscript.

1

That day the world cracked open, I was lighting matches and dropping them one by one on the cold Mexican tiles. I was thinking about bones. How fragile they are, how they can hurt, break, break a body. I couldn't figure out then how burning and the bone-strangling incidents went together, cause I hadn't done the burning yet, which changed everything. And that is the story I am trying to tell now.

Daddy was already drinking highballs with Lucky in the kitchen while Miss Jesse, the colored lady who worked for us, folded clothes upstairs. Daddy was talking C-R-A-P crap. I could barely listen without shouting out comebacks as I sat on the stairs spying. Except that if I made any commentary, I'd have gotten buttslapped by Daddy for being ungrateful. He did a lot—cooked me pancakes, lectured me about homework, and taught me how to ride horses when Mama was sick.

But he didn't know when I needed new socks, or how to get ointment and a Band-aid when I got scraped, or how to ruffle my hair and give a soft kiss on the head. What I missed most about Mama was her humming as she brushed my wild hair into shape and wrapped it into a French braid. A pang went through my gut like a knife, so I pushed the thought away, like thinking about bones.

Daddy never said that Mama had turned too selfish to get up, too making-stuff-up sick or too drugged out to cook even a poached egg. Sick. Ha. She always felt sick. Headaches, earaches, arm aches, stomach aches, back aches. Ache ache ache. She couldn't move. Couldn't paint. Had quit painting three years ago. I glanced at the framed oil painting on the stairwell wall she painted of a bushy magnolia. Only the magnolia flowers she painted purple. Always off with the colors.

It turned my stomach to hear the click clack of ice against glasses. I thought about bones click-clacking.

"So now I've got to decide—put her in the 5C ward, or leave her here," Daddy said. "With the girl."

By the girl, he meant me. By 5C he meant the psycho ward. He went on about Mama as a billow of cigarette smoke drifted out of the kitchen, filtered into the living room, and wreathed up the staircase. "She wears shades even in the house now," Daddy said.

"In the house?" Lucky said. "Damn dark as the ass end of a mule." That lawyer friend of Daddy's, Lucky, took the cake. And made questionable fashion decisions. Today from my window I'd seen him get out of the car. He wore green plaid polyester pants with a red checkered shirt. Now he continued. "It's a pure tragedy for a girl not to have a mother figure, A.J. I wouldn't tell you how to raise your child, but somebody needs to get her away from those horses and into that—what do they call that thing—cotillion classes. Teach her some manners. How to be ladylike."

"What?" Daddy said. "Cotillion?"

"Cotillion," Lucky said. "We got our girls in that thing. Teach them how to dance, how to take a compliment, answer the phone. Your girl won't give me the time of day on the phone or off. Needs to get away from that filthy barn. Not fit for no girls."

"Not fit for *any* girls," Daddy corrected him. Daddy came

from white trash like Lucky, but he'd learned how to talk right, and he urged every blessed body else to.

I'd figured out my categories of people. Poor white trash were poor like colored people, but they didn't have a good excuse for it like colored people. They lived in trailers with squeaky doors and made back steps of concrete blocks that wobbled and grumbled. White trash children's hair was greasy and bore bugs. I saw white trash people once, back when Mama didn't hurt all over. We delivered a fat, beige, and frozen Christmas turkey to this family.

They let their dead car rust up in the front yard, too. With the same hands they wiped their runny noses, they played marbles. Yessiree, in that dirt yard. Right in the middle of where they'd wrestled trashy lawn chairs out of the garbage that my daddy would never even put his hands on. And they'd set them up to sit on and play Poker and Black Jack. I made sure nobody would ever call me white trash, no sir.

"She loves horses," Daddy said. "I'm not going to keep her from that." Daddy got me in love with horses. He and I could ride for hours a day out on the country road. The arms of live oaks would swish and lean out into the road like bending ballerinas as we rode through the speckled shade. Sometimes we'd spot the bright red hurricane lilies under the shade of an oak draped in Spanish moss. I could almost whiff the sweet sour of horse sweat as I thought about it sitting on the stairs. Taste the mineral saltiness on my lips after kissing my horse Star on the neck.

Daddy and I didn't do that kind of thing anymore, though. Now seemed like things had changed too much.

"Girl's getting too old to be hanging around barefoot in a barn, A.J. Especially with no real mama, you got to get the girl some—"

"Rayann!" Daddy called. He was getting in one of those irritated drinking moods. I could tell by the way he hollered it. Sometimes he got so mad he threw things and hit anything in his way. The clacking of ice in glasses, like bones.

I stood and tore up the steps on tiptoe. Just before Mama got really sick, she had said, "There are things you just cannot forget." Like how the town she came from, Woodville, lay in a valley of springs just before the gulf coast. The earth dropped down from our town Tallahassee into a place where just underground a deep limestone spring ran. I squeaked across the upstairs tile floor on my toes.

Miss Jesse had her head turned toward the door like she knew I was coming. She was pretty for a colored lady. Kind of small but with strong arm muscles, shiny brown eyes, a sweet tulip mouth. I couldn't ever tell if she was mama or grandmama age. She lifted her eyebrows in a what-you-doing-now kinda way.

"You can't even walk through this house without acting like you sneaking up on somebody," Miss Jesse said. She stood in the bedroom next to mine smoothing out a towel on one of the twin beds. "Think you Dick Tracy or something?"

"The world is full of bones," I said, standing frozen in the doorway.

"Now what makes you talk that kind of foolishness?" she said, dropping the towel and sitting down on the bed. "I need to rest my own bones." She pulled her legs up onto the bed, pushed off her shoes and wriggled her toes. "You daddy's here drinking with that Lucky?" she asked.

I nodded and closed the door.

"What you doing?" she said, and watched me go lie down on the other bed. "You always coming up with something from the devil," she said. "What's all this about bones?"

"Nothing, Miss Jesse," I said, getting up and opening the double doors to let in some fresh air. I gazed out the balcony doors. Early May and summer had already arrived. The wisteria and azaleas gone. Honeysuckle and jasmine threw out a blanket of hot perfume. Chickadees said *dee dee dee* and flitted through the air. I did not know why I could not just purely enjoy it. "Nothing," I said again, chewing on my latest hangnail. Then I walked over to her. She looked tired. I wanted to stroke her arm, but she was colored. It wasn't allowed. Instead, I covered her feet with a towel.

"Just—" something terrible was gnawing at my stomach. I thought I would throw up. The thought of the sound of bones breaking, making me gag, scared me half to death. I covered my ears and walked over to the other bed.

I tried not to think about it. Bones. Sometimes I got hung up thinking about them. Just the thought that under all our finery, clothes, manners and smiles, under epidermis, tissue and blood as my sixth grade biology book called them, we're just bones. Easy to break, easy to crack. Cracking up. Like Mama. The thought took me all kinds of strange places. Two hundred and six bones to be exact. That's the number of bones in the human body, my biology book said. Fish bones, bare bones, bony-hipped cow bones.

"Girl, what's ailing you?" Miss Jesse said.

"I don't want to talk about it." I gasped.

"Hmm mm mm," she said, the way I'd heard colored people say when they did not approve of something.

"I hate that Lucky," I said. "He smokes too much."

"Hate's a mighty strong word," she said, sighing and closing her eyes. "Devil loves to hear you using that word." I sat down on the bed and pushed the clothes to the end.

"Well, I hate Red even more," I said. "I'd like to *kill* Red."

Miss Jesse opened one eye and glared at me. "I would like to be on a walk with him, and I'd have Daddy's hunting knife, and I would say to him, 'Let's lie down and look at the sky,' and then I would stab him right in the heart."

"You are talking the foolishest talk I ever heard," Miss Jesse said. She knew he was white trash, and I didn't have to say it to her out loud. That's why she didn't get more mad. Still, on she went. "The Lord Jesus sent you to me to try me, and if you don't hush up, I will take you over my knee." She did not mean that.

She knew how Red was, how he would get mad at somebody driving slow. One time when I was riding with him and Daddy to town, that colored fellow with the mule cart plodded along in front of us, and Red couldn't get around him. He started bumping his Duster up on the cart and blowing his horn. Calling him sorry nigger. Daddy had turned kind of pale. That Red was white trash if there ever was any. I knew my categories of people. Besides just white trash. I laid down to give it some contemplation.

You had your rich people like Mama, who'd always got what they wanted, had their hair done and nails polished every week, and they drove cars big enough to set up to eat Sunday fried chicken dinner in. Rich people wanted everything to match. Babies' booties matched hats matched dresses. Ladies purses were required to match alligator shoes. Every blasted towel matched, like in Bubba Burlow's house, the county commissioner who smoked cigars and hunted with Daddy. His wife, Sissy Burlow, had pink engraved towels all set set set in the guest bathroom smelling like they were just laundered with no yellow stains or frayed edges. Her pink shell soaps matched. You can sure tell a category of people by their towels.

And rich men. They got round and smoked cigars and

thought they smelled like gardenia perfume. They ran for public office and always won, cause they only ran against each other. They owned all God's country from the Georgia state line down to the Gulf of Mexico, from the Alabama state line over to the Atlantic Ocean. They put cows on their land, or they held hunting clubs on it. And I overheard one of Daddy's friends once at a party say they harbored a passel of women of the night over at the Redbird Cafe in Frenchtown, where all the in-town colored people stay.

People thought I was rich, but that's not the truth. I was a regular person. When you marry a poor white trash person to a rich person, and they have a child, that child evens out to a regular person.

Miss Jesse did not like me talking about killing people. She was eyeing me but good. "Girl, you are pushing your luck with Jesus," she said. "But I am too tired to argue with you, or to spank your womanish behind. Now hush while I shut my eyes for a few minutes."

I did not mind her talking to me that way. She was not what you'd call a nigger. Not that I used the word—I used the term 'you-know-what.'

"Rayann!" Daddy yelled. Miss Jesse raised her eyebrows again. I could almost hear her asking, What you done started downstairs? I raised my eyebrows in a desperate way and gave her the "Shh" finger to my lips. Miss Jesse frowned.

"Jesse! You still here?" Daddy hollered from the bottom of the stairs.

"Yes, Sir, Mr. Wood?" Miss Jesse called, sitting up fast. She walked to the door and opened it.

"Rayann up there?" he asked.

"She's in the bathroom, running herself a tub bath. She'll be out in a snap," Miss Jesse hollered. She pointed silently to the bathroom. *Get in there now!* she mouthed. Snap. Bones. The limestone spring. Sometimes the spring would eat the earth and the ground would crumble and cave in, Mama said. You'd be left with a sinkhole that filled with water. At the bottom of sinkholes, she'd said, lay things too unlucky to name out loud. So she whispered them to me: *suicide girls, babies nobody wanted, ghosts from the war between the states.* I leaped across the hallway into the bathroom. I sang a tune like I'd heard nothing of their conversation.

"How about checking on Mrs. Wood for me, please," he hollered. "And tell Rayann to get out and come down here now."

"Yes, Sir," she said, opening the bathroom door and peering in with a hard look. I splashed my face and hair to make it look like I'd been bathing.

It must have taken a long time, cause Daddy yelled, "Rayann!" I pushed off my clothes and pulled on the dirty jeans and horse sweat T-shirt just to spite Lucky. I leaped down the stairs three at the time and halted in the den. That Lucky sipped on a fresh highball. "Rayann!" Daddy said again.

"Yeah?" I said in an exaggerated you-rang-sir voice.

He opened his arms and said sweetlike, "Come here, Lollipop." I walked over and he hugged me hard. Daddy acted more like a kid than a grownup. He felt bad about his temper and couldn't help but come hugging you and admitting he was sorry he got mad. Not that he was so mad now, but he had started yelling. I wrapped my arms around him and hugged back. I wished I hadn't changed into the dirty clothes. "Why don't you check and see if everything's okay with your mother."

"Yes, Sir," I said. "After I get some milk."

Daddy turned back to Lucky and said, "Told that nigra woman to see about my wife, and the nigra up and disappeared.

Even have to check up on them at home. No telling what she's doing back there in Liz's room," Daddy said to Lucky.

"Them jigs, marching on Washington, mouthing about 'free at last.' They ain't got the sense God gave 'em. Been free since the Civil War," Lucky said, putting out his half-smoked-down cigarette.

"Don't use that word," I said. "She might hear you."

"Now, Lollipop—" Daddy said.

"She's colored," I whispered. "She is not a 'you-know-what.'" You'd think Lucky would have some discretion about using such words, being a lawyer and all. You'd think they'd have taught him some manners at law school. I bet he didn't know how a real you-know-what acted, like old Obadiah McCain who lived at the far end of Saturday Street down the road where colored people lived. He'd beat up his wife and left her for dead. Now that was a you-know-what. But that Mattie McCain did not die, she up and left, and I hope she did not take up with another you-know-what.

That was your second category of black people. The first was Miss Jesse and Mr. Nix at the hospital who gave me gum every time I went up there with Daddy. The second kind was like Obadiah McCain, a you-know-what, and the third kind I did not know any of—Negroes. They acted uppity, like those people on TV such as Martin Luther King. People who wore dapper suits and said Negroes wanted to ride the front of the bus. They stirred up trouble, wanting to be called *Negro*. People said once they got the right to ride the bus and use our restaurants, what would they want then? But honest to god, I bet they were smarter than a person like Lucky. They sure dressed better.

"She's upset about her mother," Daddy said to Lucky. "Honey, why don't you go tend to the horses?" he said to me.

Gray smoke from the cigarette he smoked floated over to me.

"Daddy, you smoke too much," I said, waving my arm around to bat away the smoke.

"Lollipop, why don't you change clothes?" he said, ignoring me. "Get into something clean. And straighten up your shoulders."

"I don't want to," I said, standing up straight, frowning. "And that's not really your business. It's what mamas tend to." I meant for that to sting. I felt mad at Daddy for listening to Lucky. But Lucky guffawed. Daddy did, too, and shook his head. He pointed down the hallway that led to Mama's room.

"Go," he said. "Now." I didn't even think of it as his room. He'd moved everything, his rusting razor and Barbasol and his chewed up toothbrush, to the downstairs half bath in the utility room. He slept on the den sofa at night when he came home. Sometimes he worked on-call at the hospital, but other times, he came home smelling like a smoke factory and a bar. It made me ache, thinking about being lonesome enough to go out to a place that made you smell bad. I could never get in a late night TV show or read a book on the sofa anymore cause it smelled of old skin.

"Go on. See about your mother, then, if that's your business." He meant business, as he would say, his brows screwed up close, his eyes bugging out like he would hit me if he wanted to, so I whirled around. "Wait," he said. He handed me the ashtray he and Lucky had used. "Empty this. Make sure you put that one out," he added, pointing to the cigarette Lucky had halfway put out in the ashtray. It still smoldered.

Without a word, I stomped off, which really came out as a slapping sound, bare feet over tiles. Out of the kitchen and back to Mama's bedroom. I heard Miss Jesse in the bathroom. Water ran in the sink, and she scooted bottles of makeup, lotions, perfumes and medicine across the marble counter.

Mama was propped up, her wine-colored satin pillows mashed behind her. Mama had always possessed smooth clear skin, dark hair and eyes blue as sky's reflection on a river. A talent for art. Money. Her family owned scads of land, and then traded money for it. She could not help me with my categories of people. She did not understand how many layers went into it. She would probably not give the colored people part the time of day.

Granddaddy was bragging once about how his daddy had been a member of the KKK. "But the KKK hang people," I'd said. Granddaddy had given me a killing look. Mama told me to hush and respect your elders. You don't understand how it was back then, she'd said, and it was an honor to be in the Klan. Honor schmonor, I'd said as I huffed out of the room.

Mama's mama had been a homely farm girl, Daddy said, and she gave Liz, as Mama was called, everything she wanted. Waited on her hand and foot. So when it came her turn, she did not ever entirely cotton to cooking or taking care of a child, though she tried early on, I'd heard Daddy tell Granddaddy once. Granddaddy was crazy as a rabid dog, people said. Built himself a house out back when he retired. Said he didn't like a phone or electricity, so there he lived in the dark until Daddy moved him to a house on the country club property. All he did there was order the electricity off and build himself a still in the living room. Granddaddy recommended that Daddy should get himself a place of his own, too.

I could not ask Maria Calphas over to play, hang around, or ride horses on account of Mama. I couldn't invite anybody. I liked Maria because her eyes sparkled big and she made a bigger smile, and she did not call me "Large," which stood for LRG which stood for Little Rich Girl, like other people did.

Mama took off the sunglasses and turned her head. Mama was always made up, but now her lipstick was smeared on lopsided.

"Well, hey, honey," she slurred, her eyes red. She gave a deep sigh. My gut burned. I put down the ashtray on her dresser, and walked over to the bed. She could hardly keep her eyes open. I remembered the time in first grade when I'd come home and she'd said, "Hey, honey," that same way, only with a spark in her eyes and without the slur. She'd taken my hand and led me to the den where she'd bought me an antique rolltop desk, only a tiny one, my size. "All your own," she'd said. She'd always made my lunches, and back then breakfast. She tried to teach me to paint like her, but I never could get the lines straight or as she said, the proportions right.

We'd cuddle on the sofa, and she'd make up songs about the silver outlining the trees, how the bass fish have skin translucent like onions, and strawberries were little worlds the color of Mars.

That came before the hypochondria, as the doctors called it. Before she would get drunk or drugged at night when Daddy had left. Before she'd cover every window in the house saying the moon would steal your eyes. The memories made me think about Mama as a heap of bones lying in the bed, so I pushed the thought away.

"Come on up here, honey," Mama slurred, holding out her arms. A part of me wanted to, wanted the old her back with her wild songs about frogs and silver trees.

"No, Mama," I said. "No. I'm too big." She let her arms flop down, and she stared at me, a sigh escaping her lopsided lipsticked lips. Then I felt mad. She was making me do things without even having to ask. Her eyes begged. I'd had it with her begging, and was sick of her sickness.

"Come on, honey, just a little hug," she said, reaching out

her right hand. Her breath smelled like booze. I swallowed.

"Your lipstick's crooked," I said. "I'll fix it." I turned to walk into the bathroom where Miss Jesse stood in the bathroom doorway.

"Rayann Wood," Miss Jesse said. "Do as your Mama says. Get up there in that bed. I'll bring you the lipstick." So I held my breath, crawled up into the bed, and hugged Mama fast, her skin still silky smooth. I could have cried, only I never did anymore. It only reminded me of how bad things had got if you'd made it to the crying phase. So I stopped tears before they reached my eye faucets.

Miss Jesse brought me a lipstick, tissue, and compact so Mama could check her makeup afterwards. Panic rose from the pit of my belly.

I tilted her head back and held her chin with my hand, rubbing hard on the lipstick staining her face the best I could and reapplied it carefully. Mama looked down her nose at me, eyelids drooping. Why do you do this? I thought to myself. You selfish mother. I pulled away, and handed her the mirror. "Take a look," I said. "See how pretty." Whirling around by the butt, I grabbed the ashtray.

"Daddy told me to empty this," I said, raising the smoking tray in the air. I jumped down from the bed, and hit the ground hard and running, and headed for the dining room. Outside, a breeze flickered over the bushes. In the dining room between the bedroom and den, a wind flew in and picked up the bottoms of the sheer curtains. In a few minutes, I'd get outside and brush my old horse, Star. The wind chimes jingled. Mockingbirds took turns at the feeder, singing *cheer up cheer cheer cheer cheer up* and pushed their babies toward the edge of the nest to fly.

I sat down at the dining room table that Mama had inherited. Her daddy had owned the Woodville pulp mill, and when her mama died, we moved into the big plantation-style house on the St. Marks River. Her daddy lived in his dark shack then. When Daddy got enough of the rotten falling down thing as he called the plantation house, and enough of Granddaddy's filth, he sold the plantation house to a Yankee from New York. He built this Spanish style house with real Mexican tiles Daddy said cost an arm and a leg. Mama had said, "Now, A.J.," when he talked money. Mama never talked about money. Daddy always did. I watched the cigarette burn in the ashtray. In the center of me, I felt like that cigarette, burning.

The long skinny dining table sat sixteen. Some supreme court justice had owned it and handed it down in Mama's family. I wanted to show it to Maria, which made me imagine bringing her home and taking her riding. Showing her the pond and how a horse feels under you. Then I thought about Mama with her glass of bourbon and her blue pills, her staggering about the house. She might complain about the heat and strip off her dress, down to her slip, right in front of Maria the way she did one time when Red was visiting. No, I couldn't do that. I picked up the cigarette to take a suck off it to try it out.

"I'm not ready to do that just yet," Daddy said. "I think Rayann can watch her this summer. See how that goes."

"You're a sucker, A.J.," Lucky said. "Need to deal with the problem." They walked into the front hallway. "Look at those pictures she used to draw."

"Paint," Daddy corrected him.

"That one there—the ocean? It's pink. Now whoever heard of a pink ocean? Everything else looks okay, but—she's a permanent case. If you won't go, why don't you find her a place? At least get ahold of some of that inheritance."

I didn't exactly know what Lucky was saying, but I knew it must have to do with bones. Mama could turn to bones, and me, too. Without really thinking about it, I held the cigarette to the edge of the table. It burned a tiny indentation, black and rounded, into the edge, and smelled like charcoal and plastic burning. Changing it forever. I liked the feeling it gave me. Warm, like blood pumping fast through your arms and legs. It blistered a black hole onto the surface of the table fast.

I heard Miss Jesse walk out the sliding glass door by Mama's room. She was sweeping the patio and allowing some fresh air in the room. I could hear her singing as she swept, a song about sweet Jesus.

Meanwhile, Daddy freshened his drink and saw Lucky out. They wandered into the front yard to stand around by Lucky's car for gosh knew how long jawing. I realized Daddy hadn't thought to find out from Miss Jesse or me how Mama was faring. I put the cigarette on the top surface of the table. It seared into the wood.

Another black hole. I burned another hole right next to it, another. I made three more, all the while thinking about children's bones, and the *Life* magazine I had seen with pictures of children in the war, running screaming from bombs. How they were getting close to being bones their own selves. Mama's bones in the bed with her wine-colored sheets. I stopped thinking and sat back. I had burnt a B into the table quick as you please. I had to burn a message into the table. BONES.

I grabbed Daddy's lighter and another whole cigarette to burn enough dots to get the word clear. Miss Jesse had stepped back into Mama's room talking to her, fluffing pillows, I hoped, and cleaning the tub while I burned. I took a suck off Daddy's cigarette and coughed and coughed until I thought I would gag. That's when I got up with the whole filthy ashtray and dumped it into the kitchen garbage, and swabbed it out in the sink with Palmolive liquid soap.

I felt better than I had in a long time. Mama would've wanted to kill me, but it made me feel clean.

Then I realized the house was starting to smell like smoke, like a fireplace that had burned something by mistake. I grabbed the Lysol spray and opened the French doors to the hallway across from the living room to let the smell out. I gave the dining room quite a drenching. I sneaked back over to the front porch area to spy on Daddy again, to see if he smelled anything burning. Probably not—he and Lucky had smoked and stunk up the house. He couldn't smell a thing.

I headed back to tell Miss Jesse I would go brush and feed Star. She had swept the whole patio, and brought the broom back into the kitchen. She stopped cold in her tracks.

"What's that smell?" she said, sniffing the air, looking at me sideways.

"Huh?" I said, washing a plate, not looking at her, rubbing my nose. "What smell?"

"Like burning wood." She stuck her nose to the air and sniffed.

"Just Daddy and Lucky smoking their *stupid* cigarettes."

"How many time I told you not to say that rude word? You need to respect your elders," Miss Jesse said, looking at me hard. "Now what's that burning smell?"

"Oh. That cigarette that was burning?" I said casually. "I forgot and dumped it into the trash can. It burned a napkin and some stinky plastic. Don't worry, I put it out. I'm going to go brush Star, Miss Jesse. I'll see you tomorrow." I hesitated. "You are coming tomorrow, aren't you?" She nodded and sighed, glancing at the clock over the stove. That's when I threw my arms around her. I had never hugged her before.

"Oh, my goodness," she said, shocked. I tried to let go, but she held onto me hard, and I let her. I let her hug on me and pat my back, and I kissed her brown cheek. It felt soft and smooth and mushy like Mama's.

2

I skipped out to the barn feeling light and dancy. I picked up Star's bridle in the tackroom behind the house and headed beyond the woods along the back fence of the yard. A warm breeze pulled the pasture pines back and forth across the sky. I bridled up Star and rode bareback, steering her off our paved drive and onto the dirt road. The dirt road was slick clay called Georgia clay, only we lived in north Florida.

Betty's Creek Road it was called. The last Indian left settled it and named her creek Betty's, Daddy had told me. When I asked him what kind of name was Betty for an Indian, he said, Betty White Cloud, and I said at least that sounded more real. He said Indians came in all varieties.

Betty's Creek Road stopped at the top of the hill, our driveway. The road followed the creek down past the woods on either side, past Miss Jesse's tiny white house behind some trees that hid a hill that tucked her house in safe. Out of sight, on down to the bottom of the road where the water emptied into a lily pad and eel pond. Colored people lived down by the pond in bright yellow, purple, and blue wood houses on Saturday Street.

Betty's Creek Road stretched past the pond under Magnolia Road, the main road to town that led straight to the hospital if you turned right, and way out into the country if you turned left.

The sun fell down warm like butter through the lettuce

green trees. A canopy of pines, sweetgums, and fat oaks shaded the road, letting in speckles of sun. The blue sky sailed overhead. A mockingbird sang *chair chair*. I could hear the creek whispering past over the rocks. I was happier outside. Trying not to think about burning BONES into the table. Past the curve in the dirt road, I saw a peculiar thing.

A colored girl walking away from me tiptoed with balance like a tightrope walker, dodging the small rocks. Down the clay road she walked in bare feet. Two white geese followed her, waddling and sounding like a band of kazoos. The girl sang a church hymn like she was rehearsing for *The Ed Sullivan Show*. Her voice was round and low. An alto in a church choir.

"*Hold thou thy cross,*" she sang. I recognized her as that girl, the fastest, strongest kickball player in school. She wore a matching orange shorts outfit with big red flowers. The boys always picked her for the team, even before boys, even though they said, *That nigger girl sure can run!* when she couldn't hear. I had learned to step out of the way at third base when she hoofed it, her long legs stretching to home runs. But nobody would talk to her. She was a colored girl, and the only colored person in the sixth grade. Except for one other colored girl in third grade who was always sick.

"*See through the gloom,*" she sang, those geese waddling and honking behind her. If she lived on Saturday Street, I would give her a ride on Star. After all, nobody would see but maybe other colored people, and what would that matter?

I had no one to play with, and not that I'd want to have anybody in the house, but I did want to show off the secret hideout I'd discovered. I'd found the old mill storehouse from when the place was a sugar mill a hundred and fifty years ago. It now hid in the overgrown woods past our house. I'd build my own home nestled inside the storehouse in case I ever needed one in the woods between our house and Miss Jesse's. But no. This girl was colored. I'd ride right past her. Maybe wave hello.

The leaves held their fifty-eight shades of green looking tender enough to eat. It had rained the afternoon before, hard and long, and the green world I loved sang, too. Early crickets *bree*'d and tree frogs sang *breek breek breek*. The smell of damp dirt caught me breathing deep. Cookie Johnson, that was her name. She hadn't seen or heard me yet. How'd she get up so close to the house, I wondered. Colored kids never came up to the house unless they wanted a job. Unless she'd been to Miss Jesse's house. But Miss Jesse was at that very moment cleaning the kitchen at our house.

"*Heaven's morning breaks,*" she belted out, throwing her arms to the cloudless sky. It reminded me of seeing her downtown in McCrory's department store with a fountain Coke stand, a sip-and-look bar where across the street stood the state capitol. A "Coloreds Only" bathroom sat outside, which my math teacher Miss Shipp said was now against the law. I liked Miss Shipp even if she did have red hair and a zillion freckles on her knuckles, and even if she did talk like a Yankee. I'd spied Cookie once the winter before scanning the Motown LP's with her eyes, deciding between Diana Ross and the Supremes and the Four Tops, all the while clutching a Sam Cooke record. Now in the warm breeze, listening to her voice, I got chill bumps. All warbly and crying out, her voice.

"*In life, in death, O Lord, abide with me.*" As she finished, Star's hooves clomping on the hard clay road caught the hidden ears of the geese, and they startled. Honked fast and loud. They collided into each other turning around to look. Cookie turned around scowling at them, then startled embarrassed when she saw me only ten feet away. She frowned.

Just when I gave an "I'm sorry" white girl look cause I had

a horse and she didn't, the bigger goose charged right at Star's chest. Star reared up, then shied sideways so fast that before I knew it, I'd been slung out and down, onto the road. I landed hard with an *oof.*

I felt embarrassed first, then mad, and my left hip smarted with pain. I sat up slow as the geese hovered and honked a circle around me. Star stood a few feet to the left side of the road, eyes huge. She breathed hard and rattly like horses do when they've seen a possum or rabbit, anything rustling that puts their minds to snakes.

"You okay?" Cookie said, standing over me. "Shoo, you crazy fools," she said, waving the geese away. She gave them a stern look and said, "I'll grab you by the neck and pitch you in the water." They ran to the right side of the road away from Star. She turned back to me. "You okay?"

"Yeah," I said, standing up and brushing off. I hobbled around to loosen up. "What you doing up here, anyway?"

"What you doing down here," she said, shifting to one side, a hand on one hip, "creeping up behind me like that." She stood about six inches taller than me, and I noticed her prettiness. She had a tulip mouth like Miss Jesse, only fuller, and kind of Chinese eyes. Almond, my mama called eyes like that. She was not scared of me one little bit. I liked her for it.

"You must live on Saturday Street," I said, brushing dried clay off my palms and jeans. I rubbed my hip and thigh where I'd landed.

She glanced over at the geese. "I don't live on no Saturday Street. I live up here." The geese stood quiet now, the smaller one preening the bigger one. She shook her finger at them, and said, "Stay over there, you fools." They ignored her just like cats do, and kept right on honking softly and preening. Turning back to me, she said, "You sure you okay?"

"Living?" I said, back to her first answer. "Up here?" I added, like what kind of answer is that. I took Star's reins and patted her sweaty neck. "It's okay, baby."

"Living with my aunt," she said, and pointed back up the road to Miss Jesse's. She said it like 'ont' instead of like 'ant.'

"Miss Jesse?" I said, feeling dizzy.

"Miss Jesse, uh huh, so what *you* doing up here?"

"Miss Jesse's your aunt?" I said. I thought about hugging Miss Jesse, and about her hugging me back, and how she took care of my family and never said a spitting word about having a niece. Did she hug her niece like she did me? Did she cook delicious meals of fried chicken and okra and squash casseroles? How could she do all that for two places? She had a secret life. One thing was certain. Colored people were a mystery. As mysterious as the markings on a turtle's back. Like they had all kind of secrets and weren't about to budge on revealing them.

"I told you already. Now you. What you doing up here?"

"I live up here. Up there," I said, pointing up the hill. "Miss Jesse works for—" I didn't want her to know about Mama.

"Your mama," Cookie said. "You the one they call Large at school."

"Don't call me that," I said irritated. I took Star's reins in my hand.

"Y'all got a color TV, right?" she said.

"Yeah." I hated to admit it. If she knew that, she must know about Mama. "Look, do you want to ride my horse?" Star had started to breathe normally. She even chewed whatever grass she'd stashed in her mouth.

"Oh, yeah, so he can throw me like he did you? No, thank you." But she looked up and down the road. Then up and down Star, then up and down me. "What if somebody saw me up on your horse?"

"So?" I shrugged. "You scared or something?" That did it. She eased up to Star's side. I pushed thoughts of Daddy driving down the road out of my mind.

"Why? You scared?" She reached out her hand to pat Star on the head. "Dang, he's big."

"Pat her neck. It makes them nervous if you go right for their head. There. Like that." The geese started honking.

"Shut up, you jealous fools," she said. They turned their butts to her.

"They your pets?" I said. "Can you pet a goose?"

"Horse hair is smooth," she said. "But his fur is all sweaty and nasty." She rubbed her hands together and balls of brown dusty sweat formed in her palm. "Yuck."

"It is not either nasty. She. It's a she. Star. Like I said, can you pet a goose?"

"I don't know," she said. "Come here, Waldo." The bigger one waddled over. "They're married."

"Married?" I said. "Geese?" I imagined a ceremony where the smaller goose wore a veil and a bigger goose held a ring in its mouth. But where in the world would he put it? Cookie would wear all black and hold the Bible and lead the ceremony.

"They stay together for life, geese. Margot, she won't go nowhere without Waldo. Somebody left them down at the pond, but they didn't know how to get on."

"Aw, who would dump these geesies," I said.

"Didn't even know how to get their own food," Cookie said. "They saw me walking by and followed me on home. Aunt Jesse won't let them up in the house, though." Then Margo waddled over.

Betty's Pond served as a dropping off place for all kinds of animals—puppies, sacks of kittens, a parakeet that died before I could pick it up, even grown dogs. One time when I rode

Star down to the pond, this brown dog with bald spots sat in the bushes whining, looking like it couldn't move except for its paws. That had happened two years before, when Mama'd just started her drinking and playing sick. I had insisted that Mama drive down and look at the dog, and we made Daddy drive down with us.

"The dog's a goner," Daddy had said. "I'll get my shotgun—"

"No!" Mama and I had said, holding hands. So he packed the dog off in the trunk of his Lincoln, cussing. He took the dog to the vet. When Daddy came home, he told us the dog had a broken back, and nothing the vet could do but put him to sleep.

"Now who would break a dog's back?" Mama had said.

"You wouldn't believe the things people will do," Daddy had said, shaking his head. I thought of bones.

"Can I pet Waldo and—?" I asked Cookie.

"Margot. No. They don't let you do that right at first. You got to be around for a while."

"Oh, I see," I said. "They have to charge you while you're on your horse and almost kill you first."

"Girl, you should have seen yourself fall, fall right off that horse. Like a sack of potatoes," she said. She leaned back and opened her mouth wide to haw haw. She did not have one filling in her head. My mouth already had six, due to soft teeth, as the dentist called it, but I suspected it could be attributed to all the chocolate I loved to eat.

"Very funny," I said. "I'm a good rider. Except when stupid geese run at my horse."

"Oooo, girl, you got some attitude," she said. "What you think, they just mean? They were protecting me, that's all." My thoughts went back to Mama. Protecting Mama. What I'd done to the table. My stomach tightened. I pushed the thought away.

"Are you going to ride this horse or not?" I said.

"No. No, I got to get going," she said, scratching her leg, glancing up the hill.

"You don't have to," I said, softening my voice. And then before I knew it would come out of my mouth, I said, "You got the most beautiful singing voice I ever heard." She smiled big now, and she blushed, I guessed. How would you know what a colored blush looked like? I wondered, but would never ask. She peered at the ground.

"I know. I'm moving to Chicago when Daddy gets out, and we're going to sing in the clubs together. He's a jamming guitar player. I'm going to do commercials for money in Chicago," she said. She closed her eyes and started singing like she was on the *Ted Mack Amateur Hour,* her hands held up, her face looking pained: *"I'm the type a guy who's always on the road..."*

You know that one?" she asked.

"Sure," I said. Then I joined in. *"I'm the type of guy who's always on the road. wherever I lay my hat, that's my home. Yeah."* For a second we stood and looked at each other. Then we both said, *Yeah,* smiled and stamped our feet, looking away.

"Girl, you know your music, now," she said, digging up a rock in the road, rolling it around with her big toe, then picking it up and tossing it into the woods.

"I got a radio. I listen to WTAL," I said.

"Yeah, that's a all right station," she said. "We listen to it at the house." I'd never thought about Miss Jesse listening to grooving songs and singing along. Chicago sounded so far away and sophisticated. I'd probably never get to go there.

"Look, I know this secret place by the creek where I sometimes go sit and cool off. You can even jump in the creek." She looked doubtful. "The geese might like it. Won't nobody see us." I never talked like that. Mama called it using double negatives. But I liked doing it.

"Well. Oh, all right," she shrugged. "You gonna ride that horse?"

"No. We can just walk over there. I don't think Star's really scared of Waldorf and—what's her name?"

"Waldo and Margot," she said.

"I think Star just got scared when Waldo charged at her. Let's go over in here." We ducked into the overgrown rut road, Cookie on the right with the geese behind her, and Star behind me. Small white moths and black butterflies flitted around us, and the sun shone full on the path. Just then I heard a car, probably Lucky's, rumble down the hill on Betty's Creek Road, and I felt relief that we had dove into the woods.

"How long you been living with Miss Jesse?" I asked.

"Since school started. That's why I came to this school. You bite your nails," she added.

"I can't help it," I said. I curled up my fingers, turned them around and looked at the ragged short nails.

"I know. Me, too. I bite mine, see?" she said. Hers were bitten down as far as mine, almost to the quick, but were more even across the tops. Mine had little jags sticking out. Right then, I felt we had made a truce. To what, I wasn't sure. She went on. "I want to get me some of that stuff you can paint on your nails that makes you stop when you put your hand to your mouth."

"That bitter stuff up at Woolworth's, the clear stuff in the bottle?" We rounded a bend, avoiding branches that had grown out into the path. The smell of leaves on the forest floor hung thick in the air.

"Yeah," she said. "But Aunt Jesse says we can't afford it right now. She say not on what your tight daddy pay her."

"Daddy ain't tight," I said. Saying ain't felt good too. But hearing about Daddy squeezed my heart. Still, I went on. "He gives me money."

"Well, he don't give it to his house cleaner." I thought about Miss Jesse's little house, which I'd only seen from the outside. I would sit in the car while Mama talked to her after bringing a Christmas present of blankets and a new bedspread. Neat and tiny. Four of her houses would have fit into one of ours. The front steps were kind of crumbly, and she owned no air conditioner, either, that I could see, and a stove top chimney poked out of the middle of the roof, so I guessed that served to keep her warm in the winters.

"Where's your daddy?" I said to change the subject.

"He's in the jailhouse," she said, matter-of-fact, like she'd said, He lives next door. "But he'll be getting out soon." She picked a wild daisy on the grassy path between us. She didn't even act ashamed to say it.

"What'd he do?" I wondered for a minute if he was a sorry, no count you-know-what. Colored people, especially men, were always going to jail. Why did they have to act so bad, I wondered.

"None of your business," she said. I wondered if she hung around uppity Negroes. I thought of Mama. I knew how this Cookie girl felt. How many times had I said that or wanted to when people asked me about Mama? So I didn't pursue that line of questioning, as Perry Mason would have said. I never asked anybody about their mama.

I could hear water chortling just ahead. *What if Daddy caught me here with a colored girl?* I worried. But something in me didn't care.

"Dang, it's cooler down here," Cookie said. We rounded a corner where ferns, green moss, and funguses grew on rocks.

Tree roots and dirt replaced grass. Sycamores and bays shaded the whole grassy bluff. The geese started honking fast, and Star picked up her pace, nudging me from behind. There lay the creek. It relaxed my back and neck to hear creek water running. A frog jumped plish into the water. The geese waddled right into the slow-moving stream. I let go of Star's reins and she wandered over to the creek and stooped to take long loud sips of the clear water.

Cookie put her toe in first, then a foot. Then another foot. "It's so clear," she said. "Not muddy like the pond." I rolled up my jeans, followed her in, let the cool water run around my ankles. I stooped and put my hands in.

"Daddy says if you put your main pulse points to something cool, it'll cool your whole body off," I said. My hands had a fish algae smell I liked.

"Your daddy a doctor?" she said.

"Hospital administrator," I said.

"Humph," she said. "My brother works over there." She found a dry grassy spot under a bay tree.

"Doing what?" I said, sitting on the muddy bank, ankles in the water.

"Cleaning," she said. I thought of Mr. Nix, the old colored man at the hospital who gave me gum and read the comic from the wrapper with me. How Daddy had fired him last year for drinking on the job. I thought of Cookie's brother, whoever he was, giving me gum, drinking on the job, then going home to tell his family he'd got fired. I thought of children starving, of children in the pictures I saw in the war after bombs, and then I thought of Cookie having nothing to eat. I stopped myself. Daddy didn't fire every colored person, just drinking colored people. Still my stomach wouldn't sit still.

"What's his name," I said.

"Ivory Jones," she said. With that, I let out a breath of relief. I didn't know him. Probably because he worked the late shift, and I rarely went to the hospital in the middle of the night.

She picked up a wet stick floating on the water and studied it. "He wants to be a nurse's aide, but they won't let him." Colored people didn't get jobs like that.

"How old is he?" I said, and wiped my hands on my jeans.

"Old enough to be mean as the devil. Sixteen. Barely." She threw the stick down the creek.

"How old are you?" I asked.

"Same as you. Thirteen."

A plane flew overhead, and a mockingbird sang a crazy repertoire of songs. Cookie waded in and sat next to me, listening to the creek rush by. She asked if you could fish in the creek, and I said probably. She talked about how the minnows in the creek reminded her of last fall when it rained for two weeks solid, and how Betty's Creek had flooded over the road to shape one big pond. She said Mr. George on Saturday Street took out his fishing pole and his tore-up lawn chair, sat himself down in the middle of the road and fished. Caught a mess of bream, she said.

I told her that was strange, but not as much as the goat bar I went to with Daddy one time. It had broken pool cues cause there wasn't room to play with regular ones, and a goat walked around the bar all the time.

"Crazy crackers," she said, shaking her head. I liked that she cussed.

"How come you don't ride the bus," I said. Everybody rode the bus who lived out where we did. I'd never seen her.

"They won't let me," she said, pushing up to stand.

"Sure they'll let you. They have to," I said. "Ain't it the law now?"

"The law don't mean they'll let me," she said. She glared at me. "The older boys. Said they didn't want no *niggers* riding on their bus." She threw a stick into the water and watched it float around the bend. "They pushed me off one day. I ain't gone back." I felt embarrassed. I stood, then stooped back down into the creek. I put my hands in the water and stared at them. They looked so pale, like little white minnows.

"Those older boys are so stupid," I said. "I hate them." I did not know what else to say. You did not talk about colored and white problems around colored people. Colored people thought different. They wanted more rights and stuff. But I knew something for the second time that day—it was wrong. What those boys did on the bus was not fair, and everybody who went along with it knew it. But you wouldn't catch me saying that aloud. Everybody would say, What are you, a nigger lover? Much worse than being called Large.

"I get a ride with my brother every day, and I don't have to take no damn bus." She peered up at the sun and asked did I know what time it was. I guessed around two, and she said she'd better be getting on home. "Saturdays Aunt Jesse gets home early. Now. Come on, you two," she said to the geese. "You ready?" she said to me.

I did not feel like going home, but I worried that Daddy or somebody might see me hanging around with a colored girl. I nodded.

On the rut road, we sang *Mr. Postman, look and see, oh yeah, if there's a letter in your bag for me* since I told her I liked the Beatles. She said Paul was a candy ass sissy, but he sure could sing. I had a terrible crush on Paul, but I did not tell her.

"How'd you find that old spot?" Cookie said, hurrying up the path.

"What old spot?" I said as we wound around the big curve.

"That crook in the creek, girl," she said.

"Riding Star," I said. "Nobody else around. So I just ride everywhere. I've got a hideout, a *secret* hideout right between your house and mine. Want to see it?"

"You mean in the woods?"

"Yeah, where the smaller creek runs down to the road. Over there. It's extra cool, too. Got walls and a doorway. No ceiling but the sky."

"How about that," she said, looking up at the sky, squinting, sounding faraway.

"Want to see it?" I said. We could see Betty's Road now, and we slowed down.

"Aunt Jesse needs me to pull weeds today," she said, glancing my way, then away. "I don't and the bugs'll get to all that lettuce."

"I'm not talking about right now," I said. "Next week. Next Monday, after school." She looked out at the clay road with a frown.

"I've got a lot of work to do," she said. I knew we could both get in big trouble, and I felt nervous, too, getting close to the road. But I liked her, and wanted to keep in secret touch with her, so I made a bargain with her.

"I'll help," I said.

"You're saying you'd come—?" she said, stopping dead in her tracks, eyebrows raised. The crickets were breeing, and I felt lightheaded. *Please,* I was thinking. "Well, maybe," she said, shrugging. "Hey, you remember The Drifters?" She started walking toward the road again. "They came out a few years ago, but I like their songs."

Then she started singing softly and I joined in, "*Under the boardwalk, down by the sea, yeah, on a blanket with my baby is where I'll be.*" As we approached the clay road, I went down to fake baritone and sang *"Out on the boardwalk,"* and Cookie rang a fake soprano, *"We'll be having some fun."*

"Girl, you got to be quiet. How you get so low, anyway?" she said. Just when I was about to say I don't know, we rounded the corner and stopped dead in our tracks. Star bumped into me. Not thirty feet up the road, Miss Jesse was walking down the hill. She had taken off her apron and glasses, and she looked like a different person. When she saw us, she stopped dead in her tracks, too. The geese kept walking and started to honk when they saw Miss Jesse, but she paid them no mind. Her mouth stood open, her hand flying halfway up to her mouth, then she dropped it. She looked from one of us to the other. Cookie and me stood still and stiff as walking stick bugs. Miss Jesse pursed her lips and put her hands on her hips while the geese walked in a circle around her. They might as well have been invisible. She put on her scold face.

"What you girls been up to?" She stared Cookie down.

"We just took a walk in the woods, Aunt Jesse," Cookie said. "We didn't do nothing."

"We were just talking is all," I said. Miss Jesse shifted feet and looked down the road to Saturday Street. Then back up towards my house. She took a deep sigh and dropped her arms.

"Get on home, Cookie. Rayann, you'd better get home, too. You in trouble." She raised her eyebrows and put her fist on her hip as she walked toward us and beckoned Cookie to her. "Your daddy found some cigarette burns or something or the other, some damage to your mama's table. He want to know did I do it. Don't know why in the world he'd think I done such a foolish thing. Burning 'BONES' into that table."

"What?" Cookie said, turning back around to look at me. "How can you burn 'bones' in a table?"

"Some fool burned the word 'bones' on the table," Miss

Jesse said, darting a sidewise look at me and putting her arm around Cookie. "Somebody been thinking a lot about bones, from my speculating."

My throat hurt like something had burned it raw. Cookie leaned into Miss Jesse, who put her arm around Cookie. All I felt was a red jealousy seep over me.

"I didn't do it," I said. I hoped I sounded convincing, but my throat pulled tight and ached. "Why would I do a thing like that?" I held onto Star's reins to keep my hands from shaking.

"They all in a tizzy up the hill. You better tell your daddy what you told me," she said, then turned around with Cookie and headed to her driveway up the hill. She turned her head around and said, "That Lucky, when he seen it, he thought your mama did it." She gave me a piercing look. "But your daddy don't. So you better get home and straighten things out then, hear?" I looked away.

"Yes, Ma'am," I said, mumbling, looking at the ground.

"Girl, you fed these geese?" I heard her say to Cookie as they all four headed up the hill to Miss Jesse's house.

"No, Ma'am, but I was getting ready to," Cookie said, "Honest."

"You best be careful..." she was saying something I couldn't quite get in a hissing whisper. Then her tone slid back down to normal. "We got to get that mess of greens out of the garden," she said, "and mulch them blueberry bushes. Got to check the peach trees for worms, too."

Then they were out of earshot, talking and planning their Sunday, I figured. I wished I was climbing their hill to home rather than heading to my big house. Even if theirs was a colored house. Little did I know then what I know now: that when you visited in colored people's houses, blood started to spill.

3

Once back in the cool dark barn, I brushed Star down. It gave me a strange good feeling when a horse about three times your size stood still while you fussed over it. Or walked when you sat on it and nudged its sides with the insides of your feet. A little harder, and it trotted. When the horse knew she was on the way home to some oats rolled in molasses, and she charged into a gallop, and you clung on to her sides with your knees. Nothing else to hang on with when a horse runs in a pure two-gaited gallop. They cut loose under you, not holding anything back, muscles in motion, you moving as they move. Like flying.

After I brushed her, I fed her oats, a treat, since in summer our pasture grew big and green. Oats we fed her only in the winter, when the grass went to brown seed. I gave her a good sweet talking to, as if I didn't have to go face Daddy inside, patted her flank, then put her in the pasture.

The late afternoon sun washed gold through the trees as I shut the back glass door into the kitchen.

"Rayann?" Daddy yelled when he heard it.

"Yes, Sir?" I said.

"Come in here, please," Daddy said, like a gun shooting out pellets fast and hard. He meant, *Get in here now.* "To the dining room."

"What is it?" I said, walking in, my voice raised high, sweet and soft.

"First off, where have you been?" he said.

"Just riding," I said.

"Just riding, huh? Well, do you know anything about this?" he said, pointing to the table where I'd burned the holes. He tried to appear adult and serious, but his bloodshot eyes gave away that he was pickled. The letters were etched clear as day—BONES. The table looked dusty with the angle of light slanting in on it. The candelabra needed polishing. I had to admire how clear the black letters showed up, even from where I stood in the doorway.

"What?" I said, holding my palms to the ceiling and letting my face go blank. Like I didn't see it. "The candelabra?"

"Come over here," he said, waving his hand quick, and letting out a big sigh. "Right here. Do you know anything about this?"

"Oh, my gosh, what is it?" I said.

"It's a damaged table, a burned table, an intentionally damaged table. And I want to know if you did it. And you'd better not be lying to me, young lady, or you're going to be in some trouble," he said. He slurred it a little, but since he was handing out a lecture, he worked on pronouncing.

I was scared of Daddy's temper. The first time I saw it I was only three, and he came home when we lived in a little apartment while he went to college. Mama had made tuna casserole, cause they were trying to save money, and he threw the whole thing, tuna and mushroom soup and noodles and casserole dish, against the wall, saying he was sick of tuna fish. That tuna fish casserole's creamy middle had oozed down to the floor while some of the noodles stuck to the wall. After Daddy stomped off into the kitchen to make a sandwich, Mama had cried and I had picked pieces of noodles stuck on the wall. Now I had to think fast. Even with the lecture tone, his voice held that don't-quite-know-what-to-do parent tone.

I didn't like lying to Daddy, but what if he found out I did lie? Even the truth meant he'd give me a whipping. Worse, if I told the truth, I could miss seeing Cookie in the woods next week.

"You think I'd do that?' I said, pointing at myself, bending over a little for emphasis. "I love that table."

"Well, I—" He looked both relieved and flabbergasted at the thought that Mama would do it.

As soon as I saw him hesitate, I said, "You think I'd mess up Mama's favorite table?" I yelled it, looking wide-eyed at him.

"Don't you yell at me, Missy," Daddy yelled. Then he took a breath, turned around and looked at the ceiling. He turned back around and let out a sigh. "Now Rayann, I know things have been upsetting you lately with your mama sick, and so forth. But you do not use that tone—"

"What the hell is going on?" a voice behind us slurred. Daddy and I turned around. Mama had walked into the room. She wore her blue flannel nightgown, which was falling off one shoulder. Her hair was mashed up on one side. I was embarrassed for her, and saw her as a clown, the way Daddy would see her. Like this sad little lady who no longer was the sexy wife he was so proud of when he married her. She held an unlit cigarette in one hand. She looked like somebody had wheeled her up from a motel room under the sea. He shook his head. Then he snickered nervouslike. She plopped back against the wall, looking bleary, but her eyes focused straight at him.

"What are you doing up?" Daddy said, moving to Mama to put his hand under her arm. "You need to get back into the bed, Liz." Mama yanked away and nearly lost her balance. She looked so tiny, her blue eyes confused and mad.

"Answer my question," she said, pointing with the unlit cigarette. "What's going on here?" Daddy ran his hand through his hair, and it stuck up like a baboon's.

"Nothing, Mama," I said. "Get some clothes on if you're going to—"

"I was asking Rayann—" Daddy interrupted. He shook his head in bewilderment.

"Asking her what?" Mama said. "Go on, Anty. Asking her what?" She looked from me to Daddy, and I looked at the floor. When nobody said anything, she said, "Where's my purse?" She looked around the room and craned her neck into the TV room. I fetched her purse from the bedroom. She put the cigarette in her mouth, and handed Daddy her purse. "Anty, I want a light." She was using Daddy's real Indian name that nobody else knew. Antelope Jumper Wood. He had told everybody his name was Allen. Just call me A.J., he'd say. Anty was her pet name for him. Daddy fished around until he found her gold lighter with her initials and lit the cigarette for her.

"Liz—" he said, then hesitated.

"What did I want to ask you?" Mama said. "I mean," she laughed and lost her footing and then got it back, "what did *you* want to ask *me*?"

"Don't worry, Mama, it's nothing," I said. "Why don't you go back to bed." She was getting the attention now, so maybe I could slip off, and he'd forget about the table incident.

"Ask me, A.J.," Mama said. Daddy looked at the floor, then at the ceiling. Then at the table.

"See?" he said. Mama wobbled over to the table, Daddy stumbling with her.

"That's the word 'bones'," she said. Then she laughed. Just a Ha. Then a ha ha ha. "You think I did that?" She turned and looked at Daddy, who, I could tell now, was sure she'd done it. If Mama'd been normal, she'd have been beside herself, wanting to clean it off, no matter who'd done it.

She'd have said, "Good Lord, look at this table!" Then

she would've gone and gotten the wood stain and the wood wax and tried to get it cleaned off, and would be fussing and chattering about how nobody respected her antiques.

"Did you do this, Liz?" Daddy said, like he was talking to a kid. She looked up at him and suddenly she understood. Hurt and confused. She turned around and looked at me. "What's this all about, Rayann, honey?" she said.

My face turned red hot, and I looked at the floor. I wanted to tell the truth and take my punishment. But maybe the best thing that had happened to me in a long time, talking to Cookie, would end. She would wait for me to come help her in the garden, and sure enough, I wouldn't appear. Nobody could keep me from my new friend. Friend? You couldn't be friends with colored people. But I liked her. I did not want to give up riding Star, either. And I did not want to explain why I burned the table, either. I didn't know myself, only that it scared me. I backed towards the doorway.

"I don't know," I said. "Can I go, Daddy?" I said. He nodded, so I ran to the kitchen. I felt empty and hungry, so I dug into some of the turkey Miss Jesse had roasted during the week. I could hear Mama.

"You all hate me, don't you? Blaming every little thing on me," she said. "You'd just like to get rid of me, wouldn't you?" Her voice would rise up into a screech every few words.

"Now stop talking like that, Liz," Daddy said. "It's just— you're sick, honey, and it makes you think that way." He knew how to put on the doctor voice all right. All Mr. Smooth and Comfort and I'm-in-charge. "Nobody wants you to go anywhere."

I shoved some turkey into my mouth and drained the milk carton. I wanted to fill myself up with something besides the empty way I felt. Then I headed up the stairs to take a bath.

"Nobody wants you to go anywhere," Daddy was saying. Mr. Smooth and Comfort, coaxing her back into bed.

I ran a good long bath to drown them out. You never knew how Mama would act. Sometimes like an important poised lady, no matter how broke down she looked. Sometimes like a crazy wailing child. I poured bubble bath that smelled like roses and threw in some Epsom salts. They were talking and yelling, but I shut it out. The year before, Daddy had moved out for a while, though he claimed he had late night on-call business. Mama had gotten bombed one night when he had disappeared. She had that thinking-of-one-thing-only focus going, and wanted to find Daddy. I took the car keys from her. She tried to call him, but she kept reaching the Emergency Room, one number off. Finally she gave up.

She reached for the bottle once more, and I snatched it from her. I slung that bourbon bottle way out into the front yard. Mama walked out there and tried to find it with a flashlight, crying and saying, *You don't love me anymore.* When she couldn't find her half-drunk bottle, she walked back in and refused to drink the water I'd poured for her.

She finally did reach Daddy on the phone somehow. And what did he do but come over to the house with another bottle and hand it right to her.

I stepped down into the bath. "You all don't love me," Mama was wailing. "Nobody treats me right around here," she said, crying. I turned the water back on hard. I sunk down into the water up to my little boobies. They had felt sore to the touch lately. And they were growing. I did not wish to think about that, so I sunk up to the neck in the bath and breathed the smell of roses, listening to the warm water run. I thought about talking to Cookie. Then I started humming *Under the boardwalk, down by the sea, yeah, on a blanket with my baby, that's where I'll be.*

I bolted up in the bed during the night. My room was lit by the moon and the vapor surrounding it high in the sky. Its fuzzy light burned in through the glass of my balcony doors. Something was off, I felt it in the core of me. At first I thought of Star. But no, in the house, something. I tiptoed downstairs like a cat. Daddy was slumped sideways on the sofa, positioned between sitting and lying, a Leaning Tower of Pisa pose. His reading lamp shone yellow in the dark room. He snored steadily, and the refrigerator clicked on and began to hum. I walked through the house to Mama's bedroom. At first I couldn't see anything but black brown darkness. Then from the white slant of light coming through the bathroom I saw her—lying on the floor near the bathroom like a heap of dirty clothes.

"Mama?" I said, standing over her. I knelt. "Mama?" I could not even hear her breathe. Then I heard it, slow and shallow. I lifted her arm and it fell back down. "Mama!" I shouted. She did not even stir. "Goddamn it, Mama." I half expected her to sit up and scold me for my language. "Goddamn it, Mama, not again." I'd had to carry her to bed before when she'd passed out in the living room after getting up from the sofa.

I pulled towels from the bathroom and laid them on the floor next to her. Then I rolled her around till her body lay on top of them. She rolled over like a sack of potatoes. "Damn, Mama, I am not no Florence Nightingale here, you understand," I said. I pulled the big white towels around her, wrapping her up. I talked aloud to keep myself from going nuts. "You look like a mummy," I said. I could hear only her shallow breath and my feet slap and squeak across the polished tile. I squatted to pick her up. I almost fell lifting her the first foot off the ground, but after that she hardly weighed anything. She never ate a thing but cheese crackers and ginger ale anymore. "You're skinny as a broomstick."

I picked her up and her feet dragged across the floor. Her head flopped across my arms. I dropped her down on the pink sheets. "I'm no heavyweight champ, either." I covered her with the satin comforter, puffing away. From the bathroom light, I could see the dark hair strewn across her face. She barely breathed at all, like she might give up and quit trying. I climbed up on the bed to study her.

The room smelled of dust, Bluegrass perfume and stale chocolate mints. Outside, the owls hoo-hooed. Raccoons and foxes bumped around in the night, looking for food outside the back window of Mama's room. She breathed too slow, with more and more time between breaths. Her face had turned nearly sheet pale, and her lips had a purple tinge. Then she stopped breathing for a couple of seconds, and I shoved her like a bag of bones. She started breathing again. I started to sweat, thinking I'd bust open from the inside.

"Damn, Mama," I said.

Mama's head was turned sideways, and her hand had flopped onto her face just under her chin, so that it looked like she was contemplating something deep. It reminded me of how we'd spent the summer in the mountains before she got so unhappy. Two summers ago, and we'd been sitting in the bar of The Blue Ridge Inn, the old hotel where we'd stayed, and her family had stayed before that. I loved the linen table cloths and napkins and heavy silverware. Daddy'd gone away on business, and Mama and I'd shared some fresh raspberries. The midmorning sun hit the crystal vase on our table and made a rainbow shadow across the wooden floor.

"What are you thinking about, Mama?" I'd said, because her head rested on her hand in that thinking-about-things way.

The smell of linen and pine wood sat in the air.

"I was just watching those people over there, the couple. Thinking about how you can tell when people are married," she said. "They don't talk to each other." She smiled at me beautiful and cheeky.

"Aren't they bored?" I said.

"They're comfortable with each other, and they don't have to talk," she said, watching another couple closer to the doors.

"They look bored to me. Are you and Daddy bored?" I said.

"No, honey," she said. Tightness showed around her mouth. "When you're comfortable together, you don't have to talk." But something in her voice made me think she was trying to convince herself. I started fidgeting, and she said, "Come over here." With that, she pulled me into her lap and enveloped me with her arms. "Pretty soon, you won't want to sit in my lap anymore." I had sat back and pressed my face into her shoulder, relaxed my back into her soft body. Out the front window, the sun had finally hit the grassy meadow. The lodge was quiet except for the dishwasher spraying in the kitchen. I sat a while and she patted my leg, staring out the window like she was searching for her lost dog. When I couldn't sit still any longer, I asked if I could go play ping pong with the kids in the rec center.

Now in the brownish black night, her mouth hung open, her hair was matted down, her whole face ashen. She was barely breathing and not stirring. "Damn, Mama," I said again. "How much did you drink?" I got up and turned on the bedside table light and ran down the hallway to wake Daddy up.

I told him Mama seemed deathly ill, and he needed to take her to the hospital. He rubbed his head hard and said Ow, then sat up. "Let me get my face washed," he said.

"Hurry, this is an emergency," I said.

"She's drunk," he sighed, his liquory breath spreading as he rubbed his head again.

"She's hardly breathing, Daddy," I said, impatient.

"I'll need to take a look at her," he said. He shuffled to the hallway. I ran ahead and jumped up in the bed. "She's probably okay, Rayann."

Daddy hated involving his own family in doctors or the hospital. When I got the measles, he refused to send me to the doctor until I took my own temperature and showed him it read 104.

He picked up her arm and tried to get a pulse. "I can hardly feel it," he muttered. He looked like he'd turned into a board, that stiff. He moved jerky and mechanical, like the Jetson's robot, Rosy. He listened close to her breathing. "Yeah," he said, standing up. "Get some clothes on. We've got to get her in."

I tore upstairs and put on some shorts, and flew back down the hallway. I met Daddy in the den. He'd changed and combed his hair in the half bath, his eyes red, lips parched, face white, and beard unshaven.

"Let's go," he said. We headed to the bedroom to get Mama. He loosened his shirt, preparing to pick Mama up. "Get me some water, Rayann."

"Water," I said.

"Yeah, I'm thirsty, go on. Use your mama's glass."

I opened their bathroom door. There it lay—the bottle with her blue pills. Capped but separate from the others and tipped over. I picked it up and shook it. Empty. I grabbed the bottle and sat, collapsing like a tent on the cold floor. Bricks, cold bricks. I felt like all the bricks of the house were falling down on me, chalky and heavy. I sat numb until Daddy said, "Rayann, hurry up!"

I stood, shaking like an old lady, and walked out holding

the bottle. "She took these," I said. My voice shook. Daddy grabbed the bottle. "All of them."

"Good god," he said. "Valium. Ten milligrams? I didn't even know she had such a dosage. Do you know how many?" I shook my head. "Let's go," he said. He moved like a robot, but not cheery like Rosy. Like a grim robot.

Unlike most people, I usually enjoyed going to the hospital. Daddy worked there, and I had gotten used to the way it worked. It created its own little world.

I created mine, too: Since my daddy had been hired as King, I was the hired Princess. I could go anywhere I wanted, spy on anyone, walk through ICU doors if I so desired. You could spend your whole life at a hospital if you think about it. Beds, cafeteria-style food with the best black-eyed peas and rice and bread pudding you ever tasted, and heat and cool under the roof. Lots of different workers around who seemed to be dating each other, or who used to date each other, or were married to each other. Once Mama had said they were all married to their work.

Tonight, though, I came in like most people who visited the hospital, smelling the cleaning fluid, then wax, then finally the blood under everything else. They would come in scared or sad, often looking like they'd lost a war. Sometimes cheery groups visited a new baby in the family. For the first time, I came in with the lost-war slump in my face.

The two EMTs who worked on Mama held their elbows in close like soldiers at attention. But when they checked Mama into the ER room where I followed like one of Cookie's geese, their elbows flew like drummers, as if they were playing their song to help people stay with the living. Daddy had excused himself to get a cup of coffee, but he'd gone to call the psychiatrist Dr. Indley, and to find the best doctor on call. I knew how it worked.

The tall tech with hair that reminded me of a beige carpet—wiry, curly and not blonde or red—had on a nametag that read SKIP. He checked Mama's blood pressure, took her pulse and her temperature. The short one with a dark straight crew cut said, "She came in with an unknown number of Valium 10 mils P.O. and high alcohol content."

"Well, that'll cork you out," Skip said. He held Mama's arm as he listened to her pulse, whistled, then turned and looked at me. I stared at him. "She was probably trying to stop the agitation. A psychosomatic history, agitation prevalent. Breath is slow and shallow, purple around the lips. I'll check the airways." He said all this like he was in an alert trance while he looked at me. It's how they worked. I'd seen it before. He looked away and tilted Mama's head back. "Lucky so far, no obstruction, but I'll need oxygen." He looked back at me and smiled. They had let me stay cause I was Mr. Wood's daughter. "You okay?" I nodded and stared at the cabinet full of syringes, scissors in wrap, needles, bottles of antiseptic and anesthetic. Sure, I was okay. I just wanted to throw up, was all. My mama had tried to kill herself because I was too chicken-hearted to admit I burned her table.

The short crewcut guy handed Skip an oxygen mask, which Skip put over Mama's face and strapped around her head. "This is your mom, right?" Skip said. I nodded. "Can you get your dad for me?" he said. I nodded again, and left the room. But as I left, I heard him say, "Looks like the guy would be in here, you know?" Walt murmured something I couldn't hear.

Daddy was walking fast down the hallway, circles under his eyes, and his hair back up like a baboon again. I wished he didn't look red in the face and smelling like he'd been drinking.

But he felt at home here, swinging his arms, craning his head in every direction, nodding to the nurse and the doctor on call as he rushed past.

"How is she?" He didn't wait for the answer, but rounded the corner into Mama's room. Skip stood erect with his elbows in again, the way everybody tucked their elbows in for a boss man.

"Mr. Wood, Sir," Skip said, "we'll need to get an IV in her and get her stomach pumped. Would you and your daughter like to sit in the waiting room?"

"Yes, we would," I said. Daddy would want to take me down to his office, but I wanted to stay right there. I got up and held Mama's limp cold and parched hand, but I couldn't think of what to tell her. *Keep breathing,* I thought.

A big aluminum coffee urn stood on a corner table in the workers' lounge and lots of Styrofoam cups were stacked beside. The lights shone fluorescent. I was freezing cold. Two puffy brown sofas sat on either side of the table, so I curled up into one and tried to get warm. Daddy got on the phone nailed to the wall. He was talking to the psychiatrist, answering his questions, asking more. I drifted off to sleep somehow. I dreamed lacy iron bars, the ones on 5C, the psych ward, covered a window. There were no screens, and the glass had been sealed tight. No breeze entered or left. Somehow, Mama's body had been burnt like a broiled chicken and she couldn't move. She didn't have anything left, just parched skin. And I held the match. I woke up with a jolt as Daddy hung up the phone. Drool ran down my chin and I blinked in the bright light.

Daddy turned around and sat down on the couch next to me. "Sugar." He put his arm around me. I leaned into him and felt his strong arm. It's my fault, I thought. Daddy cleared his throat. "If your mother makes it through this, she's going to have to go away." The lights over us buzzed. Go away? I thought. "For about a month," he added.

"Go away?" I said, sitting up and turning around to look at him. "What for?"

He told me that she'd be staying on 5C where they kept the crazy people before they decide whether they're really crazy or they get to go home. They'd keep her there until, as Daddy said in that hospital way, she recuperated from the overdose, and she'd be under observation for a possible longer stay at Chattahoochee. Everybody knew about Chattahoochee. Crazy people ended up there, two hours away from Tallahassee. I'd heard from one of the girls at school that a nurse's aide had told this lady patient he'd help her escape, and when he got her in the stairwell in the middle of the night, he raped her. Stuff like that happened all the time at Chattahoochee. Everybody knew that.

"She doesn't need to go there," I said.

"Rayann—"

"No," I said. He could not shut me up like he did at home. "NO!" I stood up and held my arms by my side, my fists balled up.

"Honey, you don't understand," he said, and leaned over, putting his hands on my shoulders. "Your mother is very sick. I'm trying to get her the best help I can, and you have to under—"

"Mr. Wood, Sir?" a nurse said. It surprised us both, but she'd come to the door while we had stood arguing. She held a tight smile on her face. Daddy followed her down the hallway the other direction. I sat back down. All I could think of was what Ralph always said to Alice: *One of these days, Alice, one of these days, Pow, right in the kisser!* I imagined having the guts to say that to Dr. Indley when he told Daddy that Mama needed to go into Chattahoochee. I picked up an old *Highlights* magazine and tried to read one of the crossword puzzles. My eyes hurt. In a little while, that tall Skip came in to get some coffee.

"Tried the coffee yet?" he said. I looked at him sidewise. "It tastes like it came out of a septic tank." I couldn't help but smile.

"Then why are you drinking it?" I said.

"Torture. Keeps me awake." He sat down on the other sofa.

"I could think of better ways to stay awake," I said.

"Yeah, like what?" he asked. I shrugged. "What do you like to do that might just keep you awake? Besides work the crossword puzzles in *Highlights*?"

"Ride horses," I said.

"Oh, yeah?" he said. He leaned back and drained his coffee, then tossed the cup into the trash can under the table. He started to ask me a question, leaning up and taking in a breath, when this tall lanky colored guy came into the room with a stack of clean ER scrubs, green, blue, aqua, and told Skip he was needed in ICU. The lanky guy glanced at me, then took a deep breath and let it go as he sat down next to me. I'd only seen colored people work as janitors in the hospital. He should probably get up and go, I thought. Daddy might decide to fire him for sitting next to me.

I didn't know what to do, so I picked up the *Time* magazine and started looking at pictures of The Rolling Stones and then of that Martin Luther King Negro in Birmingham.

Who were these people who came and went from the coffee room? Why should they be living, breathing fine and not be overdosed, maybe near dying, and not on their way to 5C and then Chattahoochee like my mama? I wondered if

Skip, or this colored guy with his beautiful amber eyes, had a mother or a brother or a dad in the hospital, would they feel as scared and numb and sad as me.

Amber. The color of the foyer light, Mama had said. A rich yellow brown. Amber. The word fit the color, warm and rich.

"How you doing?" the guy said. Amber eyes looking full on. I could not take my eyes off him. He had the clearest red complexion, almost like Indians I'd seen that one time my family went to a burial in the Everglades.

"Fine," I said. I took my eyes away, but my stomach flip-flopped. I stared at the old *Newsweek* with President Nixon's picture on it, and picked it up, acting interested. As he made his coffee, I noticed he wore those ridiculous shoes they had to wear, scrub shoes, in ER and OR. They looked like paper shower caps on their feet. Some even wore the shower caps on their heads. "Really, that's a lie," I said, surprising myself. "I am not fine. My mama's had a bad accident."

"The lady passed out?" he said, like he already knew. "You're Wood's daughter."

"How'd you know?" I said, dropping the magazine on the table.

He shrugged. "Work here."

"Yeah, I can tell by your shoes," I said, pointing at his big pastel shoes.

"Cute, huh?" he said. He held his feet up with shoes that looked like grandma slippers. I couldn't help laughing. It felt right fine to laugh. He got up with his towels and coffee and said, "I'll be back." He had big shoulders and a slow gait. Cute enough to die for. What was I thinking, my own mama could die tonight. Plus, he was colored. Light colored, but colored. I went back to the crossword puzzle.

In a few minutes, he came back. He leaned in the door, just

his top half, and he wasn't holding the coffee cup or the folded scrubs. "Your mama's okay," he said. He looked up the hall and down. "They've got to send her to ICU tonight. Then to 5C for detox." He must have seen the scared look on my face. He walked in and sat back down on the other sofa. "She's lucky. No brain damage, looks like. But she'll be here for a while."

I sat back and let go a long deep breath.

"You okay?" he said.

I nodded. "Detox?"

"She's got to dry out," he said, looking straight at me. Who the heck did this guy, this brave colored guy, think he was, talking so free. "She needs to get on the wagon, as they say." I nodded. "Permanent like." I nodded again. "You okay?" he asked.

"I'm just glad they're not sending her to Chattahoochee," I said. I could not believe myself, that I was spilling this private news to him.

"Chattahoochee?" he said, his eyebrows raised. "She's not no permanent case." He saw me sit back a little. He had audacity to give an opinion like that. He shrugged. "Just my opinion." He stood up and gave me a hand wave. "Take it easy." Then he vanished.

When Daddy came back in, he started explaining how Dr. Indley had suggested Mama be quarantined for a month.

"Quarantined?" I said. "Don't they do that to donkeys they bring back from Israel or somewhere?" I folded my arms and frowned. I felt tired.

He explained that this was a way to get her away from her daily stresses. He was talking around things, like grownups did. On and on as he paced and stared at the floor, smoothing his hair down. Words I'd heard before from being around the hospital: rehabilitation, drying out, counseling, efforts, attempts. He talked the way I'd heard doctors talk to patients' families in that distant, reasonable voice that avoided the truth. What bothered me most was that he seemed relieved, somehow. Happy.

4

I lay in bed faking sick from school the following Monday. I did not want to face hearing whatever the kids at school might say about Mama. Or worse, say behind my back. Just give out doleful looks as they passed me in the hallway thinking, "That poor kid, Large. Just because you're rich doesn't mean you're happy." I wanted my own life. Not Mama's. Not my family's.

Daddy didn't want to let me stay home. He put his hand on my forehead and said I didn't have a fever, but he said, "Today, I'll make an exception. Tomorrow, you're going in, come hell or high water."

Miss Jesse brought me soup in bed and let me watch the morning shows as she ironed. She moved her folding place to the den. I folded towels and sheets for her until she said, "Stop it, now, you're making a mess of my clean clothes."

She made my favorite, chicken and dumplings, for evening dinner. It rained after lunch, so I could not even step outside, and by mid-afternoon, she'd lost patience. "You ain't getting away with this another day," she said. I stood at the refrigerator unscrewing the milk carton, getting ready to drink out of it. She swatted my butt.

"Ow, Miss Jesse, what?" I said, rubbing my butt. It stung a little. I reached in the cabinet for a glass. "I was going to get a glass."

"You better stop that lying," she said. "Don't never pay off. And where you think you going?" She glared at my tennis shoes. "You don't need to be hanging round the clay road," she said. "You need to stay up closer to home. Can't nobody be watching you all day. I got my hands full as it is, and I don't want you busybodying around, you hear?" She was stacking bowls, and she waved them around as she talked.

"I'm not," I said. I knew she meant stay away from her house. "I'm just going down to my secret hideout. Can't a body do anything around here?"

I hoisted an old blanket from the garage, pulled the tin foil of Rice Krispies treats from my pocket, tucked it into the middle of the blanket, and headed out. Past the front, across the drive and down through the woods to my hideout and to hope for Cookie.

"Where you going with that?" Miss Jesse called out the front door.

"I told you, I'm going over to my secret place in the woods," I said.

"Well, don't be getting into no trouble," she said. "And you be back by the time I leave, you hear?" Miss Jesse had suddenly gotten real bossy with me, like I did not have a mama.

"Yes, Ma'am," I said. You never said ma'am to a colored lady, but Miss Jesse deserved a title of ma'am. But she acted like I hadn't been on my own already before Mama went into the hospital. "I'll be good. I promise."

Heaven must envelop the woods just after a summery rain, when it cools off just enough to make things bearable again after a hot dry midday. The trees hang heavy with rain water and lean into pathways. Droplets of rain hang like pearls off the ends of pine needles. I headed to the woods, the birds chattering. Petals of white honeysuckle had scattered yellow on the brown woods floor. Mushrooms grew up under fallen logs and I could smell the damp scent of rain in the woods.

My hideout was perfect. The walls, made of limerock and coquina, kept the wind out. Trees hung into the top that rose twelve feet high. I'd made a stairway to the open door with pieces of pine trunk Daddy sawed in circles from a big tree that crashed down during the flood.

I spread the blanket out onto the leafy hideout floor and sat down on its cushiony bed. School was out, so I headed to Miss Jesse's house, jumping over the creek and stepping through the woods to the barbed wire fence that separated her property from ours.

Miss Jesse's great granddaddy, Mr. McRae, had inherited the place from the old landowner, when he'd freed the old Mr. McRae from slavery. Mama said that the old Mr. McRae always worked the landowner's gardens, and gave him something back. The old Mr. McRae's son and grandson, Jesse's granddaddy and daddy, were quite the gardeners, Mama had said. They had cleared their land of woods, and made a grassy yard full of peach and plum trees. They'd dug a huge garden area every year on three acres next to the house the old Mr. McRae had built. Then Miss Jesse inherited the land.

A beat up Valiant was parked in front. What if just by stepping foot on this land, I got beat up by colored boys? I wondered. And Daddy would kill me if he saw me down here. I heard Cookie along the side and back yard singing, and my thoughts dissolved like sugar in warm tea. The garden was edged with what seemed a jillion flowers—purple pansies and yellow sunflowers in front. Further back around the sides grew orange marigolds and dark lavender. In the center, onions, green bean plants, tomatoes, squash in various shapes and heights.

"She come around here just bout midnight, make me feel SO

GOOD, She make me feel AW-right." By the time she got to the spelling part, I had leapt across the green beans, come around the tomato bushes fenced off, and on to the back where her voice lifted. I jumped out in front of her to join in with *"G-L-O-R-I-A Gloria!"*

"Girl, you like to scared me half to death," she said, standing up, taking steps back like I'd blown her nearly down. The geese charged at me, honking, but I knew their bluff and stood my ground. "Where you been?" She checked me up and down.

"Staying home," I said. "I been sick." The geese were circling, honking softly.

"You ain't sick," she said, waving her hand and stooping back down to work. "Least you don't look sick."

"The kids talking about it?" I said. I reached for Margot, but she dodged me, and they both ran off.

"It? What 'it'?" She looked annoyed.

"You know. My mama."

"Oh. Well, you know they don't talk to me anyhow," she said looking back up at me, wiping sweat off her brow. I imagined Cookie in all the lunchroom noise of talking and yelling, holding her pale green plastic tray, the smell of cafeteria pizza, her balancing the pizza, chocolate milk, and salad on the plate, and her walking down the aisle between tables looking for the other colored girl or a place off to itself to sit down.

A pang went through me. "But no, I ain't heard a word." She stood up, straddling a strawberry plant. "That's why you not at school?" she said in disbelief. I looked at the ground.

"What you want me to do?" I said, and swung my leg, changing the subject. "You know, in the garden?"

"You really going to help me?" she said. She threw some weeds into a heap beside the garden border. "You got up out of your sick bed to help me in the garden?" She grinned. "Well, that's all right, then."

She directed me to the rows of late lettuce, some dark green, some light, some red topped. "This needs picking bad, all of this. The bugs getting to it." She handed me a grocery bag, and I squatted in the dirt and started to pick.

The sun came down bright, but a cool breeze scurried through and the birds sang in the woods surrounding us, so I didn't mind. Not since Daddy had quit growing a garden, around the time Mama took to the bed, had I felt so happy. We had company the night Mama's sickness got deeper. The head of the doctors at the hospital and his wife came for dinner. We sat at the big table I later burned, Mama at one end, Daddy at the other, the doctor and his wife on one side, me on the other. They'd all had a few glasses of white wine. The smell of roast chicken and biscuits, the lights of candles, the tink of crystal came back to me. So did the minute when I dropped the raspberry jam on the Persian rug.

Mama had jumped up and yelled, and said, "What made you do that?" I had flushed from head to toe, not knowing what to say, everybody looking at me. I felt shame only. As she headed to the kitchen, Daddy had said, "She's just a child, Liz." Mama returned with a bowl sloshing with ammonia and peroxide, cleaning under me. The doctor and his wife stared at their food while Daddy told Mama to quit and eat. I had heard Miss Jesse in my head. If she were there, she'd have said, "Go ask your daddy can you be excused." So I did, and I was. By the next day, Mama was in bed, and had been ever since.

"Cookie?" came a man's voice from the house. I jumped. Somebody had seen me. I peered at the screen from a distance, trying to see in. I could only see the screen door and brown beyond, maybe a small back porch and a room with light streaming all the way from the front door beyond that.

"Huh?" She sounded flat and bored.

"I'm leaving. Be home around eleven thirty."

"Okay. Bye."

"Who's that?" I said.

"My smelly old brother," she said. "Takes up too much room." The car started and puttered away.

"You want to see the hideout?" I said.

"Yeah, when I get done with this, and you get done with that. Otherwise, Aunt Jesse will whip me." She concentrated on her weeding. The geese wandered back. "Shoo them away if they come near. Auntie will strangle them if they get in her garden."

"Does she slap your butt?" I said.

"Sometimes, why? She spanking your butt?"

"She just slapped mine today. She never did it before."

"She must be trying to help out since you don't have a mama at home," Cookie said. It was quiet except for the birds. "And you probably need it."

That meant she thought I'd done something bad, something to be ashamed of, like she knew the secrets I held inside about making Mama go crazy. She would never be my friend.

"She don't mean no harm," Cookie went on, casual. "Throw that stuff with all the holes away in the weed pile. Worms got all in it." *She don't mean no harm.* I said that over in my head a few times.

"I know," I said, tossing some leaves into the weeds. "I love Miss Jesse." I had never said that aloud.

"You told her that?" Cookie said, sitting up, looking at me like a big sister. I shook my head no. "Girl," she answered. "I tell her ever day of my life. Otherwise, I wouldn't have no life." She went back to yanking weeds and tossing them past the garden. I wanted to ask her about her mama, but didn't.

She started singing, low, almost like murmuring the way some people talk to themselves. *"...never let you go, So won't you say you love me, won't you be my little baby..."* I pulled lettuce and listened, humming low to myself. The butterflies feeding on flowers flitted past my face, and a bumblebee buzzed by. When the strawberry patch showed only rows of green with black dirt around and leaves on top, and my bag filled and spilled out the top, she said we could stop.

"You wait here," she said, taking the bag. I did not ask to go in, but tried to peer into the back screen door. White kids were not supposed to go into colored houses. Colored ladies did not like people in their houses, Mama had told me.

Cookie ran back outside and stood frowning into the garden.

"What if somebody sees me on your property?" Cookie said, cocking her head.

"Don't worry," I said. "They won't. The walls are high. Nobody's ever seen me." I thought about Miss Jesse. She'd never let me out of the house again if she caught me here. I changed the subject. "Look." I had discovered a beautiful black trumpet flower with a yellow center in the vegetable plant.

"Hollyhock," she said. "They get taller than you or me."

"I've never seen a black flower before. It's so weird."

"*Black's* all the colors combined," she said. "I learned that in Home Ec. Did you know that?" She used that Negro way when she said it.

"'Black is Beautiful' like they say on TV," I said, but the words came out tilted and not real, like when you're thinking aloud and still coating it with politeness.

"Well, it is," she said, pulling herself up, putting her hand on her hip.

"You're right. It is," I said. "*You're* pretty, anyway."

"Aw, come on," she said, turning her face away shylike and smiling. "You saying that cause you want me to go look at that place."

"Nu-uh. No, I thought so as soon as I saw you. On the road, you know," I said.

"You seen me all the time at school. You just thought of me as that colored girl." She did not give me time to protest, but broke out into *Walking the Dog.*

"Asked my mama for fifteen cents, see the elephant jump the fence," she sang and started moving around, her eyes closed as she moved her hips front to back and side to side with the music. We headed across the rut drive and toward the fence and the woods. She strutted about on the grass just her side of the fence, her hand held out like a prissy lady walking her French poodle. *"If you don't know how to do it, I'll show you how to walk the dog."*

"What a crazy song!" I said.

"Rufus Thomas sings it," she said, heading into the woods. *"Just a walkin the dog.* This the way?" she asked.

"Yeah," I said, following her. "You're the craziest girl in the whole world." I shouted it out like the best song in the world.

The geese followed us. If Cookie left their sight they both started honking loud. We jumped over the trickle of creek and got to the old millhouse hideout.

Cookie looked all around, and her voice broke off from the song. "Hey, this is all right. How do you get in?" I stepped up the logs and heaved myself into the stone house.

The geese got excited and started honking when Cookie got up into the hideout. "Shut up, fools," she said. "Go play in the water." She pointed to the trickle of stream. They both turned around and waddled toward the water. "What about the bugs?" she said.

"There's not many bugs, but I got some bug spray over here," I said, and walked to the corner of the small room, showing her a Styrofoam ice chest full of just-in-case stuff: bug spray, a kitchen knife, some Betty and Veronica comic books, matches, a pen and tablet, and my latest theft, a Miller High Life in the bottle.

"Oh, girl," she said. "It's going on here." She looked up and down. "But you need some more blankets for this itchy floor." She stared at the ceiling beams that had fallen onto the floor. "And a roof."

"I don't want no roof," I said, staring at the trees swaying from the breeze. The sky stretched clear and blanket blue beyond. As if there for proof, the moon hung upside down in the bird blue daylight like a bowl tumped out. "Just look at that moon."

"How you going to keep the rain out?" she said.

"Maybe half a roof," I conceded.

"What you doing with beer?" she said, tracing the moss that grew on the stone wall with her finger.

"Waiting for a special occasion," I said. "Like Saturday." I took out the treats I'd hidden under the blanket and sat down. "Come on," I said.

"What if somebody sees us," Cookie said.

"They won't," I said, swallowing. She plopped down.

"You look like you're setting up housekeeping," she said. "All you need is a little apron."

"I am," I said. "Just in case."

"Case of what?"

"I don't know. It's my own house. That's all." She pushed her long reddish brown legs out straight. *Maroon,* I thought to myself. I handed her the foil of treats. She took one and started to munch, and then I had one. Her legs were so long and strong,

I could not help but stare. "What's it like to be the girl all the boys pick for kick ball?"

"I don't know. I don't think about it. I just kick the ball hard and run." She munched away, looking at my legs. "You little old bitty thing," she said. "You're a little lady, aren't you?

"Cut it out," I said, drawing my legs up. "I am not. I ride horses. Just cause I'm small does not make me a lady."

"You got to put more oomph into kicking that ball. Little cracker girl," she said.

"I'm not no cracker," I said. "I'm white."

"How does it feel to be white?"

I thought about her getting shoved around on the bus, and felt foolish for saying anything about her legs.

"I don't know. I don't really want to think about it," I said. "Let's read Betty and Veronica." Cookie shook her head and rolled her eyes, but took a comic book anyway. The water from the creek between the hideout and Miss Jesse's property trickled at a pitch like the high keys on the piano. Cookie stared for a long time at one page where Archie had kissed Veronica.

"You ever kissed a boy?" she said. We were lying on our stomachs, legs in the air.

"No way," I said. I was thinking about that movie I watched with Daddy called *From Here to Eternity* where the guy and girl rolled around on the sand kissing and kissing, and a wave washed up and they just kept kissing. All I could think of was how your bathing suit would itch like crazy, and how could you keep kissing with an itchy bathing suit crotch and chest? "No, I never did. Did you?"

"No, but I thought about it." She chewed on her pointer finger. "This boy's nose all up in my way." Her eyes sparkled.

"Who?" I sat up to hear.

"This boy at church. He stays down on Saturday Street. He

is fine. Friend of my brother's."

"What's he look like?"

"Kind of cinnamon. Big. About six foot two. He's got him a cute butt, too." I laughed.

"You're not going to kiss his butt, are you?" We both broke out laughing. I took out the pen from my stash of emergency stuff and asked her could I draw on her arm. Since she'd talked about kissing, I figured maybe she'd let me draw on her.

She instructed me to draw a bracelet around her wrist. So I drew daisies with five long petals.

"Before church during our Bible lesson—" she said, starting a story about him and then stopping mid-sentence. We heard a slow rustling outside the hideout. Cookie and me looked at each other and sat closer. "What's that?" she whispered.

"Nothing," I said. "Shh." Our arms were touching. It crept slowly around the building. We sat still for a long time. Then it got quiet.

"It was probably just a dog from down on Saturday Street," I said. Still, we sat still as the late afternoon birds sang. After a while, she said she had to go.

"But you got to tell me the rest," I said.

"Nothing to tell. We kept touching legs under the table. He kept looking sideways at me. You suppose he wants to kiss me?"

"Of course. Why don't you?" I said. I figured people wanted encouragement. And afterwards she'd have some information about the people rolling on the sand.

"He's too old. Sixteen. He might try and take advantage of me." She shifted and sat up as I picked up her wrist and finished putting daisies over the front of her brown wrist. "I don't know. Maybe. How about you? You got somebody you'd like to make out with?" I flashed on that boy, man really, at the hospital, the reddish brown colored guy with amber eyes. It scared me that I thought of him first. Second I thought of Bob Woodley who sat next to or behind me. He wore glasses, was skinny and never picked early for recess teams, but then neither was I. And he was funny and smart. I'd mention him.

"Well, I don't know about making out," I said. "French kissing and tongues and all that. Anyway, I don't even know his name."

"Don't know his name?" she said.

What was I saying? "Oh, never mind. I just saw him, that's all."

"Come on now, that's not fair. I told you."

I decided to tell her just enough. "Well. He was cute. He had the prettiest complexion I've ever seen, and eyes so different. Amber. He was real nice to me when Mama got sick. At the hospital. He's too old," I said, shaking my head as I drew.

"How old is he?" she said.

"Probably eighteen. Too old. And I could never kiss him anyway." I turned her wrist over on the underside to draw daisies. Her skin was a lighter brown on the underside than on the top of her hand. "He's colored."

"Colored?" She put her head close to mine and peered into my eyes.

"I said never mind." I glanced at her, then continued to draw the daisies.

"Ooo, girl, you think you gonna try you some chocolate kisses, huh?" I shoved her hand away and she laughed. "What color is he?"

"I already told you, colored, so never mind." I dropped the pen and picked up the comic book and stared at Archie saying he didn't believe the stories in *The National Enquirer,* and Betty telling him there's a lot of strange things that happen in the world that we don't ever understand, like the two-headed man who started a barbershop quartet.

"No, girl," Cookie said. "I mean, milk chocolate, mahogany, coal, what?" She offered me the underside of her wrist again. "Does he pass the paper bag test?"

"The what?"

"If he's darker than a paper bag, my grandma said he's too dark. But she's a stuck up old fool."

I picked up the pen again to finish the daisy bracelet. The circle was almost complete. Cookie's skin passed the paper bag test on the wrist side, but not the other side. "So," Cookie insisted, "what color is he then?"

"Light brown. Kind of reddish brown, almost like Indian brown. And I don't know if he passes that dumb paper bag test or not."

"Well, you need to find out his name," she said.

"I'll never see him again, so never mind," I said. I finished up her bracelet fast. "Done," I said. "Now, I got an idea for a contest," I said to change the subject. "Let's see who can grow their nails out the quickest."

"How we gonna tell?" she said, studying her bracelet. She held her hands up to her face and studied each nail.

"Let's say when they peek over the tops of our fingers, like little mountains." She peered over at my nails.

"I don't know if I can do that," she said.

"Hypocrite. You just told me I needed more oomph to kick the ball. You say you can't keep your teeth off your nails?"

She shrugged her shoulders.

"Seriously," I said. "I'll try if you will."

"You can't cheat and get you that polish at Woolworth's," she said.

"If I do, I'll buy us both a bottle."

She looked at the circle tattoo of delicate flowers. "I like this. I'll wear it to school tomorrow." She said it with solemn eyes.

The blue jays squawked, and squirrels skittered from tree to tree. Cookie jumped up, and said, "I got to be home when Miss Jesse gets back. I'm in charge of cooking dinner, and I got to get that lettuce washed." I challenged her to meet on Saturday, late in the afternoon. She stood tall and thin and she had some chest development going on. Her big almond eyes sparkled and shined a deep brown. "I don't know. I guess so. Well, see you at school," she said.

"Yeah. Tomorrow." She jumped down, gathering up the geese at the creek. They leapt over the water and she turned around and smiled. Her dimples showed, but I could tell she felt what I did. That somehow we were being watched.

The next day, I wore Mama's perfume, Royal Secret, a rich magnolia mixed with something sharp that I'd never normally wear. Nobody said anything about Mama. By lunchtime, I walked to the cafeteria downstairs. I stood in line behind Loretta Thill and Cynthia Gentry, popular girls who already had their growth, boyfriends and pierced ears. Mama wouldn't let me pierce my ears. Even sick, she had her say. "Why do you want to put holes in your body?" she'd said. "Only nigras and people from Africa do that. You can see *National Geographic*. You want to look like them? Not my daughter. It's just plain tacky," she'd said.

"Want to sit with us, Rayann?" Cynthia said. She'd never asked me to sit with her. I liked her. But not Loretta, who made fun of everybody. She was the tallest girl in school next to Cookie, the girl equal to a boy bully. Sticks and stones may hurt your bones, and Loretta Thill could always find a way to make words do the same. She thought she'd been blessed with a great sense of humor, too, always laughing at her own jokes on other people.

"Okay," I said. I'd kind of wanted to sit with Cookie since nobody sat with her or Colleen McKracken, a country girl with hair all the way down her back, cause her daddy wouldn't let her cut it, people said. Her church believed the Bible, and it said somewhere in the New Testament that women should never cut their hair. She wore thin bobby socks, too, which looked like what they wore twenty years ago. Colleen sat at the other end of the same table with Cookie.

As we started to sit, I looked down the aisle at Cookie and waved. She gave a small wave. Loretta saw it. "You aren't going to go sit with the nigger or that religious freak, are you?" Cookie was watching Loretta. "Look at them. Table probably stinks." Her mouth pulled up on one side and she snickered. Dread ran all through me.

"No," I said. "I guess not." I sat down with my blue plastic tray next to Cynthia. Cookie stared at me, like what's wrong with you? I may as well have been alone. Cynthia and Loretta talked about their boyfriends and the combo that would play at the community center Saturday night. I took one bite of pizza, but it tasted chewy, thick and greasy. My stomach squeezed, so I spit the pizza out in my napkin.

Cookie kept looking at me, and honest to god, it made me furious to have her staring at me like What in the world are you doing? Are you a chicken? I wanted to throw a chicken at her for staring at me like that. I finally got up and dumped my tray and stomped outside where I could breathe. But try as I might—walking by the office, getting a sip of water in the hallway, I kept thinking about what I saw when she'd waved at me—the daisy tattoo bracelet still stood out clear on her wrist.

I ran out to the playground to hang on the fence, but I could not get enough air or go very far. I put my feet in the chain link fence, hung on with my fingers, and stared out at the green bushes beyond.

5

The next night, I sat doing homework in my room, the moon a fat hook in the sky. I couldn't concentrate for thinking of Cookie's hurt face, the tattoo bracelet, and talking in the hideout. I wanted to see Mama, but Daddy said be patient. For how long? I wanted to know.

Daddy sat drinking downstairs with Lucky. Daddy coughed in a way I knew meant he'd gotten onto a topic that agitated him. I was thirsty, so I decided to spy.

Since Mama had been in the hospital, Daddy hadn't acted like he missed Mama. And I had rejected Cookie at school, and she wouldn't look at me.

Honestly, it all felt like a twisted up ball of yarn sat inside me. I felt hot and mixed up. I sat near the bottom of the tile stairs. The step felt cool on my backside, good after a warm day. At least my belly felt full for a change. Daddy had come home early and made spaghetti and meatballs. The night before, he'd stayed out way past midnight, and I'd ended up snacking on ice cream and potato chips. Mama thought snacks near about came from the devil, and she allowed no Cokes in the house. She said if you ate snack food, you might as well pull a big hunk of animal fat off the meat and chew it up. How she could lecture on animal fat and slug down the bourbon, I could not figure.

I heard the *My Favorite Martian* song in the background, that cheery chorus and then Uncle Martin doing something that puzzles the humans. This meant the show had ended, which meant bath time. I'd have to walk in quietly so he wouldn't notice me.

"Well, you know, A.J., you can't be kept on hold forever," Lucky said as I stole into the TV room to watch the fearless crew waving at the camera. Daddy and Lucky stood in the kitchen.

"I've got to wait for Indley, Lucky," Daddy said. "I can't make any fast moves. This incompetence thing takes a while. Tricky to get it, too."

"I'd be on it if I were you," Lucky said. "I'd tell Indley what I had in mind, too." Indley was a skinny tall psychiatrist with clothes too big for him. He'd gone to Yale, a rich Yankee kids' school, and he always managed to work into conversations with new doctors at parties this joke about how his grandmama was Scandinavian. And she always pronounced his alma mater like "Jail." He said it all casual like, but you knew he wanted to make sure you understood where he'd gone to school. He finished with a joke about how when people asked her where he went to school, it came out as Jail.

Lucky went on. "I'd tell him Chattahoochee, too."

"Right," Daddy said. "I don't know, she seems pretty coherent to me. We'll have to see what the good doctor recommends." They were silent, so I turned the TV off, and went into the kitchen, straight to the refrigerator and poured a glass of milk.

"Rayann?" Daddy said.

"Yes, Sir?" I said, hoping he hadn't seen me spying.

"You need to get a bath now, hear?"

"Yes, Sir," I said.

"Now come give me a kiss," he said, "and say hello to Lucky." I kissed him on the cheek. It felt soft from not being shaved for a few days, not prickly like a one-day beard. He smelled like old skin, and held me too tight, so I pushed away. I left the room. He waited till he thought I was upstairs, but I tiptoed back to the doorway.

"D.T.'s are pretty rough. Yesterday she threw a lamp at me when I went to see her. Didn't hit me. Bad aim. And she's weak. But it broke on the wall."

"How's your girl doing?" Lucky said. I drained my milk glass and set it quietly on the coffee table in the TV room.

"Okay. She's tough. It's been going on a couple of years now anyway—"

"She's getting some nubs on her, isn't she?" he said.

I looked down at my chest. My cheeks burned. I wiped my mouth with the back of my hand. I noticed nobody was saying anything.

"What'd you just say?" Daddy said real low.

"Nubs. You know, buds. You know, headlights," Lucky said.

"Shit, Lucky. You better mind your own cattle. You hear me?" Daddy sounded mad.

"I'm just trying to give her a compliment," Lucky said.

I did not want to hear more, so I tore upstairs on my tiptoes. I made sure to lock the bathroom door before I took my bath.

The next afternoon at three, I stood in the bathroom remembering that I used to fancy myself a mermaid. A mermaid who rode horses. Now, I stood before the mirror, combing my hair a different way, trying to get some control over the curling brown mess. I wished the mirrors wouldn't show every blasted zit and freckle I had. Or wild hair mess. Or nubs, as Lucky had called them. I gave up on the hair problem.

I had more pressing matters to attend to anyway, as Patty Duke on TV might say. Like why Lucky felt Mama deserved a place like Chattahoochee, and what business it was of his to notice my boobs.

I knew one thing: I had to get a bra. I couldn't just dream of having seashell cups like mermaids wore in Classic comic books.

I walked into my bedroom to get the rubber band, and saw on the bed the nail polish ad in the magazine I'd flipped through. Stop Bite. Maybe if I got some Stop Bite for Cookie and me, I could give her a bottle, and we'd start up the contest. I began jumping on the bed, looking at the blue sky outside. A great day for a trip. I bounced back down and picked up the magazine, and pretended to talk to Mama in the old days, sitting cross-legged on the bed next to me.

How about a trip to Woolworth's? I imagined her saying. *Get a little lipstick, some Stop Bite, and,* I sighed. "A bra," I said aloud. My voice echoed around the room.

I fixed on how the sixteen girls who got selected as May Day princesses at the May Day celebration downtown paraded around in the park looked like they wore steel bras that poked out like gun barrels. I had hoped the ends would shoot out bullets. Girls in their white belled-out dresses, guys in white jacket tuxes hooking their arms for the girls to hold onto, just waiting to shoot off their guns.

I stood up too straight and pinched the shirt where my boobs were. I walked prissy into the bathroom and stared in the mirror. "I wouldn't mind having them if they did shoot bullets," I said, like I was talking to the old Mama. I stared at my face.

All that makeup those May attendants wore made them look like walking masks. Wouldn't it be something if they could wear masks on their faces that showed how they really felt on the inside? Some would be mean old Chinese warriors.

Others would cry like fat cartoon babies. Some would take on the faces of insects.

I pretended to hear Mama saying, *Come on, Rayann, time to go.* I grabbed my purse. I made sure to put on a thick dark shirt so nobody would see my boobs.

Daddy had given me a twenty dollar bill on Tuesday when I returned to school. He'd told me to take the bus to town if I wanted to. Miss Jesse had the day off, so I headed out to bike down Betty's Creek Road.

I zipped my bike along the dirt road passing colored children playing a game of tag at the pond. I was glad I wasn't in a car where I'd leave them to cough in a cloud of dust, the windows up and air conditioner blasting. At least Daddy and Mama usually drove slow if anybody was playing or fishing or walking down the dirt road. Not everybody did.

I hid the bike in the woods, and got on the bus at Magnolia Road. Mostly colored people rode the bus, and they sat in the back or the middle. I got on the long dark bus and sat up front. I always enjoyed the ride, not having to worry about anybody else, watching the bus driver turn right at the hospital, headed past my two-story brick school with the dark auditorium. We'd practiced for the May Pole dance in that auditorium.

You would not believe all the to-do that went on about May Day. The princesses and queen all paraded down a grassy promenade downtown at the park. They lined up in a horizontal row, the queen in her fanned-out lawn chair, while in front of her sat dozens of drooping day lilies. People had argued for months beforehand over who did decorations for the tables, dresses for the girls, the punch pouring. They fought over who'd stand in the receiving line and who'd be the end-of-line hosts.

The bus drove past the junior high and the Baptist church

where their preacher'd run off with his secretary. His daughter was supposedly picked for the May Pole dance. But then all hell broke loose, and the "May Day" families though it inappropriate for her to represent them. All the girls picked for the dance had to come from "May Day" families—rich people.

I suppose either Mama's being rich or Daddy's being a hospital administrator made me a victim. I got picked to wrap the pole. Mama insisted, because it might help Daddy's position at work. All April we'd practiced in the dim school auditorium, weaving colored ribbons around a tetherball pole. Eight girls would walk in a circle holding a pastel ribbon, alternating going over and under each other's heads to make a weave around the May Pole.

In the end, all that practice did not make up for Suzanna Stoutamire, who had brought her basset hound for lord only knows what reason, who ran out jumping for the ribbon, tripping her. She went under when she should have gone over and confused every darn one of us till the May Pole ended up looking like this oversized knitting needle some five-year-old had tried to hook stitches to. Meanwhile, the basset hound just bayed and howled.

The bus waited at the main intersection of town for the light to change. Nothing exciting there but the green Sinclair dinosaur across the street. Catty corner from that, The Floridan, a big apartment house that Mama told me to stay away from. She said only nasty old Jewish men lived there.

We headed down main street, past the bank where Mama and Daddy banked. Way down nearer the capitol, its rival, the Lewis State Bank, was run by *liberals*, Daddy said. Strange people who hung around Martin Luther King and the like.

In the next block JCPenney sat in a green store front, and Woolworth's, my destination, in a red storefront. Next to that, the Florida Theater.

We turned onto Park Avenue and stopped by the post office building. Plenty convenient and shady right there in the park, but you had to walk past the koo-koo's who'd got let out of Chattahoochee, the worst crazy hospital in the entire state. Sometimes they would ask you for two nickels. Sometimes they wanted to tell you that Jesus loved you, too. One time as Mama was mailing letters at the drop box, this crazy colored lady had pulled a knife on Mama, asking Mama if she could mail her letters for her. "No!" Mama had hollered, and gunned her engine, nearly whiplashing us away from there. No, Mama did not belong in Chattahoochee. Anyway, I knew to jump down off the bus and run to Woolworth's, and I did.

I whooshed open the door there and felt the dry of cool air conditioning hit my sweaty self. The cheap plasticy smell of all dimestores met me. I loved the records right in front, with top 40 on display. The Beatles' second album, with "Roll Over Beethoven," was featured this week. The Motown section sat separate. To the right stood the old fountain, closed now due to colored people wanting to eat there. A sign on the counter by the wheel-around stools said, "Grill Cheese Special 95 cents" and "Fountain Drinks 10 cents."

Pink, purple, and sparkly fake blue sapphires sat in a display case in the front. Behind, you could find bins of lipsticks and nail polishes.

The saleslady looked about Mama's age but without the easy life before the drink hit Mama's face. She'd pulled her hair up into a top knot, and you could see the gray and brown roots under the bleached white. She blew some hellacious bubbles with her gum as I came in, nodded, giving me the once over. When I got closer, I could see a birthmark on her chin and neck, a purple blotch.

I went straight for the Stop Bite settled in one of the white wire racks of nail polish, in its row to the right of White Wonder and Posse Pink, and to the left of Groovy Grape. I grabbed two bottles.

The sales lady watched me like a hawk, so I gave her my politest smile. Her tag said *Miss Platt.*

"I got these earrings on sale," she offered, jutting out her neck and wiggling the earring she wore for me to see. Fake rubies and pretend gold.

"Mama won't let me get my ears pierced," I said. She said it's *tacky,* almost came out of my mouth. My voice bounced back to me.

"Huh," she said, like Isn't that interesting? but she was not listening to me.

I wandered down the next aisle and found a lip-gloss in Pink Passion. I wondered what color Cookie would want, and Marie, my friend I couldn't invite over cause Mama might get drunk or take them pills and strip her clothes off and run around in a see-through slip. Maria was Greek with olive skin. Cookie's, cinnamon. I did not see lipsticks I thought either of them would like on their face. Too light. Maria could settle for something a little too light. But not Cookie. None of the colors would ever pass on a colored person's face. Where did colored people go to get makeup? Maybe they had their own secret store since they had so many colored secrets.

"Hey, Hon," the sales lady said, walking over to the orange lipsticks, picking the brightest one up, rolling it out and applying it to the back of her thumb. "I've got a new peach dress, and I can't find any lipstick to match it. How about this one?" She held out her hand. It looked like the color a clown would wear. I wanted her to leave me alone so I could go look at the bras in private.

"I think that would be perfect," I said. "Course I haven't seen the dress, but I think the color's just right for you." Miss Platt would never pass in the May Court. She would not even get to the end-of-line hosts position. I wanted her to go back up front. I hunched my shoulders in and headed to the bra section.

"Where's your mama, Hon," she said from the makeup area.

"In the hospital," I mumbled.

"Oh," she said, like that explained everything. She bustled over to me. "Are your nitties starting to poke out of your T-shirts?" she said, cocking her head to the side, smiling like she'd been nominated president after you thought you'd got it yourself.

"What?" I said, wheeling around to look at her. That hateful word nitties made me think of a sow lying on her side with ten baby pigs sucking away, fighting to get the good ones, kneading their little hooves into the mama's chest.

"I'll help you get fitted here," she said, her hand raking plastic hangers of bras across the metal rod. She picked up a measuring tape draped over a nail.

"No, thank you," I said. I imagined Mama saying that. Just like sugar.

Come on, Mama, I said, pretending, *Let's go.*

"You need to get measured, Hon," Miss Platt said, coming up behind me and around the other side of the counter.

Then my brain fastened onto Cookie. Her boobs kind of stuck out, too, even in a regular shirt. Maybe Loretta and her crowd were already talking about Cookie. And me, too. We both needed bras. Maybe if I got them together it wouldn't be so bad.

I started pushing through the tiny hangers. The sales lady crossed over to the makeup aisle and edged around the back side. She fumbled through lingerie pretending to get interested in nightgowns on sale like she wasn't spying.

How about these? Mama said in my mind, as I arrived at two white training bras, both white laced.

Okay, I said. The plain ones had stretchy material and straps appearing for all the world like a T-shirt trying to act as a hospital contraption. I got a size 28 for midget me, and a 32 for skinny tall Cookie, hoping that would do it. The sales lady put back the flannel nightgown she wouldn't have got caught dead in.

"Don't you want to try one on?" she said, pointing towards the plaid curtain that hid the dressing room. I looked at the bras. What if I had chosen the wrong size? Then I'd have to bring them back. I walked to the dressing room she had not pointed to and raked the hook across the rod to close the flowered curtain.

"Do you know how to put it on?" she said, from the other side of the curtain. I wished she'd shut up.

"Yes," I said, trying to talk quietly.

"You turn it around backwards at your waist and hook it on the middle hook," she said. "If it fits there, it'll fit when it stretches out. Or shrinks up. You know, from washing and drying. And when you develop even more than you are now. You sure you don't need some help?"

"No," I insisted, trying to keep quiet. My hand shook. "Don't try coming in here," I commanded. "I can do it." I twisted the bra around and pulled the straps up. It felt binding, but not itchy except where the sales tag dug in. Both boobs were kind of smashed across the chest. One boob pointed to the floor, and the other one went sideways towards the arm.

"If you're too big already, you need to get the next size up," she said.

I wish she'd shut up, I said to Mama in my mind. Mama would have just picked a bra out for me. I could imagine it: I'd just hide in the racks, and she'd get the bra. I'd say, *Tell the saleslady it's for your other daughter.* And Mama, my old Mama, would have done just that. She would know how to act quiet. The saleslady went on.

"But what you do to make sure it's a good fit is, before you put the straps over your shoulders, just lean forward and put your nitties into it. Then—"

"It fits," I shouted. If she said that word one more time, I thought, I'll yell. I slipped it off my shoulders and unhooked it. I'd work out the details at home.

"The 28?" she said. She must have had telescopic eyes, I thought, to see through a curtain.

"Yes, it fits," I said, rushing to get out of it and to put my shirt back on so I could leave. I could imagine Loretta or Cynthia standing outside the dressing room holding their stomachs from laughing about me getting a damn bra. Then going back to school and telling everybody what they'd heard about Rayann's nitties.

Suddenly, she pulled back the curtain and stepped in holding the measuring tape. I crossed my arms over my bare chest. I couldn't look at her, but I felt certain she was secretly laughing at my retard body. If Mama had been with me, this Miss Platt could not come in and see me half naked.

A storm welled up in me and poured out. Tears flung out near straight from my eyes, a couple hitting her blouse making dark spots there. "Oh, my—"

She dropped the tape and picked up my shirt fast, turned it right side out and pulled it over my head and shoulders. "Arms in," she said. I stuck them through, water running down my face.

"It's just..." I said.

"It's okay," she said, circling her arms around me. I never even let out a sob. I just shuddered in breaths as she patted my back in the cheap smelling fitting room of Woolworth's. She smelled like gardenias. It felt good to let go all that extra water in me. When I had finally stopped breathing heavy, she handed me the tape, and I looked into her eyes, sniffling. They were a soft brown. She stepped out of the dressing room.

"What do I do?" I said. "With the tape?" She guided me through the measurements, and sure enough, I'd picked the right size.

"Well, then, put that 32 back and we'll get you another 28," she said. I held a bra in each hand. "Maybe a different style."

"I don't want to." I said, opening the curtain.

She raised her penciled-on brows. "It's for a friend," I said.

"Okay," she said, agreeable.

At the register, I glanced at her whole body. Strong, but they'd never let her be prom queen. I studied her big birthmark that almost looked like a burn. It reminded me of the Baptist preacher's daughter, who had a small one on her cheek. I wondered how she'd felt when her daddy ran off and the May families booted her out. Maybe relieved. Miss Platt was okay.

"Seven-fifty," she said, and I handed her the money. "Thank you," the sales lady said.

"Thank you," I said. I hesitated, but couldn't think what to say. "Bye." I headed out of the store.

Let's go, honey, Mama said, pushing at my back all tender, holding the bag for me. I coughed to get rid of the sharp pain that was jabbing at my throat as I hit the hot air outside.

6

That night, the moon filled half itself in the dark sky. From my bed, I looked out the balcony window and saw the stars caught like night flowers in the branches of the oak. Mama. I wanted to see her.

Daddy was another story. He'd stayed up late every night drinking. He talked on the phone about *insanity* and *incompetence* and something about *custodians of accounts*. Wild hope starred his eyes. His rumpled hair stood up on end. Something smelled wrong, I felt it in the dark sky.

His sense of what should go on at home crumbled when it came to making decisions about Mama or me or his friends. Like he had a hunched over heart. And he was helping himself bend it over.

The next morning I got to school late, because I had to wake Daddy up to drive me there. At school we had devotionals. I hunted for Cookie everywhere on the playground. Back inside, I asked to go to the bathroom three times so I could wander around. I paced past her locker, then past classrooms. I finally saw her, sitting in science class near the back. I slid to the left of the door where Mr. Hood couldn't see me and started waving my hands. While Mr. Hood yammered on about molecules, Cookie sat, one elbow on her desk, head in her hand, staring out the door. I waved. Cookie sat up, her eyes guarded, and she glanced at Mr. Hood. Theo Styles, a regular person except for he was chubby, saw me. Maybe he'd call me a nigger lover. I could call him a fatso.

I pulled out the two bottles of Stop Bite and held them up, side by side like twins. She looked puzzled. Theo waved his pencil in front of Cookie's view, and she got curious and moved to see. I pointed at my nails, then pretended to chew mine. I held up the bottles again. She straightened and raised her brows and mouthed, Really? then pointed at herself.

After class, I met her at the locker. She was singing. *"... you know what I mean, and the way she looked was way beyond compare, So how could I dance with another...*Girl," she said, "you nearly got me in trouble."

"Sorry," I said, handing over the small bottle. Nail polish didn't cover the sorry I felt. "I got something else for you. I'll give it to you in the hideout. It's kind of, you know, private." Just then, Loretta and Cynthia, the popular girls, came through the double doors holding their books laughing. Dread rolled over me like a morning fog. "See you later," I said, "at the hideout." I walked towards them, but pretended to be in a big hurry. I burst out the double doors and stood in the white sunlight blasting down too hard white sunlight. When they'd gone down the hall and turned the corner, I walked back in. Cookie was frowning at her locker.

"Can you meet me at the hideout? Saturday?" I said. "I can help you with the garden."

"I don't know," she said, fingering the bottle of Stop Bite. "I don't know. Aren't you worried about the hoochie coo girls?" She gave me a look like she smelled a dead skunk in the road, but that it hurt her anyway. She put the Stop Bite on the top shelf of her locker and slammed the door. It sounded flimsy and tinny.

"Hoochie coo girls?" I stepped back.

"The girls you just ran from." She clicked the lock.

"Yeah, well, no," I said. "What's a hoochie coo girl?" My stomach turned, and I felt sweaty. I swallowed, and tried thinking of something else.

"You know, those girls wear tight skirts and high heels, low cut tops, prance around Frenchtown looking to make some fast money," she said. "Girls think they the cat's fur coat." She twirled the lock.

"Oh," I said. I tried to grin, but my face hurt. I was thinking about Loretta wearing a tight red skirt and high heels, a set of red earrings and a red coat with matching red fur, prancing around, then stumbling in the high heels over at Frenchtown like she was hot stuff.

"Thing I like about them, is, they don't care nothing about what other people think," Cookie said. She glanced over her books.

I cleared my throat. "I got you a bra," I said, stepping towards her, whispering and looking around. Nobody around but a couple of stupid boys at the end of the hallway.

"A bra?" she said, wrinkling her brow.

"Yeah. At Woolworth's. I got one for me, too." I stepped back.

"No kidding," she said, looking me up and down. "You got me a bra?" she said, pointing from me to her. I nodded. "You got yours on?" she said. I nodded. "And you picked me one up, too?"

"Yep. It was easier to get one for me if I got one for you, too. You feel so stupid getting them." Suddenly I felt like I'd said too much. I took a step back and started to turn around. "Well, I better go. I'll explain it later."

"Is it white?" she asked. I nodded. "Pretty?" She shifted her books to one arm.

"It's got lace on it," I said.

"Okay, then," she said, looking at my chest. "Turn around."
I turned and she said, "I see it. Lord have mercy," she said, and laughed into her hand and stomped her foot.

"You coming?" I said, turning back around to face her.

"Coming where?" she said.

"To the hideout. On Saturday like we talked about before."

She shifted her books to her side and rested them on one hip, looking back at her locker. "I don't know if Aunt Jesse or my brother would approve of you being at our house," she said, looking out the corner of her eye for my reaction. "They might think I wasn't good enough if I was hanging around with the wrong people." I looked away down the hall.

Here came Loretta and Cynthia again. Cookie looked, too. That's when I saw it—Cookie's accusing look towards me, like *What you gonna do, scaredy-cat white girl?*

"See you tomorrow?" I said, quickly.

"Hmph," she said. She waited as Loretta and Cynthia approached, then stepped in right behind them, imitating the I'm cool way they walked. Then she disappeared around the corner.

I walked down the hallway the other way and the bell rang. Kids spilled out into the hallway like a wave, shoes shuffling like surf, people charging forward as if they were one big force. I wished I could be a big wave and squash what I was afraid of. I kicked a locker at the end of the hallway. I wished I had the guts to think like a hoochie coo girl.

7

The next night I looked at the sky winking with stars and wondered if Cookie gazed out into the darkness and wondered about me. I was hoping she'd come to the hideout tomorrow.

Daddy was bustling about like a housewife with a bald shiny head, straightening pillows, arranging magazines, and setting out records to play. He seemed to have forgotten me. But that was not what bugged me. I'd been reading a romantic chapter book, the first one I'd ever tried. It featured a woman standing on a cliff, the wind blowing her hair and clothes back. I felt sure she'd never get a windburn or chapped lips.

I'd done all my homework and then some when the front door bell rang. I'd thought it might be Lucky coming in the front for a change. Daddy nearly raced to the door to answer it. "Hello! Come on in!" he said, using his company voice. I stood at the dark top of the stairs. In walked two women, one with a grocery bag, the other a bottle of wine.

"This the right kind, Al?" the woman with the bottle said, holding it up. She wore a black dress with wide sleeves that opened out at the wrist, trimmed in black fur. She paraded into the TV room with her sparkly high heels. Her long straight brown hair was teased up and frosted with white streaks.

The other woman wore a turquoise blouse with white tasseled skirt and matching vest, and white high-heeled cowgirl boots. Her eye shadow was shiny turquoise, and you'd be hard put to see her eyes for looking at the bright paint on her face.

"If it's not the right kind, we've got more," she said holding up the bag. They all opened their mouths wide and laughed.

"This isn't the kind I asked for," Daddy said, studying the green bottle the way he did when Mama used to get the wrong thing at the grocery store. But he didn't get mad. "What the hell, let's try this out." He led them into the TV room where I couldn't see.

"Gorgeous house, Al," the black dress lady said. These women reminded me of how you could smell a skunk in the woods.

"Why, thank you," he said. He failed to tell about how Mama did all the decorating, that the interior was featured once in the *Atlanta Constitution* Sunday paper, and the painting they probably looked at was painted by Mama. I felt like Mama had melted into the sky. "Y'all come on in to the kitchen and make yourselves a drink, now, hear? Then I'll give you a tour of the downstairs."

Over the next half an hour, three more showed up. I sat on the steps and read my romantic chapter book and watched. They could not see me for the shadow of the stairs.

"Hey, y'all! Ready for a real party?" It was Daddy's secretary, Rheta, swishing her hips in a jerky way. She wore an orange dress, orange hat and shoes to match. I thought of hoochie coo girls. Lucky arrived and they all crowded around the front door. He wore a light blue seersucker jacket with, of all things, brown plaid pants, and a weird white fishing hat.

"The law can go to hell tonight," Lucky said, shaping his hand into a pistol and pretending to shoot the cowgirl, who screamed and pretended to faint away dead. Lucky lifted his bottle of cane sugar-colored liquor. Mama hated Lucky.

Then came the guy Mama had said was just blind crazy. Not that she had any room to talk, mind you. Everybody called him Red, only he did not have red hair. "Whoooo!" Red yelled when they greeted him at the door. His arms were raised over his head, his fists shook, his eyes bugged out. Daddy said he'd got his nickname from his temper. He lived way out in the country, was slim and almost nice looking for a grown up. This was the guy shot out all four tires on his wife's car where they lived in the country. Tonight, Red wore blue jeans and a red checked shirt with snap buttons, and his usual wide belt with a silhouette of a rebel flag, the name "Robert E. Lee" underneath.

Red brought something in a sack. "Worked this fine stuff up at home, and you're gonna love it!" he said. Every time I saw him, I thought of a fellow sweating up a fierce red mad, shooting out four tires. And some woman watching from the window, holding the keys.

I went back upstairs to my romantic book, but this girl in the book just bawled a lot cause she didn't know if this rich guy she'd met was gonna come back from Germany. I could think of some other things worth bawling about.

Daddy and the party friends got louder over the next hour, and cranked up the record player. Herb Alpert and the Tijuana Brass, Andy Williams, Dean Martin, hokey music that grown ups liked.

"Al, where is that girl of yours?" I heard Rheta say as they headed into the kitchen. I crept down the stairs further to hear.

"Oh, she's somewhere around here. Probably out with the horses."

"This time of night?" the cowgirl outfitted woman said.

"Oh, yeah. She's on the horse, or reading, or doing homework."

"Homework?" Rheta said. "It's Friday night!"

"She's smart. So smart it scares me," Daddy said, laughing. "I'm real proud of her. Carry her picture around with me and take it out and just look at it sometimes."

"What's her name?" the black dress lady said.

"Rayann," Daddy said. "I love her but she is one armful of trouble. Thinks she's smarter than everybody else. Like all teenagers. Thing is, she *is*. Just don't want her to know it." They all laughed. My mouth went dry and I swallowed. I wanted to spit. I ran upstairs and did just that in the bathroom sink. He was bragging about me, but to people I didn't like knowing about me. I tiptoed to my bedroom and shut the door. He was dumb. Bringing all those hoochie coo women to the house. They had some nerve, making loud noise and not giving any thought to who else lived there.

I opened the balcony door and stood looking out. The moon floated almost half empty in the sky. The fireflies had just started their lazy blinking in the open drive out front and beyond in the woods. I thought of nights when Mama and I would read up in my room by a flashlight. The moon would shine milky through the glass doors. We'd run outside and catch fireflies in our hands and wait till they lit up and let them go.

I decided to sneak down to Mama's bedroom. Maybe I'd sleep in there, even though I hated the color of those sheets.

As I tiptoed down the staircase and slinked past the front of the house, I could see the back patio. The double doors from the dining room stood wide open so the music could blast through. They slow danced on the back patio. The cowgirl lady and Red, the lady dressed in black and Lucky, and Rheta and Daddy. What I saw made me freeze.

Daddy had his hands on Rheta's butt, and he groped on it like Mr. Magoo searching around for his glasses, and instead finding cantaloupes. I stood frozen, watching. It felt like my chest was opened up and all the petals of my heart were being stripped away one by one. Then Lucky said, "Okay, swap," and they each changed partners and got with the next person. Lucky kissed on the cowgirl, and the lady in black played with what was left of Daddy's hair. How could she want to play in that nasty old head? He was old. I tore to Mama's room.

It still smelled of her. I wanted Daddy to come talk to me about how we both missed Mama. If he did, he would forget about those costumed women. He'd want to get Mama out of the hospital.

Who was I kidding, I thought, lying down on her bed. I could not believe what all he had forgotten. This took the cake. I hated Mama's wine-colored covers. Still, I found myself breathing in deep, trying to smell something of her.

8

I decided to check on Mama at the hospital. I'd have to hoof it there myself. I sneaked out the front door while those party clowns stood in the kitchen Everything looks like something else, especially outside, especially when you're walking down a sandy clay road in the middle of the night with only a weak flashlight and the nearly full moon overhead. Take for instance dead logs. They fake the shape of alligators. Trees look like people, mailboxes in the distance can suddenly turn into dogs. A palmetto frond can appear as a huge old hand reaching out to get you. The night time world is a new place, ready to stalk you. I put one foot in front of the next and kept on.

The trees' shadows from the moon speckled the road. I could see Miss Jesse's porch light through the woods as I passed.

Without sight, I could hear better. And smell. I passed the fishy scent of the swamp. Cattails whispered in the late spring breeze. The night train passed in the distance of town, and I headed out to the main road, a two-mile walk. I took the road as much as I could on the way down Magnolia Road to the hospital. Only two cars passed me. When they got close, I ducked into the woods.

At the halfway mark, as Mama called it, past the second pond, the frogs started up a chorus that lullabied me. I felt tired and wanted to lie down and go to sleep. But I couldn't. Adrenaline shot through me, then left. My skin got goosebumpy and sweaty together. I started to hum nothing. What would Cookie sing, I thought. *Do you like good music, that sweet soul music. Just long as it's swinging, Oh yeah, oh-oh yeah,* I sang, trying to keep the beat as I walked.

I worked so hard at keeping the beat that when a possum ran across my feet, I screamed, tripped, and then bellyflopped in the street. My knees, palms and chin burned as I lifted up and brushed off. Couldn't stop now, even with such a bad stinging. That's when I saw the hospital's lights.

I walked straight to the Emergency Room in back. That late, I was the only soul around except for workers. The receptionist was snoring with her head on her folded arms at the typewriter. She bolted upright when she heard the door slam. She took one look at me and stood up from the typewriter desk and said, "Oh, my word. Mr. Wood's daughter. Honey, what on earth—" She pulled me into the chair by her desk asking me where I had been. I felt of my hair. Frizzy and mussed up. She threw on her glasses and stuck a thermometer in my mouth, glancing at her watch.

"I'm here to check on my mama," I mumbled around the thermometer, holding my scraped palms up so they wouldn't hurt.

"What happened to your knees? and hands?" she wanted to know. "And you're shivering," she added, wrapping a hospital gown over my bare arms. "How'd you get here? Look at those knees. And that chin." She didn't wait for me to answer. "Let me get one of the techs."

"Is Skip here?" I asked. She rushed through the double swinging doors and shouted down the hallway. I heard shouts back, and she returned, pulling the thermometer out, escorting me through the door and into a room. It must have been a slow night if they wanted to fix me up in the E.R. Or maybe I was getting princess of the hospital treatment. I sat on the cot of the small room where the white paper crinkled and wrinkled when you moved.

"How's my mama?" I wanted to know.

She only answered by saying she wanted to get a tech to see me first. She did not want to tell me. When adults avoided answers, it usually meant bad news.

"Well," Skip said as he came in the doorway. "You been partying it up too much?" He covered me with a blanket. "Haven't I told you about that?"

"How's my mama?" I asked, squirming, which made the paper crinkle.

"Your mom's okay, I think," he said, cleaning my knees with antiseptic. "But visiting hours are over, you know." He cleaned my palms and chin, and asked, "What'd you do, walk?" I nodded, and he washed me with slow careful hands, like he saw the daughter of the administrator walk to the Emergency Room every night. Then he applied some antibiotic ointment and bandages.

"Where's your dad?" he said. "Does he know you're here?" I felt a jolt go through my tired self. I didn't want to talk about what I'd seen at the house. I didn't want them calling Daddy, either.

"He's having a party at home," I said. "I just wanted to see Mama."

"Well, let's get some juice in you first, then we'll call your dad. You look pale," he said, disappearing. He left the door open, and the other tech Walt and a nurse and doctor on call gathered at the door. I guessed because I was their boss's daughter, but I crossed my legs and scowled at the floor trying not to blush. When he came back, he handed me a glass of apple juice. They all watched me drain it.

"Rayann—it's Rayann, right?" Skip said. I nodded. "Well, your dad's phone at home is busy. Who watches after you when your mom is sick?" Suddenly, I did not like being the hospital princess.

The nurse, doctor, and Skip exchanged looks. I stared at the floor. I'd just wanted to see my mother. And now all these nosy people were standing around, waiting for some answer, and I did not know it. You could hear the buzz of lights overhead, and that dadgum white paper crinkling. I kept staring at the floor.

Skip cleared his throat and said, "Well, we need to notify someone that you're up here. Who can we call?" My stomach felt queasy.

"That would be my aunt," somebody said. "My aunt, Miss Jesse, she takes care of Rayann. She cleans the house and watches after her. Only not in the middle of the night." I looked up. Out in the hall just behind the others stood the guy. Everybody turned around to look at him. It was the guy from before, the Indian brown guy with amber eyes, the one I'd told Cookie I wanted to kiss. He wore scrubs, and those funny looking shower caps on his feet. He went on. "This girl's anxious to see her mama. I'll take her up. Then we'll make sure we get her home." He said it so natural. So calm.

Crowds of people are strange. One person can change the whole way they're all thinking, and this guy had done it by talking casual. Like it was no big deal. Like he knew me on a personal basis. "Oh, okay," the nurse said, and they all started shuffling away from the door, back down the hallway. He stepped into the room while I put all the relationships together like you do with the distributive property in math and figure out the answer.

"You—you—you—" I looked at his name badge. He hadn't

had one before. Johnson, it said. "Cookie's brother?" I said. He nodded. My stomach was butterflies. I tried to hide my busted chin, and I couldn't look him in the eyes. Until I saw him trying to act cool, looking sideways and his arms folded. Eyes a little scared of me and trying to hide it. "Thanks for helping me out there," I said. His arms came down and he walked into the room and opened a cabinet like he was looking for something he couldn't find.

"That's right. My bogish sister, that's Cookie," he said. "I heard about you from my aunt. And Cookie." I sure heard about you, I wanted to say, but then I didn't, because he did not fit the description Cookie gave—smelly, bossy, mean—what all had she said?

"Is my mama going to be okay?" I said to him. I don't know why I asked; I didn't even know him or why I thought he'd know. The paper crinkled under me, so I got real still.

"I don't know myself," he said. "I know she's been through the D.T.'s. She's over that now. That's the hard part."

"What's the D.T.'s?" I said. I knew I should know, but I didn't.

"When they get you off the liquor," he said. "It's hard. Makes you cold, gives you the chill, you see things."

I felt woozy and laid down on the cot in the small room. It made a lot of noise, but I couldn't help it.

"Don't lie," I said. I braced myself for the bad news. "You don't have to lie to me—is she really crazy now?"

"What makes you think I'd lie?" he said. "What I got to lose?" He looked at me and shrugged. "Hard to say who's crazy, who's not. And when. Depends on the day sometimes—who's crazy and who ain't. I'll take you up there after they finish with you here. You want to go?"

"Yeah. Yeah, I do." I sat back up. Maybe if they'd let me see her, she wasn't that bad off. "So what's your name?" I said.

"Ivory Jones," he said. "Ivory Jones Johnson."

"How come I never seen you, but I see Cookie sometimes?" I said.

"Cause I'm working. How you think we're going to feed us all?" he said. I thought about Miss Jesse and Cookie and Ivory Jones eating dinner at night, a big dinner with all that free garden squash and tomatoes, beans and potatoes. But I guessed they still had to buy their chicken and rice.

The nurse came in and took my blood pressure. Ivory Jones pretended to clean some steely looking instruments in the sink as the cuff got tighter around my upper arm.

Skip returned to the room. "Well, no answer at home now," he said, and shrugged.

"The music is up loud," I said. "Daddy's having a little party."

"Well," Skip said, looking at Ivory Jones, who now was drying the instruments with a towel. "I agree we let her see her mom. Doctor's orders say it's okay to see relatives now." Ivory Jones nodded.

"I'll take her up there. And see to it she gets home," Ivory Jones said. Skip nodded and patted my leg.

"Take it easy on that chin," he said. "No more wild parties for you, hear?" Then he was gone.

"You not gonna tell Cookie about this, are you?" I said. "She doesn't know everything about my mama. Or me."

"Oh, you think so, huh?" Ivory Jones said, drying his hands and turning around to look at me. He put the towel down and folded his arms again. "What you think you got to hide?" He smiled, showing his teeth with a tiny split between his two front ones. He looked like Cookie in the eyes. My chest got warm, and I fidgeted with my bandages.

"Nothing," I murmured. I started tilting my head sideways

like I saw Elizabeth Taylor do to one of those guys in *Cleopatra*. Once she winked, but I thought better of that.

"Okay, and I won't tell you nothing about her wandering mama, either," he said, picking the towel back up and throwing it into the dirty laundry basket. I stood up, ready to go see Mama. "And her mama's stank-breath punk excuse for mens, either," he said, pulling the paper off the bed, bunching it up and yanking out the next clean white sheet of paper. He turned to go out the door, then turned back around. "Nothing at all."

On the way upstairs, Ivory Jones told me he ran track for school, which hooked him up with the job at the hospital. "Your daddy knows my coach who talked me up. Yeah," he said, nodding and smiling a sideways smile like he had a joke on me. "I needed a job to stay on the track team, and he talked me up to the boss man. Coach says I can get a scholarship for college, the way I run." The slow elevator took us up while I looked at his long legs. "I'm about the only black man that works here ain't in janitorial or laundry. Guess I got luck." He was talking, talking like a Negro, going on about a scholarship. To what college, I thought. I bet he had one of those dapper suits. I wanted to see him in it. Then I started to worry about his safety when I knew people didn't like uppity colored people. Ivory Jones had to tread careful.

"How come you want to work in this hospital and not A & M?" I asked.

"Black hospital ain't worth a damn," he said. "Everything's hooptie old. Equipment's outdated. Lighting's like the inside of a Coke bottle. And they don't pay." I didn't like the sound of that place, or the idea of Miss Jesse ending up in it.

"What's bogish mean?" I said.

"You mean like my sister?" he said. I nodded. He laughed

as the elevator came to a standstill. "Oh, you know. Mouthy. Bold. Acting sexy, and the bold riding along side you."

When the elevator doors stopped on the fifth floor, Ivory Jones went to the desk and talked low to the night nurse who kept nodding and talking, glancing over at me, and shaking her head yes. Ivory Jones walked me down the hall to Mama's room.

"She'll be sleeping, out cold maybe for another day or two," he said. "With that medication. But if you want to sit in there, you can. You ain't supposed to be here at night, but—" he shrugged and glanced back at the night nurse, "under the circumstances, they're making an exception. Sometimes they let kin stay. Usually not the kids."

"I'm not a kid," I said, straightening my shoulders. "I'm visiting age."

"Hey, I know you're not a kid," he said, holding his hands up. "You're a young lady." He looked me up and down fast and then cleared his throat, and dropped his arms and then folded them in front of him. "You know we got to notify your daddy you're up here." His eyebrows were raised in a kind of question.

"Okay," I said. He seemed a little fatherly to me then. It made my chest warm all over again. "And hey," I looked up the hallway and down. "Thanks." I held out my hand to shake his. I felt stupid, but I didn't know what else to do. He took my hand and shook it. A warm dry hand. He went to let go, but I held on for a second longer. He flashed a look at me that told me nothing at all, and I dropped his hand. I wondered how long I'd wait for that guy to get back from Germany if I dove into that woman's place in the romantic chapter book. Maybe a good long while.

The room smelled a little stale, like dust and Bluegrass

perfume. Something went missing in the smell. The faint scent of bourbon, gone. And no Royal Secret. No cigarette smoke. Mama lay in the bed sleeping. "Hey, Mama," I said, soft, almost asking it. She snoozed away. I eased down onto the bed, but she didn't even stir. I couldn't believe it, but she wore full makeup, even though the foundation left a mark on her neck. She hated that in other ladies. She called makeup her armor, but she said you should never look like you're wearing any, that was the trick. But that ladies who didn't wear it usually looked just plain, and a woman had to be put together, she said.

I pulled her left arm up out of the sheet like it was made of the finest crystal and held her hand. It felt cold as a china plate. Her dry hands also showed red raw scratch scabs. When Mama got agitated, her hands itched, and she clawed at them till they bled sometimes.

"Look at this hand," I said. "What a mess."

"Rayann?" she said, startled. Her eyes flew open, closed again, then opened slowly. She laughed groggylike, and struggled to sit up. "Is that you?"

"Yeah, it's me," I said. I felt sore and tired. The moon shone in the window. Suddenly, exhaustion poured over me like a bucket of warm water.

"When did you get here?" She reached out, combing her hand through my hair.

"Just now. It's late."

"What have you gotten yourself into?" she said, her voice groggy from sleep as she looked at my skinned-up self.

"I fell off Star—it's no big deal," I said. Boy, was I turning into an A-plus liar.

"Well, lean over and give your mother a hug." For a change, I did. Her ribs and shoulder blades stuck out. She felt fragile as china, too.

I decided to get some things she needed that nobody'd noticed. I walked down the hall to the nurse's station and asked the head nurse for some of the hand lotion the pharmacy sent out. "Lubriderm," I said with a doctor's tone. If you showed people you knew something, they got the idea they had to do what you told them. I'd found that out watching doctors at the hospital and observing Daddy, too. After I got the lotion, I pushed the door of the room open and sat back on the bed and lathered Mama's hands up with the lotion. She fell right back to sleep.

I looked out at the stars through the bars of the hospital room and wondered. The way the crazy summer had started out did not make things look so promising, so I just started talking to fill up the room. Have I got a lot to tell you, I said aloud to Mama's snoring. Did you know Miss Jesse's got a niece? Living with her. And she goes to school with me. I spun on, telling her about Cookie and Ivory Jones. I explained that I'd gotten a bra, but nothing about Rheta or those costume women or the party or Daddy. I felt hurting tired. I curled up at the end of the bed and sighed.

"I'm just going to rest for a minute," I said.

I woke up with a kick to the rear end. Mama, stretching before she saw me. "Rayann?" she said. She laughed, yawned and stretched her arms. "You spent the night there?"

"Yeah," I said, sitting up. The sky stretched blue out the barred window, and the sun shone in. "Did I fall asleep? Yeah, guess so."

"I thought I'd dreamed your coming here," she said. "So how did you get here anyway?" she said. She bolted upright. "And where is your father?" I started explaining that I'd gotten up in the middle of the night wanting to see her. And again,

I left out the costume ladies, Lucky, and Red. I told about walking to the ER and getting bandaged. She nodded, holding my chin, turning it side to side, inspected my face.

"Daddy said I couldn't see you for about a month," I said. I flung my arms around her, and she patted my back.

"A month?" she said. "Says who?"

"I don't know," I said, the sound muffled in her shoulder.

"Oh, what a mess. You shouldn't have done it," she said, pushing me slowly away. She shook her head slowly. "Walking down here at night. It's dangerous." I lowered my eyes. "But I'm glad you're here. They wouldn't let me see anybody, but that was for a week, not a month." She sat back in the bed. "It's been awful. Wouldn't let me have a drink, had an IV in me, and gave me this green capsule every two hours." She fiddled with her hair. "They kept taking my blood pressure. I saw bugs on the wall." She had dark circles under her eyes, but she didn't smell like liquor.

"Are you cured from drinking?" I said.

"Oh," she let out a hot sigh. "So how about finding me some coffee, hear? And a juice for you?" she said. "I could buzz for it, but they won't bring it to me. They don't want to let me leave the room yet." She shook her head. "It's like prison. I've got to get out."

I wandered down the hall to the nurse's station where the charge nurse with black glasses looked me up and down. "Miss Wood?" she said with an all business look.

"Yes, Ma'am," I said, looking innocent.

"Did you sleep okay?" She looked up at me over her glasses. She smiled like somebody had pulled each side of her mouth up with puppet strings. "Your father's been notified. We reached him this morning. He'll be here soon."

"Yes, Ma'am," I said. "Mama would like some coffee. And

I'd like some juice," I said. "Please."

She took off her glasses and gave me a you're-out-of-line-here-but-I'll-be-polite look. "She can't have coffee," the nurse said. "Doctor's orders." Too bad, I thought. Coffee would not hurt. I knew how those doctors worked, too. They'd come up with some cockamamie idea about maybe this would help and that, without ever asking the patient if it made them flat out miserable.

I knew how people like this nurse worked, too. Toe-the-liners my daddy called them. People who obeyed the rules no matter what. Daddy said those people never got ahead. Still, I knew what to do, cause I'd had teachers like that. You talk to them outside of school about other stuff. Then they somehow end up letting you get away with more.

"Yes, Ma'am, you're right," I said to her. Shepherd, her tag said. "Mrs. Shepherd," I said. She smiled at me, and I went on. "What do you think I ought to take her instead?"

"There's apple juice in the nurse's station," she said, pointing across the hall.

"Thanks a lot," I said. "I really appreciate it, Mrs. Shepherd."

"Oh, and," she said, putting her glasses back on and glancing at her watch, "you're not to spend the night here again. Your father's orders." She smiled her puppet smile. How the hell would she know my father's orders?

"Thank you," I said, sweet as chess pie. When I reached the door of the nurse's station, I laid my eyes on the coffee machine. Fast as a rabbit, I poured a big coffee and grabbed a juice. Somebody had brought donuts for the staff, so I snagged a couple. Then I heard the hall nurse ask about Mama's medication.

"She's on a really high dosage of Librium," the hall nurse said. "I wondered if we should call Indley and—"

"It's routine," the head nurse said.

"Well, I know the dosage should be high the first week, but we're on into the second week now. It seems too high."

"Let's not jump the gun. He doesn't usually make med mistakes," Mrs. Shepherd said.

"Well, I'm not a doctor, but it could keep her confused," the other nurse said.

"I'll talk to Indley," Mrs. Shepherd said. "Thank you."

Mrs. Shepherd didn't like me, and she sure had no cares for Mama. I could feel it in my skin. I'd have to watch out for her, I thought as I tucked the snacks under my shirt and held the drinks low at my side. I smuggled the goodies down the hallway.

"Look," I said, when I shut the door of Mama's room. "Goodies."

We sat on the bed and made a yummy breakfast mess. While Mama savored her coffee, I got up and opened the window. The air was fragrant with blooming magnolias and mimosas. It reminded me of how Mama and I used to ride to the gulf coast where we'd stay for a week on Alligator Point. With the windows up in early summer, we could smell the change from gardenia smell to the woody smell of the sand pines, then the brine of swamps and ocean.

My eye tried to take in every angle it could as Mama slurped coffee. I almost felt like the goodness outside could bring enough inside. "Mama, remember driving to the beach?" I said. What a bright bloom the water had made on the white sandy shore in the morning.

"Yeah, I do," she said. "The waves coming in at night like barrels." She breathed in like she could smell the beach's freedom. I remembered peering across that distance down to Mexico, the water rushing towards me, lapping at my thighs, jumping a little for joy. It made my heart leap. Then I remembered where I was.

"Mama," I said, sitting down on the bed. "You're on a high dosage of Librium."

"It helps me with the jitters," she said. "It's harder than you can imagine. Will you bring me my makeup case? It's over in the purse by the door." Suddenly I felt impatient. Why don't you get it, I thought. Mama, always the only child. Now I remembered how she could be—I want to go home, bring me coffee, get me out of here, bring me my makeup. Still, I couldn't help wanting her back.

"Mama, do you want to end up at Chattahoochee?" I said. "Get your own darn purse." She gave me a frown, sighed and got up. She looked so small in her hospital gown.

"I just want to be left alone," she said, getting back into the bed, hauling out the makeup and studying herself in her powder mirror. "I want—where is your father, anyway?" She looked at me. "I haven't seen him this week. Not since I threw that lamp at him." She went back to the mirror. "Did you know I threw a lamp at him?" I said yes, I'd heard. "He'll be worried and looking for you." She applied some lipstick.

"He's home," I said. "Don't you want to wash your face first? Daddy's talking about you going to Chattahoochee."

"Chattahoochee? Chattahoochee?" She stood up, and the makeup spilled onto the bed like a high wave full of shells emptying on shore. "He's what?"

"You heard me. If Dr. Indley okays it, Daddy might do it," I said. "I heard Daddy saying they had you on some medicine that made you loopy. The medicine you're getting is wrong. You need to stop taking it." She picked up the mirror and snapped it shut. Her jaw hung open. She stared straight in front of her. Then her mouth turned downward like the lip of a shell.

"He doesn't love me anymore." Then her brow furrowed. "He thinks he can throw me away," she said, her voice wobbling as she looked out the window. She teared up. The morning light hit her face soft and orange like the colors on a scallop shell. "Do you think I'm sagging?" she said, looking down at her body. It scared me to see her start to crying. The feeling I had came out bossylike.

"Come on, Mama, stop crying," I said, clearing off the bed and throwing the breakfast things in the trash. "You gotta stop taking that medicine." She started digging in her makeup case, and I wondered if she had the whatever it took to resist. "Just take it every other dose, okay? Can you remember that?"

"He just wants to throw me away in that..." she waved her arms around in the air, "...dungeon..." she flopped her arms down by her side, "that smells like pee. To live with all those crazy people. I want to get out," she said, tossing her purse to the floor. "I want to get out into the sunshine." Since when did she want sunshine, I wondered. Even at the beach, she stayed on the porch. Well, at least back home it would be there if she wanted it, right outside the door.

"Well, make the doctor order it," I said. "Tell him you're ready to go home."

She looked at me and said, "And I want a real bath."

A nurse came in and handed Mama a small paper container with her pills, and watched her put them into her mouth. Here we go, I thought. Then the nurse turned to me and said, "Your father just called." Meanwhile, behind her back, Mama had started spitting out the pills. A green one and a white one.

"Oh, good," I said to the nurse, trying to sound enthralled, though I really felt a thud in my stomach. Daddy would be furious at me. "Did he have any instructions?" I sounded fake.

"No," she said. "He's on the way. He wants you to meet him

in his office." Mama closed her hand on the pills and smiled. "All done, Mrs. Wood?" the nurse said. Mama nodded without a word. "Well, good." The nurse turned back to me and said, "Your mother's doing very well. It's just that the medications—" she shrugged. "Doctor's orders, you know?" I nodded as the nurse left. I'd better check on them, too.

"What in the hell possessed you to do that?" Daddy said, as we drove his big Lincoln out of the hospital parking lot. He kept combing his hands through his balding head. He looked like he'd been run over by a Jim Beam truck.

"I don't know," I said, meek. We passed the place where I'd fallen down. The tar road, the trees, the palmetto bushes, mailboxes, they all whirled by so much faster in a car. I should tell him the truth. That I'd burned the table with cigarettes. That Mama had been whisked to the hospital because of me. Couldn't he bring her home? It had all unwound like a big ball of knotted string.

"In the middle of the night?" he went on in an I-can't-believe-you voice. "What the hell—you could have been run over." We bounced down the clay road between the two sections of Betty's Pond. The sky was cloudless, pajama blue. I was supposed to meet Cookie this afternoon. "And you know you're not supposed to visit her yet. You intentionally disobeyed me. What will the doctor think when he hears you spent the night up there? How do you think this makes me look?"

He'd lied to me about not being able to see Mama yet, and he did not bother to catch a glimpse of her even thought he'd driven all the way to the hospital.

"Sorry," I said, but my voice hinted sarcasm. Yet, I really was sorry.

"Somebody acts like that, walking to a hospital in the middle of the damn night to see their sick mother." He shook his head as he stepped out of the car. "I've been thinking," he said, and turned towards the house as he shut the car door. He turned back around and bent over to point a finger at me. "I'm just wondering if you'd do better in a boarding school." I stopped dead in my tracks.

"Who made you think of that? Lucky? Or Rheta?" I said.

"Them and their *great* ideas." He did not answer me, but straightened up and looked surprised.

"What've they got to do with it?" he said, looking confused.

"Nothing," I said. I ran inside, and slammed the door behind me.

9

The simple colors of things made me tingle—the green of the leaves overhead, the chestnut of Star's flank, the soft white of the geese feathers, the cinnamon color of Cookie's cheeks. But the hues that don't have names, I worshipped. The royal blue of late afternoon we'd see in a little while, the color of forgiveness Cookie had dealt me. For some reason, she did not bring up hoochie coo girls and said nothing about 90 lb. weaklings, but she pointed out that she wore both her new bra and the Stop Bite.

Our legs swung in the air as we lay on our backs. The geese honked with us while we sang that afternoon. Margo and Waldo were forbidden to step into the hideout, so they stood around the outside, honking.

A nice breeze had risen up and cooled off the world. We shared a chocolate bar Cookie had brought. Star munched grass by the stream and waded, taking sips of water and nibbling. I'd bridled her up and brought her out in case we decided to take a ride.

"So," I said, rolling over on my belly, "How are we going to do this?"

"Do what?" she said, legs in the air, pointing skyward, then this way and that like a Weeki Wachee mermaid.

"The contest with the nails," I said, spreading my fingers.

"I started already," she said. "Stop Bite tastes like the worst piece of sour lemon you ever put your tongue to, I'm telling you the truth. Dog." She rolled down, turned over and studied her nails. "Started last night. See a difference yet?" I shook my head no. Her nails were nubs like mine. She turned over, lifted her hips and put her hands under them to point and cross her legs in different positions.

"Cheater," I said. "You got a head start."

"Well, we can start all over if you want, Miss Center of the Universe," she said.

"No. I'll start now." I opened the bottle and applied some.

"I'm warning you," Cookie said, bringing her legs back down and rolling over. "You in for a shock."

"Nothing shocks me," I said. "Not after last night."

"What happened?" she said.

"Promise you won't tell?" I said.

"Who I'm gonna tell?" she said, grabbing the last melting bit of chocolate. I realized Ivory Jones had not said anything to her. I told her about Daddy's weird party and walking to the hospital, and without saying anything about Ivory Jones, I told her about seeing Mama, her wanting to get out. And Daddy listening to Lucky about committing Mama permanently. And Daddy threatening to send me off to boarding school. I stopped talking, and the wind blew through the trees a little while. I let the Stop Bite air dry. She didn't say anything. "What you thinking?" I said.

"My daddy, he plays electric guitar," she said. She licked her palm, which had smeared chocolate on it. She stood up and opened her arms wide. "He used to fill up our house with good music." She leaned on the brick wall and lowered her voice. "Mama, she loved her family in those days. She worked days, and Daddy worked nights," she said, leaning to the left for days, leaning right for nights. "Seemed like wherever we stayed the house soaked up that music. Like a garden. Like everything in it was alive." She sat back down.

"I think my great grandma believes that," I said, sitting up.

"Believes what?" She leaned on one arm.

"Well, she's Indian. Daddy explained it to me. Everything has life in it, and we're just not fit to see it, that's what she thinks." Cookie frowned and looked at the geese. "Like this sugar mill—" I put my hands on the cold brick edge of the opening. "I mean hideout—it's got life in it. The walls of your house, you know what I mean?"

"Okay, then," Cookie said, nodding, thinking. "I can see that."

"So where is your daddy?" I said, leaning up close. She sat her butt down and leaned back.

She looked out at the trees, and her mouth tightened. "Got in some fight over in a bar where he was playing. Near Montgomery, Alabama. Somebody blamed it on Daddy, but Daddy say the man fell on his own knife," she said, glancing over to me, then back at the trees. I wondered how much blood ran on the floor of that bar room, but it was not a polite question, so I refrained from asking.

She went on. "Daddy didn't even say nothing, he said. White man, hillbilly, he was, and he died." She sat up straight and said, "He was white so Daddy didn't get no fair trial." She looked down at me, and I blinked. "He's in jail now for manslaughter," she said, low. "Seven years." She wore a sad look. I let all that settle on me and listened to the creek. That water would go on clamoring down the hill no matter what. Manslaughter. Ivory Jones had not told a lie. Cookie had looked trouble in the mouth.

"How's it feel to have your daddy in jail?" I said.

"Oh, I'm all right. Aunt Jesse, she's sweet. I miss Mama," she said. She lay down on her stomach again and looked away out the door, her voice faltering. "Mama, she left back last summer late," she said. Then she shrugged. "She just leaves once in a while. Got a restlessness in her. Said she got this job over at the Golden Goblet in the kitchen, but one day, she came home fed up. Said it wasn't no kinda decent job. So she hauled us up to Auntie's house, and now she's gone."

I remembered what Ivory Jones had told me about what bogish meant. "Is she bogish, too?" I asked. Cookie sat up straight.

"What you mean?" she said.

"Oh, you know, like Miss Jesse and Ivory Jones said—" I stooped and turned my head away, studying my newly polished nails.

"How you know my brother—he been calling me bogish? How you know Ivory Jones?" she said, then leaned away to give me a study.

I shrugged my shoulders and felt my face grow hot. I got up and went to the door to check on Star. She was grazing on patches of grass where sun came through. "I don't know," I said. "He was at the hospital the night Mama had her stomach pumped. And last night. Last night he really helped me."

"He ain't told me that," she said. She watched me staring at my feet. "You think I'm bogish?"

"I don't even know what it means," I said, glancing over at her. "Something like grown up?" I said.

"Yeah," she said. "Something like sass mouth. Sexy sass mouth."

"No. I don't think you're bogish," I said, sitting back down trying to hide my smile. "Well, maybe a little sass mouth." She shoved me, and we both laughed. I went on. "Ivory Jones, he was so nice," I said, trying to look serious, not stars-in-the-eyes. "He took me up to see my mama. I wish I had a brother," I said.

"I don't think we're talking about the same boy," she said cocking her head and studying me. "My long tall skinny drink of water brother? Nice?" she said. "He punch me in the stomach just for fun sometimes."

"He's really cute," I said. "Those amber eyes."

"Amber?" she said. Then she busted out laughing. "My big old dumb brother," she coughed. "A white girl thinks my brother is cute." She rolled all over and slapped the blanket, howling. Then she turned around at me, pushing herself up. "Amber—that—that's what you called that guy you said—I remember from before. He's the boy you want to kiss, ain't he?" Her eyes had grown huge in disbelief. "He's the one you all googly about?" I shook my head no, but I was blushing. "Don't be lying to me, girl," she said.

"Do colored people get bruises?" I said. I really wanted to change the subject.

"Course we do," she said, sounding peeved. "Even though you trying to change the subject, I'll show you." She found one on her shin and pointed it out to me. "Fell on the front steps." It looked dusky next to her cinnamon skin. "You think we don't hurt cause you think we got tough skin? Living without all that finery you got?" I shrugged. "You lazy," she said, and then tsked. "Child, please. You don't pay no attention to nothing but shaving your white legs," she said.

"I don't shave my legs," I said. "I need to. They're so hairy."

"Y'all are crazy," she said. "Nothing worse than a bunch of white people with their shiny white legs stinking up the pool." I wanted to change the subject.

"If you had a million dollars, what would you do with it?" I said.

"Girl, you all over the place." She pulled her head back to study me. "I want to be in the picture show," she said.

"There's not any colored girls in the picture show," I said. "Unless you gonna be a star like that lady who played Mammy in *Gone with the Wind.*

She shot me a hard look and rolled her eyes. Then she lifted her arms to her sides and stood up, twirling around once.

"I am going to be like Dorothy Dandridge," she said.

"Who's that?"

"You must have lived under a rock all your life." Cookie let her arms drop down in disgust. "Didn't you see her as that queen in the Tarzan movie?"

"A colored queen?"

"A Negro queen," she said, nodding. I'd never seen a Negro queen, but this idea struck me as a possibility for Cookie.

"Is she pretty?" I said.

"Is she pretty? Girl, you ain't seen pretty yet if you ain't seen Dorothy Dandridge. And since I got a voice that people swoon for," Cookie said, waving her arms as she spoke, "they'll want me in the musicals, too. That's what my church ladies say. And Miss Steward. She said I got the prettiest voice she ever heard." She lay down and lifted her legs to the sky, using her hands on her back to prop her up.

"How's that gonna get you in the picture show, bragging?" I said.

"I can make a living with my voice," Cookie said. "Aunt Jesse took me to the church down on Saturday Street first time, and I sang the solo. The ladies come up after, told me I could make a living with a voice like mine. Said I could do commercials." Then she rolled down and stood up, breaking out into the Oscar Mayer wiener song. *Oh, I wish I were an Oscar Mayer wiener,* she sang. She wobbled from dizziness and sat down. I knew she could do it, too.

I jumped out of the hideout, walked over to Star and gave

her a big hug, kissing her on the forehead. "I want to own a horse farm. Raise horses," I said. "I'll have a house full of daughters, and they'll all have their own horse. I'll show them how to ride, how to brush and feed," I said. The geese started circling. That made Star nervous. She started backing up, and flattening her ears. I hopped into the hideout, and the geese tried to follow me.

"Uh huh, and what else?" Cookie said.

"And I'll have a big library, and everybody will read at night when it's too dark to ride. We'll sit by the fire and read. Just like in *Little Men*."

"By the fire?" Cookie said. "It's too hot around here to have a fire but once or twice a year. What you talking about, little men?"

"Oh, never mind. You use a fireplace more than that. When it gets cold we'll read by the fire," I said irritated. "But I'd still have the horses and the library," I said. "You're butting in on my dream. You *are* bogish."

She ignored me until my hand went to my mouth to chew nails. The bitterness on my tongue made my face scrunch up. Cookie leaned over laughing, pointed and said, "I done told you so."

We pretended we owned our own house and divided rooms with sticks. We dreamed so long that suddenly the clouds above had grown purplish black, the fireflies were blinking and the filling moon stood in the sky. I remember the look in Cookie's eyes as we parted. Her with the geese in tow, me riding Star. Something in our looks said we were not separated by woods, the creek, or even the colors of our skin.

As soon as I crossed through the woods and got up to the pasture, the wind groaned through the oak trees, and I felt the summer sweat chilling me. Nobody knew about our hideout, our singing together, our nail polish game, or even our quibbles. We only had togetherness in secret. I tried to think of the words to the last song Cookie had sung, but I couldn't. Instead I hummed the harmony.

Ruby reds, topaz golds, and jade greens—rich and mysterious as jewels, the colors of Mama's butterfly garden, even under the floodlight. I was standing on the balcony enjoying the evening. That's when Rheta pulled into the driveway. Remembering last night was like a needle in my throat. I wanted no more to do with her after the butt-feeling costume party, so I went out back to check on Star. I wandered to the barn. As I rounded the corner of the open door to get Star's brush and curry comb, I squealed. There stood Daddy in the dark, scotch and water in hand. He jumped, and it splashed over his fingers.

"You scared me," I said, hand on my chest.

"You scared me, too," he said, shaking off his wet hand.

"So what are you doing?" I said. Maybe if I engaged him in conversation, the doorbell would ring and ring, and Rheta would give up and go away.

"Oh, just looking," he said. He opened the door to the hay storage room and stared at the ceiling. He walked back out to the tack room and put his hand on my shoulder, sipping at his drink. He looked at me strange. "Where have you been?"

"Just riding Star. I went a long way today. Through the old pastures back to the pond, way back there, you know?" Boy, I was learning how to lie lie lie.

He looked at me darkly, like he didn't believe me, but wouldn't make an issue of it. "How would you like another horse, Lollipop?" he said. He must be juiced, I thought. Calling me Lollipop—he'd not remembered his name for me since

Mama went into the hospital. And he'd threatened to send me to boarding school earlier in the day. But the thought of having another horse thrilled me.

"Really?" I said. Grownups. Who knew what they were thinking. All they wanted to do was sit around, talk small talk, and most of the time looked forward to nothing. "That would be great, Daddy. Star's lonely , I think. Could we get a younger horse?"

"I don't see why not," he said. "I forget you must get lonely around here."

"I'm fine," I said. "I'm going to feed Star now." I thought I'd better leave before he changed his mind. I headed out the door as he stood in the barn entrance.

"Getting some woman shape to you." He was looking at my chest as he took another sip. "Legs getting long, too. Don't you think you ought to cover them up?"

"Daddy, knock it off," I said, waving him away. "Oh," I said. "I almost forgot. Your secretary's here." I did not want to honor her with a name.

I thought he'd be gone by the time I harnessed Star and brought her back, but he stood, one hand in a pocket, the other holding the empty glass. "I'm going away on a trip this week," he said. "I'll need to get somebody to watch you. How about Rheta?"

"No," I said. "Not her. Miss Jesse." Then I felt greedy. It meant she'd stay with me while Cookie and Ivory Jones stayed alone. "How about somebody else from work?"

"I'll see what I can arrange," he said, and headed back to the house. I spent a long time with Star to keep from the toil of Rheta. I cleaned Star's hooves and patted her rump, scratched her forelocks. She hung her head low and half-closed her eyes. If I stopped, she'd nudge me to keep it up. It got dark, and I headed to the house. I slipped inside through the front door and on up so as not to see Rheta.

Monday, Daddy dropped me off at school. He told me the business trip would have him gone a good three days, and for me to act good. When I asked who would stay with me, he said, "I'm still working that out." I kissed him bye and told him to be careful.

I took the bus home that day. Miss Jesse was watching the TV soaps, what she called "the stories," while she steam-ironed clothes. "Your daddy left you a note," she said. "On the kitchen table."

It said, Lollipop—I've arranged for Rheta to stay with you. I'm sure you'll welcome her and treat her as family. Be my good girl. Love, Daddy.

"Like hell," I said, wadding up the note and throwing it in the trash.

"What'd you say?" Miss Jesse said from the study.

"Miss Jesse, did Daddy ask you if you could stay with me?"

"He told me some woman from work, some secretary lady was coming."

"He didn't ask you to stay?" I walked into the study.

"He didn't say nothing about that," she said, finishing up one of Daddy's shirts and putting it on a hanger, then wiping her forehead. "I've left you some chicken in there. You eat chicken, and don't be snacking all evening like you does and not eat nothing good, hear?"

"Yes, Ma'am," I said. "Can't I just stay alone? I hate Rheta."

"Course not. Now I don't want to hear that word 'hate' spilling out of your mouth again. It's a filthy nasty word. You hear me?" she said. I let out a breathy growl and headed upstairs with my books. It suddenly occurred to me that Cookie got home about now. And she did not have Miss Jesse to greet her. "Miss Jesse?" I said from upstairs.

"What's that?" she said.

"You can go home early if you want."

"You think you gonna get away with something?" she said. "Cause you won't. I am not letting the devil do his work in this house while I'm in charge."

"Don't you want to see Cookie?" I walked to the top of the stairs.

"I ain't leaving no job to go home and see about her. She can fend for herself," Miss Jesse said.

"But I'm saying, you know, Cookie doesn't have her mama, and she needs you," I said. She put the iron down then, I could hear the steam escaping, and she came to the bottom of the stairs, arms folded, and looked at me standing at the top.

"Now how in the world did you know that?" she said with a piercing look.

"I just do," I said, shrugging my shoulders. Then I turned around and ran back up to the room. She harumphed, but I didn't pay it a bit of attention.

Rheta came over when it got dark, and slammed the door, yelling, "Yoo-hoo." I was finishing science homework on cells, shading in parts with color pencils. I used green paisley swirls, purple squares, and red dots. I was looking forward to studying viruses. The book said not plant and not animal, and they acted so simple, you'd think they were stupid. But nature plays tricks that way. I wanted to see how a virus ticked.

Coloring in pencils calmed me down. I thought of Mama. I'd take her some pencils or some watercolors and a pad of paper. She had a knack for it that I did not. But I could copy anybody's signature perfect. She would color the sun with a purple ring around it, and the ocean might have pink topped waves. She knew how to put dark and light just right, too. Maybe I'd take Cookie art supplies to give to Ivory Jones. He could take them to a nurse, who could give them to Mama.

I did not answer Rheta. I heard her in the kitchen, the study, the stairs.

"Oh, there you are," she said, leaning on the door. The side seam of her skirt had turned around lopsided so that the seam was a quarter of the way around front. In my mean, tiny heart it pleased me. She took off a gold pump, curled and flexed her foot.

"Yeah," I said, glancing up. "I'm busy with homework. Then I'm going to bed." I spoke in a flat voice and kept drawing. "*Mama* likes me to go to bed around nine."

I knew deep down whatever she was scheming with Daddy, and letting him touch her butt, had to do with taking sides. It's what girls did. When two girls had a fight, girls took sides. Like when Cynthia and Loretta fought over who would get the best charm bracelet from their boyfriends. When Cynthia got a locket with her initials inscribed in it, Loretta claimed it was not pure gold. Then it was a fight. Girl against girl, and every girl in class took a side. Those with Cynthia said Loretta was jealous, those with Loretta said Cynthia had bought the locket. I personally did not care if the necklace came from a bubblegum machine and stayed out of it, except Cynthia didn't make fun of people.

I hated it, but I would play it if I had to. For now, I'd play it cool. Otherwise, Rheta would get in line with Lucky to have me sent off to a military boarding school or worse.

"Well, okay," she said, putting her foot back in her shoe. "Nine o'clock." She looked like she didn't quite know what to do.

"Fine," I said. "I've got to get this done, so I'll talk to you later."

She looked at me up and down and frowned. Then she shrugged. "Fine," she said, and headed downstairs.

Tuesday it rained all day, so at school nobody could go outside for recess. The lunchroom crowded up with restless kids smelling sour from rainy clothes drying. The screaming clattery sounds hurt my ears. On those days, you saw people you wouldn't usually see. That's how I ran into Cookie in the bathroom. She was singing, of course. *Just gimme some kinda sign, girl, oh, my baby—*

"Hey," I said. "How's the nails?" I held out my hands. "No biting, but they're not growing yet, not really."

"Mine's starting to grow." She showed me the little white curves pushing up over the tops of her fingers.

"Dang, you cheater," I said. "You got a head start on me."

"Head start? Half a day?" she said with a smirk. "You're just jealous. That stuff tastes terrible." *Show me that you're mine girl,* she crooned as she swayed her hips into the mirror.

"Daddy's out of town," I said. "Rheta's staying there." I made a face.

"Who's that?"

"The secretary I told you about, don't you remember nothing?"

"The one your daddy—" she started pretending to squeeze cantaloupes in the air. I could not help busting out laughing. "Aunt Jesse told me," she said. "She asked me how you knew all my business. I told her we talked some in the woods. When you came up to the fence by the trees near our house. She told me she didn't mind, but what about your daddy. She said it might not be safe for us to be, you know, getting together and all."

Just then the librarian walked in and looked at us from one to the other, frowning. We immediately turned to the mirrors and started washing our hands.

"Baloney," I mouthed to her.

We waited till the librarian had left, then we sang, *It's like thunder and lightning, the way you love me is frightening.*

"Hey," I said. "Why don't you come over to my house tonight?"

"What you talking about?" she said, looking me like a strict mama who's caught her daughter eating all the dessert pie before dinner.

"Rheta leaves me all alone. I'll set the ladder out so you can climb up."

She shook her head no. *I'd better knock,* she sang, then knocked on the bathroom wall four times, *on wood.*

"I'll put the ladder out anyway," I said. "Maybe you'll change your mind."

That evening Rheta came in and didn't even say Yoo-hoo. She just said, "Rayann?"

"What?" I was putting on deodorant for the first time, because I had started to stink under there. I noticed some hairs, these gross long curling things that had cropped up under my arms.

"Just checking on you," she said. She went straight to the phone in the den and called somebody. Then I smelled her cigarette. I went downstairs and fixed myself some dinner while she sat with the color TV on, a drink in her hand, talking on the phone about shopping for cars. I headed out the door. I fed Star, took the ladder around front and set it up under my balcony, and came back in to find her still sitting in the chair on the phone. I smiled and said I'd be doing homework and going to bed early and goodnight. She nodded and waved at me, then went on talking.

Upstairs, I lay on the bed and realized how things really were. It's not great to realize your daddy's not keeping his promises to your mama. I worried about what in the world he was doing until it started to rain. Rain like restless angels singing me to sleep.

I dreamed a gorilla was chasing me at school, a big hairy and mean one. I tore around the school yard, climbing the kiddy slide, but he followed me by jumping up the slidy part. Then to the kickball field and around the oak tree until somehow I got onto an elevator. Then I realized I was naked, and other kids at school rode the elevator up, too.

It started pitter-pattering with rain, hard rain as the elevator zoomed up, and I felt cold and sweaty both, so I crouched over. Then the doors opened, and people were looking at me. Then they started throwing bones at me. I hid my face in my naked knees.

Then the elevator door closed, and they were knocking and banging at the door and shouting. That's when I bolted upright and realized Cookie was standing at the door of the balcony. I was breathing hard and fast and looked down to realize with relief that I wore clothes. She stood behind the glass and said in a raspy loud whisper, "Hurry up! Let me in!" She breathed fast and hard, and kept turning and looking at the front yard.

I opened the door and she nearly collapsed inside. "Dang, girl, I didn't think you'd ever wake up," she whispered loud. "I pushed the ladder off so wouldn't nobody see it."

"I had horrible dreams," I said, rubbing my eyes. I couldn't believe she'd actually come to my house. She looked at the ceiling, the four walls, at the floor and then at the little black and white TV on the dresser. "Go on, you can sit on the bed," I said.

"Shh," Cookie said. "Keep your voice down." We sat on the bed, and I told her the dream. She laughed into her hand, quiet, and said, "You naked in the rain on an elevator." Then we both rolled on the bed laughing like in church.

"What happened to Miss Jesse?"

"She went to sleep. I can't stay long. That's your color TV?" she said, pointing at it. I told her no, it's black and white, but we could watch it low anyway.

"Rheta hasn't even bothered me since yesterday. Hasn't even come up the steps." I turned on the TV.

Andy Griffith was on. It was the show where Opie met this rich kid from the city and felt like he had to put on airs, and Andy told him just to be himself. Then Andy went to meet the dad and got all dressed up in a new suit. When he showed up, a white maid answered the door. Cookie said they must be real rich if they have a white maid.

All the men were wearing sweaters while Andy wore a suit, and he was embarrassed. He felt all awkward around the rich guys, and then Opie came in and told his dad he'd been right. He'd decided to just be himself and go in his regular clothes. This made Andy think, and then he invited all those rich men to go in his little bass boat fishing, and they all got along great. Cookie said she thought Opie's work pants, which were surely beige in real life, and plaid shirt could use a little upgrade.

At the very end, it showed Andy up close and his hair looked like a Pompadour. My grandmamma had talked about Pompadours, so I'd looked it up in the encyclopedia. Some French lady made it stylish hundreds of years ago, but it sure looked dumb to me. Cookie said, "What the hell is wrong with his hair?" She pulled up her pants till they came halfway to her chest. She flooped her hair over like a Pompadour and walked around the room like a duck. I busted out laughing so hard I could not dam it up. She started to laugh, too. We jumped on the bed crashing our backs into each other, and rolled around and around, touching hands and then covering our mouths, trying to keep silent, but it just got funnier. We laughed till tears came down our faces, and we were breathing fast and hard, her lying with her head at the foot of the bed, and mine at the top side by side.

Suddenly, the door busted open. We both bolted up fast. There stood Rheta in the doorway, staring in, looking at us both with big eyes. Cookie cleared her throat. Rheta looked from Cookie to me and back again. She cocked her head.

"Do you live near here?" she said to Cookie. Cookie looked at me.

"Yeah," I said. "Down the road."

"Well, I think you'd better get on home," Rheta said, all calm, but like Cookie might as well be a roach or something. "You can come through the house this time." She said it low, and she smiled, not a mean smile, just an I-know-what-you're-up-to-girls look. Then she left. She never said another word. I walked Cookie downstairs and out the back door, into the black air where fireflies were keeping their appointments with the night, as Mama used to say. I felt a confused feeling about Rheta then. She had not blessed us out. She did not mention it the rest of the week. She went back to pretending I was not really there, but like she was kind of nervous around me, too. Picking at her fingers and trying to think of the right thing to say. I settled for an uncomfortable and silent agreement not to talk about it. At least I hoped she would agree to that if I agreed not to push her out of the house with meanness.

10

Moonless. The sky was utter dark, thrown with stars. I strained to hear the voices that had waked me up. Daddy and Lucky. The rest of the week with Rheta had gone by like a blurry streak. Daddy had flown home, and the next week I hardly saw him. He'd worked at the hospital catching up.

Now it was Saturday night about eleven, and I lay in bed listening to Daddy and Lucky. Laughing and shouting downstairs. It sounded like a celebration. The smell of cigars slipped its way up to the second floor, hurting my throat.

Then Red showed up, and they all made toasts. I tiptoed light, so as not even to squeak on the tiles, and sat on the stairs to listen. Their conversation turned to hunting and fishing. I only caught snatches of it. I knew none of the costume ladies had gotten an invitation to this gathering. Daddy and his friends banged a bag of ice against the counter, then cracked pieces into the kitchen sink. They were fixing their own drinks, something they'd never do if women were coming. I slipped down to the middle of the steps to hear better.

Lucky was bragging. "In three days we got us a hundred quail up there at Hazel Creek in Georgia," he said. Somebody whistled through their teeth.

Then Red piped up about somebody named Bo. "Bo wouldn't go, cause he don't like niggers." Ice was tinkling into glasses.

I flushed with embarrassment thinking about Miss Jesse,

Cookie, and Ivory Jones hearing such talk in my house. The liquor cabinet doors opened with a squeak.

"There's a lot of them up at Hazel Creek," Red said.

"This week, I had a woman come over to the hospital— blackest woman you ever saw," Daddy said. "Didn't have a pot to piss in, either. And dumb, lord was she dumb. Could hardly understand anything she said. Wanted to put her son in *my* hospital." He stopped to let the others laugh and growl. "Claimed the colored hospital didn't have the right medicine. She said he'd already lost one leg, and was about to lose the other."

"That ain't all he's gonna lose," Red said, and they all laughed like they'd told a big joke. What'd you do, Al, somebody said.

"I told her we didn't take no darkies. Give them an inch, and they'll take a country mile. Put them in the schools and soon enough, they'll be wanting to eat with us."

Then Lucky said something I couldn't hear, and they roared with laughter. A part of me did not want to listen, another part said, You'd better keep both ears to it.

"I cut me off a nigger's finger once, trying to mess with me," Red said, real loud, like he was testifying to his own congregation. I stood up fast. My legs shook.

Daddy and Lucky asked Red about this finger. "I kept it in my freezer," he said.

Then it got quiet for a minute. "You don't believe me? Come on. Let's go out to my place. You can have a look, you bastards." They all placed bets about whether Red really had a finger or not.

Then the sound of the door slam echoed through the house. The car and truck vroomed off in a muffled sound. I slowly made my way down the stairs, thinking What kind of people would drive twenty blasted miles out to the country to see a finger in a freezer? Then it got so quiet. I could hear the refrigerator click on and off. Even my feet patting across the tile floor bounced off the walls and through the house. When I started thinking about how many bones are in fingers, I said aloud, "Don't!"

I got busy opening all the windows downstairs to let the smoke out, and did everything I could to keep from thinking about fingers in freezers. When I felt tired, I crawled into bed and buried my thoughts by reading a book about this boy Huck. He had a drunk daddy, and how, to escape, he killed a pig and dropped the blood around to make his daddy think he'd died. That way, his daddy would not go searching for him. I had to hand it to that boy. He cut that pig's throat, saving his own self.

When the door slammed again, the tremor of it shook through the house, even shaking the glass in the balcony window. I'd been asleep. I looked at the clock. Two hours has passed. The sky had low clouds rushing past, so no moon and no stars. Black like a giant crow's underbelly. All of them had returned. They talked louder and slower.

I was mostly suspect of Red, especially after I heard the tire-shooting story. But I'd heard others, like once when he and Daddy had gone on a hunting trip up in the Georgia mountains. Somebody passed them on a mountain road while Red was driving. Red got so furious about it, Daddy said, that Red had sped up and kept tailing the guy until he rear ended the guy. Smashed the back of that fellow's car over and over again. Daddy said he'd got sorta scared of Red that day, said you just didn't know what he'd do when. I wondered why they'd let a guy like him run free, cutting off people's fingers, and they wanted to capture Mama like fireflies in a jelly jar and keep her in a hospital just cause she acted crazy lying in bed drinking and taking pills all day. Then I remembered she was in there cause of me—they thought she might burn the house down if she'd burn holes in her table.

I listened to them in the kitchen while they made themselves another drink. I slunk down the stairs on my tiptoes slow, holding onto the banister. I eased down to the bottom, listening to Lucky talk about his bobcat prize. One time we'd all gone to Lucky's house for dinner. He had these stuffed bobcat mama and babies on the round table in the living room. His pride and joy, he said. "Aren't they beauties?" he'd said. I'd studied them—these babies with soft fur still on them. Eyes of marbles.

Daddy and Mama had agreed how beautiful these cats looked sitting on the table. When I'd said to Mama, "Why'd he kill them? I could pet them if they were alive, and they'd enjoy it," she shushed me.

"That's not polite," she'd whispered.

I sat at the bottom of the stairs listening, and all I could understand was that this kind of talk was something hard as those dead cat babies between grown men.

"Ain't you got a daughter, A.J.?" Red said. I froze.

"I thought I had a daughter," Daddy said, "She's probably asleep. Or out wandering." I stood, ready to leap up the stairs.

"Well, you got lucky then," Lucky said, laughing. "You're just down to one now."

"Only need a female around for a couple of things, and the second one is cooking," Red said. The three of them laughed out loud. My stomach soured.

"Yeah, might as well just find me a twenty-year-old whore," Daddy said. He did not speak that way around me and Mama. "I'm gonna lie down here and watch TV."

"A. J.," Red said. "Where's that girl of yours? She getting

ripe yet?"

"I just told him," Lucky said, "she's getting some buds on her." I broke out in a cold sweat. I flew up the stairs to the bathroom.

"That's it, that's it," Daddy said. "Enough of this bull crap." Soon, Daddy was snoring and Red and Lucky started wandering around downstairs. They weaved their way to the front hallway and studied one of Mama's paintings.

"She's crazy as a bedbug," Lucky said. "Look how the fruit on them apple trees is red, white and blue. Now whoever heard—"

"I'm just gonna have a look upstairs," Red said. My eyes darted around the bathroom. The window—a 15 foot drop onto concrete. The bathtub. He'd just open the shower curtain.

"She ain't up there, Red, where you going?" Lucky said.

"I'll be back," Red said. "I'm just taking a look." I could hear his voice get closer and his shoes on each step as he headed up the cold tile stairs. I thought about mice, and how they will run and hide in any hole they can find.

I crawled quick as a rabbit into the cabinet under the wide, two-sink counter and squeezed into a corner where no bottles sat. The pipe felt cold on my left shoulder. I scrunched my head down and closed the door quiet. My knees were just about in my mouth, and a bottle of old medicine dug into my butt. My skin got hot top to bottom.

I could hear Red as he pushed open the bedroom door. He walked into the bedroom. I heard him open the balcony door. Then he closed the door and headed back into the hallway, then into the extra bedroom. I saw the yellow from the light of that bedroom go on, then off. Then he walked into the bathroom.

All over my skin was throbbing and hot, so I grabbed the cold sink pipe with both hands and held on. The old bottle stung it dug in so hard. Through the louvers in the cabinet door, I could see his legs and feel the air move as he passed by the sink toward the tub and toilet room.

"Rayann?" he called, like it was a game. To keep from whimpering, I bit my knee and squeezed the metal pipe. He opened the louver doors that take you to the toilet and bathtub, and he opened the shower curtain.

"I know you must be here somewhere," he said. I bit down on my knee. Then I heard the zipper of his pants go down, and then he peed in the toilet. I felt sweat start to trickle down my arm. Then I heard the zipper go back up.

Red stood at the sink and washed his hands. I could feel the water gurgle right by my ear in the pipes. I barely breathed. He turned and walked out.

"Can't find her," Red said, on the way back down the stairs. "We'll just wait till she comes back." Lucky chuckled and said something, but I didn't hear it.

I crawled out on to the balcony, then over the railing and hung there like a bug caught in a web. I hung until my hands hurt from holding on. I quit thinking about the ten-foot drop onto grass and let go. When I hit the ground, it stung, and I rolled backwards on the soft grass. I wasn't hurt. "Damn," I said, just to know I was alive. I brushed off. Then I ran fast and hard for the woods. I tore into the briars at the edge of the road and kept going anyway, as their stickers ripped across my legs. I did not slow down, but raced toward the path. No moon. I charged forward and crashed into a tree. I collapsed and sank to the ground, hearing myself breathe hard, fast. I waited till my eyes got used to the dark without any silver light helping me along. In a few seconds, I saw the tree next to the entrance of the path. Then I saw the path and headed straight into the woods for the old sugar mill hideout.

It appeared bigger and darker in the night time. The trees stood like ghosts around it with the little light the stars offered. Tree limbs spilled long shadows like ink into the hideout. Some dog way down on Saturday Street started barking in the distance. Waldo and Margot got going across the woods, so I stood stock still. After a while the noise died down. I stood at the entranceway breathing hard.

My eyes got used to the dark even. I gritted my teeth and crawled into the hideout. I thanked Cookie and myself for the blankets we'd taken. I shook them one at a time and out dropped what I hoped was a lizard, some sticks and pine needles. I made a pillow of one blanket and folded the other in half, then curled into its middle.

The hideout smelled muffled and mildewy. To keep from thinking about spiders and ants, I got up and sprayed some bug repellent I kept in the corner ice chest. I lay on the blanketed floor, the moon shining down. I listened to the sound of water running down the creek. It began to sound like sparklers fizzing.

It was so still at first. Then it seemed like everything was moving. I thought of everything—the ocean half an hour away jumping with silver light reflecting and singing back to the stars. Mullet. Porpoises. How when the moon shone, porpoises' little hairs looked painted with phosphorous. Anything to not think about those cigar-smoking men in the house. Or burning things. If I'd just told Daddy I was the one who burned the table, Mama would be home, and none of this would have happened.

I even thought to walk to Miss Jesse's, but as soon as I crawled through the barbed wire fence, the geese started honking, so I turned around and went back.

Finally the dark overhead grew softer, fuzzier, like a weak yellow, the color of cat fur underneath. Then gray. I was waiting for orange, because that meant true day would come. I listened to creek water gushing and imagined the earth taking big gulps early in the morning so that later in the day, it would turn back its green freshness into the world. I listened for the mockingbirds to start up with *what cheer what cheer birdie birdie birdie cue cue cue cue.*

So when I heard crackling, I nearly jumped out of my skin. I waited, my heart stomping in my chest like horses galloping. I curled up and covered my head.

I do not think I'd ever heard a sweeter chorus of voices than Cookie and the geese honking. She sang *"—something inside starting to burnin, and I'm filled with desire. Could it be a devil in me, or is this the way love's supposed to be. It's like a heat wave, burning in my heart. It's like a heat wave, burning—"* She stopped.

"What you doing in there, crazy girl?" Cookie said, peeking over the doorway. I pulled the covers off and sat up, dizzy. She stepped in, and the geese honked. "Get out of here, you crazy fools," she said, kicking them back. "Before I kill you." They wandered over to the creek. The dawn was starting to crack open the sky with an orange sherbet color. Cookie took a deep breath and stretched.

I itched all over and felt irritable. "I ran away from home, nosy girl," I said, scratching at my legs. I told her about Daddy's party, about Red, and about how I'd crawled into the bathroom cabinet. I couldn't believe what she did next. She laughed. Hard. How dare she laugh, I thought. Then she put her hand out to touch my hair. I slapped it away.

"It's not funny," I said. "They were talking about whores and how they'd cut off a colored person's finger and—" I choked, swallowing the sob that surged up my throat.

"Hey," she said, rubbing the hand I'd slapped. She frowned

and looked at me up and down, then at the woods towards her house.

"That's the first time you never had anything to say," I said. I laughed, the way you do when you're wanting to cry and start laughing for no crazy reason. She knelt across from me and touched my hair again.

"Your hair's almost nappy," she said. I put my head in my hands. I drew in a shuddery breath and let it go. "Still," she said, "it's kinda soft."

"Get your hand off me, it stinks," I said, pushing her off. I felt so tired and dirty.

"Come over to my house," she said. I shook my head no. My legs itched all over. She knew white people didn't go into colored houses. I scratched a rash of bites on my ankle. Once, Mama and I had driven over to Miss Jesse's house to pick up some beans she'd shelled for extra money. "Can we go in and get her, Mama?" I'd said then.

"No," Mama had said, touching my arm as I opened the car door. "Rayann," she'd said, like I'd said a bad cuss word. Like how could I even think that.

"You can get breakfast," Cookie said now, ignoring my silence. My stomach did feel all bunched up. I stretched my legs out. Covered with red bumps. The skin felt itchy, sore and pestery. "Girl, your legs a mess!" she said. "You look like a chicken pox fell on you." She put a finger to my shin. "Do they itch bad or hurt?"

"Itch," I growled.

"You need to get some alcohol on those bites," she said, "down at my house." She stood up and offered me a hand.

Daddy told me never to drink or eat after a colored person, I thought to say, but did not. I didn't even make sense to myself. I looked away and did not take her hand. Miss Jesse cooked our food, so why couldn't I eat hers? I saw a hurt look run across her eyes. She pulled her hand back and folded her arms. Then her mouth widened and thinned into disgust.

"Oh, I see," she said. "Miss Rayann's just too good. She can't live at home, and she can't stay with us." She laughed then, a bitter laugh. "Hmm umm," she said, shaking her head. Only the sound of the creek gurgled, running, and the cardinals steering other things away from their nests, feeding their babies. "Wait a minute," she said, starting a list with her fingers. "You done ate after me. You slept under my blanket by the looks of it there," she said gesturing at the blanket on the ground. "Aunt Jesse, she always in your house, and cooking your food, and you done ate a lot of that, too." She put her hands to her hips now. "Seems to me you done broke most of them precious lady rules of yours." The woods got a jazzy weirdness to them, and I scratched at my bites, looked at my sorry red swelling legs. "Well," Cookie said. "Starve if you want to." She jumped out the doorway. "And let those bites burn you up, too."

"Wait," I said. She turned around, scowling. "What y'all got to eat?"

"Peaches and eggs and cinnamon toast," she said, her eyes challenging. "Brown eggs. We ain't got no white eggs." She turned her back to me, her shoulders high. She walked towards the creek. "Come on, you fools," she said to the geese. "I am so tired of you, I could kick you into tomorrow."

"Wait," I said crawling out the doorway and stumbling at a run to catch up with her. "You shouldn't talk so mean to those geese." But she didn't hear me, resuming her song where she'd left off, singing and swaying her way through the woods, *Don't pass up this chance, It sounds like a new romance, heat wave, burnin, burnin....*

11

The air around Miss Jesse's smelled like cologne—peach and tea olive blossoms. Bees thrummed fat and lazy, and the sun shone on the steps of the concrete porch where I stood while Cookie tried to talk Miss Jesse into letting me stay. I could barely see all the way through the screen door to the back of the tiny house.

Cookie spoke from the kitchen back door. I could only see her shadow. Her voice got high in that begging please way, while Miss Jesse talked in a low voice I could not decipher. Eventually Cookie opened up the screechy screen door. She grinned and said, "Come on in."

The living room sized up to about my bathroom and held five chairs plus a sofa. None of them matched, but every piece of furniture held a bright color of turquoise or ruby red, and looked neat and tidy. The house smelled like cooking oil, Clorox bleach and wood floor, the way Miss Jesse always smelled to me.

Next to the small fireplace, somebody'd tacked up camera pictures on the wall. No frames. One featured six colored men dressed in suits and a drum set that said, "Mt. Sinai AME Gospel Band." The picture next to it showed younger guys. They all sported ruffles on their shirts, and each one held a guitar. Under the picture, I read, "The Tribulations."

"That's my daddy in both those pictures," Cookie said. "Two bands he played in. He's the one next to the end, the tall one here in the church band," she said, pointing to the gospel band. "See him?" I moved in close and squinted. She couldn't have looked more like him. Tall and rangy with long legs and those almond eyes like Cookie and Ivory Jones both had. "And here he is with this rhythm and blues band. They all younger, but he's the best."

On the hearth of the fireplace sat this huge conch shell somebody'd written on in paint. "Myrtle Beach, 1945." I picked it up. I couldn't hear the ocean. I didn't know whether Miss Jesse owned an inside toilet, but I'd seen her outhouse in the back yard. I figured I'd ask about the outhouse later, but I wanted to clean my hands. "Can I wash up?" I said. I figured I better go ahead and face the outhouse deal now. Just then, Miss Jesse's small crisp-dressed self walked into the living room.

"Baby, what—" she said, looking me up and down. She looked prim as always, dressed in a turquoise dress, but in house slippers. "Just look at you. Bites on your legs and leaves in your hair." She pulled a twig out of my hair and ran her pointer finger down the back side of my leg. "Cookie, get the rubbing alcohol and a washrag. Better, y'all go in the bathroom, and Rayann, you get washed up. Take a cool bath. Hot water's only going to make you itch like a summer dog with fleas. Cookie, you put some alcohol on them bites while I get this toast out."

When Miss Jesse pointed me towards the hall where the bedrooms and bathroom were, I was relieved I did not have to use an outhouse. I shooed Cookie out of the bathroom. The tub looked just like a normal tub, only brown. The toilet, too. What a relief. I got cleaned up, and then put the alcohol on. Its coolness gave me goosebumps.

Then I sat at the table and gobbled down some canned peaches. And that cinnamon toast Cookie had mentioned, which turned out to be crunchy, sweet and buttery, too. Miss

Jesse was watching me out the corner of her eye.

"Your daddy carrying on last night up the hill?" she said, filling up my milk glass after I drained it. She had tiny hands for such a bossy woman. How'd she ever get all her work done with such tiny hands?

"Yes'm," I said. "You know Lucky, his lawyer friend Mama hates?"

"That loudmouth fellow with the glasses?" she said. "One don't know how to match nothing?"

"Yeah," I said. "Yeah, him."

"Uh huh," she said. "What he said? Go on."

"Well, him and Red, you know Red?" I said. "Always wears blue jeans?"

"Oh, you ain't saying," she said, and shook her head. "That man is the seven-headed red dragon." She shook her head. "Sent by the Devil himself. What he's doing at your house? Go on."

"Him and Lucky and Daddy were all drinking and talking in the house last night. Talking about—well, whores and excuse me for saying it, uh—colored people, and—I don't know, I got scared. Daddy went to sleep, then Red walked upstairs to find me, and I got real scared then. So I hid in the cabinet under the sink."

"You ain't saying," Miss Jesse said.

"Tell about the man's finger," Cookie said. I did not want to talk about that in front of Miss Jesse.

So Cookie told it. "This Red man say he found this colored man stealing, and he tried to cut off his finger, and couldn't get it off, so he cut off his whole hand." Miss Jesse began to look at Cookie sternlike, and I knew she was asking herself what on earth I was doing sitting at her table.

"No, it was not the hand. He said, finger," I said, holding up my pinky. Maybe a little finger counted for less. "Cookie told it wrong, Miss Jesse, it was a finger." Miss Jesse put her hand on her hip and still gave Cookie an eye-slitted look.

"Those white people, I tell you they think they can—" Miss Jesse started in, and then darted her eyes at me and stopped. She turned around to head back into the kitchen, seemed to think better of it, set the milk jug on the table, and looked square at me, her arms folded.

"Don't you have nobody you can stay with?" She said it exasperated.

I ran that one around in my head. Only Granddaddy who lived on a golf course with no electricity and ran a still in his living room. "Mama's mama's dead," I said. "Daddy's, too. Besides, I got Star, Mama, a house I love—"

"You love that house so much, how come you leaving it every chance you get? Be hiding out in your room?" Cookie said. By now she'd perched up on one foot in the chair across from me at the table, crunching cinnamon toast, looking at me hard.

I stared right back. Miss Jesse pushed things around on the table, wanting to hear what I'd say. I'd seen Miss Jesse hang around a room rearranging things, acting busy just to hear what Daddy or Mama had to say. What would I do without the woods if I left? I loved the woods and all that was in them— June bugs, beetles, banana spiders. The jagged shape of turkey oak leaves. Robins, mourning doves, and—Star, I loved my horse. And now a friend and a hideout. I tried to think of how to make my mouth tell it like my heart knew it, but nothing would come out.

"Why'n y'all womens leave her alone?" came a male voice from the bedroom just off the dining area. I flushed like crazy. Ivory Jones, just getting up, I guessed. "She's hungry and tired, probably," he went on. "Can't think, eat, and y'all talking all nosy and needling her. Just leave the girl alone a minute."

"You ain't the boss of me," Cookie said, twisting in her chair towards Ivory Jones' voice.

"I don't want to be harboring nobody whose daddy's friends hate colored folks, nephew," Miss Jesse said, turning to walk back into the kitchen. She turned back and looked at me. "No offense, darling." Then she turned to him and said, "It might be your finger next."

"Oh, that's the way those white men talk," he said, coming into the living room, buttoning up a shirt. My heart nearly leaped out of its chest catching a glimpse of his bare chest, all light brown and hardly any hair and shaped all in boy curves and carved out muscles. I felt warm in strange places. "They talking trash to each other," he said, glancing at me, then slapping Cookie on the head. Then he turned to talk to Miss Jesse. "You know that Red is lying through his cracker teeth. He wandered on into the hospital about a month ago. Probably looking for Mr. Wood. When old Pig come in."

"You mean that old hophead hangs out with Sammy Sam?" Cookie said. I had never heard them talk like this. I guessed that was the way colored people talked to just each other in their own house.

"Yeah, old Pig," Ivory Jones said. "Come in with his finger all messed up. Hacked it with a machete in his sugar cane patch. Probably hitting the juice too hard. Had a piece of that finger in his bloody handkerchief, talking about sew it back on. They couldn't do that, so the doctor gave the finger to Red. Just for kicks. You know how they are." He glanced at me. "That's all it amounts to."

Everybody got so quiet you could hear the crows high in the trees scheming to steal from the corn in Miss Jesse's garden.

Miss Jesse looked at Ivory Jones a long time, like she wanted to say something but did not. Then she said, "Hmph," and told him to sit down and eat breakfast.

Somehow a piece of me relaxed. I almost felt sorry for Red, Lucky, and Daddy. In my house making up junk to brag on. I wanted to leap out of my chair and hug Ivory Jones. Instead I drank my milk.

"I need you to carry me up to the market and get some beans," Miss Jesse called from the kitchen. Ivory Jones rolled his eyes.

"I got to work on my day off, looks like," Ivory Jones said, biting into his toast. "Carrying my auntie around in a ugly brown rustmobile." He rolled his eyes again.

"Ain't going to take all day, and you loves an excuse to drive a car, so you can hush that talk right now," Miss Jesse said. I thought they'd forgotten about Daddy and sending me home. Miss Jesse turned to me and said, "How's your mama doing?"

"I don't know," I said. "I saw her that one night when I walked up to the hospital. Daddy yelled at me. I haven't seen her since. I wish I could," I said, my blue and white chipped plate in my hand, headed for the kitchen. I realized they were eating off of the china that we used to own. I even remembered the chip on the side of the plate. Mama must have given it to Miss Jesse. "I want to take her some paints and stuff," I said.

"That's a good idea," Miss Jesse said, wiping her hands on her apron and wheeling around to talk to me. "She loves them paints. I think you need to take the bus downtown to see your mama. Soon. Today. Tell her what all's going on at home."

I sat back down at the table. We each perched quiet and still, Cookie and me, Ivory sitting back in his chair and folding his arms, frowning.

"But Aunt Jesse," Cookie pleaded. We sat still as we could

in case it would help our chances for my staying. Miss Jesse walked back into the dining area.

Just when I knew she'd point her finger towards my house and send me on home, Miss Jesse turned to Cookie and wagged a finger. "I'll let her stay." Then she turned to me and wagged her finger. "I can't be letting you stay out in them woods." I could hear mosquitoes on the screen door pinging and whining. "Well." She sighed from the bottom of her stomach like she did sometimes when she ironed and watched the stories. "Just for *today*," she said, pointing first a finger at Cookie, then at me. "Just for today. You hear me, Cookie Johnson? And Rayann, you need to go home tonight."

She shook her head and walked into the kitchen saying "Umm mm mm," and started banging pots and pans around. Cookie jumped softly into the air and held her two thumbs up to me. Miss Jesse went on. "Your daddy will be worried sick about you if you don't go home. And I'll carry you if you won't go your own self. Your daddy'll be laying up in the house all day if he had a wild night." At that I rolled my eyes and acted like I was going to throw up. Cookie covered her mouth to keep from laughing. Miss Jesse turned on the water and said over the hissing sound, "Ain't nobody gonna do you no harm up there tonight."

Cookie straightened up. "Yes, Ma'am," she said, sweet and high pitched like an eight-year-old child.

"Thank you, Miss Jesse," I said, scratching at the mosquito bites on my legs. She rounded the corner, and peered at me, concerned. She knew the tone of my voice.

"What's wrong?" she said, frowning. The bites were making me miserable. "Time for some kerosene," Miss Jesse said. "Fetch that gas can for me, Ivory Jones," she said, "and bring me a rag." He did what he was told, and Miss Jesse swabbed my bites with the stuff. They stung like the dickens. Then, like magic, they stopped itching altogether.

Summer was sliding in. Hot and wet as tears. The sun blazed on Miss Jesse's garden. A wind came out of the swamp and slapped the green stalks of sugar cane together. Cookie and me drained the sweet ice tea, but still it felt too hot to hang around the yard, and we had our orders from Miss Jesse. Inside, it was curtainy, dark and stifling, but Miss Jesse had instructed us to stay put. We passed the time playing cards, putting ice on our foreheads, and listening to songs on Cookie's record player. Ivory Jones and Miss Jesse returned from the downtown market and were unloading the groceries.

"Get on out of this house," Miss Jesse said, shooing us towards the screen door. The honeysuckle and mimosa tree hung, swaying in the slightest bit of breeze while the crickets played their background music. The geese stayed cool under the shade and panted like dogs. We brought the record player on the porch and listened to Ray Charles while we argued over whose fingernails had grown longer. "Don't y'all girls be fighting out there," Miss Jesse said. Then out burst Ivory Jones through the door he'd set swinging. He tossed a football in the air.

"Let's play football!" I said, jumping up.

"No," Cookie said. "Go on," she said, batting a hand like to shoo him away. "Go *on*. We're playing our own game. Get your own friend."

"You scared I'll make a cream of the both of you?" Ivory Jones said, tossing the ball into the air, then glancing at Cookie with raised eyebrows. She didn't say anything, but crossed her arms and gave him a look that would fry meat. He craned his neck to stick his face closer to hers. "Huh?" he said.

"Come on," I said. "Let's play football."

"Oh, all right." Cookie sighed and dropped her arms. She stomped to the front yard where the grass had been mowed flat like a field. The Chiffons crooned out *Doo lang doo lang doo lang, He's so fine, Doo lang do lang do lang, Wish he were mine.*

Ivory Jones showed us how to play center, quarterback and receiver. Then he explained how to play defense, which meant tackling. He got us into a pattern of Cookie as quarterback, himself as receiver, and me on defense. After Ivory Jones hiked the ball to Cookie and before she could get the ball out of her hands, I leapt into the air and tackled her around the waist. Her eyes got big, and the whump of her back on the ground surprised us both.

"Dang, girl," she said.

"Sorry," I said, giving her a hand up. "I didn't mean—did I hurt you?"

"You can't hurt Cookie," Ivory Jones said, picking up the ball that rolled beside us. He twirled it in the air and said, "She's too mean." Cookie stood up holding my hand with one hand, and quick as the wind, she punched her brother hard in the stomach with the other. He doubled over and covered his belly with his arms.

"Ivory Jones?" she said. "You hurt?" He stood up grinning.

"You can't hurt a fly," he said. Then she hit him again, and they tumbled on the ground laughing. At first it scared me to see them tussling on the ground like that. Then they were laughing. I felt like I'd interrupted a private moment. I wanted a brother so bad I could taste it. Or just to roll on the ground like that with Ivory Jones.

He stood and gave Cookie a hand up. In the next formation, Cookie threw one to Ivory Jones, and I lit out after him. He must have been running slow. If he'd run fast, I'd never have caught him. He was long-legged fast. But I surprised him when I leaped into the air and grabbed him from the back around the chest. We sailed toward the ground, only because the force of my body was nearly rushing sideways. We hit the ground together hard, but I did not care.

Somehow he got turned around, and seemed like I had landed smack dab in the middle of his chest. It felt hard but soft at the same time. It took the breath out of both of us, and we laid staring, surprised at each other, neither of us making an effort to move.

I will never forget it, how that singer was crooning on the record player, and Cookie with him; *I just can't wait to be held in his arms. If I were a queen..."* I felt his boy body under me. I did not want to move, and neither did he by the looks of it. Until the ball hit us both, Wham, upside the head. Then Cookie said, "Hey! What y'all doing laying all up on each other?" She came to stand over us, scowling, her shadow on our faces. I rolled off, and we both stood up fast, brushing grass from our clothes.

She directed her look at Ivory Jones. "You getting all light struck?" she said. She picked the ball up from where it had rolled and hooked it under her arm. She stared Ivory Jones down. He looked like a kid who'd eaten all five pieces of gum in the pack.

What's light struck, I wanted to say, but did not. It had something to do with me.

"Just let it lay," Ivory Jones said, brushing off. "You the most bogish—" Then he ran at her and tackled her. Cookie started laughing in spite of herself until he snatched the ball and ran off with it. She threw him down and snatched the ball back, stood, and walked away like that African queen I'd expected she could play in the picture show. That seemed to settle something I did not understand, me being white and all, but I was glad we got back to playing football.

We threw and caught and flung each other down all afternoon. We fell in dirt and grass, and it smelled clean and scary together. The geese chased us around, especially Margot, tugging at my shirt until Cookie said, "Get out of here, Margot, don't be bothering her." She tossed the football in the air.

"She's not bothering me," I said. I patted Margot's smooth thin head. She'd finally let me start petting her.

"Neither is Ivory Jones, falling all on you by the looks of it," she said. And to him she said, "And since when did you get so sweet as to let people catch you?" She threw the football at him. "You better watch out, boy, slowing down and getting all sweet on little Rayann." He gave her a daggery look.

"You can see that Cookie is good at running her mouth if not the ball," he said, and stripped the ball right out of her hands. Then, sudden as a cat, he bounded up the steps of the porch. He came back out, cleaned up and dressed for work. He waved bye and drove off.

When it got too hot, Cookie and me drank more tea and shared a big loot of blueberries from the side yard bushes. The light started to grow fainter, and then turned a darker blue. I played with the geese as the day finally cooled, and a breeze came up. At twilight, we ate grill cheese sandwiches and watched the tiniest sliver of a new moon rise.

Cookie and I were hanging around on the concrete porch, her in the rocking chair, me on the block steps, singing my favorite song of the week; *I don't like you, but I love you...You really got a hold on me.* Miss Jesse came out to have her usual smoke of cigar and sit in the creaky old rocker. The crickets were singing, cicadas crackling, and a breeze blew up to cool off the world. I could hear the creek just barely chirping a trickling song across the woods.

"Okay, Rayann, time for you to get on home," Miss Jesse said. Cookie stood up and started in.

"But—"

"No buts," Miss Jesse said. "You can walk her across the woods, but you come right back, Cookie. You hear?"

"Yes, Ma'am," she said.

Once in the woods, we stood by the creek catching tadpoles to let them go again.

"What you pouting about?" Cookie said. I hadn't realized I was. I'd thought how normal Cookie's family seemed. Nobody was drinking a lot and fighting mean and talking bad about girls. Even without a real mama or daddy around.

"I don't know. Nothing." I shrugged and sat down.

"Don't want to go home?" Cookie said. I shook my head no. She went on. "Miss Jesse said your daddy won't be worth a wet rag. Sneak in the back way if you're scared."

"It ain't that," I said. Usually this time of day I might give Star a little grain and talk to her. I'd practice cheerleader stunts in the front yard by the grass or turn on TV to watch *Lucy* or *My Favorite Martian* or *The Honeymooners*. Or even turn on the sprinklers if the grass needed watering just to smell the light fresh smell. Not tonight.

Suddenly it seemed like everybody had somebody. A nice home with card playing and plans for Sunday School. I started to spill it out. "It's all my fault," I said. "And Mama's going to go to Chattahoochee. Daddy's planning it. And it started as my fault."

"Chattahoochee?" Cookie said. "That's for crazy people. I mean really crazy people. Dang, girl." She sat down. "How's she getting there? When?"

"I don't know. I just know he's planning it. I don't know why he thinks she needs to go," I said. I did not want to tell her about my burning the table.

"Why's it your fault?" she said.

"I'm not a good daughter," I said. "And now I don't know if Red's going to be there, too. I don't want nothing to do with him."

"Well," she said. Then it got quiet except for the creek running.

"I guess I got to go," I said.

"Wait," Cookie said. "If you want to, I mean if you're too scared to go home, I can sneak you in and let you sleep on the floor."

"Really?" I said. I sat up and looked at her to be sure.

"Yeah, but we got to be real quiet. And you need to stay low till we go off to church tomorrow morning. Then you can leave out the back." I listened to her plan and said okay. What a relief. I could stay away another night.

I sneaked up to the top of the hill through the woods and walked back toward the pastures to feed Star. Then I returned to the hideout. As soon as I thought it might be late enough, I sneaked back to Cookie's window and tapped with a stick. She tapped back, and that meant she'd unlocked the screen on the back door so I could go in.

And that is how I ended up sleeping on the floor of a colored house. As I fell asleep, I heard an owl in a nearby tree start to *hoo-hoo Ah, hoo-hoo hoo Ah.* Soon I could hear Cookie snoring. I followed right behind her.

12

The next morning, I woke up to clattering in the kitchen and the smell of sausage cooking, which somehow did not bring me comfort. A bad feeling fell over me, like it just poured down from the sky and seeped through the mattress to me. I lay between the bed and the wall, knowing I'd have to stay still and wait until everybody left for church.

I crawled under the bed and peeked out so I could see. Ivory Jones and Cookie were getting ready for Sunday school, their legs walking between the bathroom and bedrooms. They brushed their teeth, ran tap water, flushed the toilet. Miss Jesse already had put on her powder blue Sunday dress, which I could barely see the bottom of.

Cookie argued that she did not feel like feeding Margot and Waldo, but Miss Jesse told her to shut her mouth and move her feet. So Cookie, wearing her bright orange Sunday dress, skipped back to the bedroom, jumped onto the bed, reached down and touched my foot. Then she skipped to the living room, and out the door. I wondered if I could stay one more night in the hideout with just some blankets.

Then I heard a sound, like something wild. I lay still and listened. Then something wailed, some sound that slashed through this perfect Sunday morning. It was Cookie. Screaming. Ivory Jones tore out the door. I peeked out long enough to see him running by in a blur wearing his black Sunday suit. I felt hot and cold together, frozen under the bed.

"What on Jesus' earth?" said Miss Jesse as she flew past the opening from the bedrooms to the dining room. I crawled out and peeked around the doorway to see her charge through the screen door and outside. She held her favorite yellow vase that she'd put fresh daisies in the day before. I scrambled through the living room and onto the porch to see Ivory Jones and Miss Jesse stop dead in their tracks halfway down the yard. Just beyond them by the rut driveway was Cookie. "No! He's dead! No! No! No!" Cookie screamed. She ran in a circle around a white heap of feathers on the road. There was blood on Cookie's hands and on the front of her orange dress. And white feathers stuck to the blood smeared on her neck. She flopped down and hugged the white thing, and got up again, more bloody and feathery.

My knees caved in, and I sat right down on the front steps. Ivory Jones ran towards Cookie. Cookie got up and screamed "No! No! No!"

Waldo's head lay at an impossible tilt up and away from his body. His beak pointed towards the house. His wings were spread out like he'd fallen splat on his stomach in a belly flop. Even from where I stood, I could see his eyes staring at the Sunday blue sky. All around, the ground was wet and dark.

"Cut his throat," I heard Ivory Jones say. "Tried to cut off his head."

"Oh, my sweet Cookie," Miss Jesse said. She handed the vase to Ivory Jones, and held her arms out to Cookie. Cookie backed away, arms out in front of her, pink palms out but bloody, a few downy feathers stuck to her fingers. She said, "No! No! No!"

Miss Jesse grabbed Cookie's wrists and drew her in. She put one arm around Cookie and said, "Now settle down, baby, settle down," as Cookie sobbed into her auntie's neck.

Ivory Jones stood frozen. I was twisted up inside. Something awful was trying to squeeze out of me. I put my hand to my mouth to keep in whatever wanted to come out. I tasted dirt, so I spit. It felt good to spit, so I spit again. That's when Ivory Jones saw me and looked surprised, not knowing I'd spent the night.

"It's okay, baby girl," Miss Jesse was saying. "It's okay." Miss Jesse's apron was bloody now as Cookie cried in her arms.

"Who would do a thing like that?" Ivory Jones said, and turned to look at me. Like what the hell you doing here, seemed like.

Then I felt tickling at my feet. Margot was honking a scream herself, trying to fly up into my arms. "Margot!" I said. I scooped her up, and she buried her beak and face in my chest, all trembly and hard muscle tense, still honking in a panic.

Miss Jesse looked at me for the first time. "Girl, what on this earth are you doing here?"

"I-I—" I said, Margot flopping, held against my chest.

"You been home?" she said. I shook my head no and made a point to look at Margot so I would not have to see the look in Miss Jesse's eyes. "Get that filthy goose out of your arms," she said, and turned to Ivory Jones. "Ivory Jones, Lord have mercy, boy, see to her. Bury the goose. Then see her out of this yard. Take her home if you have to. Walk her through the woods and watch her go up the steps." She moved her hands like I was something smelling bad that she wanted out of the way.

I headed up the porch with Margot still shaking in my arms, now biting at my neck. Miss Jesse guided Cookie, limp and weak, back to the house.

"You okay?" Ivory Jones said. I stopped at the foot of the steps and turned to look at him. His voice did not accuse. "You got to put that goose down," he said. I was squeezing Margot as hard as she was biting me on the neck. I put her down.

"Scat, goose," he said, shooing her under the shade of the mimosa. The sky had a brilliant blue against the peach-colored blossoms. How could this day be so pretty? Margot waddled frantic right back up to me, honking in a high screech, trembling. She walked around and around me, rubbing up on my legs.

Miss Jesse had an arm around Cookie as they walked inside. I searched Ivory Jones' serious face as he frowned down at me.

"Who would do that?" I said, choking, afraid of who did it and why and what they'd do next. "Who would do such a thing?" He didn't say, but glanced back at the spot on the road where the dead Waldo lay. Margot flew into me, and I picked her up and cuddled her in my chest. She nestled into my neck and honked soft and fast. "Do you think it hurt bad, when he died?" I said.

"You stayed here last night?" he said, studying Margot and me, then ducking under the house to get the shovel.

"Yeah," I said. "Cookie sneaked me in."

He shook his head, then gestured for me to go with him. "Come on. Let's bury that goose. On second thought," he said, "take *this* goose out back so it won't get all in my way." Then he said, "Go on. What you staring at? Just take the goose out back." When I didn't move, he said, "Come on," and he grabbed my arm with his hand and pulled me out back where I let Margot down. I sat under the tree, and Margot stayed not six inches from my heels. My face flushed up and things spun in the heat.

That was the quietest house after Ivory Jones, Cookie, and Miss Jesse got cleaned up. I could smell that the sausage had burned up. The blue jays screeched as Ivory Jones dug the grave in the side yard. Cookie said nothing, just stared out the back door at the bare field beyond Margot and me. I could hear the water running in the kitchen where Miss Jesse was preparing to soak the bloody clothes in lye.

"Guess we'll skip church this morning," Cookie murmured to no one in particular.

"No, Ma'am," Miss Jesse said. She had recovered the yellow vase from the yard where Ivory Jones had set it down. She'd picked a whole slough of tea olive blossoms, white and sweet smelling, and had put them in the vase along with the daisies. She set the vase carefully on the kitchen counter and pulled at the stems, adjusting her arrangement. Then she stepped back and looked at it.

"We will be attending church this morning," Miss Jesse said finally. "And it's time for Rayann to go home."

"But Aunt J—"

"We will *be,*" she said it again, slow and firm, "attending *church* this morning." Then she picked up the arrangement to take it to the dining table. I said good-bye to Cookie through the screen, then got up and blocked Margot from going into the side yard where Ivory Jones was putting Waldo into the grave.

"You can have her," said Miss Jesse, standing at the bottom of the back steps.

"The goose?" I said, picking her up and holding her close.

"Yeah, you can have her," she said with a wave of her hand.

"No, Auntie," Cookie said. She stood with the screen door open on the back porch. She started to cry again.

"Hush, up, Cookie," Miss Jesse said. "That damn goose will be back. You need to get ahold of yourself. We got church to attend." Miss Jesse turned around, shaded her eyes and looked hard at Cookie, whose lip trembled. Miss Jesse's face softened. Then she walked back to the screen door and put her arm around Cookie. "Oh, little pearl," Miss Jesse said, and Cookie leaned into her aunt. "You are precious as a pearl. I didn't mean it, baby. You can keep her for your own self." Then Miss Jesse stood up straight, like she'd made a decision. "Now. Hush this talk, and get ready for church." Then she walked inside so I could say bye to Cookie. Margot would not stay away from me.

"You can borrow her for now," Cookie said wiping her eyes with her arm. "Maybe she needs to go away for a while." She sniffed.

"Okay," I said. "I'll bring her back real soon. I think she's confused. I'll take good care of her, don't worry." I hoped she didn't hear my voice shaking, or see my whole self shuddering. I hugged Cookie quick around the neck. I did not know what to say, or what else to do. "Bye," I said. "See you at school."

"Bye," she said, and patted Margot's head. "Don't be a fool, you hear me?" she said to Margot.

I headed home holding Margot, Ivory Jones looking solemn as he walked ahead of me, escorting me through the woods. Not only did I not know what to expect at home, but I had a goose with me. And why on earth had someone killed Waldo? The geese always stayed with Cookie, they never wandered off. And now I had taken Cookie's only comfort left. I couldn't believe how hot and then cold I felt. The sky spinned around some.

Ivory Jones jumped over the creek, and then spied the old mill hideout, looked inside and called it a clubhouse. Suddenly it looked shrunken and strange, and it wouldn't stand still. Shrunken, like the shacks I'd seen in New Orleans when we went one time on a business trip with Daddy.

Suddenly Margot flew out of my arms and straight into the hideout, right at Ivory Jones' neck. It played a trick of the imagination and I stopped cold, just in the middle of my step. The quick flash sprung up into my head a picture of Mama and

Daddy at home, fighting. Daddy's white work shirt, Mama's white button-down blouse. Daddy shaking Mama, just for a split second, the vision, and the fear that seared through me.

"No!" I said. The world spinned around. Someone was walking towards me. A football player. A skeleton of bones dressed in a football uniform. No, a suit, a blue suit of bones. Tailor a suit in bones, a navy blue suit. Little boy blue, come blow your bones. To market, to market to bloody a white goose.

By the graveyard, tomb filled with bones. Brown, skin of brown, charcoal, burnt wood. Burnt BONES in a brown table. Ladybug, ladybug, fly away home, your house is on fire, your children will burn. Black. Everything black.

I came to right away, and Ivory Jones stooped over me. "Just stay there a minute," he said, pushing me back down.

"What happened?" I said.

"You just fainted away," he said. "You feel okay?"

"Yeah," I said. "Move, I want to get up."

"You sure?" By way of answer, I stood up and brushed off. I guess he figured I must be okay, and said, "You shoulda seen your face. Got white as a paper towel. Your eyes rolled back and blam—straight down. You sure you all right?" He stood beside me.

"Everything's wrong," I said, putting my hand to my head. "Just everything." We stood listening to the sounds of the woods for a minute. He put his hand on my shoulder.

"Sit down," he said. "I don't want you fainting on me again." We both sat down.

"I shouldn't have spent the night," I said. "And Waldo's dead."

"You didn't kill Waldo," he said. "You think that goose's

blood got something to do with you?" He pulled back away from me and looked. He shook his head No. "Could be anybody coming after us. Course you shouldn't have spent the night. Your daddy—what he's going to do?"

"I don't know," I said. "That's the whole thing. I don't know." I put my head in my hands. I didn't understand anything. If I had just not burned those letters into the table. Whoever said sticks and stones may break my bones, but words can never touch me was a liar. "Is Cookie going to be okay? Maybe you should take Margot."

"Naw. Cookie's okay. She's got Auntie taking care of her," he said.

"Well, who do you think would do something that mean?" I said.

"Those damn honky bastards down at—" He broke off and looked away. "I don't know. Better not say just yet. Better not jump to conclusions." His eyes clouded so I couldn't tell anything.

"Honky?" I said. I was shaking my head. "White people? Why would they just come kill a goose?"

"Girl, you are one naive—" he said. He turned to me propped on one arm and frowned, shaking his head. "Go turn on your TV set. Open your eyes. Read the paper. Look what's going on around you," he said, his one arm waving wildly. I thought of Red bragging about cutting off that colored man's finger.

"Oh, my god," I said. "You think they killed him just to—"

"They sent us a warning," he said, looking flatly at me.

"Oh, no. They won't do that. Why would they kill—" I said. Who was this "they" I was talking about?

Then he laughed. Long and hard so that he held his side. I had to sit there and watch him laugh at my stupidity. When he quit laughing it got quiet. Just birds and the creek.

"Well, then—" I didn't know what to say.

"We'd better go," he said, pointing in the direction of the house through the woods. He stood up and held out a hand to help me up like he had Cookie the day before, the long time ago day when we had just hung around playing football.

Margot had come back, and she was honking up a storm. I started making up my alibi: I'd decided to camp out in the woods, and left Daddy a note he must not have found. Under the fruit bowl in the living room. Maybe it got lost Friday, did he do anything at home Friday with some of his friends? I rehearsed it in my head. We stopped at the edge of the clearing. Across the lane, Daddy's car sat parked in the driveway.

"Oh, my god," I said. "I'm in trouble."

"Go on now," he said. "Good luck."

"Ivory Jones—" I still didn't know what to say about anything. So I just waved. "Thanks." He nodded, hands in his pockets, and turned to head back through the woods.

When I walked in, I heard a voice in the kitchen. It stopped when the door shut. I held Margot in my arms, petting her and telling her everything would be okay. Daddy came round the corner, phone at his ear, the cord stretched as far as it would go. He looked half beat up tired with circles under his eyes and an unshaved face.

"Rayann," he said. "Where in the hell—" Then he hung up the phone and ran up to me and hugged me, goose and all. "Where the hell have you been? My god in heaven." I didn't say anything, and he sighed and ran his hand through his hair. "Where have you been?" He pulled away from me. Now he frowned, a mad frown. "I've been worried sick about you. I was just about to call the authorities. Where'd that damn goose come from?"

"Didn't you get my note?" I said. I backed up a little. "I been camping out for two days. In the woods near the creek," I lied. Margot was honking and squirming, so I put her down.

"What note?" he said, looking around the kitchen like it might appear out of thin air. I certainly wished it would. "And get this goose out of here," he said, pointing at Margot as she pecked at his ankles. "What the hell's this goose?"

"I left the note under the fruit bowl," I said, lifting up the bowl, "Friday." He was combing his hand through his hair. "Maybe somebody who came over Friday might have moved it."

He kicked Margot, not hard, but I still ran over and picked her up. "Well then, you should have waited till I got home," he said, walking away. "And *asked* me then. Not *told* me in a note. Who leaves a note that could disappear?" he said, using first one arm then the other for emphasis. "Mysteriously. Into thin air." He was pacing and waving his arms fast and furious in the TV room now. "What the hell were you thinking? I have been half crazy looking for you this morning. In the barn, in the pasture, at the hospital."

He looked at me standing in the doorway between the kitchen and the TV room where the telephone hung. He instinctively put his hand on the phone. He took in a deep breath, and shook his head, dropping his hand. "You have no sense. No sense at all." He let out his breath, shaking his head, then wiping it with his hand.

Those words hurt. Hurt me in the stomach till it bunched up tight. I still felt dizzy. I thought at least I had some sense. But maybe I didn't. If I'd thought through anything at all, Mama wouldn't be in the hospital, and maybe Waldo would be alive.

"Are you turning into one of those juvenile delinquents? I'll be goddamned if I'll have a juvenile delinquent living under my roof," he said, pointing to himself. "And where the hell did this goose come from?" He pointed to Margot, who was waddling around looking for crumbs on the coffee table.

"I don't know," I said meekly, picking her up and setting her outside the TV room glass door on the back patio. "It followed me home from the creek."

"Well, that does it," he said, like the goose had made the decision for him. "I'm calling the boarding schools," he said, picking up a piece of paper with his handwriting on it. I knew, cause he had beautiful squarish cursive writing, and he wrote thick and bold . He put on his reading glasses and stared at the paper. "I found a couple in Georgia, and one in South Carolina. There's one in Alabama, too." He raised his eyebrows and looked at me from behind his glasses with cold brown eyes. "I've just about had it." He dropped the paper.

I didn't say a thing. "Don't think I won't do it tomorrow when I get to work, either," he said, pointing a finger and punctuating each point as he said it. Then he pointed to the stairs. "Now get upstairs and stay there. I don't want you in my sight for the rest of the day."

"But how'm I gonna eat?" I said.

"That's it, enough. Get out of my sight," he said. It dawned on me he'd only gotten worried this morning, which meant he'd been out all weekend. He'd come in this morning, I hadn't been around, and then he got worried. He felt bad and was taking it out on me.

"Hypocrite," I said on the stairs where I knew he could not hear me.

13

I'm just a girl, not a girl like my mama. A mama who's crazy. A mama who's got a talent for painting and drawing. Maybe I had some talent that was still a mystery to me. I just had not discovered it yet. Or maybe I was just a regular girl.

I was thinking all this as I walked into Mama's room at the hospital the next afternoon. The light was warming up the room. A doily sat under the blue glass vase full of pink roses Daddy had sent her last week. Mama was not in the bed. She held a notebook pad and pencil, and sat cross-legged in the visitor's chair. Her pencil moved back and forth, side to side. I stood for a minute in the doorway, just watching her. Her almost smile. Blue eyes. She didn't look crazy anyway.

I'm just a girl who's not allowed to pick her own best friend. Now that's enough to make you crazy.

When Mama saw me, she startled. She stood up and opened her arms, then beckoned me with her hands. She was smiling. When was the last time I'd seen her smile? "Hey, honey," she said. "You look thin. Are you eating okay?"

I did not want to tell her about those awful men in her house, or about staying at Miss Jesse's. But I realized I had been missing some meals lately on account of it. I had smelled black-eyed peas and rice stewing in the kitchen on the ground floor.

"Yes, Mama," I lied. "I just ate some roast beef and mashed potatoes that Miss Jesse made on Friday." My stomach rumbled a little, and the menu I'd just spilled out so easily sounded delicious.

"You drawing?" I said, sitting on the bed. Three writing pencils and one green crayon sat on the table beside her.

"Yep," she said, sitting down. "A nurse got me these from pediatrics. It helps rest my mind." The pencil whished back and forth, side to side, and it made me sleepy. It reminded me of her lying down to settle me for a nap when I'd been young, and how she would draw. The sound would sing me to sleep. I lay down now in the hospital bed, my head at the foot of it, close to Mama's chair. She held up one painting she'd finished earlier for me to see.

A huge hand held a woman who lay sleeping in its palm. The woman wore an emerald green dress with high heels to match. She looked like a May Queen type only grown up. It looked a little scary, that tiny lady sleeping in the big hairy hand. But she did a great job drawing it. It made chills run down my back.

"It's beautiful," I said, reaching out and touching the dress. "And look what I brought you," I said. I sat up and handed her the bag of paints, colored pencils and sketch pad I'd brought her from home.

"Oh, good," she said, opening it, then clapping her hands. Then she took the paints out and started unscrewing the tops. I could smell the acrylic paint, which made my eyes heavy with sleepiness. "Honey, I've got to get out of here," Mama said. "Can you help me?" I opened my eyes and looked at her. I could tell the thought made her agitated.

She stared at me with eyes wide open. "This painting," she said. "You know I always fooled around with pictures," she shrugged and laughed. I wiggled on the bed and got my legs tangled in the sheets. *You've got to get me out of here.* This talk made me nervous. She stood up and untangled my legs without ever looking directly at me. She sat back down. I stood up and went to the window.

"I just got a goose," I said. She only stirred up the paints and turned to a new page to paint and waited. That didn't shock her, so I went on. "I got a goose from Miss Jesse's." She nodded and smiled, swinging her leg and dipping the brush into the paint. I was fiddling with the window opener, trying to get it open. The metal surprised me, so cold and hard, but finally it gave.

"They don't open, honey," Mama said. "Just in case somebody decides to—you know—" she dropped her brush, pushed up her sleeve and waved her hands around, then laughed a little. "Jump."

I thought about how I'd jumped out the balcony window. And how I'd fainted thinking about mixed up nursery rhymes the day before. What the hell, I thought. What I got to lose? I gushed it all out. How I'd gotten the goose because of the dead Waldo, how I'd been there because I'd spent the night, how I'd spent the night because of the men in the house and the finger story. I worried that this would set her off, set her back, but I needed to tell her. I even told her Daddy had said he'd put me in reform school, and that he was looking now.

I stopped there. I did not tell her about that woman Rheta who Daddy was feeling on, or how she'd stayed with me while Daddy left town, or how she caught me and Cookie in my room. Or how Waldo died. I was panting by the time I finished. My chest heaved up and down. I had been pacing back and forth in the room. I glanced at Mama. She was not kneading her hands like she did when she was about to go crazy. She had painted the whole time I talked, and now she put down the brush and stared at me. She stared at her lap and then shook her head.

"I wish I'd had the sense to do something like that when I was your age. Sneak out the balcony. Sleep outside in the woods. Go to a colored house for help. I'm proud of you. I'm glad it was Miss Jesse's." I looked away. I felt too tender to move. She never talked to me this honest.

She stood up and moved to the window and looked out. "I need to get out of here," she said. She was no different from me. Needing to jump out a window. *I need to get out of here. Can you help me?*

She stayed a long time there looking out at I don't know what. She sat back down and began to paint a deep brown back and forth, side to side with the brush.

I figured that was all the conversation of this sort she could stand for now. But it amounted to a lot. I never thought she'd say those things to me after I'd spent the night in a colored person's house. *I'm proud of you.* Sticks and stones may break my bones, but words, *I'm proud of you*, will never hurt me.

She dropped her brush again and said, "Now. You're not going to want to stay for dinner, are you?" I was starving, and it must have showed in my face when she mentioned dinner. "I can hear your stomach growling," she said, pushing the button to call the nurse, and giving a short laugh. "They might say I'm crazy, but I'm still your mother. I'll call the nurse and tell her you'll be here for dinner."

Even though it was hospital food, I ate everything on my plate, the peas and rice, smothered chicken and yeast rolls, even all the bread pudding. And it seemed delicious to me, too. Mama painted her way through the whole lunchtime taking nibbles off her plate here and there.

"I'm glad I'm here," I finally said. Mama told me to fetch her purse. She gave me fifty cents and told me to bring her some cigarettes from the gift shop. I knew I couldn't, but I'd just steal some from Daddy's desk drawer if I could get into the office.

I asked if I could get a comic book, and she gave me another quarter. I walked the stairs down to Daddy's office. I went straight to the secretarial desk, Rheta's desk. That area didn't get locked up till the night shift at 11, even though Daddy's got locked when he left, around six on an early day. Nobody was around, so I went through the drawers. I found a half pack of cigarettes and took it. I admit it—I thoroughly enjoyed the feeling it gave me, snitching a little something from her.

When I opened the bottom drawer, I saw a manila file folder that said, "Applications—Rayann." I took it out and opened it up. Applications to boarding schools. I froze. To my horror, I saw she'd typed in all the blanks of information about me. About the only thing missing was Daddy's signature. I stuck the folder in the back of my pants and pulled my shirt over it. I took them to the back where I knew the garbage got collected and taken off. I tore every sheet of paper into tiny pieces, then threw the thick file in the big incinerator bin.

I got back to Mama's room as she said she was putting the finishing touches on her newest painting. "Look," she said. She turned it around. It was pretty and horrible. It scared me. Maybe she needed to stay here a while.

A dark brown background of woods all streaky and fuzzy set off a woman in stark white hanging from a rope from a tree. The woman had dark hair like Mama's, and the dress looked like a May Day affair. Below her, a man in bright red crouched holding his head in his hands. White tombstones dotted the background. It's what brought the dress to life. Black crosses stuck up from each white tombstone. I couldn't take my eyes off it. The trees looked soft, like the dress and the woman's hair. Even the man's overalls looked soft.

"Mama, you're not thinking of dying, are you?" I said. Maybe she was crazy, but she was my mama.

A regular girl knows when to stop thinking and do something. I did something I should have been doing all along.

Big as I was, I sat down in Mama's lap.

"I'll get you out of here," I said. I did not know how I'd do it. "I promise." But I would do it. All those boarding school applications flashed in my head and my stomach pulled tight. I picked up the pad of paper and put a brush in my hand. I took my other hand and placed Mama's hand around mine. I was nearly as big as she was.

"Show me how to paint like you," I said. I really knew I never could, that my talent was for imitating handwriting, but I wanted to know how it felt to be her. She held onto me with her left arm, just sitting still for a minute. Then she started moving her hand and my hand across the page, telling me how she got something in her head first and drew the main idea, and this time it happened to be the ocean. Then she slowed her arm down and made small strokes to draw a boat. She said then she worked around those main ideas that way. I felt her breath on the side of my face, warm and wet as the nighttime breeze off the Gulf of Mexico.

14

Two barn owls who lived in the woods began to call. It wasn't dark or evening. It wasn't that time that colors seep into the sky like plums, bruises, or the deep ocean. But it felt that way to me. Instead, the sky called out a bluebird color, while the owl's voices floated out from the dark oaks like oboes in the school band, calling and echoing each other's calls.

More owls joined in as Margot and I walked towards the creek and crossed over. I was terrified at what I might find just past the woods at Cookie's. She had not attended school for two days, and Miss Jesse had not showed up for work. Their whole world could be ruined. Mama's painting crossed my mind. The woman in the tree would fade out and then fade in as Cookie, then Miss Jesse and then Ivory Jones. I'd be crouched in the red overalls below. I pushed the thought aside and crossed the barbed wire fence that separated the woods from Miss Jesse's place.

I squinted into the brightness to see Miss Jesse's white house and the fruit trees around it—hot, yellow and dry. Early summer had set in, but not the everyday thunderstorms that cooled off the world. Down on the rut road, only a dark blotch told what had happened last weekend. Margot waddled over to where Waldo had laid. She honked softly. I called her back, but she did not hear me.

No one was in sight, not in the garden on the woods side of the house, or in the front where the grass stood. Not in the back where the sugar cane grew like giant grass, tall and green. Through the screen door, I could see that the front door stood open to the inside.

"Hello?" I said. Nothing but the mockingbirds and owls. Crickets and wind whispered through the dry grass. "Hello?" I said again. Nothing but bees buzzing nearby around the tea olive tree. I tiptoed up the concrete steps and stood, my heart pounding. No one sat watching TV in the little living room or ate a snack in the dining room. No movement in the kitchen beyond. I opened the front screen door. The sun slanted in through the window of the dining area. The clean scent of Miss Jesse's house met me, but not anything else. The screen door slammed behind me.

Suddenly, a scream came from the back, outside. Then I yelled and dashed back out the screen door, jumping off the five-foot high porch on to the ground, landing in dirt and grass. I lay there for a second spitting dirt and feeling dazed. Just as I decided to get up and get lost, a voice came behind me.

"Oh, it's you," Cookie said, a scowl covering her face as she peered over the porch at me below. "You like to scared me to death."

I sat up and turned around. "You're not dead," I said, relieved. "You're not dead."

"No, I ain't dead, how about you?" She leapt down the steps, reached out and pulled me up with her hand, warm and slightly sweaty. "You look a little dead, but then all white people looks a little dead, so pale and all." She said it without sparkling eyes. It stung a little.

"Well, hey Margot," she said, her face brightening into a smile, her arms open to that goose, who was honking and hissing and smelling swampy like the creek. "You want to go pick some mulberries?" she said, scooping up Margot, the sun glaring on our faces.

It occurred to me that she was well. I thought at least she'd been sick or something. And where was Miss Jesse, I wondered.

Maybe out back where they were picking the mysterious mulberries. I knew nothing about mulberries, I'd only heard of them.

"Okay," I said, shrugging.

She gave me a hard up and down look. "Okay, then. Follow me." I walked behind her into the house and to the kitchen where she pulled out an iron skillet with her one free arm. With the other, she held Margot like a baby. "Put the mulberries in here. I'm collecting them to make a pie."

Then I followed her out the back door where she turned the corner to the other side of the house, the one I'd never really paid attention to except in the night when I tapped at her window. There stood a mulberry tree. Tall as the house. I felt baking hot, even though May was pushing its tail end through the door, and school had not yet let out for the summer. What had Cookie been doing the days she'd not been at school? How come she hadn't answered me when I called to her? Maybe she was trying to get rid of me like Daddy was.

"How come you didn't answer me when I called you?" I said as she put Margot down. She climbed into a high branch of the tree. She straddled a thick branch, and started picking the berries. They looked like blackberries to me. I'd never seen berries growing on a tree before.

"I didn't hear you," she said, looking down at me, then back to her work. "I been practicing for my church solo. I didn't hear you till I quit singing and heard the screen door slam." She shrugged. "I just been out here picking these mulberries." She picked berries and put them in a chicken boiling pot she had situated in the crook of the tree.

I couldn't stand not knowing any more.

"Where's Miss Jesse?" I said, my head cocked to one side as I looked up at her straddling the branch. "She didn't come to work yesterday. Or today."

Cookie looked down at me disgusted like. "Who you, the boss man?" she said, popping a couple of berries into her mouth. "These so sweet. You tasted them yet?" I ignored her.

"Well," I said, shifting the frying pan from on hand to the other. "Well, after, you know, what happened to Waldo—"

"You mean Aunt Jesse ain't there to clean your family's drawers?"

"No, that's not—"

"Clean them for nothing? Excuse me, half of nothing, what your daddy pay. She's over to the new restaurant downtown working in the kitchen." My heart sunk. I'd lost Miss Jesse. The only good thing about going home now.

"Cause of Waldo?" I said. I felt confused. "I should never have spent the night." I shook my head and glanced up at her. She glared at me. A bevy of gray birds flew up frantic in the still and sizzling hot air and streaked away in the whitish sky.

"Waldo ain't got nothing to do with it, girl," she said, leaning down below that branch, so close I could almost feel her breath on my face from where I stood on the ground, picking berries. "It ain't got nothing to do with you."

I flinched, then she swung back up and started picking again. Margot sat panting under the tree.

"You think you the center of the whole world," she said, shaking her head. "You think you got to have Miss Jesse at your house to clean up after your mess, and if she ain't there, it's cause *Rayann* slept in a *colored* house." I didn't know what to say, but I could tell by the fast way she talked, that she was working herself up into a broiling mad. I wiped the streak of sweat that ran down my face. I had lost the person I needed at my house. And I was about to get shunted off to reform school.

"Truth is, Waldo died cause *niggers*—" she said, drawing it out in a nasal imitation of nasty-nice talking white people. She stopped to see if I was shocked. I was. "—ain't supposed to ride in the *front* of the bus," she continued. "Ain't supposed to attend no *white* schools. Ain't supposed to eat no *lunch* at the Woolworth's. Ain't allowed to sit *downstairs* at the movie theater." With each point, she'd pick a berry and throw it hard into the pot. "Ain't got the right to *speak up* when Mr. Wood promised Aunt Miss Jesse fifteen dollars a *day*, and then don't pay nothing but a damn *eight*."

She jumped down from the tree and stood right next to me. I stared at the berries, focusing on studying them for the best ones, picking only those. Cookie stood watching me, her breath coming quick. I was ashamed that my daddy had not kept to his promise. It seemed, somehow, like my fault. I did not say anything, just slid away from her, keeping one eye on her and one eye on those black mulberries, putting them in the heavy frying pan. Cookie went on.

"The ones who killed Waldo. They left a note down in the mailbox." She pointed towards the front drive, down the hill where the mailbox leaned. She wiped her brow.

"They who?" I said, stopping, still staring at the berries. A bitter dry taste sprung up in my mouth.

"Those *white* boys," she said, raising both her arms up for emphasis.

"What white boys?" I said, scared to look in her eyes.

"Those white boys been driving up and down Saturday Street on Sunday mornings. They saw Waldo walking with me and Ivory Jones and my auntie a few weeks ago. And then they killed him," she said kicking a root of the tree. "Note said,

'This is what happens to nigger geese who chase white people in their trucks. And this is what happens to those who causing trouble.'"

In a flash I thought about it in reverse. What if some colored family decided my family was white trash just cause our goose was chasing their car. What if they killed our goose for it, and we couldn't do anything about it? But it would never happen, cause we were white.

I was trying to figure out how this stuff went together. A hot wind blew up and did not really cool off my sweating neck. I smelled like b.o., but I kept picking berries so as not to upset Cookie. I felt their plump pulp grown around each seed "I might be able to get some money from Mama," I offered.

"You ain't heard nothing I said, have you?" she said, leaning up against the tree, arms folded.

"Yeah, I did. I'm listening," I said, aggravated now. Something in me knew I could not offer her money. Sweat ran down her face and she blinked. I licked my lips as I watched the sweat run down to her mouth. I wanted to go wipe it off for her, but she would just push me away. The other half of me wanted to scream and slap her face.

"You sweating up a storm, girl," I said, trying to joke around. I put down my pan and walked inside, turned on the water and listened to it gush. It made me think of *Baby It's You*, and it dawned on me that Cookie was singing again. I grabbed a glass and poured her some water. I took it outside and had a sip. It washed some of the sour taste down. I didn't dare offer it to her. She looked over and took the water glass from me. She gulped down the whole glass. Then she took a deep sigh and wiped her mouth. Only the gnats whined around our faces, and the afternoon birds chirped in the woods beyond.

"I never knew you could eat mulberries," I said, smelling

one. "They look like blackberries."

"They're sweet. They don't smell. Taste one, go on," she said, eating one herself. I did.

"Sweeter than blackberries," I said. I thought about the red blackberries I'd seen by the creek on my walk to Cookie's. I'd be cooler if I hung around over there for a while. I wondered where Ivory Jones was, and if he wanted to go over and fish in the pond down the hill. Just him and me. Cookie was scaring me. She was making me madder than fire, picking and lecturing about white people. I was trying to hold my temper like good girls did, like Mama had taught me. Ivory Jones and me, we could eat some sweet mulberries and maybe even swim. "Hey, where's Ivory Jones?" I asked.

"Those berries sweet like my brother," Cookie said, cutting her eyes over at me. "Is that right, Rayann? Is my brother sweet and dark like mulberries?"

"I don't know what you're talking about," I said.

"He's at work, you love-struck girl." She laughed, lifted herself off the tree trunk and gave me a shove and said, "You sweet on my mulberry black brother, you *lily* white child."

I threw down the heavy frying pan with a thonk. The berries flew up and back down, some spilling out. I turned to her and took her shoulders hard.

"I can't help what color I am," I said, "and yeah, I love him," I said, shaking her on the love. "And I love you, too. And I love Miss Jesse, too." With each love I shook her again. Each time, she winced a little. "Can't you see that?" I shoved once more and she backed away frowning. She leaned back against the tree, and then slid down it till her butt hit the ground.

"When my mama's sick, I don't have nobody." I leaned over to yell at her. "At least you have Miss Jesse." My face was red hot, and spit flew out of my mouth. "And now Daddy's going to send me away to reform school."

She leaned back against the tree and took another deep sigh. She put her head in her hands and pushed her face up so that it looked like a carnival mask grin. Then she dropped her head in her hands and was quiet.

I thrashed across the woods, fists balled, Margot at my heels. I reached the creek and then took off my sneakers and walked into the creek and cooled my feet and ankles. "You might as well go back there, Margot," I said. "I'll be leaving, and you can't come with me." I squatted down and wondered if anybody else in the world ever told people they loved them by shaking them. I sat my butt down smack in the middle of the creek and splashed water all over.

How stupid to think you could make friends with a colored girl. I let the steam come off me as I sat in the water. Margot sat her fat wet butt self down in my lap. "Great," I said to her out loud.

I sat in the creek, the dank, dirt smell of its banks, a grassy smell mixed in. Margot got up and wandered down the creek farther. Cookie didn't even get to see her mama in the hospital. Her daddy was in jail. At least mine was home. Still, she had Miss Jesse. And a brother. She'd let me go home with her when I didn't have any place to go. She'd shared her brother with me, even though she felt jealous about it. I cupped my hands and filled them with creek water. Then I spread my fingers and let the water run through my fingers. I had to go back. I had lost my temper in a dumb way.

I stood up, staring at the trees and thinking about their mercy in the summer heat. The creek was a mercy, too. I walked back to Miss Jesse's house to the back yard. There sat Cookie, Margot beside her. Cookie just stared at the ground where I'd left her. She looked up.

"Dang," she said, studying me up and down in a curious way. "You look like something the dog drug up out of the water." She looked drug around her own self, her hair astray, her face sweaty and cloudy. She looked away, shrugged her shoulders and looked back. "I didn't know you had it in you." She grinned.

"I'm sorry," I said. "I don't know what got into me."

"Come on," she said, standing up. "Let's finish picking these berries before the birds get them all." We picked up our pots and got to work.

We picked in silence for a while until the air suddenly got cool. A dark cloud pushed its way overhead and hid the sun. Cookie finally broke the silence. "Reform school, you said?"

Next thing I knew, I was telling her all Daddy had said, and about Mama's painting. I hoped those stupid boys' note wouldn't keep her from school. I begged her to come back and finish the year out. I kept popping the sweet mulberries into my mouth. "There's only three days left. You can stand that," I said.

We picked berries under the tree a long time, and for a while, I forgot who we were, a black girl and a white girl forgiving each other, sitting under a mulberry tree letting the cloud grow darker and heavier around us. Then it started to rain. "Blessed relief," Cookie said. And we let the rain fall on us and cool us down.

After a while, we went inside to get towels to dry off. In the kitchen, a note caught my eye. It was written in the dark green pen my daddy always used at work. I walked over to the counter. Cookie was in the bathroom getting towels and singing Aretha's saddest song, *Sad as a gypsy serenading the moon, Skylark, I don't know if you can find these things, oh, my heart is riding on your wings.* The note was written in slanted block letters like Daddy always wrote. It said, "This is what happens to nigger geese who chase white people in their vehicles. And this is what happens to those who cause trouble."

"It can't be," I said out loud. That's when I got a chill, and could not stop shaking. After I dried off with a thin blue-flowered towel that used to hang in my bathroom, another thing Mama must have given Miss Jesse, I told Cookie I had to go home and get warm.

15

After I got to the clearing, I listened for home, Margot behind me. In the dusk, all I could hear was the wind in the trees, the drops of rain that had sat on the leaves pattering to the ground. The house stood dark and the drive was empty. I shivered with cold right there in the early summer. My fingers grew cold, and even my toes froze in their shoes.

I walked into the house and sniffed. Sour. Dirty dishes. I walked into the kitchen. Stacks of dishes were heaped up in the sink. In the refrigerator, some leftover canned spaghetti, but none of the good chicken or cake or green beans that Miss Jesse cooked.

"Girl, you pale as a gardenia blossom," I said, imitating Miss Jesse's voice. "Get yourself a warm bath, and I don't mean later."

"Yes, Miss Jesse," I said, answering myself, bounding up the steps to get into the tub. Then I ran a bath, and talked to Miss Jesse as I did it. "Mama's gone, and Daddy's been confused," I said. "And now I'm alone in this house, and I don't know when anybody will be home. You're gone, and there's not much food, either. And I don't know who left that note for y'all."

Go on, Miss Jesse said in my mind. *The water's warm, and you're shivering like a skinny blade of grass.*

I sniffed, getting ready to cry. She shouldn't call me skinny like that, I thought.

Ain't nothing like a summer bath in warm water somebody else done heated up for you, now. Hold up your arms and get out of these wet clothes. Now, that's it. Just step on in. And don't that feel grand?

I shut my eyes, and since it did feel so good, I only squeezed out a few tears.

After I bathed and got out, I picked up my math homework and did it all, including the extra credit problems. Then I set out my clothes for the next day, gathered everything together for school—books, pencils, paper, everything. It helped me to think at least something could be put to order. And I turned on the black and white TV that sat on the dresser. As I contemplated whether to heat up the SpaghettiOs or make some mac and cheese from the box, I watched TV. Willy the Weatherman sat giving the nightly news. He played the organ in the morning, which I liked considerably, and wore a different colored hat for each of the days of the week. I knew that from watching the color TV.

On color or black and white TV, there was trouble. Trouble in Birmingham and Montgomery. The policemen were chasing colored people with big shiny sticks. They clobbered these colored people over and over, like those colored people hadn't felt it the first time. German Shepherds growled and showed their fangy teeth. One colored lady who'd got hit in the head bled from the forehead. She screamed, "Jesus, save me, Lord Jesus."

I had seen this kind of trouble before on TV. One day when Miss Jesse had a stack of ironing to do, she'd stood in front of the big color TV. She'd watched the colored people demonstrating. She had both eyes stuck to the TV. I had felt embarrassed then. I mean, what'd you say to your favorite person in the house, the one who fed you, the one who cleaned your room, your kitchen, your bathroom, your clothes? The one who knew you, and all the goings on in your house? I'm sorry my people are beating up on your people? I'm sorry you have to clean my family's drawers?

I could remember things I'd heard white people say, too. Like this one lady at the hospital waiting room said once, "If they're so unhappy, just let's send them on back to Africa where they came from in the first place."

But Miss Jesse had rocked me to sleep, she had let me stay at her house when I was in danger. My whole body got hot and then froze as I watched all those people, black and white, in a big mess, while policemen who looked mad beat up on colored people.

Just as I stood to turn off the TV, fetch something to eat, and call the hospital about visiting hours, I heard a car door slam.

I peered out the window and spied Daddy's arm hanging over Rheta. She had driven him home in her big old car. She wore the craziest looking, shortest dress I'd ever seen. It was covered with big sprigs of what looked like peacock feathers. All over it. She carried what looked like a clasp purse with gold letters on the front in her other arm. Tiger-striped high heels. I watched her laughing and half-steering Daddy into the house.

When they got inside, I stayed at the top of the stairs to listen. "Oh, honey," Daddy said. "Can you find us something to eat? I'm just starved." The feet of the sofa scraped across the floor when he sat down, and he let out the same groan he used to use with Mama.

"Fighting those hospital niggers has me starved. As if it wasn't hard enough already." What did he mean? Did he mean Ivory Jones? My heart squeezed. I thought of police dogs and the bloody-headed woman screaming for Jesus.

"Don't worry, Allen," she said with a fake soothing voice of a mama that put me somehow right on edge. "I'll see what I can find here." I could hear the suck of the refrigerator door. "What you could use is a little feminine spirit around this house."

"Did you check on the insurance policy?" he said. "In all the hoopla in front of the hospital, I forgot it."

"Yeah," she said. "Covers you and the girl." I could hear her high heels clicking across the tile floor in the kitchen.

"Can you see if there's some bourbon in there? I'd like to have another drink, sugar britches." I was no longer hungry. But I stood at the top of the stairs to wait till they hopefully cleared out so I could get to the kitchen.

She clacked out to the sofa to give him the drink, then clacked back to the kitchen. "Indley's got the paperwork on her in the pipeline. And now," she said, and paused, "a toast to us." I heard the tink of their glasses, the clack of her heels back to the kitchen, then the suck of the refrigerator again.

"Where is that girl of yours, anyway?" she said. "Nothing in the fridge. I wonder what she's been doing for food." She headed back across the floor, and I realized she was aiming for the bottom of the stairs. I stood up and flew to my room, shut the door with a quiet click and slid slowly under the cool sheets of the bed. I stared at the TV. Soon I heard knocking. "You in there?" she said.

"Yeah," I said. If I didn't speak up, Daddy might send me off sooner.

"Well, how about opening the door?" I walked to the door, opened it, and sat back on my bed. There she stood in that kooky dress, the smell of cigarettes seeping into the room. "Hello." She said it cool.

"Hello," I said, staring again at the TV. Willie the Weatherman was giving the local news. He wore his yellow hat, I guessed, cause it looked white on the black and white TV. He sure tore up those piano keys when he played on TV.

"Well—how are you?" she said like a challenge, folding her arms and looking at me sideways with suspicion, then darting her eyes around the room. I knew she could not have much experience with kids the way she talked.

"Fine." Willie the Weatherman told of how to expect more of this rain we'd been having, and that it would start up again tonight. We stood a good chance of afternoon showers again tomorrow.

"Would you like something to eat?" she said. "I found some ham and peas." My mouth started to water. I'd forgotten about that ham from the week before. Mama said I needed to eat better.

"Okay," I said, shrugging and looking back at the TV. I figured if she was cooking, I'd eat. But I would not sit at the table with them. "I'll have a plate up here."

When I went down to get a plate, I smelled a burnt smell. Daddy acted cheery, pulled me to him, and hugged me till it hurt. "Here you are, you troublemaker," he said. He asked me how my day had been. Sometimes he forgot what exactly he was mad at me about.

"Fine," I said. He weaved a little as he walked to the kitchen sink and didn't quite focus, but I figured he wouldn't be yelling at me drunk and would be on good behavior for his unwanted-by-me house guest. He wouldn't mention the applications being missing if he knew it.

So he started talking to Rheta about his afternoon as I put the leftovers on my plate. She had burnt the canned black-eyed peas, but she had sliced the ham, which you could hardly mess up. It smelled salty and bacony, even though everything else smelled of char.

"They don't *just* want to work at the hospital in the office and professional staff, those damn coloreds want their people to come to our hospital for service," Daddy said. "Next thing you know, they'll be taking over everything." He looked at me, then piled burnt peas on his plate. "It's not right. What they don't realize is, they're not like us. Don't know how to dress, don't bathe, can't talk. They just don't have the brains for it. Never will."

"I think it's those communists putting things in their heads," Rheta said, getting her own plate. "It's the outside agitators just coming in and making trouble, trying to ruin this country from the inside out. Those Russians want us to crumble right into their hands." With that, she made fists and then opened them up to show us crumbled in the Russians' hands. "Did you see the car drive by with the sign said 'FREEDOM—IT'S NOW OR NEVER'?"

It disgusted Daddy so bad, he picked up his knife and slammed the sharp end into the table. He glared at me in the eye and said, "Don't look to me like nobody needs set free," he said. "Niggers are free to pack their bags and catch the next Trailways bus out of here," he said. "They can free their asses right on up to New York or Chicago, or wherever it is they want to go. I know one thing, they're coming into my hospital over my dead body," Daddy said, thumping his chest. I went cold. Dead bodies, Waldo's dead body. I felt sweaty and dizzy. Miss Jesse had first cooked the food he was putting on his plate and shoveling into his mouth. I left the room with my plate not saying a thank you or good night.

I thought of Cookie sitting under the mulberry tree as I walked up the steps with my plate, head in her hands, and how just about everybody grown up I knew thought like Daddy. When I took my plate upstairs I sat out on the balcony floor to eat. Most of the food tasted charcoalish. A gust of wind blew by, making a whooshing sound in the trees, the kind just before a storm. It blew dark petals off the tall crepe myrtle bush in front of my window. Hot pink petals drifted to the ground. I wondered if Cookie saw them the same way I did.

16

I walked down the dirt road to catch the bus to see Mama. Mama wasn't really free, I thought as I passed Saturday Street and headed toward Magnolia Road. That is why I had decided to go to the bank first and find out whatall Mama had there before it got stolen.

When I got on the bus, I lost my freedom there right away. The driver, who had curly little ears that sat below his hat, told me to sit up front near him. Mostly colored people rode the bus, and a white person drove. The colored people usually sat in the back, except for some of the black college girls who went to the Negro college on the other side of town. Sometimes they would sit up front and get into trouble. For so many people who rode the bus all the time, it struck me how quiet it usually was. It smelled barely of diesel and the seats felt comfortable. Not a lot of people were riding that day, so I didn't know why he'd want me to sit up close, but I didn't argue.

At the last roundabout stop that dropped people off at Tharpe Street near Frenchtown, where downtown colored people lived, I could see a big bunch of people crowded around by the downtown city pool. Mostly colored people. Police cars, too.

The bus squealed to a stop, and the windows rattled. Outside the pool, all these grown kids, the Negro college kids, traipsed up and down the front sidewalk holding up signs. The city pools had been closed for a year. Daddy had said the city commission people didn't want their kids swimming with filthy colored people. No telling how many diseases they carried, he'd said.

Now I could see the signs. Homemade with cardboard and markers, and held up with plywood sticks. They said, SEGREGATION IS WRONG, and WE ARE ALL BROTHERS IN CHRIST, and FREEDOM NOW. The next thing I saw made my stomach pitch and turn and squeeze up tight. Just next to the swarm of colored people marching, stood a smaller crowd of white people looking madder than heck. They held baseball bats and sticks and lumber pieces. Lots of screaming "Damn niggers" and yelling "Swim in your own pools" came from the crowd holding their rough weapons. If the police had not formed a line between the two groups, a flat out brawl would have busted out.

A white lady sitting near me said, "If it weren't for those Yankee agitators getting all in here and keeping things stirred up, we wouldn't have this kind of trouble." The bus driver said, "Now they want to swim with us. Next thing you know, they'll want to be in bed with us."

I glanced past the middle to the back of the bus where colored people sat to see if they'd heard these remarks. Everybody was looking silently out at the goings on. One old black man was staring straight in front of him, pretending he did not see or hear anything. He looked tired, and his shoulders sagged. He did not even glance at me when I looked at him. The bus hissed, and started to go forward.

This one colored lady, about Miss Jesse's age, stared at the whole thing as it went by us on the bus. She held her chin high, and her shoulders back. She glanced at me, and glanced away quickly. I turned back around and sat quiet the rest of the way to the bank.

Inside the cool, dry bank building, I saw no colored people. The bank smelled like a new building, always clean and fresh. It reminded me of the hospital, how everything under the tiles and paint smelled like blood. How silly, there's no blood in a bank, I told myself.

I passed a line of cashiers and kept going to the safety deposit boxes. I thought I remembered Mama and me going to the safety deposit box once, and it took a key. I pretended I knew exactly what I intended to do. That's something I'd learned to do when I would grocery shop for Mama sick in the bed. So that people would not question a young girl doing grown up things like buying groceries, you just had to act like you knew exactly what you were doing.

"Hello there, honey, what can I do for you?" said the woman at the door of the safety deposit area. Even though she sported a dull gold beehive nearly a foot tall and almost that wide, I recognized her. Mrs. Moncrief. At one time, she and Mama had been friends. Sorority sisters. Roommates in college. Way before Mama went to bed for a few years.

Mrs. Moncrief had had some sort of problem with her husband that she and Mama whispered about in the TV room. Then she got a divorce, which Mama said was a crying shame, cause then her friend had to go to work. Today she wore some jangling bracelets that banged around as she put her hands on the cardboard box full of keys. The keys sat in envelopes lined all in rows with numbers on them.

"I'm here to check Mama's box," I said. "She asked me to check on things for her." Mrs. Moncrief squinted at me, as if she'd maybe seen me one hundred years ago. She didn't know me. I cleared my throat and deepened my voice. "Elizabeth Roberts Wood."

"Oh ... Lizbeth. Lizbeth's daughter? Rayann! I hardly

recognized you! Look how you've grown!" she said. "You remember me? Agatha Moncrief?" I nodded my head, and she lowered her voice. "Your Mama had the most talent of anybody I'd ever seen. She could put together the most gorgeous flower arrangement out of what was growing outside in the yard. And the art work she did," she shook her head. "How is your mama?" She lowered her voice again. I couldn't tell if her eyes showed concern or nosiness.

I looked her right in the eyes, smiled and said, "She's just fine." I was not lying, I told myself. "She's just started painting again, you know. She sent me down here to get some things out of the box." I couldn't believe how grown up I was acting.

She took me into the safety deposit box vault. The walls were completely covered with small boxes, each one decorated with a brass handle to slide it out and engraved with a fancy number. She found the box—1861—and I memorized it for good. My heart beat fast as I took out the key. The key I'd found in Mama's underwear drawer, a place Daddy would never think to look for something private and important of Mama's. Mrs. Moncrief had to open the box with her key, and the one I had in my pocket. We both slipped in our keys and turned them. The lock gave, and she pulled the drawer out for me. I tried to stifle a sigh of relief as she handed me the heavy metal box.

"It's terrible, that Writ of Incompetence thing," Mrs. Moncrief said, glancing back at the doorway.

"Yes," I said. *What was she talking about?* I wondered. I smiled at her, but it was a trembling smile. She backed away from me and cocked her head. She glanced back at the doorway, and walked over to it. She fiddled with her bracelets nervously, taking them off, putting them back on, like she was trying to make up her mind. Now I remembered. One night she'd showed up in the middle of the night with her baby and a black eye. She needed a place to stay, and Daddy was out of town, so Mama set her up in the guest room. I remember Mama promising never to speak a word of it to anybody. And she didn't—not even to me. Finally Mrs. Moncrief looked back over at me all sad and let out a deep breath. She locked the glass door of the vault and walked over to me.

"Cause when that goes through, honey, all *this*," she pointed into the box, "will be *his*." Her eyebrows raised up, and she looked at me like she was searching for something in my face. I cleared my throat. Stay cool, I thought. I sat down at the table.

"His?" I said.

"Your daddy's," she said, firmly. "Well, technically it's yours—you're the beneficiary on your mother's account," she said. "But your father, since he's got the Writ of Incompetence, if that goes through, he takes charge of the account for your mother and yourself." I looked at the long thin box. It felt like a bucket of ice cold water had dropped onto my head. Of course, I thought. That's why he wants me to go to boarding school. Then he can have the money.

"I'm not real clear on what the Writ of—" I said.

"Incompetence," she half-whispered, glancing again back at the doorway. "Well, I'm not sure of all the legalities of it, but if he can prove she's incompetent in any way—old age, physical illness, or—"she swallowed, glancing down at me, and then back at the doorway, "mental illness, and they can prove it—" She shrugged. "It's his."

Finally, somebody trying to help Mama. "How can they prove she's crazy?" I said, swallowing hard. I hated to say it out loud. But I knew she knew. I started fiddling with the bank book on the top of the pile of papers.

"Doctor's letters, that kind of thing," she said.

"Oh, yeah," I said, as if I knew.

"Well, Mama is not crazy," I said, sitting up straight. She patted me on the shoulder.

"Uh huh," she said. "Good luck. I'd better get back to my office in case anybody comes in," she said. "You take as long as you'd like." She locked the door behind her and winked at me.

"Thanks, Mrs. Moncrief," I said. It came out thick, like something was stuck in my throat. Her high heels click-clacked across the tile floor, echoing from wall to wall in the vault. Good. I was alone. First I found an envelope with official looking papers in it that said Deed and Title. I'd have to ask Mama what that meant.

Then I opened the bank book. Mama's name appeared at the top. My heart went into my throat when I saw how much money was entered into the account—$250,000. It seemed like a lot.

Next, I found an envelope at the very bottom of the box that said, "Mad Money" on the front scripted in Mama's handwriting. It held a whole passel of money rolled up in it. I looked around me in the little room without even moving my head. I had to act cool. Nobody around. I counted the money. $2,000. My heart beat fast, and the money was slippery in my hands. That couldn't be right. I counted it again, licking my fingers as I counted, tasting the inky paper. Two thousand dollars, all in fifty dollar bills.

I looked around the room again hardly moving a muscle. I licked the envelope and pasted it shut with the money in it. I slipped the envelope into the front of my underwear, and pulled up the waist. I put the bank book inside the center of my bra. I stood up to see if it would all stay and to make sure nothing poked out.

Then I sat at the table and wrote down the names of things on the paper called Titles and Deeds to ask Mama about them.

I was trying to read the second paragraph of one Deed when I heard the door unlock, and Mrs. Moncrief walked back in. I told her I was finished. She looked worried.

"Honey, now don't you repeat what I told you," she said. "I could get into big trouble here."

"Oh, of course not," I answered. Boy, I was turning into a professional liar. But I wouldn't tell on her. I'd just tell what needed told. I would have given her a hug, but I didn't want her to know I was stealing, so I held out my hand for a handshake, and then squeezed her hand with both of mine and thanked her for her help. She smelled like gardenias.

"Call me if you need anything," she said. "Your mama helped me through some things before." I nodded as she opened the door, saying *Have a nice day*. I waved, swallowing my bitterness and gratefulness down.

Back on the bus, I sat quietlike down in the middle by myself so as not to cause any attention. Just in case the money fell out. A baby in the back of the bus was crying, probably cause it was so hot. Some colored people were whispering to each other. When the bus passed by the pool, everyone had disappeared.

"Guess they arrested those nigras," the bus driver said, loud and flat, but I detected a glee underneath.

The colored people stopped talking then, and the ones who hadn't been, started darting their eyes at the pool. Didn't the bus driver know he stank bad, and needed to be arrested himself for bad hygiene? Lord knows a body's got to wear some deodorant.

I watched out the window as the green of summer whirled past. I touched the cash money envelope in the front of my underwear. It crinkled as I touched it. Then I scratched my face and felt the hard bank book cover in the center of my bra. I didn't know what in the hell's nation I was doing, but doing something was better than doing nothing. Maybe those college Negroes walking around outside the city pool right here in town figured the same.

That afternoon, the five o'clock traffic was winding its way down, and the hospital messengers dashed across the street on their nightly trip to the pharmacy to get extra medicine and bandages not supplied in the hospital. I headed to the entrance. I pushed my stomach out to hold onto the envelope of money. I nearly turned around when I saw the front doors. At the hospital, usually one security guy stood around talking to visitors or reading the paper or flirting with the young candy stripers. Two real policemen stood at the hospital entrance in their dark uniforms holding night sticks.

I hesitated only a step, though. Once more, I'd decided to act grown up cool. They didn't know what was stuck in the waist of my underwear or in my bra. Besides, I was the administrator's daughter. I stuck another smile on my face and walked right past them.

The receptionist Marlene sat at the front desk. I liked her nail polish, called Impossible Pink, because it looked so pink it did seem impossible. She always smelled of Tigress cologne. I asked her why real policemen were standing out front. I hoped she'd know something, being a good gossip, as Mama had always said, but she never stopped me from going anywhere in the hospital.

"Oh, honey, those colored people are all over it now," she said, shaking her head, and then lifting her Impossible Pink finger in a just-a-second pose and answered a ringing phone. When she transferred the call, she said, "Those colored people want to use the *hospital* now, of all things." She smacked her

Juicy Fruit gum, what she always chewed, and it made my mouth water.

"But why are the police here? There aren't any pickets or anything," I said.

"Well, it's just a precaution, you know. They took a bunch of coloreds from the pool and put them in jail. Jail's full up now. But rumor has it," she said, and leaned over to whisper it to me, "they're coming *here* next. Your daddy had me call the station for extra protection."

"Oh," I said, trying to sound natural. I felt relieved that nothing had happened really, but then worried about Ivory Jones.

"Well, thanks, Marlene. I'm going to go see Mama now." I waved good-bye as natural as I could and headed up the elevator to 5C.

The night time nurse stood in the station. Good, I thought, I'd get into Mama's room easily. The nurse smiled bigger than usual. "You coming for dinner, Rayann?" I hadn't thought of it, but I nodded, and she said, "I'll call downstairs and tell them to fix you a plate. Meatloaf tonight," she said. "You can go on down now." She pointed towards Mama's room with a smile on her face like I had a birthday present I was fixing to open, and she knew what was in it.

When I walked inside Mama's room, I couldn't believe what I saw. Paintings and colors applied to things everywhere in the room. She'd cut scraps from the newspaper and framed them in pictures of zig zags and dots and other geometric shapes. She'd painted rocks to look like wild turtles, and sticks to look like snakes. She had sketched wolves with big teeth, and Adam and Eve in the garden with the snake wrapped around the tree, drooling and grinning.

And green things. Pots of plants sat in the window sill, on

the table and even on the floor. And flowers. Yellow and pink and purple and beige and deep red blossomed in tinted glass vases placed carefully all over the room in huge arrangements.

"Rayann," Mama said, like she hadn't seen me in months. She stood up from where she knelt on the floor. She had laid an old sheet there and brushed it with paint. She wore work pants and a shirt, and her hair was combed into a neat pageboy. She hugged me.

"Oh," I said, looking around. "Wow." I walked around the room, touching the plants and peering close at all the paintings she'd done. She even had gotten ahold of an oxygen mask and painted a boy's you-know-what on it. How embarrassing. Still, I loved the room, and hugged myself. I stood up and hovered like a bee, smelling flower arrangement after flower arrangement. Then I remembered the money in my pants waist.

"How did you get all this stuff in here?" I asked her.

"Oh, nurses and aides brought flowers from empty rooms," she said. "I guess the workers here thought I was about to die or something," she said, and laughed loud and long, a music I hadn't heard in a while. "And Miss Jesse's nephew, that nice Ivory Jones?" she said, and I nodded. "He brought the plants from Miss Jesse. Wasn't that thoughtful of him?" Ivory Jones helped her create this whole world in her tiny room while outside it, he could be getting arrested.

"Yes, it was. What happened? I mean—how did you get yourself—well?"

She shrugged and put her arm around me. "A miracle, I guess." She shut the room door and said, "I stopped taking all that medicine. Makes me like a zombie. I did what you said and only take it every other time. I don't seem to need so much of it now." She shrugged and smiled at me. "What's the matter?" she said, squatting to work on her sheet spattered with paint of all colors, her knees cracking as she knelt down.

"But what if you get sick again?" I said, pacing, touching the money bag. "What if you need that medicine?"

"Let's just hope for the best, honey," she said. "I'm trying." She reached up to grab my hand and squeeze. "You know, sometimes at night I still hear voices." She sat down all the way and crossed her legs. "But I just get up and paint now." She waved the paint brush around. "Just get up and paint."

"Yeah, I guess that makes sense," I said, sitting down next to her. I did not want to get my hopes up too much. I loved the chemical smell of acrylic paint she used, and took in a deep breath.

"I think something at home has been making me sick," she said, painting a pink mouth on the gorilla she was creating on the sheet.

"You mean Daddy?" I said. It was the first time we'd talked about this.

She nodded and sighed. "I don't know. I just don't know."

"I do," I said, my voice angry.

She looked at me surprised. "Well, I still love him."

"Well, look here." I pulled out the money from my waist. "See this? It's your money. And Daddy's trying to get your other money."

"Honey, what on earth are you talking about?" She put the paint brush down and looked at me like I was the crazy one. "Where'd you get this big fat—that's my Mad Money! How'd you get to it?" she said, reaching for it. Just then the nurse's aide knocked on the door and said, "Mrs. Wood? Dinner for you and a guest?"

Mama's eyes got big. She leaned over and whispered. "I'm not supposed to have anything extra in here. I mean other than this stuff," she said, waving her arm across the room. She stood up and lifted the mattress away from the frame on the bottom of the bed. "Put it under here," she whispered. I shoved the envelope in. Then we both turned towards the door. "Yes, bring it right in," she said, a singsong in her voice. I knew where I'd learned how to tell white lies and to steal with such an easy way now.

We sat on the floor of Mama's garden hospital room again cross-legged and ate. The meatloaf and mashed potatoes tasted like cardboard. I kept pushing them around on my plate making scary buildings and mountains with them until Mama told me to settle down. But the black-eyed peas and mustard greens had ham seasoning in them, and we cleaned our plates of them. Then we enjoyed bread pudding for dessert. It melted all rich, creamy and cinnamony in our mouths. While we ate, I told her how Daddy had quit paying Miss Jesse.

"Are you sure, Rayann?" she said. "Is that what *they* told you?"

"Mama, do you think Miss Jesse would lie to us?" I spooned another creamy mouthful in.

"Well, you never know about some colored people," she said. I thought about how she said herself, *You can't teach an old dog new tricks.*

"Mama," I said firmly, putting down my bowl. "I know. They are *not* lying. Ivory Jones eats like crazy, I've seen him take the milk carton out of the refrigerator and drink half of it right then. And Cookie, she's tall, and she can eat a lot of chicken and greens. And there's clothes, and—"

"You spend a lot of time around them?" she said, looking suspicious.

"Dang," I said, wiping my mouth with my hand.

"Don't do that," she said, handing me a napkin. "How many times have I told you not to use your sleeve or your hand.

Honestly."

"Mama, it's been hard by myself at the house," I said. I put down the dish. Mama stared into space as I went on. "Daddy, well—" I didn't want to go on. I didn't want to upset her, or tell her about that damn Rheta and the costume lady party. She listened, cocking her head to one side. "Miss Jesse's gone to work for Angelo's restaurant kitchen downtown."

"She has?" Mama frowned and shook her head. She stood up and pulled the money out of the mattress and began to count out the whole thing on the floor. "Is it all here?" she said, counting the fifties out in a pile.

"But here's the thing." I reached out and touched her on the arm to get her looking me in the eye. "Daddy's trying to get your *other* money."

With that, she stopped counting, put the money into two piles and looked up at me and said, "Don't let me forget, I've counted to eight hundred here." Then she turned to me and said, "Now what's this?"

"I think Daddy's trying to get your money. I took this," I said as I pulled the bank book out of my bra now. "I didn't try to get any of that money out, though."

"What?" she said, grabbing her account book. "You can't. Nobody can." She flipped through it, looking for the balance. "Only I can withdraw from this—"

"No, Mama. That's what I'm trying to tell you. Daddy's getting up this Declaration of Incompetence, see," I said. "So *you* can't get to it."

Mama was counting the rest of her two thousand dollars in cash. I figured she had to deal with just one thing at a time, so I waited as patient as I could, though I wanted to scream.

"Two thousand," she said, looking at me as she returned the money to the envelope. Her hands shook. "What on earth are you talking about?"

So I explained what the safety deposit box lady had told me. How if you get a doctor and some other people to say you can't take care of yourself or your money. "And then the money goes to Daddy to supposedly take care of you. You go to Chattahoochee and I go to reform school." I realized I had waved my arms all around as she watched like she didn't believe it. "Mrs. Moncrief, your friend, told me all this." I folded my arms. She kept half the money, and gave me the envelope back.

"Chattahoochee!?" She stood up. "And then the money goes to *him* to supposedly take care of us. *I* go to Chattahoochee and *you* to reform school? Agatha Moncrief told you, huh?" She touched the dirt of the aloe plant someone had given her. She took the Styrofoam water pitcher that was supposed to serve as her water holder and poured water into the plant. "Are you sure, Rayann?"

"Mama, it's what Mrs. Moncrief told me. She works at the bank, you know."

She played with the furry leaves of her African violets, three of them with flowers of pink, purple and white. She stood quiet for a while, running her fingers over the leaves. "You take a little money to Jesse," she said. You could have knocked me over with a feather at that remark. "If we owe her money, we need to give her some. No," she said as she held up the money she'd hung onto and shrugged. "I'll give Ivory Jones some money for bringing the flowers. Then it won't seem like a handout. You know how proud Miss Jesse is." I tucked the money back into my waistband. "And you put the rest away where nobody, I mean nobody, knows where it is but you. Understand?" She put the rest in her purse.

"What about the other thing?" I said, stuffing all the money into my shorts. "Chattahoochee. And the Incompetent thing."

"I don't believe it. I just don't—why would he?" The silence in the room brought out the buzzing of the fluorescent light by her bed. "How could he?" I'd let her figure it out herself. Then I thought again. Maybe I'd not done right not telling her some things.

"Mama," I said. "There's some stuff I haven't told you." I stood up as she stared at me from the other side of the room. She sat down in the chair and crossed her legs, composing herself. I cleared my throat and shook my legs, rubbed them awake and ready, and then sat on the bed while she watched. I went ahead and told her I thought Daddy *might* be running around, and that I heard him and Dr. Indley planning on how to get her put away, and how he and Lucky were working up the Incompetence thing.

Mama stood up and was looking me square in the face. She sat down on the bed next to me. "Are you sure your father did all this?" I looked at her and nodded. She began to shake herself. In the chest. Crying. Deep, heavy sobs, her hands in her face. I froze up when she did. I didn't like getting so close to her, because when she hurt, I hurt even more. I never wanted my mama hurt. I got so scared when she was hurt that I felt split in two, and it was easier for me to get fighting mad. At least then I felt like I could do something about it. I couldn't, though. I was only scared. Maybe she'd get sick again. "That scoundrel," she said.

"Mama, it's okay," I said. Those words seemed weak and silly. But that was the truth. She was somehow painting and planting and healing herself without anybody else's help. At least I hoped so. My throat felt sticky and I had to swallow a lot to keep from crying my own self.

She walked into the bathroom and got tissue to wipe her face. She blew her nose. "I'll be all right. Just give me a few minutes." She fished in her purse. "How about finding yourself a book or some cards and we'll read or play Go Fishing, huh?" I knew she wanted to be alone, so I got up and headed on a magazine hunt around the hospital. I shut the door and felt the whoosh as it closed.

I searched high and low, from the E.R. waiting room to the cancer ward to labor and delivery. Finally I found an old beat up *Highlights* magazine in the surgical waiting area and brought it back to the room. Mama was trimming a few yellow leaves off her plants. She asked me about my summer plans, and how school was going, and all those things mamas ask. We talked for a while, never opening the magazine, but she combed my hair and said I was growing like a weed, and to pick out some patterns and material and she'd get herself a machine somehow and start sewing me some clothes. I told her what I wanted—two pairs of culottes and I'd buy blouses to match.

I lay down on the bed and she rubbed my back. Eventually, she said, "I need to get out of this place as soon as I can. I want you to find out what you can about this Declaration of Incompetence." I tried to stay awake. I imagined myself floating on a cloud, Mama rubbing my back. I fell asleep while she was talking.

When she woke me up a little while later, she said it was time to go, the last bus would arrive in fifteen minutes. I promised I'd find out all I could.

On the way out, I nodded to the policeman at the front door while I patted my stomach where I held the money. Only one policeman stood guard at the front this late. Out in the cool night, I felt relieved that Ivory Jones would get paid for doing something Miss Jesse had been thoughty enough to dream up. The crickets and cicadas had started up their own concert. The oak tree in the parking lot held a nest of woodpeckers who were slumbering now. I turned on the faucet outside in the front and splashed some water in the bird bath just to make sure they had water.

I prayed to God that somebody thoughty as Miss Jesse would never have to wash anybody's but her own underdrawers again. At least not if she wasn't getting full pay for it. I walked down the sidewalk in the twilight to the huddle of people under the bus stop waiting for the last bus to carry them home.

17

School had finally let out. What a relief. No homework, no lunchroom food, no Loretta and Cynthia to worry about. Cookie had finished out the year, and she and I celebrated the event by hanging around the small creek with Margot, dangling our feet in the water, cooling off by splashing our necks and arms with water. A family of crows had just flown over making big squawking *caw caw caw caw* sounds.

The green world worked invisible while we basked in it.

"I want to go downtown," Cookie said.

"What for?" I said. I felt content to splash in the water and think about green.

"I don't know. Get me some new music. A new 45. Aunt Jesse gave me two dollars for this week. Maybe Count Basie, or a new Motown record." She was banging sticks on my head, restless. If I thought we had all summer to wade, I wouldn't have minded, but big envelopes from boarding schools had started coming in the mail. I'd confiscate them and then rip them up and throw them in the outside garbage. Still, just in case this was the only fun I might have all summer, I'd go.

"Hey—we can stop by the Levy pool," I said. Cookie said okay, so we put on our shoes to go ask Miss Jesse for permission. Since Daddy worked all day, I still took it upon myself to pretend that Miss Jesse was in charge of me.

"Yeah," Cookie went on, "and we can go down by the railroad tracks, by Gramlings. Jojo's on the other side of the tracks," she said, slipping on her sandals. I'd never seen that place, but I felt ready enough for a summer adventure. "You can get a chocolate soda. And any popsicle you want at Jojo's, banana, orange, grape, even orange sherbet. And hey—can I wear that lime green shirt of yours?"

I didn't know about that. I had never loaned Cookie any clothes. I stared at the short green plants that grew near the creek. "Well, if you're careful with it. And you have to ask please." I was putting on my Keds.

"Well, please, then. You know it looks better on me. You're too skinny for it," she said.

"Stuck up," I said.

Miss Jesse did not share our enthusiasm about going downtown together. "If you trouble trouble, trouble will always trouble you," she said, pointing her finger at us both, keeping time with the song of her words as she shook that finger. She had been sitting on the sofa next to the shaky legged coffee table until we came in. Then she sat up to fold laundry and watch the Saturday cartoons on their tiny black and white TV. She did not look the fifty-three years old Cookie had told me she was. She looked maybe in her forties like Mama. Ivory Jones was just getting up since he'd worked till midnight.

"Oh, come on, Aunt Jesse," he said from the kitchen where he got himself some corn flakes and buttoned up his shirt. He buttoned his shirts all the way up but for one button at the top. "What if Martin Luther King said that kind of talk?"

"I ain't raising no Martin Luther King, I'm raising a girl and half-raising another one. Two girl children looking for trouble, and one big mouthed boy," she said, yanking out a towel, matching up the ends, folding it up tight and patting it down.

"What if we're extra careful?" Cookie said, kneeling on the

floor by Miss Jesse. "What if we promise we won't sit in the wrong seats or pull the cord too soon or—"

"Or sass the driver," I said.

"That ain't even my whole concern," she said, frowning, pulling out some of Ivory Jones' shorts and flapping them. "How about all that disturbance downtown past few years. How about them people caught fire on the bus. And if that ain't enough, how about all the beatings over yonder in Alabama?" She folded one thing and picked up another, flapping it out hard. "Even here—things going on here, too. Rocks throwed in the Reverend Steele's house."

"That's last year you talking about, Aunt Jesse," Ivory Jones said.

"That's right. And it could happen today," she said, pulling out one of Cookie's nightgowns and shaking the static from it. It smelled clean and mild, like Ivory soap flakes.

"I'll protect her, Miss Jesse," I said from where I stood behind Cookie. They all laughed a little at that. Miss Jesse studied me up and down.

"You mama done paid Ivory Jones a whole lot for them flowers," she said. "Don't tell me you didn't have nothing to do with it."

"No, Ma'am, I did not," I said, darting a look at Miss Jesse, who showed with her eyes she did not believe me. I shrugged. "Well, maybe I reminded Mama that Daddy owed you some money." I shifted back and forth on my feet. "And that you'd quit on us." The room got still then. Quiet. Usually Cookie would have something smart to say. "I don't blame you for quitting," I said.

"Honey, you like my own baby sometimes, troublesome as you is," Miss Jesse said.

"You can't keep them from growing up sometime," Ivory

Jones said, taking a bite of his corn flakes. "Looks to me like they're both getting their growth. Time to let loose, Auntie."

"You don't need to speed up the devil's work, Ivory Jones," Miss Jesse said. Then she lay down on the sofa. She did not seem the type to lie around on the sofa, but I figured she was home and tired. She said, "Oh, me. All right then. Do what you gonna do, you gonna do it anyway." She let her arm sail out and flop down beside the sofa, while she covered the other arm over her face. "I'm too old to argue." Then she sat up with a groan. "Come over here, the both of you." She waited while we came to stand in front of her. She held up her hand to list off the rules. "Be careful. Be quiet, don't walk together," she was saying, holding up her fingers and pointing to each one. "Don't laugh, don't touch each other," she said, then went to the other hand. "Don't let each other out of your sight. And for goodness sakes, mind your manners."

"Yes, Ma'am," Cookie said, and we jumped up and headed out the door. But not before we both got a slice of Miss Jesse's pound cake, all smooth and creamy and tasting just a little bit like lemon. We rolled two pieces up in napkins and hurried out.

"Stay away from that pool where all that protesting is going on, too, now, you hear?" she said.

"Yes, Ma'am," we said in unison. We took off running, laughing like birds in flight.

We got on the bus with Cookie stepping in first, then me. "Ten cents," he said, pointing his hand at the slot. When I came behind her, he said, "That'll be ten cents, honey." He watched me go to the back of the bus to sit with Cookie. I loved the smell of the bus, the old leather seats, the wear of them. The bus driver motioned for me to come to the front of the bus and talk to him.

"You sit up here behind me," he said. "Colored folks mostly sits in the back." *Duh*, I wanted to say. Then I wanted to say, *I will sit with my friend where it's dangerous.* Instead, I sat down right behind him without a word so as not to cause any trouble. At Tharpe Street by the pool, I stepped down the stairs. Cookie got off behind me. I walked a few feet ahead of her on the sidewalk, pretending not to know her.

We dove off the sidewalk out of the hot sun and stepped into a grove of big trees and shade on the front side of the pool. Then we sneaked around on the other side of the trees away from the street. We stayed close together where people could not see us from the road. We walked to the edge of the trees and peered out at the picketers by the pool. One policeman stood nearby with a gun in his holster.

You could hear the sounds of their feet shuffling around as they walked near about silent. The picketers held up their FREEDOM NOW signs and paraded in the hot sun. Two ladies, one black and one white, stood and talked to a white guy, like they were trying to explain something to him. "Let's go see," Cookie said. We walked out into the sunlight together. Not touching each other or looking at each other at all. But I could feel her standing there, like you know when somebody's hand is an inch away from your arm, and the hair stands up to meet it.

"It's just ridiculous," the white lady said. She wore all white linen, like a nun's outfit, but not an official one, one she'd decided on herself. "The commissioners have got to discuss this. The taxpayers are spending twenty thousand dollars a year to maintain these pools, and because of what they call 'old southern ways,' which are nice words for racism, it's all going to waste." I had never heard a white lady talk like that before. Or like she knew what she was talking about. Or who dressed that way, either. I wondered if my mama knew her.

"It's about freedom," the black lady was saying. "We're citizens of the United States, the state of Florida, the city of Tallahassee. We have the right to use the city's facilities as citizens." I'd never heard a colored lady talk that way, either, to a white man. Like she knew what she was talking about, and not afraid to say it. All clear and stuff. And wearing a satin blue button-up dress.

The guy had a sign that said "Press Pass," and he held a pad in his hand. He wrote furious fast and nodded as he scribbled. Cookie and me moved at the same time, drawn to the three grownups talking, like that one black lady's words had made us brave. We started walking up to them at the same time, at the same pace, like we were twins or something, even if we were opposites—one tall, one short, one brown, one beige. All three grown ups stared at us. Cookie and I stood together, our hands behind our backs, arms nearly touching, and I swear I could feel her electricity on me.

"We're not doing nothing," I said. "We're just listening."

"See," the white nun outfit lady said, pointing to us and talking to the man. "The children don't have prejudices; it's only the adults who do." Cookie and I looked at each other and moved a little closer together, touching arms. Then the policeman shouted out to us from the right by the picketers.

"Hey! What are you kids doing around here?" He headed over to us.

"They want to swim, can't you see?" the white lady was saying.

"You kids better get out of here," he said, ignoring her, looking at me. "Pool's not open. This is not a mixed swimming pool." He was glancing at Cookie and then looking away.

Cookie grabbed my hand, and we took off running.

I heard the white lady in linen. "Leave those children alone!" To the press pass man she said, "See what I mean about the intolerance..."

Meanwhile, we were running as fast as we could to the next block, towards Branch Street. I felt free for some strange reason. I guess cause Cookie had a wild free look in her eyes.

Once out of the park, we walked into a grove of shade trees, panting. A warm breeze had come up, and the moss in the oak trees swayed.

We skipped down towards Branch Street and got on opposite sides of the road with crepe myrtled sidewalks. We headed towards Frenchtown. Cookie jumped up in the air and swatted a crepe myrtle blossom. It snowed its dark pink petals down onto her hair and shoulders. I had to admit, there was something thrilling about being that close to trouble and still getting away. But then I remembered Miss Jesse, my promises to her, and her voice barking out instructions to us before we left.

"We better watch out," I said. A lawn mower buzzed a block down, and a screen door slammed up the street. Long sidewalks stretched in front of us on both sides of the road. "Let's run. Have a race. And don't stink up my shirt."

"Shut up, fool," Cookie said, running across the street, slugging me in the arm, and then dashing back across. So I took off down the sidewalk, Cookie speeding way ahead of me with her long long legs across the street. About five blocks into the edge of Frenchtown, we spread way apart on either side of the road, me behind Cookie. We pretended not to know each other and slowed to a walk, panting and wiping sweat. Then we headed downtown.

As soon as the street was clear of people for a block on the Woolworth's side, Cookie said, "Let's go to Woolworth's and get cooled off. Then we can go down to Jojo's and get a drink by the railroad." My mouth watered for a Yoohoo, all creamy and sweet. She looked up the street and down the street, then grabbed my hand and pulled me into Woolworth's glass doors. Since we were supposed to walk separately, we split up right away.

As usual, Woolworth's was bright, empty, and you could see all the way to the back where toys and cheap lamps were displayed. At the register, a new cashier lady glared at us. She wore crazy white-blonde hair and white nail polish. Her eyes stayed glued on us, so we split up.

Cookie walked to the Motown section. I shuffled to the other side where the Top 40s sat. Cookie found a Ray Charles album and a new Supremes 45. I was opening all the Yardley colors when I noticed the saleslady following behind Cookie in the store.

I walked to the front of the store where teen clothes hung on low racks. "Do you like these?" I said to get the saleslady off Cookie's backside. I held up a red, squareneck shirt.

"Ooo, yeah, lemme see," Cookie said, walking over with her records. The saleslady scowled and followed Cookie over.

"I saw y'all stealing stuff," the saleslady said. Miss Blackstock, her tag said.

"Huh?" I said. Cookie looked hurt.

"We didn't take nothing," she said. Miss Blackstock raised her eyebrows and spoke to me.

"I saw her," Miss Blackstock pointed at Cookie.

"You can frisk us if you want," I said, sarcastic, holding up my hand with the lipstick in it. Cookie did the same with her records.

"Humph," said Miss Blackstock, and she walked away. Cookie and I exchanged looks, and then decided to leave.

That cashier lady stared through Cookie at the cash register that same way the bus driver had. As Cookie counted out her money in pennies and quarters that Miss Jesse had given her, the woman rolled her eyes, put her hand on her hip and let her breath out hard. I stood a few feet away. Cookie was buying the red shirt, not paying a bit of attention to that disgusted cashier.

Afterwards, Cookie pushed out the door into the heat. Then I walked out, hot and wet like a towel after a bath. "Ignorant," was all Cookie said.

We headed casual as we could with our Woolworth sacks, across the park but separate. We found ourselves walking down the hill to Gramlings Feed Store. Cookie walked on the other side of the street, cooled in shade of the pecan trees. The doors always stood wide open, and you could see way to the darkened cool back of the store. Mr. Gramling had thrown cracked corn on the pavement for the pigeons. New saddles and bridles hung on the far wall.

I walked up to the door closest to the railroad tracks and took a big whiff. I loved the smell of hay and of oats, corn and molasses. You could nearly taste the heavy sweet molasses if you smelled deep enough. Just past the store lay the railroad tracks. Across the tracks and up the hill, the Negro college was nestled under trees, another part of colored town foreign to me. I felt hot and thirsty all of a sudden.

"What you doing?" Cookie yelled in a stage whisper from across the street.

"Just smelling," I said. She gave a big come on gesture, so we headed to the tracks. Dragonflies buzzed around and landed on the rocks spread out under the tracks.

"I heard people can find Indian arrowheads in these rocks if they look hard," Cookie said, picking up flinty rocks and dropping them. They almost sounded like glass wind chimes when they struck each other. My tongue felt thick and fuzzy.

"Well, I'm thirsty, I don't want to look for no damn arrowheads," I said, "Let's go." Big crows and blue jays sat like jewels on the telephone wires as we hopped across the tracks. Now we were on the Negro college side of downtown. Bushes of lantana and wild willows billowed up toward the sky. I could see sky all around, so I was staring up.

That's why I missed the cove of pavement with a wall around it covered in kudzu. I did not see, either, the kids' bikes, or the colored kids, three girls and two boys, hanging around the wall until I heard them screaming for glee. They were playing the statue game where somebody swings you around. You're thrown in midair, and where you land, you freeze like a statue for as long as you can. They were listening to WANM, the colored station, on the transistor radio.

"Hey!" said the older boy I figured to be about thirteen. "Long-legged! Turn around." I realized Cookie and I weren't even trying to walk separate anymore. I knew he was referring to Cookie. He would not talk to me anyway. He had not gotten his growth, and was showing off for the others. Cookie ignored him.

"Ooo, you be moving it, girl," the other, taller guy said.

"Hey, long-legged pretty girl," the smaller guy tried again. "What you doing with that white bitch?"

Cookie stopped quick and wheeled around. We stood just a two-room distance from them. "Going to the store, black boy," she said. "We thirsty, is that against the law?" All the kids hooted.

"Ooo, lord, girl, you better watch your mouth," the oldest girl said, shoving the smaller guy. I started feeling a little dizzy.

"Maybe I should go back," I said. But Cookie ignored me. She dropped her Woolworth's bag, and put her hands on her hips. "Keep it up and I'll have to whup your ass," she called out to the whole group.

"Really," I said, "I'll just go back." I started to turn around. She grabbed my arm and held tight.

"No, no need to worry," Cookie said. "They just talking." All the same, she glanced with her forehead furrowed, looking back as she picked up her bag. Then we walked away. A truck with a loud muffler drove past, and a couple of dogs barked at it. As we opened the screen door to the inside of Jojo's, a cool and dark country store feeling waved over me. The smell of cement floor cooled me off. Layers of Dove soap and the cheap no-name brands covered the top shelf. There sat a row of roach-killing sprays and bottles, then mousetraps, then motor oil and batteries. And beer. In the corners, stacks and stacks of Black Label, Old Milwaukee and Schlitz Malt Liquor, heaped up from the floor to the ceiling.

Jojo's felt cool and safe. I wanted to loiter there all day long. The Coke ice box buzzed loud and hard. I could have sat on top of the doors and cooled off for hours. We dropped our sacks and leaned into the coke ice box. I got a Nehi Grape soda, and Cookie got an Orange Crush.

"Now don't be spilling that orange soda on my lime green shirt," I said.

"Girl," she said, and shook her head.

Jojo stood at the cash register wearing a purple horse jockey hat. She held a fly swatter in her hand. She stared at me and Cookie like we were a huge rhinoceros in her store. It was a sharp look, like she suspected we'd knock everything over with our big tusks. She ate from a paper plate of lima beans and ham. It was quiet in the store this time of day, too hot for anybody to want to walk to a store for anything.

I paid for my drink, and Cookie paid for hers. I went back

over to the Coke machine and leaned up on it. That and the fat round fan in the corner of the room cooled us off. I thought about getting something to eat.

"I'm starved," Cookie said, over by the crackers and candy rack. I knew she didn't have much money left after buying her records, bus fare and orange soda.

"What you want? I'll get it," I said. We bought some pork rinds and shared them while Jojo adjusted her purple cap and watched us like a hawk. I felt a little irritated at Cookie. She'd bought the shirt I found earlier, and now I was buying her something to eat with the money she'd have had if she hadn't bought that shirt.

"If y'all looking to cause trouble, don't think twice on it cause I will call the police," Jojo said. "I don't want no rioting in my place. I got a respectable business here I got to keep up." She was wiping the counter down now. "And don't y'all be loitering, neither. Maybe y'all need to move on along, hear?" She peered out the window at the kids across the road, and up the road on the other side of the tracks. Cookie rolled her eyes, grabbed our sacks and motioned for me to come on outside.

The screen door slammed behind us as we crossed the street and headed back to the cove. One thing was coming clear—I was not trusted here any more than Cookie was at Woolworth's.

When we arrived back at the kudzu wall, those kids were dancing something they called the Tighten Up. It looked real good, and I wanted to stay and watch. But the younger girl saw us and stopped. "What you hanging around her for?" she said. "She must be white trash or something, hanging around you." Cookie hesitated. She'd never looked uncertain. Then she recovered her dignity. She took in a breath.

"What you just call her, girl," Cookie said, pulling off the last of her orange soda, and setting down her bottle, her fists clinched. She walked right up to that girl. "Want to see what some trash looks like, go look in the mirror," Cookie said. "Say it again. Say it again so I can kick your ass."

I was surprised at Cookie acting like she wanted a fight. She did not want a fight. It was what she had to say. It kind of scared me, and it seemed like bad manners to talk that way, but still, I swear to god, it made me swell up inside from happiness, somebody taking up for me like that.

"Cookie, why don't we just go," I said, putting my grape soda bottle down on the pavement, then picking it back up again.

"Girl must be giving you some money," the bigger of the boys said, "or some white poontang."

But nobody laughed, and the oldest black girl said, "All right, y'all, this ain't necessary. Ain't no reason—"

"Look out!" the smaller boy said, "Nigger knockers!" With that, a green Ford pickup roared straight towards us like a train coming head on, and we were tied to the tracks. I heard the rebel yell. And the horn blasting, not letting up at all, just laying on that horn. Three white teenage boys sat in the cab, and five or six in the back bed. Then a strange thing happened. All the colored people ran off in different directions, like they knew what to do. I stood frozen like one of those dumbass statues in the middle of the cove, watching that truck come right at me.

Cookie yelled, "Rayann, run!" I set off towards the front of Gramlings but Cookie grabbed me and pulled me with her to hide behind a concrete block wall a few feet away. One of the white boys in the truck bed threw something, and Cookie ducked, so it smacked me in the face. It was a blue balloon that busted warm like a slap of water, stinging all over my face. It smelled weird, not like water. Then he shouted, "You're worse than the niggers! You nigger loving bitch!" He shouted, then laughed, high-pitched and fast, like a real maniac. I could see a wildness in his eyes, and how he did not look at me like a person looks at another person. Just a wild, slit-eyed look that he held on me as they drove off. I leaned against the wall, still holding the empty grape soda bottle and the Woolworth's sack in my hand. It was quiet for a minute as the warm water ran down my face and neck.

"Damn, girl," she said, sniffing. "They nigger-knocked you." I was choking, and confused, a taste of salt and something sticky I did not like on my face. My legs shook, and my hand must have, too, cause I heard the bottle clank to the ground and the paper sack crackle as it fell. My stomach was boiling. "Damn rednecks," Cookie said. She got up real close and smelled.

"Dang, girl, they knocked you with their piss." With that, the big wide sky whitened into a blaze, and the telephone lines crisscrossed so the crows and jays on the line seemed to whirl sitting still. I leaned over and threw up. I hated everybody— those guys in the truck, Mama for being gone, Daddy for changing his self. For a split second, I even hated Cookie. I threw up all my hate, gloppy purple and beige mixed together, grape soda and pork skins on the tar and grass area behind the feed store. I let it all come up. I threw up until I was wretching out nothing. I hated those boys in the truck thinking I was dirty and barefooted and stupid and diseased. Those other kids had disappeared, but Cookie stood over me, holding back my hair, and saying, "You done yet? Get it all out." And I finally stopped heaving. I pushed Cookie's hand away, and stood up, dizzy. Turning around in a stagger, I looked at her sharp. "Why'd you bring me down here?" I choked out.

She backed up, a hurt look in her eyes. Her mouth opened in surprise. "What?" She turned and looked over at Gramlings.

"You—what?" Then she straightened up and put a hand on her hip. Her eyes turned to slits. "What you said? Ain't nobody drug you here." She came right up in my face. "Miss Jesse's right—you a trouble. Trouble's trouble." Then she whirled around. "White girl," she added, then folded her arms and stared across at the railroad track.

She trotted across the street so as not to be seen with me, and started to stomp back up the hill. I walked with a new kind of shock up to Gramlings to wash my face at the hose outside. Pee, piss as Cookie had called it. I held the old rotting green hose over me and let the cold water drench my head. I started to feel better. Cooler. I let the water rinse out my mouth. The water splattered all over my shirt. I didn't care.

As I cooled off, I started to want to apologize to her. That's when I noticed something red hanging out of the shopping bag. That red shirt. I pulled it out of my bag, confused. I looked across the street at her.

I watched as Cookie stood across the street, arms folded, her pretty red brown face scowling. Her head hung low, her shoulders slumped. She looked like she did not know what to do for the first time in her life. She checked down the street, and up the street, those large, Indian eyes of hers looking surprised. She glanced back across the street at me. Then she scowled more, a worried scowl, and dropped her arms and ran across the street towards me. Sweat poured down the front of her face, down her cheeks like tears, but it was not tears. Still, it shocked me. It looked that scary, all that water running from her forehead to her neck.

'I'm sorry,' I wanted to say. Instead I said, "This is yours." I handed the shirt out to her.

"No," she said, arms folded, looking at the sky. "No, I got it for you. I thought it might look good, you know, with that real light skin of yours."

"Oh," I said. I couldn't bear to look at her, but when I did, her face was a mask.

"Here," I said. I handed her the hose. "That shirt," I said, pointing to the lime green one she was wearing. "That shirt looks great on you. Maybe you should keep it."

Her face turned up out of the scowl and relaxed, and she held out her hand for the hose. A hungry squad of coal black crows and jewel blue jays swooped down after the cracked corn on the pavement near us, chasing off the pigeons. Cookie was drenched, and she stared at me, and I guess I was dripping wet, and water was running all down my face, too. We stood face to face, our masks washed off.

18

Colored people could stay in church half the afternoon. They must have been making some kind of good fun in church that white people did not. White people would not want to stay at church all day, sitting still, quiet, elbows in and knees together, singing hallelujah and looking miserable all the while, and listening to the pastor talk about loving your neighbor.

I was holding my love doll in the hideout. A real doll. A doll that Cookie would make fun of, but I didn't care. A cloth doll with embroidered eyes that did not close. She felt squishy. Holding her made me feel better, since Margot had stayed home. Margot always made me laugh, wagging her tail, walking ducky and breathing loud like a little kid. But since she was sleeping in the barn, I brought the doll.

Suddenly, Cookie stood in the doorway. "Where that doll come from?" she said. Her appearance meant that Sunday church and dinner down on Saturday Street was over. Cookie only gave away that she'd been in church because she still wore the yellow skirt with lace and black patent leather shoes that set off her Sunday outfit. "Full of color, that doll," she said, touching the dress. "All water blue and yellow and black rickrack, too. And look, she got your light skin. That hair-do you got, too, turned under at your chin. Look at that." She ran her hand across the doll.

"My grandma made it for me years ago," I said. "It's a love doll. She said I got stuff to learn about love." I gave Cookie the once over. "Ain't you hot?" I could hear Mama in my head telling me not to say ain't, but I was sounding more like Cookie, and she was sounding more like me, what happens with friends. Today, we were trying to forget about getting nigger knocked.

"Yeah, I'm hot," she said, and shucked off the shoes. We walked over to the creek and put our feet in. "That's better." Cookie's transistor radio blasted out WTAL-AM, which had just finished playing The Dixie Cups new song and Cookie had sung *Going to the chapel and we're gonna get married.*

I had brought a pair of high heels stolen from Mama's closet and a pair that Rheta had left once at the house. Mama's feet were so small they seemed too light to hold her on the earth. So I could probably fit into those, and Cookie into Rheta's. Cookie's had turquoise with the toes peeking out, mine gold sparkles. Cookie was now singing, *I wanna hold your hand, I wanna hold your hand,* even though she restated her opinions about the Beatles sounding too sweet and boring to her. "They got a rhythm going, though," she said, swishing her hips back and forth. "They just need to cut loose and holler more."

"Lookit," I said, and held up the shoes for her to see.

"I'll take the gold ones!" she said, splashing and getting out of the water to grab them.

"No," I said. "Those are mine. And they came from my house." I held them close. They had giant gold sparkles on them. I handed her Rheta's turquoise ones, and put on the gold ones myself. The turquoise ones fit her perfect, and her brown skin glowed in them. Even the gold ones were too big for me.

"They don't fit you, Miss-Big-for-her-Britches," Cookie said. When she saw my disappointment, she said, "Let's put some paper towels in them." We'd brought paper towels to our hideout, so put them to use. She slid her foot from side to side into the shoe until her toes felt comfortable. Mine didn't slide off, even though I was stomping around in the woods with them.

"You still play with dolls?" Cookie said. I was holding tight to that love doll still. "Girl, you a thirteen-year-old baby."

"Reminds me of my great grandma." I hugged the doll, then put it into the back waistband of my shorts. Then an idea fell upon Cookie.

"Let's take a walk down Saturday Street," she said.

"I don't know. I don't want—do those guys come nigger knocking on Saturday Street?"

"Girl, you so scared. You really are a big old baby," she said. "Carry dolls and afraid of some—well," she said looking at my face and then softening, "Maybe you're right." She had gotten better about not ribbing me like she had at first. She flopped down, looking like she'd given up on something.

The truth of it, I really was ready for an adventure. I had expected her to argue me into going. Summertime had draped itself over us in a sexy way. I knew Ivory Jones liked to hang around with that Johnny, the guy Cookie had her eye on. And I knew Johnny lived on Saturday Street.

"Oh, come on," I said, "Let's go down there. I want to practice wearing these high heels, how about you?" Maybe we'd see Ivory Jones with eyes like Brazilian amber.

"Let's go," she said, jumping up, brushing off her shorts.

We clomped down the dusty dirt road that cut through the swamp of green lily pads and paper white flowers. We passed purple thistles in the brush by the road, the bullfrogs chugging lazy and low. Cookie sang *I held my nose I took a drink, I didn't know if it was day or night, I started kissing everything in sight.* We were falling sideways off the high heels every now and again, cussing, and laughing a lot. We finally turned onto Saturday Street.

The road dusted up from dirt, and the houses sat small, painted colorful as a wheelbarrow full of flowers—bright blue or pink or yellow. We were in a colored neighborhood where white people could zoom their cars through.

Cookie took my arms with her hand, and we stood at the end of the dirt street, just looking. "I hope the VooDoo Lady ain't home," she said.

"Who-oo?" I said.

"VooDoo Lady," she said, pointing to the red house down about the middle of the rutted road. "She ain't nothing to be scared of. She's real skinny and bushy haired. Look like a Q-tip that done blew up," she said. She started walking down Saturday Street, pulling me along with her.

"One time she went over to the Post Office," she said, pulling my arm as she skipped along. "Held her gourds like they was Aaron's rod, holding them gourds up over her shoulders, shaking them so they rattled like a snake. And when the postman say, 'Can I help you,' she say, 'No, you got evil thoughts in your head.'"

I stopped, which yanked Cookie to a halt, and I said, "Maybe we should go back now. These high heels kind of hurt." She pulled me on, and continued her story. "So she goes to the other guy and she shakes them gourds at him. He laughs at her. Then, half hour later, he doubled over with the stomach ache and flat on his back at the hospital. Pendicitis."

"Well, let's go back, then," I said, stopping like a horse and pulling around the other way slow.

"Come on, don't be a chicken liver," Cookie said, tugging me the other way. I let her take us clomping and falling off the high heels down Saturday Street. Both of us in shorts, wobbling down the dusty dirt street in gold sparkly and turquoise satin high heels. We matched the houses, painted in dark coral and mustard yellow and lime green with dark shutters and tiny windows you could hardly see into or out of. Wood houses with sitting porches on the front.

Then we got to Johnny's house. Two stories high, red-bricked, and bigger than the ones on either side. Johnny and Ivory Jones were scrubbing circles of bubbles like clouds on Johnny's daddy's sky blue Valiant. My stomach went upside down.

"Hooo, girl," Johnny said when he stood up, looking straight at Cookie. He was sixteen and cute with a big smile. He could not take his eyes off Cookie. Her boobies already looked like ice cream licked down some in the cones. I got a shock knowing all of a sudden that my boobies were starting to push out more than ever, more than chocolate kisses.

I saw Ivory Jones staring at me up and down, with a look cool as Alaska with his eyes like Brazil. I got a weak-kneed feeling come over me, and it felt scary and good at the same time. I could not help myself—I wanted him to keep looking. So I stuck my hip out to one side and pushed my chest out a little. I did not know exactly what I was doing, but I wanted more.

"What y'all doing down here?" Ivory Jones said. His arm muscles looked carved. Skin smooth like my mama's nightgown. But a wrinkled up frown sat on his face, kind of like a daddy.

"Whatever we want to do," Cookie said to Ivory Jones. "You ain't my boss, boy."

"She your sister, the one them old women call 'bogish,' ain't she?" Johnny said. Ivory Jones didn't say anything, but nodded his head and smirked. Johnny looked back at Cookie. "Come on over here and help me foam up this car," he went on. I am not sure Ivory Jones liked this, but by the way his Brazil eyes half closed, my stomach did the twist. Cookie grabbed me by the arm again, and we tottered up the driveway.

"I'm gonna be a singer in Chicago," Cookie announced to Johnny. "You want to hear me sing?"

"I heard you sing in church. Go on, now, sing us some sweet music, something with soul," Johnny said. Cookie stepped back from the rest of us, pulled her wisps of hair out of her face and cleared her throat. She broke out into *Baby baby sweet baby*. Singing and swaying, like she forgot we stood on this earth at all. She could act like she was entertaining for the stars and moon children. I did not know how she did that so natural.

I wobbled over to where Ivory Jones was scrubbing the car like clouds on the bluebird Valiant. He stood up and squirted the hose on the wet car, looked at me, then dropped that hose and walked to the other side of the car. With his arms folded, he leaned on the dry side of the car near the trunk. Cookie sang in her low alto, and twitched her hips for Johnny. Every now and again Johnny would grin, clap and say, "Sing it, girl."

I clomped over to Ivory Jones and leaned on the car next to him. Almost touching. He did not move a muscle. My heart pounded in my chest. I could feel the love doll pressing against the car and my back. I folded my arms like his and leaned back further on the car. Then he opened his arms and put his hand around behind my back and rested his hand on the car trunk behind me. I could smell some kind of piney cologne smell and his man skin.

"Looks like those high heels hurt," he said, his eyes dancing. I shrugged, then agreed yes, they did. "Why don't you take them off, then." So I shucked them on the trunk of the car. I was a lot shorter then, way shorter than Ivory Jones.

"Have you seen the garden in my mama's room?" I asked him.

"Yeah," he said. "She's good with those plants. Might just help make her well. The painting, too."

"You think so?" I said. "You really think she can get well?"

"Well, yeah," he said, "I think she's well enough already." I moved over a little closer to him, touching his hip to my side. Our sides touched, and my heart pounded and the butterflies danced in my belly. I stood letting it thrill me, his smell all up in my nose.

"I think she's getting well myself," I said, trying to stay collected. "But I think my daddy is trying to take her money." I surprised myself, telling him all this. I had not even told Cookie yet. Maybe because he acted so grown up, had turned sixteen and shaved.

"What makes you say that?" he said.

All of a sudden, Cookie had stopped singing. I watched Johnny and Cookie walk beside Johnny's house. They started kissing to beat the band. Their mouths were open and busy. I turned bright red. Cookie was getting her first kiss and looking like she went way on past just liking it. Ivory Jones did not see them and was looking at me with his Brazil eyes and chuckling.

"Come on over here," he said. He took me by the hand around the other side of the car. His hand surprised me with its softness and hardness at the same time. "You ever kissed a boy?" he said, standing beside me leaning up on the side of the car.

I shook my head no, studying his pretty pink lower lip, then his pretty brownish upper lip. "But you can show me," I said. I could not believe I had said it. Then he pulled his head back away and studied me close.

"What do you want with me?" he said, looking at my eyes. "You just curious?" I didn't know what to say. I didn't know myself. Everything waited inside me. Waited to explode like

Easter Sunday at church during the Gloria in Excelsis song. I shook my head no.

"It's you I want to kiss. That's all. What do you want with me?" I said.

He ignored that, and said, "And what do you think your daddy would do if he ever found out?"

"Cut off my tongue, probably," I said. "And burn you at the stake." He laughed and moved around in front of me, putting his arm on my waist. I thought I would bust, it felt so good. I put my hands on his arms.

"I'll show you if you can keep it a secret," he said.

"I can keep secrets," I said. He leaned over and put his warm lips on mine. Then he backed away. "You're trying too hard now. Just relax. Let your mouth relax. You're all puckered up. That ain't the way you kiss." He ran his finger over my lips. "Soft, keep them soft." I put my arms around his neck, closed my eyes and tilted my head up and tried to relax. I felt his lips on mine. I thought of the inside of a peach that's been warmed up by the sun, the shock of its tartness all warm, then the sweet juice. I do not know how long we stood there practicing a kiss, kissing, whatever we were doing, but it only made me wish for more. He seemed to like it, too, because he didn't stop, and he pressed up next to me.

All of a sudden, out came the VooDoo Lady from her scarlet fever red house next door. "Ahaaah Ohaaa," she hollered. A rattling noise went with it that sounded like an excited rattlesnake. She held gourds over her head and shook them fast. "Take you crazy girl baby out of here and wash that car on the street before I hexes on you. Get the girl baby," she said. Then, I hardly could believe what she did next—she started swinging a chicken's foot tied with red string over her head. Every last word she said was nonsense, and I understood it all.

I pushed away from Ivory Jones.

"I gotta go," I said. Those white guys would surely be driving by any second, and what would they do this time? What had I been doing down here? My daddy *would* cut off my tongue. Nobody kissed colored guys. Just like you should not feel a woman's butt like it was melons if she was not your wife. I put my hand to my mouth. It had tasted delicious. I had to go.

"It's just the VooDoo Lady," Ivory Jones said. I could tell by his look he did not want me to go. "She won't hurt you."

"I gotta go," I said, backing away.

"Girl, come back here," Ivory Jones said soft. "You are some kind of skittish." But I backed away up the direction of Saturday Street. "Don't forget your shoes," Ivory Jones said, his face scrunched.

"Come on back here, girl," I heard Cookie say. "Chicken liver baby." But I was already running out past the driveway. I grabbed those gold sparkle shoes and shoved my feet into them, clomping my hurting toes down the dirt road of Saturday Street, hearing Ivory Jones' voice lilting across the swamp, using his big brother voice on Cookie, saying, "Aunt Jesse's going to get all over you."

"No, she ain't. You the one's been kissing on a white girl. Just look what you done," Cookie said. "Just look."

"Go on, now, and catch her," Ivory Jones said. I had never heard him sound so bossy.

But I did not care. I ran past the Saturday Street stop sign where I did not stop. I ran past the rotting damp smell of dirt, past the standout purple thistles, past the bullfrogs and lily pads. There, one of my shoes flipped off, and I fell on the hard clay road. I stood up and took off the other shoe, not going back for the first one. I did not look back.

I put the one shoe back on and hobbled fast up the rocky

slick road of clay, hoping no car would go by. I passed Cookie's and Ivory Jones' driveway with that one high heel pinching my toes. The one gold heel shoe was smeared in mud now, so I shook that shoe off and kept racing.

When I got to the hideout, I took the love doll out of my back waistband and buried my face in her and lay down on my stomach. I realized I wanted Ivory Jones and me to be two halves of an orange, a highway that went both ways. I wanted two shoes that fit. But then I had a flash of how people gave Cookie looks on the bus, I bet it equaled the same treatment for Ivory Jones. I was not supposed to love this boy-man. He'd had all kinds of kisses from girls by now, probably a lot better at kissing relaxed than me.

I walked to the creek to splash water on my face, then back to the hideout where I held my doll and laid on my back looking at the green leaves that made an umbrella over the hideout. Holding my love doll tight tight tight, thinking about Cookie kissing Johnny for the longest minute in the world. Then here she came barefoot, holding one broken gold shoe and singing *I started kissing everything in sight.* She danced around with my shoe, flinging mud and shaking her hips all around crazyish, looking all sexy like somebody you see on the *Amateur Hour* on Sunday night TV.

Then we looked at each other and for no reason at all we both started laughing and rolling on the ground like water running down the creek between our two houses.

19

People mostly judge the book by its cover, so I dressed in my finest daytime shift. A red and white one with a square neck, and dark school loafers, it being the second Monday after the end of school. I found one of Mama's purses to match. I even put a ten dollar bill in the purse. I put the bank book in, too.

I took the bus up to the bank. I'd find out as much as I could about that Declaration of Incompetence. And speaking of growing up, I had discovered that I already needed a bigger bra. I was suddenly expanding out like a volcano eruption. I planned to stop by Penney's to pick one up. If time permitted, I would stop by Elinor's Flowers and buy Mama potted zinnias. She loved the hot pink ones.

At the Tharpe Street stop, the morning sun was still flying up like a yellow canary. Two picketers held their signs and walked in a big circle. So early, I figured nobody was heckling them yet, and no police were in sight.

When I walked into the bank, the temperature was already rising into the fry-an-egg-on-pavement zone. Even at ten in the morning. Inside, though, it felt crisp cool with the air conditioning. I walked over to a teller with smooth brown hair, the smell of gardenias around her window.

"Please, Ma'am," I said. "I'd like to see Mr. Marshall." I'd looked it up and found out he was the bank president.

"Excuse me?" she said. She raised her eyebrows and sat

back, looking me over.

"Where is Mr. Marshall, please?" I said.

"He's a very busy man," she said. "I'm not sure—"

"I need to see him," I said, trying to hold my shoulders back and high, and lift my chin up. "I need to see Mr. Marshall, please."

"Well, all right," she said. "I'll see what I can do." She walked across the lobby and entered a glassed-in office. She talked to some man who looked kind of familiar. He was too pretty for a man, with neatly styled dark hair and a straight long nose. Too neat if you ask me. His office smelled like the paper room at school.

He stood up and looked at his watch and gave me one of those smiles that wasn't really a smile. I had seen him before. He'd attended Daddy's hospital office party last Christmas with his wife. Now he was giving me that up and down look that I'd noticed Ivory Jones and other boys giving me lately. He was looking so hard at my boobies that I looked down to see if I had a spot on my dress. I did not, so I folded my arms over my chest and sat down.

"What can I do for you? Is it Rayann Wood? Al's daughter? I recognize you, I think." He sat down himself, and I remembered him. He'd brought his wife to the office party, but he'd stood in the kitchen real close to that friend of Rheta's, the cowgirl outfit one, telling her about his record albums or something. Then he'd led her back into the bigger party where I'd watched him slide his hand down her back. I swear, didn't his wife have her eyes open?

"Yes, Sir," I said. "I want to know what a Declaration of Incompetence is and how you get one." He raised his eyebrows again.

"You must be talking about your daddy's legal matters," he

said. He gave me a piercing look.

I looked right back into his eyes. "Yes, Sir," I said. "Who decides whether she's incompetent? I'm just wondering. Curious, you know."

"The court decides," he said. "Your daddy's lawyer requests it, then three people have to interview your mother. Decide whether she's capable of taking care of herself or not." That would be Lucky, Daddy's lawyer, I thought. Now I remembered. Lucky had mentioned hunting with Ray Marshall. He was looking at my chest again. "You're mighty young to march in here like this." I folded my arms over my chest and stood up.

"My mama says I'm precocious," I said, and walked out. I didn't know if I was more scared he'd tell Daddy, or more just plain mad, mad enough to spit in his face. I walked out the lobby to catch the bus to see Mama.

Instead, I walked up a block and crossed the street to Penney's where I bought myself two bras, slipping into the changing booths. I hoped not to be noticed as I tried them on. The sales lady told me I had not even needed to get a training bra the first time, I could have just skipped on over to the next size. Fine, I thought, thanks for noticing. I changed out of the Woolworth's bra in Penney's dressing room and slipped on the new one, stuffing the other two into the red purse after I paid cash for the new ones.

Next, I bought Mama the zinnias. I didn't know whether or not to tell Mama all I'd just learned. Maybe if one lawyer could draw up a lie on paper about Mama, another one could draw up a paper that told the truth.

I needed somebody to talk to but who, I wondered as I walked to the bus stop with the flowers, my new bra looking weird, jutting me out more. Seemed like every blessed body in town was friends with Daddy.

When I got on the bus, I remembered Ivory Jones would be working in the afternoon. I hadn't laid eyes on him since I had run away from Saturday Street that day, but I thought, well, you got to see him sometime, Rayann. At least I'd have on a proper dress. I fished around in that red purse and sure enough, found a lipstick. I smeared a little Raspberry Relish on my mouth, and wiped most of it off. Then I tried putting it on again, but lighter this time. I looked in the mirror where the bus driver was always glancing to see to the back of the bus. I surprised myself. I looked like Mama in the eyes and cheekbones. Homelier, but the resemblance surprised me.

When I arrived at the hospital that evening, the two policemen stood at the doorway again, even though no trouble had occurred at all. Not till I got to the 5C ward. Up there, a knot of hospital workers stood around at the nurse's station talking. When I pushed through the doors, everybody turned and looked. Then they scattered fast as sand crabs. The evening nurse in charge, Delmara, came over to me.

"You look pretty today, Rayann," she said, guiding me away from the station where all the people had stood. "I need to tell you something," she said, looking concerned. "Before you go in."

"Okay," I said. "Go ahead." My back tensed up.

"Your mother," she said. "She's been crying all day."

"Is that all?" I said. My back relaxed. She looked at me funny.

"Well, since she woke up, she's just cried and wept buckets," she said. "Nobody, not even serious medication has stopped her from crying. She should be asleep, but somehow—" She broke off and looked down the corridor

"She's sad," I said. Delmara looked at me like how obvious

can you get. But wouldn't anybody who'd found out the person she loved the most was trying to get rid of her so he could have her money? Besides, I knew Mama. Her true feelings followed way behind big things happening. I said, "She knows Daddy doesn't love her, so she's sad." Delmara backed up, surprised I'd talk about her boss and my daddy that way. Then she took a sigh.

"Well, I'm afraid it's even more complicated than that," she said. "She seems to be back in a state. The doctor wants her sedated. He also wants her visitations to be limited. That is, she's to see no one."

"I've *got* to see her," I said. "I won't upset her."

"I know," she said. "But don't come up here during day shift," she said raising her eyebrows. "They take doctors literally. And be sure not to say anything to your mother to make it worse. I've never seen her quite like this."

Sane, you mean, sane and sad, I thought as I went into the room full of beautiful green plants and colorful flowers. "Mama?" I said. She was lying on her bed on her side, her back to the door. I set the zinnias down at the entrance. She turned to look at me, her face blotched in shades of red, but she was not crying. "You okay?" I said, walking towards the bed slowly.

"Oh, you've got my red purse," she said, her voice weak and hoarse. "You look nice in that dress." I let out a sigh. She was her old self. Just a really sad one this time, not scared like when she went crazy.

"They're worried about you," I said, sitting down on the bed. "The nurses and all."

"Oh, I know it," she said. "I can't stop crying." With that, she teared up again. "Your father...I don't know what happened, Rayann. There was a time when he loved me." She started to sob for a minute. "He really did. I guess I wasn't a very good wife."

"Mama, stop it," I said. "Remember everything I told you that he's doing now. Come on." I thought for a minute. "I shouldn't have told you he's trying to take your money." She dabbed at her eyes.

"You know, you're right," she said. "You have to keep reminding me. I tend to remember the good times, like that Christmas we had when we first moved into the house, remember? And we put up the silver on the tree—" she started to cry. "I don't know what I'm going to do," she said. "I just don't know what to do."

I felt scared, then impatient. "Mama, that doesn't sound like the daddy I know." I felt guilty for saying such a thing. I loved my daddy, even though he didn't take good care of me, and he was trying to get rid of Mama.

"What do you mean?" she said.

"Maybe he's bad for your health." Guilty guilty guilty.

"But you don't know," she said, "You don't know what it's like for a woman without a man." She was sobbing again. "You just don't know. All our friends, well, they're his friends. They'll never invite me to anything. They'll not want me to go out with them. I'll just be alone." This made me want to kick the side of the bed.

"Well, if they don't invite you just cause you don't have him there, then they never were your friends," I said. "But they will invite you. You'll see."

"You don't understand how it is for a grown woman," she repeated, "without a man."

"Yes, I do," I said. I didn't. But I was remembering the way that bank man was looking at me like I was not a human being at all, just something kind of in his way except to look at like I did not have any clothes on at all. It somehow seemed the same.

I wondered if that was how Cookie or Ivory Jones or Miss Jesse felt when they rode the bus and the driver collected their money. Not like they didn't have any clothes on, but like they weren't human beings. Just kind of like bugs you want to flick away from your face. Like the "nigger knocker" boy—how he looked at me and Cookie, too.

"Are you taking medicine?" I asked. She opened a drawer, and I peered inside.

"Look in my makeup bag," she said, smiling through her tears. "Go on. Look." I did, and saw about fifty pills and capsules, some small, some big, some in ovals and others big and round, some orange, white, green, blue and yellow. They filled the bottom of the bag.

"Oh, my god," I said. "That's a lot of medicine."

"I'm not taking it," she said. "They want to give me a shot of Haldol, but I don't want it." Haldol, I knew from just hanging around the hospital, sedated you silly, so you didn't know what in the heck you were doing or saying. Especially an injection.

"Then stop crying," I said. "You've got to stop!" I thought hard. How would I get her mind onto something that made her happy, the way she used to do me when I was little. "Look what I brought you." I pointed to the zinnias I'd left by the door.

"Zinnias," she said. "You know how I love those. Let me get some water on them." She got up and got busy with her plants, talking to them like pets. Gradually she sniffed a little less, checking the soil, sniffling a little less, and spraying the leaves with a spray bottle full of water.

I slipped out to see about getting dinner so I could maybe keep her from crying again. That's when I saw him—Ivory Jones. Standing at the station. Most of the other people except him and the charge nurse had scattered. I stopped cold, then started sweating at the neck. I could tell he'd been standing there a while. He was playing with a paper clip he'd undone by the time I got to the station. He looked up, and then tried to look all casual. Or maybe it was me trying to look casual. But I was not. I gulped and said Hey, and tried to smile.

He nodded and stood up straight, checking out my shoes, my dress and my lipstick. We could not really talk too much anyway in public, but he made sure I saw him raise his eyebrows over my dressed-upness. I told the aide on duty that I would like to eat dinner with Mama, and to please not give her a shot, because she had stopped crying.

"She's just sad, anyway," I said. "She needs to cry."

The nurse just nodded and glanced at Ivory Jones. He cleared his throat.

"Miss Wood," he said. I thought he was talking about Mama, so I just stood there looking at him stupidly.

"He's talking to you," the nurse's aide said to me.

"Huh?" I said.

"Miss Wood, if you'd like, I can take you downstairs and you can tell the kitchen you'd like to have dinner here," he said in a formal way.

"I can call down, Ivory Jones," the aide said. By his face, I could tell he wanted to talk to me.

"Well, that's okay," I said. "I need to tell them I have a special diet tonight." I knew about special diets from hearing Daddy talk. "Yeah, if you'll take me down there—I know where the cafeteria is, but not the kitchen," I said to Ivory Jones.

So we headed down to the doorway. Once past it, I hit the elevator, but he shook his head no. He motioned for me to use the stairs. He glanced up and down the corridor. Nobody around, so we practically dove in.

We headed down the stairs to the fourth floor, and he

stopped midway where the stairs took a turn. "You all dressed up," he teased. "Where you going in that uptown outfit and that red lipstick?" I rolled my eyes. I could feel my hands sweating, and my heart thumping underneath that new bra. Then he got that worried wrinkle I'd noticed in his brow. "Your mother's doctor wants her moved to Goodwood Manor," he said, so low I barely heard him. I took a step closer to him.

My heart sunk. Patients staying in Goodwood Manor were nearly always on their way to Chattahoochee. "But how can he?' I said, leaning back on the wall.

"That doctor's in cahoots with your daddy," Ivory Jones said, peering up and down the steps. "I saw them headed out together yesterday afternoon with their golf clubs." Just then the fourth floor stair door squealed open, and Ivory Jones motioned for me to head down towards the noise just as he headed up the steps. "Go," he said, when I did not move. So I walked slowly down the steps, even though my legs were weak from this news and from standing so close to Ivory Jones. I walked slow while a nurse walked up the stairs past me, and out the door of the fifth floor.

Ivory Jones caught up with me, and that's when I knew. He really did care about me. He was risking things for me. My heart bloomed heat.

"Ivory Jones," I said in a whisper. "About the other day—"

"Shh," he said, looking up and down the stairs. "Girl, you crazy? Don't talk about that here."

"No, I am not crazy, and neither is my mama," I said. Too loud, probably.

"We can't talk about that now," he said. He took my sweating hand and gave it a squeeze and then let go. He looked at me with a study. "You going to keep a secret, aren't you?" I nodded. "I looked at your mama's chart. They've written orders to give her a Haldol injection as needed. That way, they'll keep her doped up. Then they planning to move her soon."

I leaned back against the wall. "I can't let that happen," I said. "They think it's worse, when she's just sad. She's realized Daddy's trying to get her money." Then I told him about finding out about the Power of Attorney and the Declaration of Incompetence.

"So then it all makes sense," Ivory Jones said, looking at the wall. "He's having her sent over there to make it look serious." He went on. "You know that day head nurse?"

I nodded. "Miss No Coffee?"

"Yeah. I don't trust her. And did you know the social worker came by?"

"What did she say?"

"She looked at your mama's paintings," he said. "She said your mama's crazy. She recommended Good Manor, too, like Dr. Indley. Next step—" he shrugged his shoulders and shook his head— "Chattahoochee."

I sunk against the wall. My mind raced. That Dr. Indley, he'd probably tell Daddy all the wild things Mama had done. I had tried and tried to forget them, so when they came back to me, they flooded me with shame. That time she got drunk, then naked, and Daddy had to chase her all over to get her into the tub. The time she answered the door for the mailman in her underwear. I remembered them when I thought about how Daddy or anybody might think her crazy. Sure he could say she was crazy. Sure he'd made orders to send her off.

You couldn't stop doctors' orders. Doctors in a hospital were like Zeus in the heavens or Neptune in the seas. No—no, they weren't. I remembered once when I was hanging around in the pharmacy, and that doctor had ordered the exact wrong drug for a cancer patient. Instead of something that would help with the pain, he ordered a stimulant. So the pharmacist called the doctor, and got the doctor's permission to change the order himself by starting a new doctor's order sheet. They weren't gods if you could change their words. Their orders. Their written orders.

"I know," I said, pushing up from the wall. "When they're giving meds, you make sure the nurse's station is empty," I whispered. I stepped up to look at the stairs, and then down. I went on. "Then you make sure her chart is on the desk. And then I'll go change it."

"Change it? You can't do that. It's illegal," he said. Then his voice pitch went up high. His eyebrows raised up. "You get caught, and you could go to *jail.*"

His voice made me scared. Then mad. "No, *you* might go to jail, but not me," I said. He got a hurt look in his eyes and stared at the floor. I'd told a terrible truth the wrong way. "I didn't mean—uh, I'm sorry," I said.

The door opened again with a high-pitched squeak, and I walked slowly down to the third floor, while somebody on the fourth passed me by fast. I felt sure Ivory Jones would stomp away and not come back.

Then there he stood, beside me on the landing between the second and the third floors. "There you are," I said grabbing his upper arm with my hand and squeezing. He shook me off.

"Don't do that," he said. He backed away and pointed down the stairs, so we began walking again slow. "I can get everybody out of there," he said as we headed down, "but I don't know *nothing* about you changing no chart, you hear me?" We stopped at the landing and stood face to face. "You're right. I could go to jail," he said.

"Put her chart on the desk," I whispered. "I'm a great forger. It's my talent." He shook his head 'No.' "Please," I said. "This is life and death, Ivory Jones. This is not playing."

"I know that," he said. "And what about *my* life and death? Does that matter to you at all, Miss Wood?" The good clean smell of his piney cologne spilled over me, and I so respected him for his standing up to me. I wished I hadn't asked him to stick his neck out for me. I flushed and didn't say a thing. The door of the second floor opened, and we headed on down together, all the way to the first floor without a word.

Mama had stopped crying, and had bathed. She had not put on any makeup except fresh lipstick, and she looked serene as an angel. We ate vegetable beef soup and cornbread as we sat on the floor again, and then played cards for a while. Mama told me she tossed and turned at night, not sleeping, so I went to the gift shop to find her a good book. Anything could get her upset again. The gift shop offered only romantic stories or cowboy stories, so I passed those up and went to the magazines. I bought her a *Time* with pictures of Martin Luther King in Alabama and Georgia on the inside. In the surgical waiting room, I found a book about this lady who'd traveled around the world and had her own airplane, so I took it.

I kept checking my watch for 8 p.m. when they gave pills. Then I took the magazine and book back to Mama's room and waited for medication hour, when I knew nurses would leave the desk area. Meanwhile, Mama dozed off to sleep reading the magazine.

At 8, I walked slow and quiet, toe to heel like my grandma had showed me years ago, the way Indians walked in the woods to keep the animals from hearing them. The nurse's station stood empty. When I got to the desk, I peered over.

There it sat—Mama's chart. A pen right next to it. "Thank you, Ivory Jones," I whispered. I looked one way up the hall, the other way down the hall. Then I eased around to the other side of the desk, and pretended I was just sitting in the nurse's station doodling.

I opened her chart and saw at the top of a fresh page Dr. Indley's scribbles. "Haldol I.M. 10 p.m., PRN agitation. Evaluate PRN." I knew what that meant, having wandered around a hospital being nosy all my life, and learning how to read doctors' hen scratch for writing; give her a Haldol shot I.M., that meant intramuscularly, at bedtime, then as needed when she cries or gets upset; evaluate PRN, that meant as needed.

I tore the page off with all four copies that went with it and folded it, then stuck it in the back strap of my new bra, which was not easy to do without it bumping out. I finally folded it two times and slid the whole thing under the arm part of the bra. I knew where each copy was supposed to go—one stayed with her chart, one went to the pharmacy, one to the doctor, and the other for permanent records.

I found a new sheet and wrote like Dr. Indley, like little mountains. Like I said before, I was good at forging signatures. I'd copied people's handwriting at school during play periods. "Haldol P.O. PRN agitation." Then I signed the doctor's signature and date. The nurses had so many charts to keep up with every day, and the shifts changed every 8 hours, so the night nurse wouldn't know that I'd changed anything.

The orders still said, Haldol, but Haldol by mouth. That way Mama could drop it into the bottom of her makeup bag with the assortment of other pills. And it said "as needed for agitation." Nothing about an evaluation. It would take Dr. Indley several days, a week, maybe even longer for him to think up something more sly than that. At least that was what I hoped. In my head I thanked Ivory Jones for risking so much.

I went and told Mama good night, and left the hospital as the stars had barely started to twinkle, before the last bus headed away, before the sun had refused to give all its orange in the clouds away to the twilight.

20

That Saturday, anything akin to cool early summer weather had taken its leave. Cookie and I sat on Star's bare back snacking on boiled peanuts that Miss Jesse had made. Margot honked from the ground, begging for the soft salty nuts. I dreamed of swimming in Wakulla Springs, which was about as cold as the water got in Florida, down into the low seventies. But Cookie couldn't go with me, and I didn't have anybody to take me anyway. Still, I'd bought a two-piece bathing suit I was itching to wear. I was afraid maybe Ivory Jones thought of me as just this punky little girl. Maybe if he saw me in my new suit, he wouldn't think that. But he'd have only been allowed to go to the Springs if he'd gotten a job in the kitchen, or outside chopping wood, or around the hotel cleaning the floors.

"I wish we could go swimming," I said. "Cool off."

"I wish we could get a drink of liquor," Cookie said.

"Liquor?" I said. "What for?"

"Oh, I don't know. It's Saturday evening, *that's* what for," she said, steering Star's nose towards her house. "Let's go get some lunch, or dinner, or a snack." So I followed her to Miss Jesse's house. I stood in the hot front yard with Star while Cookie went inside to see if I could eat lunch there.

Miss Jesse and Ivory Jones were having some heated words in the living room. I scooted up close to the front steps to listen.

"You don't need to be getting in all that mess, unless you want to lose your job," Miss Jesse was saying.

"I might have some what's called real money and a better job some day if more of us would stand up and fight for what's fair," Ivory Jones said, loud. I'd never heard him shout before.

"I don't know what you think you'd get out of this here thing," Miss Jesse said. Star munched on grass, and his breath smelled fragrant, all grassy and molasses warm. "All these college kids raising cane. I understand what they trying to do, now, but they don't have to *stay* here. You do," she said. "Son, you could lose your job. Worse, get sent to jail," she said in a high pitch. Jail. I could go to jail, he could go to jail. It had only been a couple of days since the doctor's order had gotten changed, but I hadn't heard anything about it. Then Miss Jesse lowered her voice pitch and said, "And you some kind of fool if you don't know what that's like. All you got to do is read your daddy's letters."

"Auntie, you don't hear *nothing* the Reverend Steele says?" Ivory Jones said with a pretend patience. "All that stuff about suffering and filling the jails."

"You know that Mrs. Steele—she can't get no teaching job cause of all that. They'll punish you some way or the other. Let them college kids fill up the jailhouse if they want to," she said. "I don't want you down there, though. Now just let it be, nephew. Let it be."

"Auntie—"

"Don't you Auntie me," she said, sternlike. "I catch you at one of them demonstrations, I *will* tan your hide. You ain't too old for that." I could just about imagine Cookie snickering at the thought of it. "Nobody under my roof goes out looking for trouble, you understand? You saw what they done to that goose. The good Lord knows they wouldn't think two shakes of a rattler's tail before they did something like that to *you*." It was quiet, and then I heard a murmur out of Ivory Jones.

The screen door slapped the back door frame as he walked out. So I took Star around back to avoid Miss Jesse's yelling, and to see Ivory Jones.

He was drinking a glass of cold tea, sitting on the back step. He did not have on a shirt. Boy, did he look good. He was full of muscles but skinny in the right places, too. I wanted to put my chest up next to his. I wanted to kiss him again and again, the way it made me feel all over. I wished we could go swimming together.

"Hey," I said.

"Well, hey, troublemaker," he said. "You ain't got caught by the hospital yet?"

"Well, no," I said, shifting from foot to foot, and then tying Star up at the mulberry tree. I got her some water. She sounded like a giant mosquito when she sucked up that water through her lips. I cleared my throat. "I wrote my own prescription," I said. "Haldol p.o., prn." He nodded and looked up at the cloudless sky. I went on. "I appreciate what you did and all," I said, looking at his lips and trying to act sexy. "I really do." He waved his hand and looked back towards the door where Miss Jesse and Cookie were having loud words about Cookie's messy room.

"Just too hot, that's all," he murmured. Then he shouted towards the door, "Why don't you go on uptown with Johnny, Aunt Jesse?" Then he glanced at me and said, "It'd cool her off a little. A walk around Woolworth's in the air conditioning. She'd have a heyday in the pillow department. That woman loves pillows more than she loves God." He laughed a little bit. Then he drained his glass.

"I wish we could go swimming," I said, looking up at him in that way I'd seen women on the TV stories look at men when they were flirting it up.

"Swimming, huh?" he said, all cool like. "Little girl like you, you know how to swim?" I stood up tall and stuck out my chest some and kicked my hip out to the side.

"Seems like you need to cool off your own self," I said. He snickered and put the glass down on the step. Just then Johnny pulled up in the rut road and honked the horn. Cookie went out to the car and started a play hand fight with him. Here came Miss Jesse, purse on her arm, shooing Cookie away.

"Get away from that window," Miss Jesse said. "I'm going to town. That's okay, Johnny?" He yes ma'amed her, though I knew he just wanted to stay and play hand fight games with Cookie.

Cookie came around back and said, "She's leaving to go downtown. You want a sandwich? Aunt Jesse said okay." I nodded.

"Well, come in here and make it," she said. "What do you think, I'm your maid?" Ivory Jones followed Cookie, so I followed the two of them inside to make a sandwich. "Bye, Aunt Jesse," Cookie called out as the car drove off. While we ate peanut butter and banana sandwiches, Ivory Jones poured some tea, sat down in a living room chair and tipped the chair back watching baseball on TV.

"Why don't you go talk to that Ellis fellow up at the Ellis State Bank," he said, not looking at us, but at the TV screen.

"Who you talking to?" Cookie said. "You got the worst manners on god's earth." Ivory Jones threw a pillow at her.

"Not you, Miss Queen of Everything," he said. "Believe it or not, I was not addressing her majesty. Rayann," he said.

"Yeah?" I said. Peanut butter filled my mouth.

"Mr. Ellis, he might know a banker's way or a lawyer or a doctor, somebody who can help you with this money thing."

"Do you know him?" I said.

"No, but we all do," he said, meaning colored people. "Before I got that money from your mama that was supposed to be from your daddy and going to Aunt Jesse—"

"You ain't supposed to tell that," Cookie said, her mouth fuller than mine even. Bread crumbs flew as she spit out the words. "You were sworn to secrecy, boy."

"She already told me, you fool," he said to Cookie. "Talk about bad manners. Look at that mess hanging out of your mouth." Then he said, "As I was saying, before Aunt Jesse got her new job, she was applying for a loan from Ellis State Bank. He loans money to people fallen on hard times, or just people can't get a loan elsewise, or people working for the movement. And people in trouble with the law. He knows a lawyer works for free. In some cases." He never took his eyes off the TV while he talked to me.

"What movement?' I said.

"Civil Rights," Cookie and Ivory Jones said at the same time.

"Oh," I said, feeling more stupid than ever. "But why would he help me?" I said.

He shrugged. "Don't know that he would. But I got a hunch he might know something you could try."

As I was thanking him, Cookie interrupted and said, "Ivory Jones, don't you have liquor stashed away somewhere?" He looked guarded all of a sudden, darting his eyes sideways at us.

"You been snooping?" he said.

"I saw you with a bottle one night," Cookie said. "I ain't no fool. Why don't you give us some?"

"I want to go swimming," I said, dreamy and flirty. "In the pool downtown by Tharpe Street."

"Closed," Ivory Jones said. "You know that. Them people won't let us swim there."

"Not me," I said. "Them." I wanted to see his chest again, to swim in the pool with him. When nobody could see us. "Hey," I said. "Why don't we go at night when nobody's around?"

"Can't we have some liquor, please, Ivory Jones," Cookie said. "I know you got some. Just a nip."

"What you talking 'nip.' Nip. Y'all is both bogish," Ivory Jones said. "Both wanting to get into a heap of trouble and hardly teenagers. Not but just peeking over into teenage, just practicing at it."

"Oh, cause you turned sixteen this year, you so grown up," Cookie said. "Well, you're good enough to kiss a thirteen-year-old, I seen that with my own two eyes." She pointed two fingers towards her eyes and swaggered. I looked away.

Ivory Jones leapt off the sofa to tackle Cookie. She raced out the back door, yelling that she was going to get the mail. She ran all the way down the hill from the house. Ivory Jones came back in and glanced at me, then laid down on the sofa to keep his eyes practically nailed to that baseball game, like it had to be the most interesting thing on this earth.

I finished up my sandwich and took my plate to the kitchen. Not because I had good manners or nothing, but I did not know what to say to Ivory Jones after the kissing talk that made him chase Cookie. Maybe he didn't like how young I was. I walked outside and patted Star. She was sweating bad. I took the garden bucket, filled it up with water from the pump in the back yard and poured it over her back. She shook her withers but did not shy away.

Myself, I felt hot enough to just combust from the inside out. Then I stuck my head under the pump and let some water gush down over my head.

Next thing I knew, Cookie was bounding back up the drive, singing, *Baby, Now that I've found you I won't let you go.* She was leaping and jumping so that Star stepped away from her sideways, and Margot started honking.

"Ivory Jones! Ivory Jones!" she yelled, waving a letter around in her hand. She'd ripped the envelope open. She swung open the back screen door and shouted. "A letter from Daddy!" Ivory Jones tore out the back door, his eyes bright. He grabbed the envelope and opened up the carefully folded letter. His lips moved as he read.

Meanwhile, Cookie hopped her way over to me, picked me up, hugged me to her and twirled me around. "Daddy's gonna be free!" she said. "They're going to let him out! Early! Every time I feel the spirit!" Then she broke out into some gospel tune, *Every time I hear the music moving in my heart.*

One look at Ivory Jones' face led me to believe she had read the letter right. "Hot damn," he said. He and his sister said Hoo hoo!, hugged each other, twirling round and round. A bitter taste like metal crept into my mouth.

"We're going to Chicago. He's going to take me," Cookie yelled. "Finally, I get to go to Chicago. I'm gonna sing in his band, and do commercials, too. Get out of this tired little place." It hit me so hard, I sat down. I loved our woods and hideout. The molasses sweetness of sweaty Star. She thought of it all as a tired little place.

While they whooped it up, I watched and wished I felt so happy about it. But I tucked it away. I tried to get inside them and feel what they felt. Free. Their daddy free. I patted Margot's feathery back. A good, flying away feeling, free.

I knew already that Ivory Jones intended on staying with his Aunt Jesse to finish high school. There was talk that he could maybe even get accepted into a white college in Florida with his track running. I stood up and hugged them both.

"We got to celebrate this," Ivory Jones said, falling down on the grass near the horse.

"Where's your liquor?" Cookie said, flopping down beside him.

"Liquor? Girl, who you think you talking to, the package store delivery boy?" He was laughing, though.

"Let's go swimming, too," I tried, flopping down beside them. The clover and grass smelled good together, all greeny, and the clover was silky and cool.

"We got to wait till night time," Ivory Jones said.

"Night time?" Cookie said, and her shoulders sagged. "That's such a long time away."

"Meet tonight," he said, ignoring her whine. "At Johnny's. Say around nine," Ivory Jones said.

"Nine," Cookie said. "That's Aunt Jesse's bedtime."

"That's just what I'm saying. Wait till Auntie is sleeping, and then we go jooking," he said. He laughed and rolled around on the grass. "Daddy's free. I can't hardly believe it. One month. Wonder if he looks the same."

"Maybe he got fat," Cookie said, and we all laughed. "Okay, then," she said, rolling over to me and getting serious. "You got to come get me, cause I sure ain't going up there to get you." Usually we'd feel bad about this, but this afternoon, we laughed it away, and decided to meet in the middle at the hideout.

Everybody is cryin' they can't get a break, Tell me what's the matter? Everything seems to ache is what Cookie sang from the hideout. I made my way through the woods path of last year's pine straw, sweet gum and oak leaves. The crickets sang a chorus in the background. I held a flashlight, even though the moon lit the path through the trees above. I knew she was rehearsing for singing in the blues band with her daddy. Dreaming and singing.

"Johnny won't let no goose in that car," she said when she saw Margot with me. "And Ivory Jones said we ain't swimming." I climbed in the hideout and pulled up my shirt and showed her my new green swim suit top. The cicadas whirred an early evening song.

"We'll just see about that," I said. "And look," I said, and pulled Daddy's thin bourbon bottle out of the waist of my pants and held it out to her. It glooshed around in the bottle, almost sounding like low notes on a xylophone. I'd taken it from the liquor cabinet, about three-quarters full.

"Girl, you stole that?" she said, leaning up against the cool stone wall.

"Yep," I said. "The liquor, but not the bathing suit. You like it?" I danced around like a ballerina holding the bottle by the neck.

"Yeah, that's nice," she said. "What you brought the bottle for?"

"So we could have our own," I said, unscrewing the cap. "Just you and me. Come on, try it." I held it out for her.

"You try it first," she said, waving it away. So I smelled at the top. It wrenched my stomach and smelled poisonous.

"Blech," I said. "Here." I shoved it over her way.

"You going to be a baby?" she said. "Why'd you bring it if you're not going to drink it?"

I took a tiny sip. "Damn, it burns," I said. I could feel it fall from my throat down the chest and into my stomach, burning everything along the way. Even with that tiny swallow.

"You got to do better than that," Cookie said. "That was a baby sip."

So I put the bottle to my lips, tilted my head back, took a deep breath and gulped. I thought lava was tumbling down me. I coughed it up into my nose and throat, and gagged, and then heaved a cough so as not to get sick. "Oh, god," I said, "it tastes like sink cleaner."

"That's it," she said laughing. "My turn." She took the bottle and gave herself a sip.

"Huh uh. Baby sip. You got to do better than that," I said, mimicking her.

So she upended the bottle, and took two big swigs. Cookie's eyes watered as she held the liquor in her cheeks like a greedy squirrel with a whole feast of acorns. I laughed hard. I had started feeling just a little floaty and warm. She started laughing and the bourbon squirted all out of her mouth.

"Damn, girl, I can't be swallowing that nasty stuff and you laughing," she said. Then she took another smaller sip and another, and coughed. "Do taste like sink cleaner. Your turn," she said, handing it to me.

We took a few more sips and watched the sky go from deep blue to purple. Cookie went back to her song, *Baby even though you don't need me, you don't need me.* This time, the bourbon didn't burn as bad. Cookie looked at the wind up alarm clock she'd brought from home.

"We got to leave here in a few minutes if we gonna catch them. Down at Saturday Street," she said. "That's where we meet them."

"I'm going to miss you so bad," I said. "When you leave."

She looked over at me. We were both becoming just silhouettes in the night, but I knew I'd surprised her. Then she took another swig and said, "Oh, you'll be fine. You got my aunt and you got Ivory Jones. You got a lot."

"That's not the same, and you know it," I said, taking a swig myself. It wasn't burning too bad now. "School." I squeezed my face shut. In my mind I thought of all those clusters of big kids I'd seen standing out in front of the junior high before classes started. All their little groups dressing up for each other and talking about each other, all that.

"Aw, girl, you've been changing," she said. "You've loosened up. I bet you have lots of friends next year. And you got some meat to your bones, too, a little boobies." She laughed.

"Oh, shut up," I said. She hummed a little and the tree frogs started up their own chorus in the distance. "You've changed, too, I added. "You're nicer. More opened up." I thought about how she'd even listen to my radio station and sing songs I liked, and how she hardly ever teased me to my face anymore about being prissy. "Your singing is even better. Your voice is getting deeper, like a woman."

"You think people change?" she said, sliding her butt down the cool stones to sit. "Or stay the way they always were?"

"I don't know," I said, turning the flashlight off and on at the wall, and then looking up at the twilit sky slowly revealing itself. "Maybe both, huh?"

"Yeah, maybe both. Like the stars. Like your Mama," she said. "Now, she's changing, right? And, well. I'll see, maybe like my daddy."

"I hope your mama changes, too," I said. "You ain't heard anything about her?" I flicked the flashlight on.

"Girl, she roams," she said, waving her hand, the big shadow of it falling long fingered on the hideout wall. "She might be in New York, she might be in Cuba, she might even be in Chicago. Just no telling." All my jealousy of Cookie for leaving me vanished like her huge hand movements across the hideout wall. She went silent.

"I hope she stays in Chicago. Then you could meet up with her when you're singing blues in a bar somewhere," I said. "And she could get back with your daddy."

"Well, that's where she'd be, in some jook joint," Cookie

said, laughing rough. I wanted to change the subject from anything that might mess up our evening out, so I said what was on my mind.

"Well, here's the thing: I want to be blood brothers."

"Blood brothers?" she said, suspicious. "Girl, you always springing up stuff on me."

"You and me, blood brothers."

"You mean where you make yourself bleed and touch fingers and all that?" she said.

"Yeah," I said.

"Yeah, well, I'd lose a drop of blood for you." My insides relaxed. She stood and held out her hand to get me standing. "Come on, we got to go, or we'll miss our jooking ride. I'm gonna be *mad* if I miss that ride." I took her hand and stood up. I put the small bourbon bottle, about a third of the way empty now, back in my waistband, and turned the flashlight off, then back on.

As we walked down the road, I held the flashlight with one hand, and Cookie's hand with the other. We sang *I don't know why, but I'm feeling so sad. I long to try something I've never had,* even though Cookie said Billie Holiday didn't really sing blues. I did not care, I just loved hearing Cookie's voice singing whatever in the world. I told her so, too, and she did not say anything back, but kept right on singing. A little louder maybe.

Down on Saturday Street, the guys were already sitting in the sky-blue Valiant, both in the front seat. "It's about time," Ivory Jones said. His voice sounded a little slippery. "We was gonna go on without you."

"You better not be leaving me," Cookie said as she halted by his side of the car, peering in at Johnny, who was leaning his head back taking a swig of wine. "Y'all going to make us sit in the back?" she said.

"Girl, you want to catch the ride, you got to sit where we tell you," Johnny said.

"You know Rayann needs to duck down in case anybody sees her riding with us," Ivory Jones said. Then he took the half drunk wine bottle from Johnny and had a long drink.

"What's that got to do with me?" Cookie said, her hand on her hip.

"Get in," Ivory Jones said. "We'll trade later, and you can sit up front. You don't like that arrangement, you can find your bogish self another ride."

I pulled out the bottle and showed that good Kentucky bourbon to them. "I bet you'll take us if I give you some of this," I said, jumping up and down by the hood of the car, flashing it in front of the car windshield where both of them could get a look of it.

"Hoo, girl," Johnny said. "That's the good stuff. Stop that jumping, you want to break that frankincense and myrrh? Where you get that fine bourbon?"

"She stole it," Cookie said.

"Stole it?" Ivory Jones said.

"From my liquor cabinet at home," I said. "It's not as bad as it sounds."

"Girl, you bad enough," Ivory Jones said.

"She's bad," Johnny said. He held up their bottle of cheap wine. "Got to be badder than this, bro. Come here, girl, give me that bottle."

With that, Ivory Jones and Johnny starting hoo hooing and clapping, and Cookie and me got in the back seat. I handed the bottle into the front.

"Now don't drink all of it," Cookie said. "Save some for us, you old pigs."

They started drinking right away and did not really cough or gag like we had. Smooth, they both said, smooth going down.

"Come on, let's get going," Cookie said. "I don't want to be hanging around this tired old place. And turn on the radio."

"She the boss at your house?" Johnny asked Ivory Jones.

"She *thinks* she is," he said, turning around, swatting at Cookie.

"Give us that bottle," Cookie said, dodging his swing.

"Say please," Ivory Jones said, mimicking Miss Jesse. "Mind your manners."

"Please," she said. When she got the bottle, she added, "You stupid." He leaped back as if to take the bottle, but didn't really try to get it.

We rode down the dirt street, radio on to *Summer's here, and the time is right for dancing in the street.* Johnny turned the nose of the car out to Betty's Creek Road, then to Magnolia Road. That's when Ivory Jones turned around all solemn, lowering the radio volume, and gave me some instructions.

"Now if any cars come by—I mean any—you duck, soon as you see headlights. Got it?" he said.

"Got it," I said.

"We better go the back roads, Johnny," Ivory Jones said.

"Aw, come on, you tired ass brother," Cookie said. "I want to go downtown."

"Maybe later," Ivory Jones said, taking a long draw off the bottle. "After all the rednecks have gone to bed." Everybody laughed, and I felt lightheaded.

"Can we at least go over to the A & M?" Cookie said. She meant the black college across town.

"Can't do any harm at the college," Johnny agreed. "Let's go."

We sped past the old Floridan Hotel while I laid down on the floor looking up. The moon was nearly full, and the silhouette of the hotel loomed huge in the darkest sapphire sky.

"We're passing the Florida Theatre now," Cookie said, "so stay down." Black and white together went to the movies. It was just that colored people had to sit in the balcony. It got to baking hot-as-the-devil up there in the summertime, I heard.

"I'm hot, let's go swimming," I complained. But I was not unhappy. I was savoring the whole upside down trip uptown. Watching the huge old oak trees reach their hopeful way towards the moon. I laid upside down in a car with people I loved and was feeling like I might finally be a teenager. I thought of Mama and how she would disapprove of my drinking, my riding around with older black guys, maybe even of making friends with Cookie. Then it hit me. I was not my mama. I might look like her, but I was not her. Something in it gave me a magical feeling that shot through my arms and fingers and on out the window.

When we passed the state capitol, I sat up on the floor and stretched my neck to see the two coppery domes of the senate and the house gleaming in the moonlight. Then my stomach left me as we headed down the hill towards the south side of town. We passed Gramlings, the railroad tracks and Jojo's.

"Okay, you can get up now," Ivory Jones said, turning around in the seat. I sat up and the blood rushed away from my face. I felt dizzy savoring the sight of it all. The summer breeze on my face, brought up from the gulf just a ways down the road, felt like black silk in the night.

Just as we got to the college, Johnny turned off the radio and Cookie started belting out songs. We'd been passing the bottle from the front to the back. I began to sing with Cookie. The guys must have been feeling pretty good, cause even they started singing along with us.

Oh when the saints go marching in, oh when the saints go marching in, we sang, all of us, loud and sloppy. Sometimes we even harmonized, doing rounds with Cookie's bossy instructions. We made our way up the steep hill to the front of the campus singing it. Then we switched to something I didn't know that had one line I could follow in it, so I sang it with them, *I know I done you wrong.*

We drove around the campus, but didn't really see anybody much. Then we launched into *Jesus loves the little children, all the children of the world.* When we got to the next part, we sang the colors real loud: *Red and yellow, BLACK and WHITE, they are precious in his sight, Jesus loves the little children of the world.*

"Let's go over to State," Cookie said, which meant she wanted to drive by the white state college. So we breezed through the fountain area by the front of the school, circling it. A few couples sat out front, so I ducked while we passed through, even though people said the white college was turning liberal.

The first time colored people decided to stage a sit-in it had been just spitting distance from the fountain, right across the street and down the hill at the diner. White students had joined them at the protest, I'd heard from Ivory Jones. I could hear the shimmying sound of water falling as we drove around the fountain like a big slow merry-go-round. Cookie told Johnny that people were staring, so we headed back out towards Frenchtown.

Meanwhile we were almost done drinking the bourbon in the bottle. All through Frenchtown we sang *I don't even know how to kiss your lips...Are you ready...to fall in love...* The music was warming me and chilling me together, like the night.

We passed through Frenchtown, and ended up on Tharpe

Street. "Let's go by the pool," I said.

"One track minded," Cookie said.

"I just want to swim. So bad," I said. I was swimming in my head and molassesy all over. My fingers felt a little numb to the touch. "Please let's swim."

"Pull over, Johnny, I need to pee," Cookie said. So Johnny slowed down to look for a place to stop.

"You better make it quick," Ivory Jones said. His voice sounded kind of fuzzy and playful. "We haven't got all night for you to goof around going pee."

"Hush up, you ain't let me ride in the front all night. So stop trying to be my boss, cause you're *not*," Cookie said. "Pull over, Johnny."

We pulled into the dirt road by the swimming pool. Johnny stopped the car with a squeak of the brakes. Moss hung from the oaks and a fog hung over the whole area.

"Come on, Rayann, let's go," she said.

We got out, and she weaved and stumbled past the oaks to the pine trees where we'd hid in the daytime to keep people from seeing us together. But now it did not seem to matter at all. I could not stop laughing. I kept on snickering at nothing at all. She peed and I thought of Star and how she peed like a water fountain. I laughed till I had to pee, too. Meanwhile, I could see the guys finishing off the last of the bourbon. Then they got out of the car, each door slamming one after the other.

"Let's swim," I said, freer than I ever felt in the day time and not dizzy and light from liquor. "Come on." I shucked my shirt and my shorts to reveal my new two-piece bathing suit.

"Lord have mercy," Johnny said, staggering a little as I did so. "This girl's equipped to swim in that closed up pool. She is dressed *down*."

"Well, what are y'all waiting for?" I said. "Let's just jump over the top and swim."

"Nobody else got a bathing suit, Missy," Cookie said.

"Well, did that ever stop you before?" I asked. "Go in your clothes." Then I headed over to the chain link fence and climbed over it, using the holes for ladder rungs. It stood about four feet high, so I dropped onto the concrete. "See, easy," I said. Johnny followed behind me.

"We going to swim in the public pool," Johnny said. "No matter what all those folks say, we gonna do it."

"Y'all just watch out and be quiet," Ivory Jones said in his fuzzy voice. But he was next over the fence. He dove in first. I could only see his shadow self breaking the moon's roundness into inky silver lines and him disappearing underneath the water.

He surfaced in the deep end, and said, "Feels *so* good." Then he swam the length of the pool, so Cookie came over the fence, and the rest of us dove in and splashed around. The water was clean and full of chlorine, just like the ladies from the weeks before had said. All ready for swimming. Cookie and I practiced handstands in the warm water. We acted like Weeki Wachee mermaids, doing all kinds of stunts with our legs held together tight, while Johnny and Ivory Jones raced from one end of the pool to the other.

When we complained that they were messing up our pretty routines, they practiced cannon balls in the deep end. I guess we started getting loud, cause Ivory Jones kept saying, "Y'all keep it down!"

A breeze came up, and the moon shone bright in the sky. I agreed with Ivory Jones that nothing felt as good as a nighttime swim after a hot summer day that had finally given up its ghost. Cookie complained that her clothes made her heavy, and she wished she'd worn a bathing suit under her clothes, too.

"What's that?" Ivory Jones said. Said it in a loud whisper. We all looked around. A small dot of light was coming slowly towards us from the baseball field on the west side of the pool.

"It's a flashlight," Johnny said. Johnny, Ivory Jones and Cookie were racing to the side of the pool.

"Hey!" a man's voice called out. The light came at us faster. "What's y'all doing in that pool?" A white man voice. The light jiggled as he ran towards us. "Nobody's allowed in that pool, don't you know that?" I did not want anymore pee thrown in my face, so I hopped out quick, too. He got near the fence, and I could see the outline of his pants.

"Hey! Colored's ain't allowed in this pool!" he said. "You damn Negroes, get the hell out. I'm going to call the law and have you all arrested!" the voice said as we headed over the fence, all of us leaping fast. My bathing suit got caught going across, and it ripped, but everybody was hauling ass fast as possible, squishing wet clothes not slowing them down a bit, running to the parking lot on the north side of the pool, not saying a word, just breathing hard.

"My clothes," I said, mostly to myself. Nobody paid it any mind at all, and Johnny started up the car as we all panted fast and hard, not talking. The flashlight was headed our way, so Johnny just drove straight over the curb and onto the grass between a couple of big old oak trees and squeal-tired back onto Tharpe Street.

I might have enjoyed the carnival ride aspect of it, bouncing high in the back seat, joggling up next to Cookie, hitting my head on the ceiling if I had not felt so afraid. We headed straight down the road towards home, fast as we dared. Nobody said a word as we turned back onto Main Street, headed north and then east towards Magnolia Road.

I did not feel right again until we turned onto our own dirt road towards all of our houses and Betty's Creek. I felt chilled to the bone with the cool night air, and me in just a bathing suit. All I heard was sniffling from pool water in our noses and the moon shining its one huge eye on each of us all the way home.

21

Word got around fast. The KKK had dumped dirt full up in all the public swimming pools. The word spread so rapid that when Daddy and Rheta came in on Sunday evening, Daddy knew all about it. Not twenty-four hours later.

I'd brought Margot up to my room where I dressed her in a red polka dot doll's hat. She liked dressing up for some reason. She hissed and waddled around the room in the doll hat. When I heard Daddy's car tires snapping twigs in the driveway, I raced downstairs and put the goose outside. I did not want them to know I was home or to bother me if I could help it. But I sure sat at the top of the stairs, listening out for whatever they might be doing and saying. I heard them open the door and walk in.

"But how did they find out?" Rheta said, opening the cabinets and the liquor cabinet door.

"Who?" Daddy said. "Rheta, make some sense here." The tiles were cold on my butt through my thin pj's.

"Whoever put the dirt in the pools," she said. "How did they find out about the incident with the coloreds swimming in the pool? Did you say you wanted a drink of bourbon?"

"On the rocks is fine," he said. "One of the neighbors caught some of them red-handed, swimming in the Tharpe Street pool. In the middle of the night. Three niggers, and he thinks he saw a naked white girl in there with them." I broke out into a sweat. My clothes. Would the police figure out these clothes belonged to Rayann Wood, and come tell my daddy?

"A white girl naked?!" Rheta said. "Must have been pure trash." Rheta went on, bottles clanking as she talked. "I could have sworn I bought a new bottle of bourbon and put it in here. Can you imagine? Swimming with the coloreds. So this neighbor, he put the dirt in the pool?"

"No, you're not listening to me, Rheta," he said. He was beginning to sound like the daddy I knew who talked to Mama. "He called the sheriff, old Coulter, you know. Coulter sicced the Klan on it. That's what I heard. Said he didn't want nobody swimming in the pool. That whatever the Klan did would put a stop to it. You should see that damn pool. Whoever dumped the dirt had it figured out. Cut holes in all the fences, curled them back, brought trucks full of dirt. Heaped it in there. A mountain of clay, climbing to the sky, right there in the pool," he said, laughing.

I thought of a heap of us piled high high high as the sky. All us in jail after they fed us bread and water. That's what they did to Hosea Williams who was working for the movement. Ivory Jones told me so. They'd feed us bread and water for a while, and then when nobody bothered to make our bail, they'd just give us water till we starved to death.

"Seems a little extreme to me," Rheta said. "I mean, fill the pool with dirt when our tax dollars—" It went quiet except for the sucking noise of the refrigerator door going open. "Would you look at this? Nothing much to eat," she said. "Too bad that maid of yours quit. She sure could cook. You just want to go out and get a bite to eat? Morrison's or somewhere?"

"Yeah, all right," Daddy said. "I'm going to see about this goose begging at the back door," Daddy said. "That darn Rayann, she must not have fed him. Rayann!" he said. I was not about to answer. "What's that damn thing on its head? That girl is never home anymore," he went on, "especially since school's let out."

"Honey, don't worry about the goose. That goose looks well fed to me. Why don't we go eat ourselves, huh?" Rheta said. "How's the incompetence thing going anyway?"

Daddy said, "She'll move shortly after the hearing next week. Everybody's approved it. It's a done deal now." He had a sadness and embarrassment in his voice. "Too much to handle. Think I've found a place for Rayann. School up in Tennessee. Ready?"

"You going to keep the house?" Rheta asked.

I didn't want to hear anything else. I felt heavy and tired enough to sleep for a hundred years. I went quietly back to my room. I had to go see that man at the Ellis State Bank. Tomorrow. Then I'd stop by and see what the heck the pool looked like, all that dirt in it. I'd try to find my clothes, too.

There was no breeze, and it hadn't rained in a while. Add that to the heat and wetness weighing down all around, and you had regular oven and steam bath weather. It was the next morning, and the creek sent just a plea of a trickle down its sandy bed. Still, when you got about a foot from it, suddenly it behaved like a refrigerator, just cooling things down.

From the trail next to the creek, I gave the hoo hoo hoo-hoo mourning dove sound. I repeated it six times loud. My signal to Cookie to come out to the hideout if she heard me. Margot honked away like she knew I was calling Cookie, and she was helping me call. It was Monday after our Saturday night swim, and I hadn't seen hide nor hair of her since. For the first time, it occurred to me they could have gotten caught; Johnny, Ivory Jones, and Cookie.

Then here she came, thrashing through the woods at me, standing in the trail.

"Hey," she said, all subdued-like in her shorts. Her eyes looked swollen and tired.

"Hey," I said. We made our way to the hideout, Margot leading the way. "Did y'all get caught?'

"No, she said. "Miss Jesse was asleep, but me and Ivory Jones had to hide those clothes. I just threw them in the washer machine this morning. Mixed them up with the rest of the dirty clothes. They hanging out to dry. Hey now," she stopped at the hideout doorway while I went on in. She looked down at the ground, crossed her legs, one over the other where she stood. She grabbed a dogwood branch hanging into the hideout. "I'm afraid they'll catch us." She pulled a leaf off the tree and started tearing pieces off it and tossing them to the ground. "Did you have a stomach ache the next day?"

"Yeah," I said. "And a headache. Can't you come into the hideout?" Margot hopped in and sat down in my lap. Cookie threw her dogwood leaf parts down and stepped up and in. I went on. "They have my clothes, probably. Remember, I left them by the pine trees. Did you hear that somebody put dirt in the pool?" I sat down.

"Yeah," she said, sitting herself.

"I heard Daddy telling that trashy Rheta woman that there were three black kids and one white child who was naked," I said. "I was *not* naked."

"You kidding me," she said, sober. "Well, up at church, the folks saying it was all white kids—three white boys and a little white girl. Saying the boys made the white girl get naked. Saying the KKK is just looking for an excuse to close down that pool permanent."

"They thought you were a boy?" I said.

"I know one thing, I ain't no *boy*," she said, pointing at her chest. "I hope they don't find out the real truth, though.

You know the A & M people, and that Reverend Steele? They fixing to go protest over at the pool. Said they fed up. Want to go swimming in the public swimming pool." "I hope they do," I said, sighing. "Well, I got things to do." Then I told her about how I would be headed downtown to talk to the banker man that Ivory Jones told me about the other morning. How after that, I would walk by the pool and take a look.

"Girl. You should be glad you're going away to school if you got to be around that damn woman." She didn't like Rheta at all. Then she looked at the sky, and I thought of really having to live with Rheta. What if she moved in and took Mama's place? Cookie said, "It's dangerous over there at the pool. Don't go." Then Margot got up and plopped down in Cookie's lap. Cookie patted Margot, and then looked up at me as something dawned on her. "Don't you know I want to go, too? I might just catch the bus downtown and see you there."

"Well, okay then," I said, remembering the guy who swopped me with the pee balloon. "But don't act like you know me," I said, quick, holding my palms like to hold her back. I could have cried, saying that. I looked up at her as she stood to leave, Margot jumping out of her lap. Cookie turned and looked at me. I had never seen her eyes to look so hurt.

"Girl, you really something, ain't you. Maybe you never really been my friend at all if you don't want to be seen with me now. Maybe I won't go at all." She turned and stepped out of the hideout and walked home, Margot following her close. Damn, I felt stupid. And heavy, tired.

After that, I had nothing to do but try to check with the guy Ivory Jones had told me about who might give me some lawyer help. I took the bus. Downtown at the Ellis State Bank, things were bustling. I had never seen colored people in a bank before, and here they all were in the teller line at the desks where they loan you money, at the information desk, at the checking account desk, everywhere. White people, too, but I was used to that. I walked up to a teller line with about five people waiting and heard all kinds of talk.

I froze when I realized it all centered around the swimming pool incident.

"Yes, just piled a whole truckload of dirt in that pool," one black man said. "They must really not want nobody in that swimming pool."

The lady behind him said, "They going to demonstrate this afternoon. Those young kids from over at the A and M. Say they fed up with it."

"You know it's getting bad," one other lady said. "Don't you know there's gonna be a retaliation sure as I'm standing here. God bless us all," she said, and the other two nodded and murmured uh huh, and "you know that's right."

When I asked the teller if I could see Mr. Ellis, he laughed a little and said, "He's a busy man. You'll have to make an appointment."

"This is important," I said, snitching a hard peppermint candy from the white bowl next to him. I did not like him laughing at me just because I was a kid. I was also scared to the toes for Johnny, Ivory Jones, Cookie and me. I spoke in my most grown up voice. "And I need to see him soon. May I just wait till he's got a free minute? I took the bus from all the way out in the country."

"Well," he said, looking me over. I wore the red dress I'd selected for the other bank, with my new bra. I was relieved I had it on, because I did not want to look like a naked white trash girl. "Okay, let me see what I can do." He got on the phone and talked with one person. Then he dialed another number.

Then he hung up and said, "If you'll go down that hallway, next to the last door on the right, that's his secretary's office. She can help you out." I thanked him and he winked at me. He had a skinny rectangle face and slitty eyes. I headed back through the hallway.

"Mamie Smithers" was the name on the plate at the desk where the secretary sat. She had it good, and she knew it. Curly red hair and a big smile. The deep green carpet smelled new, the chairs looked cushiony, and squiggly paintings like I'd never seen before hung on the walls. I'd always seen pictures in banks of mountains and paintings of rich or pretty people, but never these bright pictures of squiggles and lines and bubbles. It all made me feel nice and cool while it must have been about 95 degrees outside. She told me politely to please have a seat, and I might have to wait for a while.

"That's just fine," I said, trying to act as dignified as I could. I read, or pretended to read all those grown up magazines like *Woman's Day* and *Forbes* and *Life*. Somebody had gone to the war and had taken a lot of pictures in *Life*. Terrible pictures of bleeding people, of shot people, of crying people. It featured a story about the Dr. Martin Luther King, too, and his picture sat next to the Malcolm X picture. I thought they were both very handsome, and hoped someday I'd get to meet both of them.

I let my imagination run wild then. I'd take the train up to Chicago to see Cookie, and they would both be there in the bar listening to Cookie singing. That Mr. King and Mr. X would be sitting there, and I'd march right up to them and say, "I swam in an all white pool with that girl." They would both be glad to meet me, would stand and bow like gentlemen, and I would be a grown up lady by then with a smart black skirt and white blouse on, and I'd bow back and give them my hand and say, "Rayann Wood. Nice to meet you." And they would let me sit down with them, and they would offer me a nice bourbon, though I would say, "No, thank you. I don't drink bourbon anymore, but a nice glass of red wine would be so nice." And then they would tell me they needed young people like me who read *Life* magazine and wore smart clothes in the movement. I heard somebody calling my name.

"Miss Wood?" the secretary Mamie said. "Mr. Ellis can see you now." She pointed to the closed office door.

"Thank you," I said. I stood and waited as an older colored lady with a cane left the office door open, and she headed out to the main lobby. Even though I had felt nervous, when I walked into his office and saw Mr. Ellis, I no longer felt that way. He was white sure enough, and had sandy hair, and laugh creases around his eyes, dark green eyes like a lake. A lake that would make you feel like you could dive in on a hot day.

"Pleased to meet you. Miss Wood, is it?" he said, holding his hand out and offering me the chair across from his desk. He lit a cigarette. I loved the smell when the cigarette just took the flame. It reminded me of a fireplace.

"Well, what can I do for you today? I heard it's a matter of some urgency?"

"Yes, Sir," I said. "My daddy wants to commit my mama into a crazy person home, a bad one, Chattahoochee, cause he wants her money, but she's not crazy, and I was wondering if you have a lawyer or know of a doctor I could talk to who might help me convince the judge my mama is not crazy. Otherwise, Daddy might take all her money and I'd be left going to a reform school, and my colored friends, I know I'm not supposed to have any," I took a breath, "but I do, and they told me maybe you could help me out." I had blurted it all out in almost one breath, and I sat back into the big cushiony chair to take a deep breath.

"Let's back up a little," he said, leaning in, taking an inhale off his smoke. "Rayann Wood. Who're your parents again?"

"Elizabeth Wood and A.J. Wood," I said. He sat back in his chair.

"Oh, Al Wood? Hospital administrator," he said.

"Yes," I said. "Do you know them?"

He cleared his throat and said, "Yes, yes I do. So you indicated that you think your mother is not mentally ill?" I nodded and he went on. "What makes you think that?" he said.

"She's been getting better. In the hospital. She stopped taking her medicine, she started a garden in her room up there—she was born with a green thumb, people say. She started painting again. They're weird paintings, but still, I like them, and people say she's good. And well, I'm her daughter. I've known her crazy, and I could tell you when she was having a spell, but I know she's well now. But the doctor's going to order her to Goodwood, and then to Chattahoochee. And then Daddy's going to get that Declaration of Incompetence going, and have those other people swear she's crazy. I just don't know what to do."

"You say your mother's in the hospital?" he said, frowning.

"Yes, Sir."

"With what?" he said.

"With nothing," I said, shrugging.

"What floor?" he said.

"5C, where they put crazy people," I said. He raised his eyebrows.

"What was she admitted for?" he asked. I told him about Mama taking too many pills.

"But that was two months ago. She needs to get out now. She's not sick. And Daddy thinks she is sick. But she's not, like I said. She's getting better."

"Are you aware that people in 5C can leave anytime they wish?" he said. He folded his arms. All the blood ran out of my face. What was he talking about? *I've got to get out of here,* Mama'd said over again.

"What?" I said. He stood up and took another drag off his cigarette.

"No one can keep a patient against their own will," he said as he looked out the window. He turned around to look at me. "Not even up in 5C. It's the law." Suddenly I could hear the secretary's typewriter going. Ding, it went as it hit the end of the line. I swallowed.

"But—" I said. I felt dizzy. I gripped the arms of the cushiony chair. Did Mama know this? If she could get out, then I needed to tell her. And soon. Mr. Ellis was looking at me with his head cocked to the side.

"Is everything okay?" he said. I stood up.

"Yes. Fine." I froze for a minute, just standing like my back was made of lead. "Thank you very much for your time."

"Well, I don't know that I did anything," he chuckled. "Let me know if I can help you further. Do you think your mother knows this?"

"No, Sir," I said. "No, Sir, not at all." I thought back over the times she'd gone in. *You need to stay here until you feel better,* Daddy had said before.

"Well, tell your father hello for me, will you?" he said. Daddy didn't like Mr. Ellis. I'd heard him talk about him before as a liberal.

"I'd rather keep this talk between us for now," I said, "if that's okay."

He nodded. "Certainly."

"Thank you," I said again. I don't exactly know what for. For not looking at my chest. For listening.

Outside, the electric clock at Daddy's bank down the street said ninety-five degrees. It really had turned into a sweatbox outside. Next, I had to go to the hospital, and then to the pool to see if the rumors were true. But first, I bought myself a big Coke at Woolworth's and drank it all down at once. I was tired and confused, but this new news gave me a little energy.

I stood in the elevator alone, slowly headed up the five floors of the hospital. For the first time, I knew. If I were a horse who could talk like Mr. Ed, or a wise space creature like the guy in *My Favorite Martian,* I could still not know where or how to reach my very own father. There was no use in expecting anything anymore. I got off the elevator and headed for Mama's room.

"Just a moment, Miss Wood," said the head nurse on 5C when I passed the nurse's station. She picked up the phone and called someone while I stood looking around the station for any signs that would tell me that as a patient you could leave anytime you wished to. She hung up. "Your father would like to see you in his office," she said, smiling like she had a block of ice hidden under her skull.

I felt nothing as I headed back down to his office. Just numbness. Daddy got up and shut the door to his office when I walked in. He pulled out the five carbon copies of a doctor's order sheet. "You've got some explaining to do." He put the sheets in my hand.

"I don't know what you're talking about," I said.

"Yes, you do," he said. I shook my head and shrugged my shoulders. Numb. Like I watched myself from above. He stood up and yanked the copies out of my hand. "The nurse's aide saw you swap this in for Indley's orders," he said. He turned around and walked to his chair and sat. I couldn't say anything.

He picked up the phone and dialed.

"Yes, the Chattanooga School for Girls?" He looked at me like he had me now. "Yes, yes. This is Al Wood in Tallahassee, Florida?" He waited a minute, looking at me so hard, I stared out the window. "Yes, this is Mr. Wood. I spoke with you yesterday. I've changed my mind. I'd like to enroll my daughter in *summer school* if I may."

It was quiet for that minute. I smelled Daddy's office of new upholstery and plastic carpet covers. "Will two days from today be soon enough?" he said. "I'll bring her to you myself. Yes, I can finish up the paperwork when we arrive. Thank you."

He put down the phone. "Now get out of here," he said, pointing to the door. "I don't want to hear a word out of you. This is a federal offense," he said, waving the doctor's order around. "You could go to prison for something like this." I stood up and turned around, headed to the door. "You'd better go home and get packed. We're leaving in the morning. Early. And hey—look at me," he said.

I turned around and stared so as not to exactly look. He pointed at me. "You will *not* go up and talk to your mother. I will have the police escort you out if I so much as hear a word about your heading *up* the elevator, and not *out* the front door." The fire in my belly flared up. I looked at him hard and full at the eyes.

"You killed the other goose, didn't you?" I said. A look of confusion came over him. Then he looked uncomfortable, and squirmed a little in his desk. He fiddled with his desk pen. He cleared his throat and frowned at his pen, preparing a lecture.

"Sometimes—"

"You killed Waldo," I said.

"That was Lucky and Red's idea," he said quick and sharp. "Lucky saw you hanging around that colored girl, and Red took it upon himself to—" He looked down.

Then I walked out and shut the door. I didn't feel anything. I was going to the pool to at least say goodbye to Cookie.

22

I fell asleep on the bus. Its grumbly hum is a strange lullaby. The sun beat down hard and intense. The bus driver woke me up for my stop, and my hair was wet from sweating. I got off the bus, and there sat the pool, a mountain of red clay piled into it. My heart leapt into my throat, then thudded to the pit of my belly—if I hadn't insisted we go swimming that night, this mound of dirt would not be heaped here. None of this would have happened.

The bus drove off, and then I could hear the sound of clapping and chanting. With each word, a clap, over and over.

WE WANT FREEdom
WE WANT FREEdom
WE WANT FREEdom.

It came from the pool area where a big knot of colored people walked, about a hundred or more, clapping in a circle. I headed back under the oak trees along the lane that ran beside the pool. That way I could watch what went on and stay cool, and hopefully not get spotted. A bigger circle of clappers and chanters surrounded a smaller circle of sign holders at the pool entrance.

The signs said, WE WANT TO SWIM and SEGREGATION IS WRONG and FREEDOM NOW. One policeman leaned on the shady side of the building, wiping his forehead with a handkerchief, his arms folded, dark circles of sweat underneath his arms. I figured he must be trying to escape the heat.

About ten white people speckled the circle of colored people shouting and singing. One I recognized as that white nun-looking lady I'd seen before at the pool talking to the newspaper guy. Most of the others looked like college people. All ages, sizes, shapes, men and women. And hot. Wiping foreheads, soaking their shirts, kicking off their shoes as they walked. But no Cookie anywhere.

I looked all around on the black dirt and leafy ground and then spotted them a few trees over—my clothes! The clothes I'd shucked those few nights before. So I walked slowly kind of sideways over to where they stuck wrinkled and sucked to the earth, dirty and muddy now from sitting in the weather a few days. After a month, they'd be buried. This brought me to the idea of digging a hole slowly with my toes and stuffing them in it. I started to dig the hole nonchalant as Mama would say, hands behind my back, glancing around at the trees, using my toes as I sat behind the tree, the crowd chanting, "We want freedom."

I dug slowly, wondering what in the world I could do to stop Daddy from sending me away and putting Mama in the real crazy person hospital. How could I get to talk to her before I left? I wondered if Cookie was really going to show up today, or if she'd maybe already come and gone, or Miss Jesse had told her she couldn't ride the bus to town with all this mess going on. If Miss Jesse knew I'd been the cause of all this mess, she'd turn me over her knee. Worse, she'd stop seeing me and wouldn't let Cookie see me either.

"Look at what you done caused," she'd say to me. "I think the devil hisself has got into you." I felt a hot shame come over me. Then a hot truth struck through me—maybe the real reason I was burying these clothes was that I didn't want to admit in public that Cookie was my friend. Maybe I was no different than Daddy. While I was thinking all this, I wiped sweat off my face and neck. I patted dirt over the clothes now, still burying the evidence with my toes. Then I noticed all the white people who'd started to show up at the pool.

"Go on home," I suddenly heard, and "Yeah, git your asses off this property," someone else said. The knot of sign holders and singing clappers, black and white, stood partially facing and partially ignoring another group just past the pool. This other group was the new shouting group. A clot of a dozen white men and a couple of white women who stood about six feet from the singing clappers and sign holders. "Yeah, get your asses off this property," said someone else. Other shouts I couldn't quite make out. The members of the shouting group, each and every one held a bat, a knife, or an ax handle. The one guy in front with a white T-shirt and beige pants brandished a four-foot club. "You got your own pool!" he shouted. His face was tomato red.

Just then, Willie the Weatherman in his heavy black squared glasses and this other guy who reported the news on TV drove up and got out of this green car. They both had hung heavy cameras around their necks. Then men with sticks and clubs all kept yelling and waving their weapons around. The policeman still stood by the side of the building, not doing anything but watching, his arms folded.

I patted down the last of the dirt over my wet smelly shorts and shirt. Since it made a bump in the dirt, I then piled leaves on top of that. Not a soul paid any attention to anything I might have been doing.

"What you doing?" came a sudden voice from behind me.

I jumped and felt my face grow hot. It was Cookie, standing behind the next oak tree over, peering out. "Oh, dang," I said, putting my hand to my chest. "It's you." Then I whispered. "I'm burying those clothes." She nodded and looked at the bunch at the pool.

"Whatever you do, stay back," she said.

"Don't worry," I said. We watched as the picketers continued to sing and clap and chant, even louder now. And one of the white men swung his club around in a circle. Cookie and I stood behind our separate trees, watching. "Why doesn't that policeman do something?" I said. "Those guys have weapons."

Willie the Weatherman must have been thinking the same thing, cause he ran over to the police officer and shouted to him. "Hey! How about breaking this thing up before some real trouble breaks out!" Then Willie pointed to the knot of white men. "Those men are armed!"

The policeman unfolded his arms and let them drop like two dead eels hanging by his sides. "It ain't none of my business—I can't do nothing!" he said all flatlike, and with that, he turned around and walked away from the trouble towards Tharpe Street.

I thought of all the times Miss Jesse kept coming to our house and never got paid enough. Or of Mama trapped maybe forever in the hospital when she could have walked out any time. Of Waldo getting killed for no good reason. *Go home and pack,* Daddy had said. He was mad, too. Felt like none of his family was his business. When was I going to be somebody's business? When is Mama going to be somebody's business? Or Jesse and Cookie and Ivory Jones?

"Kill the niggerloving sons of bitches!" the man with the swinging club yelled.

But it did not matter. Because you could feel by the very wind the big shift coming, coming from behind the pool where came this tall black lady wearing all red, and bringing up a whole passel of more people behind her. Chanting and holding signs. They came from down the street that ran on the back side of the pool. I had never in my life seen so many Negro people. It amounted to about five churches worth of people on a Christmas Sunday, all those people stretched like a sea serpent down the road, then curving onto the next street, stretching a whole two blocks behind that. They sang, "We Shall Overcome," and carried signs that read NO VIOLENCE and WE'RE CITIZENS TOO and WE WANT OUR RIGHTS. They headed up the lane near Cookie and me.

Then I felt something on my arm. It was Cookie, her brown arm touching me light on the shoulder as she stood beside me, us still behind the oak tree, which was wide enough to hide us both. I leaned in a little closer to her, even though we both were sticky with sweat.

"I am not believing this," she murmured.

"Me, either," I said.

Soon, must have been five hundred colored people and a few salt sprinkles of white people with them, standing there clapping their hands and saying,

WE WANT FREEdom
WE WANT FREEdom
WE WANT FREEdom.

Then here came the sound of sirens, all up and down the street from every direction. Policemen, all white I noticed for the first time, jumped out of cars and unholstered their guns. They surrounded the hundreds of people shouting for freedom, and the men with the weapons crying, "Kill them!"

One policeman stood on a car with a bullhorn and said, "Disperse immediately or we'll use tear gas."

"What's that?" I whispered. She explained it was a gas bomb the police used to make people throw up and cry and stuff. "Will it kill us?" I was afraid.

"No. They say you wish you was dead if you get sprayed. But just for a little while," Cookie said.

"How do you know all this?" I said, grabbing her hand in mine.

"Learned it in Sunday School," she said.

"Y'all have the strangest church," I said.

"Teaching us safety," she said. "Everybody knows the police using it in Alabama, Georgia, Mississippi. All over." Suddenly, I realized this was happening everywhere.

Looking at those people's faces who were shouting for freedom reminded me that I'd gotten splatted in the face with that boy's pee. My stomach turned as I remembered the ammonia smell of it, the burning feel of it on the side of my face. And that white boy, he would have done it again and again to Cookie or to Ivory Jones, or to Miss Jesse, and not thought a thing about it. People like him, people like Lucky and Red, would keep Cookie and me behind trees and out of pools forever if they could. They would leave Mama in the hospital forever. And that policeman, he'd said nothing he could do about it.

I just walked out from behind that oak tree straight towards the swarm of people.

"Don't!" Cookie said. She came from behind the tree and grabbed my hand and pulled. I yanked away.

I said, "Don't you want to swim in the pool? Don't you want freedom?"

"We're liable to get hurt," she said, pointing to the new bigger group of white people walking across the softball field on the opposite side of the pool. A squarish shaped crowd of people moved like one big floating building. They carried sticks and bats like a marching army headed towards the pool.

"I don't care," I said. I yanked away from Cookie, tromped

out from behind the tree and fell into the back side of the shouters and clappers who now had formed a circle big as a pool. Cookie ran out after me. She stood for a minute looking at me. I started clapping and chanting. I could feel everybody's clapping hands around me, the vibrations of it. The dust rose as they stomped in a circle. Cookie shrugged at me, smiled like What the heck? She gave me a little shove to get us into the circle. Then she started clapping, and we all sang,

WE WANT FREEdom
WE WANT FREEdom
WE WANT FREEdom.

I had never felt so alive in my life, and I had never meant anything so much. We stomped around in a circle, and I could feel the stomp into the earth that all those feet made. The circle went round and the dust went round and up like a prayer lifting.

All those people, young like the college girl, old like the great grandmamas at Cookie's church, and people in between, even a few kids my age and younger, a few white men and women about college age there, too, all in this big circle, looking scared and brave at the same time. Some I'd never seen, others who I'd seen at the vegetable market buying fruit on a Saturday in regular clothes, a few on TV like the Reverend Steele in nice suits, a few who I'd seen sweeping the floor and emptying garbage at school in uniforms, all clapping and chanting together in a pool-big circle. I wondered if anybody would recognize me as the girl who swam in the pool that night, or as the hospital administrator's girl, or as the crazy lady's daughter.

Somehow it didn't matter. None of those things was all of me. And that cheered me. I wished Ivory Jones could be here, the one of us who most talked about the Reverend Martin Luther King, and here, right here in the pool where Ivory Jones had swum, not on TV, but right here, he could have marched, too.

Then the big long row of white people, mostly men, arrived at the pool and stood like a square up next to the circle. Looking spit mad. They stood close, a few feet away, shouting at the whole herd of us, saying, "Go home! Get back where you belong, niggers!"

They wagged their fists towards us, and they hollered and yelled so that spit flew out of their mouths. I was terrified, but like everybody else in the circle, I kept clapping and shouting, looking in front of me and not to the sides, thinking about what I heard in Sunday School about Jesus walking on the water.

Miss Selfe, the Sunday school teacher, had told us Jesus said if you calm yourself, the seas will calm. He said you could do it, too, walk on the water. But you don't want to mess up like old Saint Peter, who, when he thought too much about all that water slapping up around him, well, he sank. All those people walking in a circle, I could feel it, had calmed themselves enough to walk up a huge storm. I knew it. I could feel it without touching a thing.

But there came the smell of something changing, changing like night into day. Then the storm turned into a hurricane. Somebody from the square group around our circle started hitting. I heard a crack and a scream and a couple of thuds, and another crack. Screaming and shouting and hitting. Then everybody seemed to be running in all directions. That's when somebody fell on me. I went face first into the dirt with them on top of me.

Whatever fell on me was dead weight, and I pushed it off me, and sat up.

Cookie.

She had rolled off me. Onto her back on the ground, shoulders limp, her head flopped to one side. I screamed.

Somebody stepped on her hand, which was loose as rubber.

"Stop!" I shouted. I didn't think, but gathered her up to me. I pulled her arms across her body and leaned over her, lifting her up into my arms. She felt like a heavy Raggedy Ann doll. All I could think to do was to hold her. What was wrong? Why was she so limp, and her eyes closed? Somebody whammed into the back of me and ran off.

"Cookie?" I said, my voice shaking like crazy. "Cookie, do you hear me?" She didn't move, didn't open her eyes. She was bleeding from the forehead, blood streaming all down her face, down her neck and onto her clothes. I laid her down and put my head on her chest. I couldn't hear her heart, but I felt it, softly beating on my cheek. "Oh, thank the lord," I said. I shook all over now. People were still shouting and screaming all around me, stepping on us. Sirens yowled from down the street in both directions.

I felt something warm and wet. Blood. I pulled my hand out from under Cookie's neck to look at it. All over my palm. "Oh, god," I said to myself, wiping it on my shirt and shorts now. Would Cookie die in my arms, all because I wanted to get involved in a demonstration? I looked around.

"Somebody help!" I yelled. Then somebody tripped over us and went onto their back, and got up and ran. Somebody else was yelling loud. I heard what I thought were gun shots. People really started to scream then, and ran out from the area in all directions. Somebody's purse smacked me on the side of the head, and somebody else pushed into my side. "Somebody HELP!" I shouted at the top of my lungs. Another person stepped on my thigh. I looked down at my friend Cookie, limp now, and started to cry. "HELP ME!" I said. I felt like soon we might both drown in blood.

23

Nobody heard. But I heard everybody. Everybody else screaming and stumbling around terrified, too. *I'm sorry, Cookie. I'm sorry,* I said. *God,* I said, *spare her. Help me out, here, will you?* Then just to prove God could be anything, I saw a face I recognized, coming my direction. The blue-gray uniform looked familiar. The white pool maintenance man who used to work at the hospital. I grabbed hold of his uniform leg and said, "Help me!" I did not let go till he paid some attention. His city worker name tag stitched on the chest of his uniform said "Cliff."

"Hey, let go!" His eyes looked scared and they darted around at the big mess of people scrambling to get away.

"She's bleeding, from the head. Please help me," I said. "Help me get her to the hospital. Can't you see she's been hit?"

He could not *not* look at her, so he did. I clung tight to his pants leg. His forehead wrinkles changed from mad to scared to sad, just like his eyes did.

"All right, then," he said, plunging his hands into his pockets and pulling out a set of keys. "But you'll have to carry her. And I ain't taking her up front. She'll have to ride in the truck bed."

He headed off for the city truck behind the pool, away from all the people. I tried to stand up with Cookie, my arms under her arms, and I fell back down. I stood up again, and picked Cookie's tall self up in my arms and started to walk. I staggered a few steps, and nearly toppled. Cliff had turned around and saw me.

"All right, all right, I'll carry her," he said, shaking his head.

"Just get her legs," I said. I swear even if I'd had to stagger all the way, I had the strength to have carried her myself a few steps at the time. Cliff picked up her legs when we got to the truck, but I know I could have lifted her into the bed myself. She still seemed like a rag doll, plopping all arms and legs akimbo into the truck bed. I crawled into the back with her, cradling her head.

"What you doing?" he said when I put her bleeding head in my lap.

"Riding back here," I said. "To protect her head." The truck ridges poked into my skinny butt.

"Suit yourself," he said, slamming the tailgate shut. "Where to?"

"The hospital," I shouted.

"A & M, then?"

"No, Sir," I said, clearing my throat to say it loud and clear. I'd take her to my hospital. I knew everybody there. I'd figure out a way to get her treated somehow. "Tallahassee Memorial."

"I ain't delivering this girl to Memorial," he said, opening the tailgate again, shaking his head. "Wouldn't nobody help her. Might as well get on out, then." He held onto the tailgate and waited, looking at me sternlike.

I hesitated a second. "Take us anyway," I said. "Take us to Memorial. You know my dad is the administrator." I swallowed hard, cause I was bluffing. Daddy would never in a million years agree. "Please, Sir," I said. I managed a smile just as the only A & M ambulance flew past us, sirens and lights going full blast. Cliff slammed the door shut, shook his head and got into the truck and headed across town. Every time he rode over a bump, my butt jumped up and slammed back down onto those hard truck bed ridges. I could feel warmth in my lap, maybe the warmth of Cookie's head, or maybe the blood oozing slowly out of the middle of the top of her head. Panic sent a heat down through me. But I wouldn't dare move. Instead I gripped the side of the truck with my hands, making sure Cookie's head always stayed in my lap.

We got out to the street that ran north to south, the one Cookie and I had taken uptown that day past the crepe myrtles and sidewalks. I remembered us laughing. How the pink blossoms had fallen into her hair and around her shoulders.

I whispered, "Please don't die." A Memorial ambulance drove past us, sirens whining.

Like a flash, I remembered. It was a chicken bone. Caught in the throat. Mama's throat. Mama strangling. Daddy leaving. Daddy thinking she was faking. Mama and Daddy mad at the dinner table, arguing over something, Daddy shaking shaking shaking her, her mouth full of food, chicken. Her inhaling it, her eyes big. Daddy's disgust. Melodrama, he said. Melodrama. His back turning to the door. His back to her. To us. Her eyes saying Help. Me reaching into her mouth and pulling out the meat, the bone, too. Mama choking. That was when she took to the bed. And stayed for three years. And then I burned BONES into the table with the cigarette. The chemical smell memory of it made me almost gag.

I felt the warm blood seep through my clothes. *God,* I said, *I know I deserve to die instead because I got Cookie involved with this, but if you're really there, if you're listening, please don't let her die.* Maybe they would arrest me and send me to jail. I looked down at Cookie, whose eyes were shut. *Or me, either, God. Don't let me die, either.*

"Wha' happened?" Cookie said, mumbling it out, her eyes suddenly flung wide open. She tried to sit up, and I pulled her back down into my lap. "Shee-face—mess-" she said, bringing her hands to her face.

"Your face is fine," I said, grabbing her hands and pulling them down from her face so she wouldn't touch her head. "You're going to be fine," I said. "Just stay lying down. You need to lie down." I could not believe this stuff was coming out of my mouth. How calm I had turned. We were at the bottom of a hill, passing the main city cemetery, a white graveyard, just in front of a colored one. "You're going to be fine. You just got hit in the head, and I'm taking you to the hospital."

She looked at me with wide dazed eyes. "Rayann—scared." She shut her eyes, then opened them again, shutting them, then forcing them to open. "Die?" I thought she said. I could not tell, her words were blurring together. She lifted her hands up to touch her head, but I grabbed them and pulled them down.

"You're not dying," I said, shaking my head no and sounding like she was being unreasonable. "Don't touch your head, okay?"

"Kay," she managed, sounding so tired it almost sounded wistful. She squinted at the oak trees overhead, and started to close her eyes again. "Rayann?" she said, opening them again.

"Yeah?" I said.

"Don't be lying." She grabbed my hand and gripped hard. I wanted Miss Jesse. I wanted a Coca Cola. I did not want to be here.

We were crossing Main Street and passing Woolworth's where Cookie had bought me that blouse. Down the hill from that, Gramlings and JoJo's where Cookie had defended me against the kids, where she handed me the hose after I got knocked. "We'll be there in just a couple of minutes," I said.

We got to the back side of Memorial where the Emergency technicians always brought ambulances and then checked them into the Emergency Room. The ambulance that had left the pool just before we had was parked right in front of us.

The Emergency tech, the tall one, Skip, who had helped with Mama when she took all those pills, was carrying a stretcher into the back door. On it lay one of the white guys who'd been yelling and screaming the loudest. Suddenly, I was filled with strength. I could feel it in my arms and legs and face. A slow fire. A slow rage, burning good.

"Hey!" I yelled. Skip turned around and saw me and nodded. I waved, standing in the truck. "Over here—I need help!" He lifted his eyebrows, hesitated, shifted the stretcher in his hands and said something to another tech.

"I'll be right there," he shouted to me. He talked one of the policemen at the door into taking his side of the stretcher on into the Emergency Room.

That tall Skip jogged over to the truck as Cliff stepped out and slammed the door. Skip nodded at Cliff and peered in. "How'd she get here?" Skip asked, leaning into the truck. He picked up Cookie's head to look at the back of it. I noticed her forehead was starting to swell. I sat down so Cookie's head could lay in my lap instead of the hard metal truckbed.

"I told her y'all wouldn't let her in," said Cliff. "Then this one here," he said, pointing at me, "tells me her daddy's the chief here, so I figured—"

"He is," said Skip as he leapt into the truck, wiping his hands with Cookie's blood onto his pants. He checked Cookie's pulse. "Looks like a concussion," he said. "Or maybe a contusion," he added grimly. "How long's she been out?" he said, looking me over, blood all over my clothes and arms.

"She conked out in the middle of all the people throwing rocks and holding bats and hitting with sticks, and—"

"Over at Levy pool," Cliff said, shaking his head. "Been all kinds of trouble over there."

"Yes, I know," Skip said. "We're starting to get a few here. Not the Negroes of course." He glanced at me, then away. Some blue jays squawked in the pine trees behind the hospital.

"Then she woke up once we got moving," I added.

"Did she speak?" said Skip.

"Yeah, a little," I said.

"Open her eyes?" he said.

"Yeah, but seemed like she was fighting to get them open."

Skip looked around, all around, at the emergency doors, at people along the corner of the building, at Cliff, then back at me.

"I can't take her in, you know that," Skip said, shaking his head slowly.

"Help me," I said, not really saying but demanding, even with my shaky voice. "Please help me, Skip." I was not used to asking like this, my fists balled up like a boxer.

"I'll treat her out here," he said, holding his palms out in front of him as if to stop me, like I was a prize fighter coming towards him or something. "But you'll have to help me." I started to thank him and he interrupted. "She needs stitches and we need to wake her up," he said. "By the way." He stopped and looked at me curious. "How do you know her?"

"She's my friend," I said. I had never said this aloud, not to anyone. It felt good to say it, the truth. I said it again, louder, and I slapped my chest with a bloody hand as I spoke. "She is my friend, my best friend, and she lives across the woods from me. Please. Please help her."

"I'll need to leave her in the truck," Skip said, looking over at Cliff.

"Oh, all right," said Cliff, waving his hand like he'd given up. "Can't go back to work anyway."

"I'll be right back," said Skip, leaping out of the truck. "We need to keep her from going into shock." He walked with long strides back through the hospital glass doors.

"Cookie," I said, staring down into her face, holding onto her chin. Nothing. "Cookie!" I yelled into her face.

"Wha—" she said, turning to the side in a groan, her head still in my lap.

"Wake up," I said. I remembered now from hanging around in E.R. that you needed to keep people with concussions alert. "You have to wake up! Open your eyes."

"Rayann," she said, slow as a drunk person, holding up her hand looking for mine in desperation. Her hand was cold. Shock I knew from being around hospital language all my life. I couldn't let her get too cold. She'd be more likely to pass out that way. "Wha's happing, wh-wha happened?" she tried to sit up, and I pushed her back down. The truckbed felt hard against my knees.

"Just stay awake," I said. "They're going to treat you soon. Give you some stitches. I brought you to Memorial. They'll treat you out here. In the truck." She tried to sit up, then lay back down with a sigh.

Skip came out with a stretcher and a nurse's aide who had a blanket, a pillow and even towels. He slid the stretcher into the center of the truckbed. Together we picked Cookie up and moved her onto the stretcher. I tried to be careful and move her head and her neck together. Then he covered her with a blanket. As I tucked it in around her, Skip explained that we'd have to wait and see. "What hit you?' Skip asked Cookie.

"I can't remember," Cookie said as she fell back to sleep. If this were a contusion, Skip said, it was more serious.

"A contusion means the skull is cracked," he said. He looked at my shorts and then I looked down. Blood everywhere. "I'm a little worried about the loss of blood." We both touched one of her arms. Cold and dry. "Try to keep her warm. And awake."

I crawled into the stretcher and under the blanket with her. She watched every move I made, but she didn't move. There wasn't much room, but her body felt cold. I turned towards her, crooked my head into her neck, and put my arm around her chest to try and keep her warm. Her legs went way on past mine. I hoped Cliff and Skip wouldn't tell me to get out. They didn't.

"That's the best way I can think of to keep her warm," Skip said, and headed back inside. I looked at the blue sky and at the flat white building beside us that now shaded the truck where we lay and wondered why it was still daytime. Cookie sighed, and so did I. Seemed like a lot of time had gone by already, and she was just getting treated. I tried to think of something to talk about. Anything to keep her awake.

"Wake up," I said, calling in her ear. I lifted her hand as she woke up. "Look at these nails! You need some polish, girl. No reason to grow these nails out if you're not going to show them off." She let out a short laugh and struggled to put her hand in her pocket. She muttered and groaned, and it took her a long time to struggle with the pocket.

"Here," she said. She slowly pulled out a bottle of Chichi Pink. As usual, she was carrying a small bottle of polish in her right pocket. She carried lipstick in her left pocket. I opened it, propped it on her chest, and started putting a sloppy coat on her nails, even though we were both lying down.

"Let's sing," I said. "I'll start." I began a low one she might follow. *Coming to you on a dusty road, Good loving, I got a ton of love, You didn't have to love me like you did but you did yes you did. And I thank you,* I sang. Even the Temptations didn't work. It only served as a lullaby to make her eyes blink and blink and then close up tight.

"I'm thirsty," Cookie said, licking her lips. They were parched and cracked. I realized I wanted a Coca Cola, so she really must have. Bad. It was all in the world that I wanted. Her eyes shut again. I'd try to get Cliff the maintenance man to get me a Coke, and I'd let Cookie have most of it.

"Mr. Cliff, Sir," I called. He stood out behind the truck, watching nurses, doctors, techs, sick people coming and going from the hospital. "Could you get me a Coke? I'm awful thirsty in here."

"What am I supposed to get it with?' he said, grumpy, walking over to peer inside the truck where we lay. I reached around and dove into my shorts pocket.

"I got a dime," I said, and handed it to him. "And here," I added. "Get yourself one, too." I sounded like one of the ladies from the Garden Club.

"Cup of coffee is what I need," he said. "How's that girl doing? She ain't dripping blood on my truckbed, is she? The city sure won't like that." He stood with his hands in his pockets, peering over with a wrinkled brow and sad eyes, looking for all the world like he wanted to help but did not know how to.

"Oh, no Sir," I said. "But I am really really thirsty." I licked my dry lips and wiped sweat off my neck. I handed him the dimes, and he disappeared into the hospital.

"I'm getting you something to drink," I said to Cookie. I shook her shoulder a little. "Wake up, I need to talk to you." Her eyes opened, and she smiled like it took sheer effort for her to do just that.

"I heard you," she said, licking her lips. "Telling him I'm your friend. Didn't kill you?" I sat up and tucked her in. I stared down at all the sand that had collected in the grooves in the truck. I had to think of something to keep her awake. I picked up her hands, one at a time, talked and blew on her nails to dry them.

"Ever been to the beach?' I said. She nodded, opening her eyes and peering at me. "Well, you know how when you see shells all over the sand, clam shells, conch shells, even periwinkle shells, and how you want to find one that's perfect?" She looked at me like What are you talking about? I didn't know. I chattered, trying to keep her awake. "Well, you know how you look and look, and they're all broken? And then you realize everything's pretty much broken, but it's still fun trying to find the perfect shell? Then you look out at the water, and you look way out, way way out, and you just see more water and more sky?"

She watched as I waved with my arms in the air, making big gestures to give her something to look at. "And you wonder about all those people who live on the other side of that water?" I had thought about this a lot, but never talked about it.

"Yeah?" she said, turning her head sideways like an Egyptian. She smiled, like people do when they know your silly ways. "What of it?" She was talking, but shutting her eyes when I didn't speak. I kept on.

"Well, you think about yourself and how little you are. You know, insignificant. You wonder, now who in this world am I? Nothing much."

"You thinking up a hurricane, girl," Cookie said.

"But thing is," I said, leaning close to her. "It's a good feeling. You think, well, isn't much that's *that* important anyway, is it?" I laid back down. "I mean, it puts it in perspective."

"What you talking about?" she murmured. No more fresh blood was seeping out of her head. A dark mass of clotted blood had started to form on the top.

"Oh, nothing," I said. "Do you know I don't like your

brother? He's a pain in the butt." I couldn't believe what was coming out of my mouth. "I am really tired of him."

With that she let out a huff of a chuckle. "Uh, huh—sounds like you going to marry him." She licked her lips and started to shut her eyes again.

"Well, maybe I will," I said. "But I really can't stand to look at him anymore. Do you think we'd have cute children?"

She opened her eyes again and looked into mine, puzzled. "Children?" She started to close them again.

"How come when a colored person gets with a white person, they don't have striped children, like the shells on the beach. Or spots like you see on a dog?" I said.

"You gonna have four," she said. "one striped, one spotted—" she started to drift off.

"That's just two," I said, shaking her.

"One four-legged and one just plain crazy like you," she said, opening her eyes and smiling again.

"I am not crazy," I said.

"Yes, you are," she said. "Wanting to marry my stinky brother. He farts, too, you know." I was overjoyed that she was talking a little more, so I picked up each hand and wiggled it a little.

"Your nails are dry, I think," I said, fishing in her purse, the one she always slung across her shoulder, now beside me. "And I did not say I wanted to marry him. And he does not fart. Well, he wouldn't fart around me."

"You prissy," she said. "You the prissiest girl I ever met. Acting like you don't let no gas once in a while." I pulled out her new makeup case.

"I'm going to make up your face," I said. "I'll be gentle. You'll look splendid by the time I finish with you." Splendid? Where did that word pop out from? I got to work, pulling the covers up to her chin.

"What you putting makeup on me for?" she said. "You put that pink stuff on and I'll look dead."

"No, it won't," I said. "It'll look good." For a change, I'd get to see what she did look like with me making her up, and she couldn't stop me. That would surely keep her awake. "You got to close your eyes, but you can't fall asleep." I softly put some turquoise shadow on her lids. "Are you going to marry Johnny?" I asked.

She opened her eyes anyway. "Johnny?" she mumbled. "Girl, I'm going to Chicago. Meet a nice rich man. Get a big old house. Big house on the lake. Five bedrooms. Biggest album collection in the North." She closed her eyes, and I smoothed out the turquoise on her eyelids.

"That looks sensational on your skin," I said. I did not know why I was talking like a fashion magazine. "You going to marry a white man?" I pulled out the lipstick. Maybe this would help her cracked lips.

"No way," she said. The weather was cooling off some now that the sky was corralling and the sun sailing further west in it. I could hear the five o'clock traffic starting up on the road in front of the hospital, even though the morning shift people had left an hour ago, replaced already by the evening shift at the hospital. But visiting hours had started, and people were beginning to filter into the back doors of the hospital to come visit relatives and whatall. I wondered if Daddy had heard anything about me sitting in a truck outside the hospital yet.

"Be still, I can't get your lips if you're talking," I said. "And open your eyes. Colored men don't have any money." She pushed my hand weakly away. It didn't matter anyhow, the lipstick was going on clumpy because of her cracked lips.

"Be still? You wanted me to talk a minute ago. You don't

know nothing, girl," she said. "Up there, colored men's got money." Just then Cliff stuck his head over the side of the truck.

"Got your girl there some water," he said, handing me the water. He was all right after all. "And your Coke."

I tilted Cookie's head up a little and put a cup to her lips. She drank it all down fast. Then she started shivering. Sometimes that happened when people in shock drank liquid. It cooled her off too much, and she needed to get warm. I opened my Coke fast and drank half of it, then lay down next to her, rubbing each arm under the blanket to heat her up.

"Tell me about Chicago," I said. "I bet you haven't ever been there yet. How do you know they got rich colored men?"

"Daddy told me," she said, her teeth chattering. This scared me, but she kept talking. "He say there's musicians everywhere. White people go hear you sing in clubs. Pay you good. And commercials. Say if you sing solo, pays a whole month's rent."

"But they don't have a darn beach," I said. "How you going to get that house on the beach? And there's no creeks up there, either. Just buildings." I rubbed her hands and tucked the blanket under her feet.

"Got a big lake. Ice skating lake. Can't see the other side. Like the beach."

About that time, Skip came out to the truck. His EMT uniform had some blood on it, and I realized he wasn't just helping us out, he was working his regular job, too. He jumped into the truck easily, and handed me some hospital scrubs and told me to put them on. "Then you can take your clothes out to the laundry. How's she doing?"

"Staying awake. Even talking some," I said. "But I can't get her warm. She stopped bleeding on her forehead." He picked up her head and leaned over to look at the back of her head. The pillow had dried blood all over it.

"Stopped bleeding in the back, too," he said. His voice sounded hopeful. At least I wanted it to. He handed her a hospital gown and said, "Can you take off your clothes and put this on?" Cookie nodded. "We're going to have to put some stitches in your head. It won't hurt. Your head's too hard," he joked. "You won't feel a thing. I'll get out while you change, then Rayann can take your clothes over to the laundry." He looked at me to make sure I was listening. I nodded.

I helped Cookie get out of her clothes and into the gown. As I took mine off, Cookie said, "Dang, girl, you got a lot of blood on you. That's my blood?" She looked alarmed.

I held up my pinky. "Hold up a pinky," I said. She did. I touched mine to hers. "Guess this makes us blood brothers." She smiled and shut her eyes as I put on the scrubs. They felt crisp and light. When I picked up our clothes, they were heavy with dried blood. My stomach turned over, and I had to swallow hard and tell myself to settle down. Skip and Cliff were talking in a low conversation. At one point I heard Cliff whistle through his teeth.

When I jumped out with the heavy clothes, I headed to the front of the truck. Skip sat on the left fender while Cliff, in his gray maintenance outfit, stood with the cup of coffee and leaned into the driver's side of the truck. Skip's navy uniformed back faced me, so he couldn't see me coming from around the right side.

"Thing is, I think he was involved in the riot today," Skip was saying to Cliff. "And not on *this* side of the issue, if you know what I mean. Digging dirt, in other words."

"Whew doggies," Cliff said. "And the girl's mama's crazy, they say?" My ears picked up at that.

"Looks like she's not. Who's to say. Seems he's trying to put her away, though."

"Oh, look who's here," Cliff said loud, cutting in, a little cheery and smiling at me the way grownups do when they don't want kids to hear what they're talking about.

"Oh," Skip said, whirling around. "Oh. How—how's your friend."

"She's awake. She doesn't want me to go off. What are you talking about?"

"Oh, just some people we know in common," Skip said. "I'll get started with the stitches. I'm worried about blood loss. One of the others—" He broke off. "Heard one of the others in the riot didn't make it," he said, looking away, over at Cliff. "Older guy got hit hard with a bat in the back of the head. Cracked his skull. He just died over at A & M. Got the words from the nurses there." We all stared down on the tar drive at our feet and didn't say anything. "Well, why don't you get those things to the laundry?" he added.

"Is she going to be okay?" I said.

He shrugged, frowned and looked worried. "I am concerned about the blood loss. I don't know how we'll do it, but she needs a transfusion, I think."

"It's okay if I leave her?" I wondered out loud.

"I think you ought to take a break, yeah," he said.

"Can I give my blood?" I said. I didn't know her blood type, but I thought I'd give it a shot.

"We'll worry about that aspect of it after we work out these other things," he said, sweeping his eyes across the building and landing on the administrative end. I looked over there, too, then.

"Just for a few minutes," I said. "I probably ought to call her aunt. And find her brother if he's here."

"Sure. Take those clothes over to the laundry. I won't leave her till you get back. Promise." With that, I headed inside with the clothes.

The laundry room had been my most favorite place to visit when I was younger. Piles and piles of white sheets strewn all over the floor, and a line of huge washers and dryers always churning. I was never allowed to jump and play in the sheets, but I still enjoyed wandering back there and watching the ladies pull things out, throw them in, pull them out, fold them up. I liked the smell of the clean towels coming out of the dryer.

Today, I took the bloody clothes right to the head launderer, a colored lady named Ollie Mae who I'd seen Ivory Jones visiting with in the hospital hallways.

"What in the world's you got?" she said. "Goodness, girl." She grabbed my bloody hands and studied them.

"My friend got hit and she bled a lot," I said. "They sent me back here to get them cleaned."

"Sure thing," said Ollie Mae. She took the clothes and threw them on the floor, then grabbed me by the wrists and took me to the big sink where they washed things that couldn't go in regular laundry. She turned on the warm water and handed me the antiseptic soap and said, "Wash those hands and arms."

"Do you know where Ivory Jones is working today?"

"He's in surgery," she said. I was surprised. He usually had kitchen duty during the afternoon, cause Daddy didn't like colored people on the floors during the day. But Ivory Jones had gotten this reputation as a great athlete. He'd broken all the track records in the Big Bend area, and even white men talked about him like he was sent from God. I nodded and headed for second floor surgery.

"Rayann?" Ivory Jones said, wiping his hands on a towel. He'd come out of surgery and into the waiting room where I'd sent for him. He looked around at all the people looking up at him, and he pointed to the hallway. We walked to the supply closet, and he shut the door. His voice sounded worried. It wasn't normal to be pulled out of surgery. His hardset jaw let me know he was confused and worried.

"Are you okay?" He looked me head to toe.

"Cookie. She got hit in the head." I felt dizzy. There wasn't enough air in the supply room. Then I blurted it all out between his shushes to quiet me down, how we met at the pool, joined in the demonstration, the riot broke out, and Cookie got clubbed. "I was so scared," I said. "She started bleeding and she passed out and I found this guy to bring her to the hospital—"

"She's here now?" He sounded scared. He leaned into me and pointed down. I nodded. "Show me! Quick!"

We hurried downstairs. "Why'd you bring her here? They won't treat her!" he said, waving his arms in exasperation. At the bottom of the steps, I'd run out of breath. As we pushed onto the floor from the stairwell, I followed him into the Pre-Op Room. I wasn't supposed to be there. Luckily, no one else was in the room.

I told him she was in the parking lot but was being treated anyway, and how she might need a blood transfusion.

"Here?" he said. I nodded. "They're sewing her up now?" I nodded.

"I'm going to try to get her admitted," I said.

"I'm going to see about her," he said, throwing the towel into the laundry bin, taking off his funny cap and shoes and tossing them into the garbage. He mumbled, "Don't waste your time trying to get crackers to do anything. Hear?" he said, wheeling around and running for the stairs. Cookie would have Ivory Jones to look after her. I'd have no one after today. I decided to go see Mama now, fast. I might not get the chance again.

"I'll be back as soon as I can," I called out, pushing the elevator button up to Mama's room. It felt hot and humid and still in the hospital. I could barely breathe.

Up on 5C, nobody walked around except one nurse in the hallway fiddling with her meds cart. I headed past two wheelchairs, and it dawned on me. Why did people on the psych ward get wheeled around anyway? Why were people always trying to convince them they were helpless? It made me mad.

I sneaked past the nurse's station and knocked on Mama's heavy wooden door. She said singsongy, "Come in." She was painting a big landscape of crows on a black piano where a woman in red sat playing. Right next to a white hospital. A black crow was perched on the woman's shoulder. Mama's TV screen blinked on, sound down low, and a commercial for Exedrin played. *Please, mother, I'd rather do it myself!* the lady on TV said, pinching her nose, her eyes squinted closed.

"Hey!" Mama said. I hugged her, then stepped back.

"What is it?" she said, putting down her paint brush and wiping her hands on a rag. Out her square window, you could see tree tops straight ahead. Summer green. As long as you didn't look at all the windows on the fifth floor, reminding you of where you were, it didn't bother me.

"Mama, you can go," I said.

"What?" she said, looking at me, like I'd waked her up out of a dream, like she always got into when she painted.

"You can leave. You've always been able to leave." She put her paint brush down and wiped her hands.

"What are you talking about?" she said.

Then I told her how I'd gone to see Mr. Ellis at the bank, and how he'd told me you could not hold a psychiatric patient in this hospital without their consent. Her face registered hurt. A blank hurt. She stared out the window.

"Is your father around?" she said softly. I told her I didn't know. I told her how Cookie had gotten injured in the riot and was outside getting treated.

"My goodness," she said, but she just sat there, staring out the window. She looked like somebody had told her *to* leave, not told her she *could* leave. It confused me and worried me. She got up and started putting her art supplies away.

"Does your father know you found this out?" she said. I told her no. She started to move around like Rosie the Robot, only not as cheery or as fast. "You haven't talked with your father about any of this, have you?"

I blew up.

"What difference does that make?" I said. My breath was coming fast and hard, and I felt dizzy.

"Rayann, I'm surprised at you," Mama said, her brow wrinkled. "Of course it makes—"

"Mama, you just don't know everything," I said, waving my arms around in frustration. "You don't know what all's happened." I paced the floor and she sat in her chair watching me.

"Slow down," she said. "You need to slow down and take some breaths." She did not seem to understand. She sat pale and confused looking, and she needed to wake up and do something.

"Did you know he has a *girlfriend* while you're sitting here in the hospital?" I said. She stood up slow. "Just listen," I said, pacing as she stood holding the arm of the chair. "All these people came to the house. There were girls, Daddy's secretary and some of her hoochie coo friends, and they started drinking and—"

"Who?" Mama said.

"Lucky and Red and Daddy and some... Rheta and some other women."

"Oh, my god," Mama said, sitting down and putting her hand to her head. She frowned, and wrung her hands. "Go on." She looked up like an angel had come for a visitation like in the Bible, her eyes so pure and pained by the light.

"They were all dancing, slow dancing, and changing partners and putting their hands all over each other, and kissing, and Daddy—"

"Kissing?" Mama said, slow and puzzledlike.

"Kissing and rubbing up on each other," I said. I was panting.

"Where were you?" she said.

"Watching. From the living room."

Mama's face fell. She stared at the wall, frozen. "Oh, I can't stand it," she said. "Did he know you were home?"

"Mama, how should I know?" I said, angry. Then I realized she had a hurt look in her eyes. "There's more," I said, making my voice go down softer. She looked up at me and took in a deep breath and let it go.

"Go on," she said, turning in and going stiff as a shell. I told her about Red coming upstairs looking for me while Daddy was at the house, and how Daddy had fallen asleep so had not stopped him. Mama stood up and walked to the window.

"Good lord," she said, walking back to the chair and sitting down again, staring at *The Secret Storm* on TV. I was gasping for breath. I couldn't seem to get any oxygen.

"And you're not crazy, really. Because it was me who wrote 'bones' into the table. I burned your table."

"That's what I thought," Mama said with a piercing look at me, "but I'm glad to hear you say it." Her face softened then, and she flashed a weak smile.

Then I blurted out how he was going to take me to reform school tomorrow and have her committed next week.

"See what happens," I got out, "when you're gone, Mama? I need you at home. Miss Jesse can't—"

With that, Mama got up again slow. The room was spinning some, so I held onto the bed. She picked up her purse and went to the bathroom mirror and started to fluff up her hair. She turned sideways and gave herself a once-over. She picked up the purse, got out her lipstick and put some on. Then she threw it in the purse and snapped it shut. I thought about Cookie. I could hardly breathe.

"Where are you going?" I said.

"Downstairs," she said. "But I'll be back for you soon." I couldn't move. I should never have told her all this. She kissed me on the cheek, her smile apologetic as she put her hand through my hair, but her eyes stared into space. Then she put her purse under her arm and walked out.

I stood there for a minute watching the late afternoon gold of the sun hit the tile floor of the room. A meds cart wheeled down the hallway, and I could hear the elevator ding as the doors opened and then shut.

I wanted to lie down and just breathe, but I couldn't. There was Cookie—I needed to go back to check on her. I headed down the hall myself. Why was it so stuffy, I wondered. I couldn't breathe. On the elevator, it felt like I was being carried up up up and down down down. My head reeled. I thought about being stuck on it forever. The metal walls blurred and spinned out of control, and then went blank.

24

They told me I collapsed on the elevator. That it happened to be visiting hours, and when all those visitors stood there and the doors opened, people squealed and hollered, cause there I lay like a dead person on the floor. I have to believe this, since I don't remember a thing.

Or anything else that happened. Until the morning sunshine of the minute when I woke up the next day, feeling the summer on my face, the hard hospital bed under me, and the tightness of an IV needle taped onto my arm. My mouth had never felt so dry. I struggled to sit up, and I heard Mama. She sat in the chair next to me and put her arm on mine.

"Hey, honey," she said. She had checked out of the hospital, I could tell. She wore her favorite silk shantung shift with matching green shoes and purse. Her hair was sprayed and stylish. How'd she do that so fast? "How do you feel?" she said. "Would you like some water?" I nodded, so she poured some for me, and I drank it all down. She refilled the Styrofoam cup, and I drank some more. "You were dehydrated and—" she hesitated, "starving, they said. I wish I'd known." She looked away. "How do you feel?" I eyed some cheese grits in the breakfast I'd been sent. How much time had gone by? A whole day?

"I'm okay," I said. "Can I have some of that cheese grits?" She handed me the bowl of grits and a spoon. I bolted upright in terror. "Where's Cookie?"

"Your friend is okay," she said. "Her brother donated his blood. They gave her a transfusion downstairs, stitched her up and sent her on home." She patted my arm.

"In the truck?" I said.

"In the Emergency Room," she said with a smile. "I made your father let her in." She raised her eyebrows and her eyes sparkled. "Eat first, then we'll talk," she said pointing to the grits.

I felt the cheesy grits slide down my throat. I ate the whole bowl, then sat back and sighed. I suddenly felt a deep ache in my chest, and I sat up straight.

"Did you go home? What happened?" She shrugged.

"Hey, hey," she said, patting my shoulder and pushing me back down onto the bed. "Honey, sit back. Relax. You've been through a lot." I stared at her, and she cleared her throat. "I spoke with your father. I told him I knew everything. I told him to help out that little girl, or I'd make a divorce so bad the judge would have him walk out without the shirt on his back." She said it all so cool and crisp.

"Divorce?" I said, my throat thickening.

"Your father told me he was furious that these colored people—Cookie—had tried to put you between him and yourself. He said they've been a bad influence on you. You're never home, he says, you're irritable. And they're teaching you to lie, and he thinks maybe steal."

"*What?*" I said, and kicked the covers.

"Lie down now," she said, pulling the covers back over me. "I'm just telling you what he told me," she said. The hospital door whooshed open. "I made sure he let you have the visitors you want up here."

"You just love to faint, don't you?" a familiar voice called. Cookie. Mama smiled as Cookie walked into the room with

Miss Jesse. They wore their Sunday dresses, and Cookie's head was covered with a big white bandage. Her dress had blue and yellow stripes, and her shoes matched the blue. Her forehead was swollen. One stitch crept its way out of the bandage covering her scalp, but otherwise she had no marks on her face.

"Oh, my god! Cookie!" I said. I opened my arms up, and Cookie ran to the bed and we hugged. Her arms felt cool and dry while I felt sweaty and hot. Miss Jesse grabbed my hand with her warm dry hand and squeezed. Then she and Mama walked out of the room together. "You're okay." I burst into tears.

"Stop that," Cookie said, and started eye watering her ownself. I pulled up the sheet, and she shucked her shoes and crawled in with me like I had with her just the day before. She showed me her nails that I had painted.

"You were fixing me up for the funeral I ain't ready for yet, girl," she said. We hugged and let our tears run down our cheeks and onto our necks, our noses all sniffling and wet. Cookie sat up, and we looked at each other and started laughing. "You look a sight," she said.

"Well, you've looked better," I said. "And you smell like hospital bandages."

"You're looking at the first Negro to ever get treated at Tallahassee Memorial," she said, sitting up tall. "They got my picture in the newspaper."

"No kidding," I said in wonderment. "Ew, was there blood all over your face?"

"Course not. Girl, you so vain," she said. "Vain and prissy. After I got cleaned up and was fixing to leave, a swarm of people stood outside the front who'd heard about it. That's why I left out the back."

"But—how'd you get fixed up?" I said.

"Girl, all of a sudden, they was taking me into the E.R., and fixing me all up. Didn't ever put me out, but they took pictures of me, and let me fall asleep. Then all these people come in and they cut my hair off with a razor. Then they put peroxide in my head—you know I'm gonna have a red-haired streak for the next six months, girl. Dang."

Cookie told me about her transfusion and her X-rays and her 17 stitches in her scalp. She even gave me a peek of her bald head and stitches.

"But wait," I said. "Tell me everything. How long did you wait till they brought you in?"

"I don't know," she said. "I fell asleep when you left, and next thing I knew, Ivory Jones and that Skip fellow was standing over me, carrying me inside. I thought I would die lying there in that little room waiting and waiting."

"I'm sorry," I said.

"All of a sudden I woke up, and this tiny white lady is holding my hand," Cookie went on. "She say she's your mama. She didn't tell me you were down there at the same time on the elevator fainted away. Your mama held my hand while they stitched me up till Miss Jesse got there."

"Really?" I said. I could not believe it. I tried to picture Mama standing there while Cookie got stitched up, holding her hand.

"Didn't hurt at all getting stitched up. Doctor said your head don't feel pain like the rest of you. Then they held me in there for another hour till they said I was going to be fine."

"Thank the angels' stars and Mary's moon," I said. "I'm just glad you're okay."

"Somebody got killed in that riot," she said, a little gloomy. "Guess I got lucky." She told me about Ivory Jones and Miss Jesse taking her home. She brightened then, and said how

Ivory Jones treated her good and spoiled for once in her life, and even brought her some chocolate. "That's when he told me you'd fainted on the elevator."

"He was there?" I said.

"He heard," she said. She touched her swollen forehead and winced. "I'm gonna have a headache for a week, they said. Got to take aspirin all the time. Anyway, he came up here to your room when you were conked out. Just to check on you. We all got worried about you, too. They said you was all dehydrated and half-starved. Dang, girl."

"I missed the whole thing," I said.

"And now they're saying your daddy's gonna be in big trouble for letting me in. And other people say he's in big trouble cause the federal government people's coming down to make y'all take us in the hospital. It's all on the TV news this morning." She reached for the TV and turned it on to *The Love of Life*. The sun pierced my eyes. I felt a pang for my daddy; I could not help it. He sat right in the middle of one big mess.

A commercial break came and the noontime farm report and news would show next. I didn't want to see it. "Turn it off," I said. Daddy in trouble. "Turn it off, please." Cookie jumped up and snapped it off and sat back down on the bed.

I looked out the window. No bars. The way the sun came in the window from the east, I figured I was on 3A. Good. All I had was the disease of wanting to get out.

"I just want to go home," I said. Cookie squeezed my hand.

"I know," she said.

The next day, I walked down Betty's Creek Road to the swamp and the dusty dog-barking road past Miss Jesse's just to think. A warm breeze rustled the marsh grasses. I'd miss that sound if I were leaving. Mama had said that now Daddy might get half of their combined money from the divorce, and that we had a choice. Sell the land and Star and keep the house, or move altogether. I'd miss the eely smelling swamp, the mosquitoes it bred. I'd even miss looking for snakes. I didn't want to give up this place.

I watched a heron lift and fly off, and it made me think of Cookie's leaving for Chicago. I wished I had some big wings. But I held more the position of a goose than a heron, walking the earth with toes turned inward. I headed up the road to Miss Jesse's, checking behind me at my tracks in the clay. They were pigeon-toed all right.

When the swampy smell of eel left my nose and the scent of green trees and grass growing met me, I heard voices and laughter. A guitar somebody was strumming and picking at the entrance to Miss Jesse's drive. I recognized Cookie's laugh. Ivory Jones' too. And I heard a deep warm voice. It reminded me that the world was blue and green and growing.

Four and five hundred miles, and don't know nobody. No, the road ain't for me no more, sugar, I heard. Then I saw him. He looked young, Cookie's daddy. Powerful and musclely with chocolate brown skin, smooth and unlined. He had this smile that made you want to grin, all buck-tooth and cuteness. He stood leaning on the gray fence post by Miss Jesse's driveway entrance. He wore this black beret, the kind you wear tilted on your head. He had a soft voice, too. He did not look like a criminal. Cookie and Ivory Jones sat under him, his audience.

He saw me on the clay road and nodded, smiled. Not afraid to speak like a lot of colored men. Cookie and Ivory Jones turned and saw me, then beckoned me over. Ivory Jones stood up and walked over to me. I could not help how my stomach flipped every time I saw him.

"This my friend I been telling you about, Daddy," I heard

Cookie say. Ivory Jones hugged me.

"You okay, Sister?" Ivory Jones said. I nodded. He surprised me hugging me in front of Cookie and their daddy. He smelled like clean soap.

"Thanks for everything, Ivory Jones," I said. "I'm sorry I left Cookie."

"Come on," he said. "Meet Daddy."

Cookie put her arm around me and said, "This is the girl got me in all that trouble, and then saved my life."

"Well, I am sure happy to meet you," he said. "Willie Johnson." He shook my hand. He had big strong hands and calluses on his fingertips. I sat with Cookie on the ground, and Ivory Jones leaned on the fence post as their father told stories while he played chords on the guitar about being a road musician.

"Daddy, you had a rough life?" Cookie egged him on.

"Rough life?" He strummed the guitar. He cocked his head and looked at the blue sky. "Yeah, pretty rough. *Sometimes we had money,*" he sang and strummed once, "*Sometimes we didn't.*" He strummed a few chords, loud and confident. "*Sometimes we had food, sometimes we didn't.*"

Then he talked about Howlin Wolf, his hero, and how he was scared to death of the man. He sang and strummed. "*People b'lieve in magic then, say, Man play like that, he done sold his soul to the devil.*" Cookie's daddy's eyes were chocolate brown and teased like hers. In fact he even reminded me of a guy version of Cookie as he went on about Howlin Wolf.

"*Had the most beautiful skin you ever seen. Look like you can blow on it and it'd riffle.*"

He had Cookie's smallish nose, the devil-may-care attitude and this talent for performing without being afraid. I'd miss all that.

"Daddy, what's gonna be the name of our band in Chicago?" Cookie said.

"How about 'Chicago Blues Stars?'" he said. She smiled. Ivory Jones stood up and brushed off his pants. I stood up, too. I wanted to go see Miss Jesse. The thought of Cookie leaving made me feel restless and hot.

As Ivory Jones and I walked up the hill, butterflies of yellow and blue and mottled brown flittered in the field beside us, coming to rest on hot pink flowers. The breeze blew across the tall grass leaning it towards the house.

"You doing okay?" I asked Ivory Jones.

"Yeah. Good to have Daddy here. He's ready to leave, though. Get back to his music." I stopped to watch a butterfly stick its feeder into a flower and sip the nectar out. Ivory Jones stopped and watched, too. "Never saw that before."

"I'm glad you're staying," I said. He put his hand on my shoulder and squeezed.

Up at the house, Miss Jesse was watering the sugarcane patch with an old hose Mama had given her. I hovered right up next to her.

"Well then, I reckon you owned up to your Mama about messing up her fine table," she said, eyeing me sideways. So she'd always known for sure and never tattled on me. Cookie probably knew too. And Ivory Jones. And they never said a word.

"I love you, Miss Jesse," I said, putting my arm around her slim waist. She rested her arm on my shoulder.

"You loving up to me, huh, since you gonna be losing your friend?" she said.

"No, always did," I said. Then she dropped the hose and hugged me full on.

"I know you gonna miss her. I am, too. Blue-eyed Jesus and

the Lord have mercy, I will miss that child! My little pearl."

"Can I be your pearl, too?" I said.

"You done been my pearl all along," she said. She pulled me away from her and looked me in the eye. "Now it's God's will this child's got to go. She's got the gift of music in her throat, she's got to go on and use it for the Lord's good."

I studied a sugar cane stalk instead of looking at her. I did not like Miss Jesse talking about God's will. As far as I was concerned, Miss Jesse was like God. "I know," I said, making two cane branches rub together and squawk out their eerie music. I picked up the hose and watered the sugar cane.

It reminded me of when we had a cane patch ourselves, Mama, Daddy and me, a long time ago. Before we got Star. How Daddy used the tractor to plow it and then plant the cane, then Mama and I watered it like crazy all summer when it turned bright green, and then we harvested it in the fall as it turned purple. When they cut it, they laughed. Once they even danced and kissed to the weird cane screeching music in the middle of the cane field. How could they decide to end it so quick?

"Seems like Mama and Daddy're all of a sudden getting a divorce," I said.

"Ain't no sudden to it," she said, stooping down in the dirt to pull weeds. "Water over there," she said, pointing to the next row of cane. "They been working on it for years."

"I thought—"

"Don't have nothing to do with you," she said. "Or what you thought," she said, shaking her finger at me. "Sometimes something's done died already," she said. She moved to the next row to yank weeds. "Don't be a rascal, put the hose to the plants. Good, keep watering. Makes weeds pull up easier."

"Why were they living together, then, if they didn't love

each other?" I said.

Miss Jesse sat up and looked across the way into the meadow. She thought for a minute. Then she leaned over and went back to weed pulling. "Watch what you're watering there," she said, pointing to the potatoes in the next row over. She cleared her throat, then went on.

"My daddy, he got sick, and I took care of him," she said. "He went to the doctor, and got some medicine, then he got worse. Got another doctor, got sicker, got more medicine. Kept on and on. Two years that went on, and he got weaker and skinnier." She was yanking weeds and rubbing her nose. "I felt sorrow hanging on my shoulder heavy, all the time. Then one morning, I walked into his room, and his feet was cold and his face had took on peace. All I felt was Thank you, Lord. The suffering is over. All the sadness had done been squeezed out of me already. You understand what I'm saying?"

"Yes, Ma'am," I said. I didn't exactly, but then somehow, it was like something with wings came and pulled something off me and flew away with it. I watered another row and listened to the wind make the sugar cane song. I took in a deep breath of dark black dirt.

For the first time, I used the road to walk home from Miss Jesse's. I no longer had to hide by walking through the woods. As I turned onto the lane to head up our driveway, I saw this black car, headlights on, pulling out of our front drive. The license plate showed a Duval County tag. That meant it had come from Jacksonville. I ran home.

"Mama?" I called when I got in the door.

"Yes?" she said, frowning, her hands in the sink.

"Who was that in the black car?"

"Oh," she said, clearing her throat nervously, "government

people. They want to talk to your father." She wiped her hands on a towel.

"The people who want Daddy to take colored people into the hospital?" I said.

She shook her head No. "He's got money trouble at the hospital, too," she said. "Shoo, now, go on upstairs and get cleaned up. We've got dinner in a bit and a lot to work out."

When we sat down to eat, I realized how much I had missed Mama's good home cooking. We had broiled chicken, new potatoes and green beans. A typical Mama dinner from long time ago. Nothing ever tasted as good as Mama's cooking, so I was in heaven. She said looked like I had started to put a little weight on before school started up again.

Mama had set a notepad and pen down beside her. We were making a list of what to keep of the antiques in the house. We listed only the furniture we'd keep so as not to have to list the items we'd have to lose. Mama had another list, too, of places to go searching for a job.

"Do you want to keep your canopy bed?" she asked. I shrugged my shoulders as the back door opened, then I realized I could let the bed go. I shook my head, "No." I heard Daddy clear his throat and close the door. He walked slowly into the kitchen. Mama's back went stiff.

"Hi, Daddy," I said. Mama said Hello. His shoulders were slumped. The wrinkles around his eyes and mouth had deepened all of sudden. He looked like he'd been in the hen house late and ate the chicken, then realized the chicken had been his best friend.

"I've just come to pick up some things," he said, low, taking off his hat and holding it.

"Help yourself," Mama said, cool. "We're just having dinner."

Daddy put an envelope down by her plate without looking at her, and then he disappeared to the back of the house. Mama glanced at me, then fiddled with her knife and shook her head.

"He looks terrible," she said. I nodded and kept eating. I could not help feeling my heart squeeze out sadness. She opened the official looking envelope, then stood up and walked over to the sink to read it.

When Daddy reappeared, he held an overnight bag. He said, "Well, Lollipop, you ready for school?"

"Yes, Sir," I smiled. I felt hot all over. *No thanks to you,* I thought. *Or thanks to you.* I didn't want to love him so much. I put my eyes to the table. I couldn't bear to look at the many puzzles in his eyes. He headed out the door.

"Oh, Al?" Mama said. "The I.R.S. came by. They're doing an audit and said they wanted to talk to you."

Daddy cleared his throat from the darkened doorway. "Well, they can reach me at the hospital for now."

"Daddy?" I said, my heart thumping in my throat.

"Yes?"

"Can you go riding with me sometime soon, before we sell Star?"

"Sure, honey," he said. "I'd love to." Then the door opened and closed behind him.

Mama started tearing up the letter into long strips at the sink. "Son of a bitch," she said. She never talked like that. She turned the faucet on and ran water over the shreds of paper. I wondered what in the heck she was doing. I got up and stood beside her. Without looking at me, she started stuffing the envelope down the disposal. "We'll just see if this fancy new disposal he ordered works."

"What is it, Mama?" I said as she reached for the switch. My stomach twisted. She paused her hand in midair. "He's going to sue me for all my money." Then she put on the disposal. "There goes his finger," she said, and smiled weirdlike. She held up a strip of wet paper. "And here goes another finger." She repeated that until the whole letter was gone. She'd gone through ten fingers and a couple of toes when, strange as it may seem, I thought of what Cookie would do when I told her that story. I just started laughing. Mama looked at me and laughed. Then we doubled over with laughing so hard.

I'm leaving this tired ass town, Cookie sang the next morning as she jumped down the steps of the hideout. We'd decided to meet one last time before she left. She sang it because she did not want my being sad to bring her down when she was bursting from inside with excitement. She had shucked the bandage and covered her head, wearing a beret like her daddy's, only hers was purple and black plaid. She looked back at me, guiltylike. "You *know* I been saying that. That I´m gonna leave," she said, picking up Margot, who'd tagged along behind her as she sang.

"I know," I said. "You're gonna do great. You'll meet all those singers and learn how to play the drums like you always wanted to, and the piano, too. I'm happy for you." She smelled like Woodhue perfume, which had a lid made of real wood, a going away present I gave her.

"We'll see each other again," she said. We crossed the trickling creek and headed for her house.

"You coming down here? Maybe next summer?" I said. I hoped she'd get there, it'd be hotter than here, and she'd take the train back in a week. The heat was already making me sweat.

"Maybe you can come up and stay with me," she said. "Take the train." The thought scared me and thrilled me. I'd never gone to a real city before, and I'd only taken the train once from

Valdosta to Thomasville, Georgia, only about 30 miles away.

"Well, if you'll meet me at the station," I said. We'd reached the barb wire fence where the woods separated the far side of Miss Jesse's yard. Out in the front of the yard in the near distance, Johnny's car sat with all the car doors and the trunk open. Miss Jesse, Johnny, Ivory Jones and Mr. Johnson all stood around it laughing and talking like they were at a church picnic. *There she is,* somebody said.

"Hey," Cookie said, turning around to me, holding out her pinky finger. "Blood brothers." I touched my pinky to hers.

"Blood sisters," I said.

"Write me," she said. "And don't let my stupid brother get away with nothing now that he's going to college on a scholarship and getting all big headed," she grinned. She saw my shoulders sag and said, "Oh, don't go getting all mushy on me." She put Margot down and gave me a tight squeeze hug.

"I'm not," I said, picking feathers off her blouse. "I'm going to work on getting enough money to get my horse back, you watch."

"I got no doubt," Cookie said. You could hardly tell she had a swollen brow and a head full of stitches. She looked uptown cool in her black skirt and the lime green shirt I'd given her. She pushed her hip out and said, "And when you come up, you can listen to me singing with my Daddy's band." She whirled around like a ballerina and skipped to the car.

"I got no doubt," I said, picking up Margot, whose webbed feet were kicking, wanting to follow Cookie. She turned around and waved.

I stood a ways back and watched her family say bye. Ivory Jones ran by the car and waved as it headed out of the yard. Miss Jesse sent her a kiss and waved. I waved with the rest of them as the car rolled down the rut road and out of sight.

I felt a little like the world had opened up and swallowed a big something without even a whisper. I turned and headed to the woods with Margot, singing *Tell Mama, all about it, Tell Mama, please, Tell Mama, now I'll make everything all right.*

Epilogue

That night at 11, Ivory Jones and I sneaked out and climbed onto my roof to watch the stars when he got off work. He put his arm under my neck, and we lay there watching the night sky.

"Black velveteen sky," I said.

"And glittering white stars," he said. He told me then he'd been offered a full scholarship to the local black college for the year after next.

"So you'll be staying around for a while?" I said, my throat hurting a little.

"Reckon so," he said. Neither of us felt much like talking, so we just stared at the sky. I was still so young, and he was almost in college. I was white, and he was black. I ached for answers.

"Ivory Jones, do you think we have souls that are hard, like a skillet? Or just fragile, you know... fragile as wings. Like on those butterflies we saw the other day in Miss Jesse's meadow," I said out of the blue.

"Girl, you know there ain't no answering that question. Why don't you ask that when you're a hundred and five?" he said. Then he leaned over and kissed me, his lips soft and wet and sweet.

I found myself singing, *Come on and take a chance and get with this dance. Wah Wah Wah Watusi.* I stared into the night thinking about the mysteries of the world. Why people keep separated from each other, how the stars landed floating in the sky, why girls love boys, why we can't hold onto water. Why I loved the place I called home, why we dream. *Nothing happens when you got to say No.*

I dreamed Cookie and me built a big house with a porch where we could sit and listen to the creek, right on the spot of our hideout. When we're old, a hundred and five, I thought, we'll rock on that porch and our great-grandchildren will be racing around and playing cards and tag football together, and maybe they won't just be black or white, but shades of ebony, mahogany, and pistachio.

We'll tell them our stories about riding Star, about the married geese and about tromping down the road in high heel shoes. We'll tell them about the goose murder, about me getting knocked, about swimming in the pool and causing a riot that got Cookie hurt, and a lot more. And they will laugh, and they won't believe it, times will have changed so much. Now that's a place I could call home.

About Mary Jane Ryals

Author of nonfiction, poetry, and short stories; editor at *The Apalachee Review* literary magazine; and research associate at Florida State University's College of Business, Mary Jane Ryals was also appointed Florida Big Bend Poet Laureate for 2008-2012.

She is the 2006 winner of the Second Annual Yellow Jacket Press Chapbook Contest for Florida Poets for her collection, *Music in Arabic.* Her short story collection, *A Messy Job I Never Did See a Girl Do,* is available from Livingston Press, and her nonfiction book, *Getting into the Intercultural Groove: Intercultural Communication for Everyone,* was released in 2006 from Kendall/Hunt Publishing Company. Kitsune Books published her first bound poetry collection, *The Moving Waters.*

A native Floridian, Ryals enjoys hiking, kayaking, and horseback riding. Ryals holds a Ph.D. from Florida State University, where she teaches writing in both the FSU College of Business and the university's Valencia, Spain program. She has traveled extensively in Western Europe, Mexico, Northern Africa, Singapore, and Vietnam. She currently lives in Tallahassee, FL with her husband, writer Michael Trammel, and their daughter Ariel. Their son Dylan lives in Asheville, North Carolina.

Of her writing, Ryals says, "Place creates character and culture. The more I travel, the more the gifts of humor and joy shower down. And the more my own small town upbringing returns to me like boats on water. Luckily, in my upbringing, my parents gave their lives generously to me, my two sisters, and brother. Rayann is not me, and neither are her parents mine. I have written this novel in close first person so that I can become the character, and so that the reader can understand, too, what times were like in the turbulent yet exciting 1960s. I bow to the black and white friends who taught me how to be in this world, and to my Spanish friends who have showed me how to make a festival of this full, brief moment we occupy on earth."

CPSIA information can be obtained at www.ICGtesting.com
Printed in the USA
LVOW052335040912

297363LV00001B/248/P